D1124294

LIVING SPECTRES

a Chesterton Holte,
Gentleman Haunt Mystery

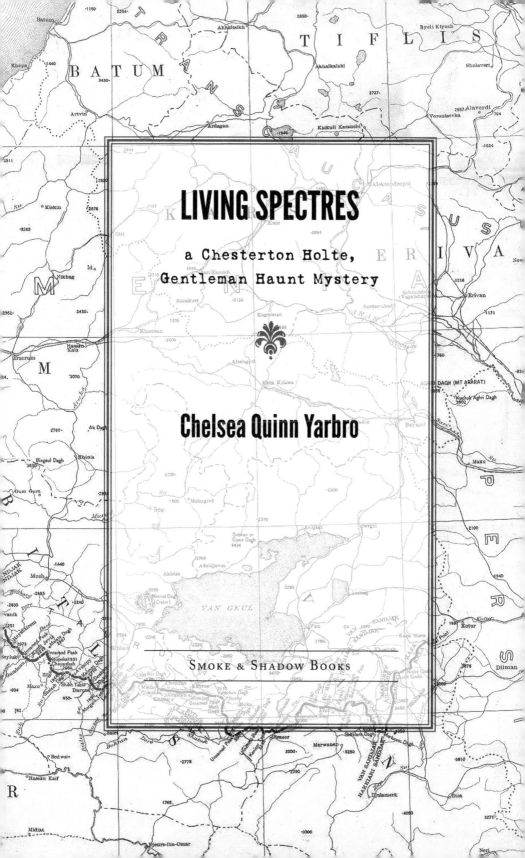

LIVING SPECTRES

a Chesterton Holte,
Gentleman Haunt Mystery

Chelsea Quinn Yarbro

Smoke & Shadow Books

Smoke & Shadow Books
Cleveland Writers Press Inc.
31501 Roberta Dr.
Bay Village, OH 44140
www.clevelandwriterspress.com

Printed in the United States of America

First Edition: October 2016
10 9 8 7 6 5 4 3 2 1
Smoke & Shadow Books is an imprint and trademark
of Cleveland Writers Press Inc.

The publisher is not responsible for websites
(or their content) that are not owned by the publisher.
Library of Congress Cataloging-in-Publication Data on file with publisher.

Hardcover ISBN-13: 978-1-943052-36-3
eBook ISBN-13: 978-1-943052-37-0

Cover Design by Patricia Saxton
Edited by Patrick J. LoBrutto

For
Maureen and David

ONE

"How is the packing going?" Chesterton Holte asked as he emerged from the corner of Poppy Thornton's bedroom; his form was insubstantial but sufficient to be familiar to her. Outside the front-garden window—and somewhat visible through Holte's nonmaterial form—was a cluster of three poplars, the edges of their leaves hinting that autumn was on its way, and that the very warm afternoon which enveloped Philadelphia would soon be a thing of the past; occasional clouds gliding through the skies were starting to gather together, bringing the threat of rain and blustery wind. Holte found this change mildly surprising, unaware that he had been gone long enough for the leaves to start to turn, but in the last two days that he had been returning sporadically to Josephine Dritchner's house, he had begun to think that he had been away longer than he had first assumed.

"Does this mean you've decided to rejoin me, or are you just stopping by? I was beginning to think that the charms of Philadelphia were starting to pall on you. Either that, or you were avoiding me because of the move. I wouldn't blame you if that were the case." Poppea Millicent Thornton looked up from her perch on the upholstered stool in front of her vanity and gestured to the stack of boxes standing in the opposite corner of the room, each one carefully labeled and closed with glue-backed paper shipping tape.

"How long ago did you decide on this?" he asked, aware that the packing must mean something more than a vacation.

"About six weeks ago, when Aunt Esther made the offer that I live at her house. She saw at once how things were with Aunt Jo and me. She's still at sea until tomorrow, and won't be back here until Friday."

"Matters are not well, then." Holte moved a little nearer to Poppy. "I gather you're making progress on your move?"

"Simply oodles," Poppy replied sardonically, then shook her head. "You see how well it's going, and this is my fourth day of it, and I have six more days to go before I have to be out; I had no idea I had so many things to take with me," she said, sounding a bit forlorn. "I've been at this since breakfast, and those eight boxes are all I've managed to get packed; I'm taking today and half of tomorrow off—without pay. Yesterday Lowenthal told me to go home; I was too distracted to finish my story on the latest arrests in the counterfeit antiques scandal, and he was right. I spent the last weekend sorting through all my books and papers; those boxes are in the library. This week, I've sorted through most of my seasonal clothes. At this rate, it's going to take me ten more days to be ready to leave, and I'm scheduled to go next Monday. Lowenthal is giving me the Monday off to do it, thank goodness. Even though I'm planning to move by increments, it's going to take time."

"Next Monday? So soon?" he asked.

"It isn't soon to me." She sighed and asked a second time, "So, are you back at last? And where have you been?"

"It's likely I'll be around," he said, answering her first question. "Have you missed me?" Holte seemed genuinely curious, although it was hard to tell since his features were a blur, and the tone of his voice was echoey.

"In a manner of speaking; after all, you saved my life," Poppy answered.

Holte did the equivalent of a shrug. "By the way, what do you mean by *at last?*" he inquired politely. "How long have I been gone?"

"Most of June and all of July and August," she told him. "We're just into September. It's the second. I move on the eighth."

His features were not clear, but there was an attitude of surprise in his posture. "I hadn't realized it had been so long." He drifted pensively toward the ceiling, thinking, that explains the changing leaves. He felt nonplused, and it took him a little time to compose himself sufficiently to resume the appearance of his living self, however flimsily.

Poppy observed his rematerialization with an unanticipated sense of respite. "What were you doing? I thought you might be gone for good."

"Not yet; I was trying to find Alexandre and Yvette Bastin." There was a note of chagrin in his voice.

"In the dimension of ghosts?" she asked.

"Yes." He descended and went back toward the window. "They sheltered me for several days in 1915, and when one of my German counterparts found out, he killed them in a fit of pique, because I was already gone by the time he arrived. I knew I had to search them out, not an easy thing for those without physicality."

"How could you make recompense to them for that?" Poppy could not see how he could—as he called it—balance the books with ghosts.

"As I'm doing with you, because of your father; I am sorry that he was shot on my behalf, as I am sorry about the Bastins," he said with a careful gesture. "The Bastins have a grown son, who is in a...facility." He glided back toward her.

The reporter in her was becoming more forceful, and she could not keep from asking, "What kind of facility?"

"One for those with...mental problems: an asylum, in fact." He turned away, looking downcast. "Reynard—the son—was damaged by the Great War, and had become unable to care for himself; he's hardly the only one to have such trouble. There are thousands like him, as well as more thousands of damaged refugees. I was hoping that I could alleviate some of his misery, but he began screaming when I finally tried to introduce myself; the nurses had to come and sedate him. I will have to find another way to aid him."

"Why did that take so long?" Poppy persisted.

Holte bent as if to apologize. "One loses track of time in the dimension of ghosts. It took quite a while to locate Alexandre and Yvette, and more time again to find Reynard."

"Why was that? I understand about the ghosts, at least I suppose I do,"—she waved at the air to encourage him to comment, to no avail—"but what makes it difficult for you to locate the living?" She was a bit surprised that he was so reluctant to tell her, but then, she told herself, he had been gone almost three months, pursuing his other obligations, and that might account for his reticence.

"I can find those whom I know, in my way, but when I don't know them, it's harder to get a fix on them. It took me a while to locate you at first, and I knew where to begin." He sidled over to the chair and tried to settle into it, but ended up about four inches above the seat. "Without some connection, I'm like a bloodhound without a scent to track."

"So it took over two months to accomplish finding Reynard, and it didn't go well. I'm sorry the son isn't able to cooperate with you. That must be difficult for you." She got to her feet and went to pick up another packing box from the stack in front of the closet. "You'll have to pardon me, but I should keep at it."

"I'd help if I could," he said, sounding a bit chagrined.

"Noncorporeal," she said. "I know: it's the nature of ghosts." Poppy was unnerved to hear how readily she said it; during the time he had been gone, she had got out of the habit of thinking of him as anything more than an illusion. But now, she had the odd sensation that they were resuming a conversation that was much more recent than the three months that had gone by. His reality, if such a word was applicable for a self-proclaimed ghost, perplexed her, because it assumed he was what he claimed to be; she had come to accept his affirmations last spring, but in his absence, her doubts had sprouted anew—after all, it was 1924, and no one believed in ghosts any more—and now she would have to give up her dubiety again. She went to her chest- of-drawers, opened the next-to-lowest drawer, and began to remove sweaters and vests from it, placing them in the packing box with a kind of automatic neatness.

"Is your Aunt Jo still miffed at your decision to leave? I'm guessing that she isn't taking it well," Holte ventured, becoming more than a pale smudge in the air near her bedroom chair, but once again fading from full materialization as he drifted around the room. Fortunately, his face was clearer, making it easier for Poppy to read his expressions.

"Not miffed any more: resigned and fatalistic. She says no good will come of it." Shortly before Holte had gone on the ninth of June, Poppy had broached the possibility of her departure to her aunt, and had been greeted with disgruntled animadversions on the evils of such a move. "When Aunt Esther made her offer, Aunt Jo gave in to tirades at first, but that didn't last very long. She hasn't resorted to a rant for more than a month now, though she does spend a lot of time in the music room, playing dirges, or in the sitting room, expressing her dismay to Duchess and drinking sherry. She won't talk to anyone outside the family and her immediate circle of friends, not even the minister at Saint Clement's, and she's known him for thirty years." Poppy was often amazed at the patience of the elderly spaniel; Duchess did not become alarmed when Josephine wept and declaimed for her missing son, but would wag her tail and offer a crooning howl from time to time. "She is afraid that my association with Aunt Esther will lead me into all kinds of folly."

Holte moved toward the end of Poppy's bed. "That's very like her—meaning your aunt, not Duchess."

"It certainly is. Occasionally Aunt Jo still reminds me of her worries for me. She's afraid I'll ruin my reputation, living in Aunt Esther's house. But she also knows I can't stay here—she can't bear hearing that I hold Stacy responsible for what happened, which I do—and, ye gods, living with Tobias and his family is out of the question; even Aunt Jo knows that would be a disaster." The very thought of living under the same roof with her unctuous older brother dismayed her; the actuality would be unendurable for both of them.

"Is that the only reason she doesn't want you here?" He drifted over to her side, hovering about a foot away from her.

"Her disapproval of what I do for a living has contributed to her wanting me gone, but the primary reason, of course, is the same reason I think I ought to go: Stacy." She finished unloading the drawer, closed it, and opened the one below, where her cold weather jackets and coats were stored.

"Oho," Holte said, moving back to her side. "Tell me more."

Poppy tried not to sigh, and nearly succeeded. "She declares that Stacy is falsely accused, and that it's my fault," she told him, managing a lop-sided smile. "If I hadn't involved the police, Aunt Jo is certain that Stacy would not have fled to wherever he has gone. She believes if I had kept quiet about it—although that was impossible, considering what happened—Stacy would still be here, and exonerated of all wrong-doing."

"She's deluded: the District Attorney was after him, and not for an ill-considered..." Holte shook his misty head. "Does your aunt understand that Stacy locked you in a warehouse basement, tied to a chair, and left you there, no one knowing where you were? Does she comprehend how easily you could have died?" His non-voice had a quality of resentment to it; he drifted a short distance away from her.

"Well, because of you, and, thanks to your efforts, and the efforts of Inspector J. B. Loring, I didn't," she said, shuddering a bit at the memory; she rubbed absentmindedly at her wrists, as if the scabs from the ropes still bound her. "But no, she doesn't see it that way—she's convinced herself that it was one of his pranks that got out of hand."

Holte made a kind of sound that would have been a sarcastic laugh if he had been alive. "That's quite a feat, in its own way, turning attempted murder into a bit of scampery."

Poppy reached for a crayon to label the box before her. "Well, it's that or admit that her youngest son is a criminal, and that is more than she's capable of doing."

Holte nodded. "She's quite resourceful, in her own way."

"And to make it more difficult, she is distressed that I'm going to Aunt Esther's because she takes it as a criticism of my time here—she's convinced that staying with Aunt Esther will guarantee that I will be an old maid, the worst fate for a woman, so far as Aunt Jo is concerned." She gave a single laugh. "Josephine and Esther: for two sisters, they are as different as—"

"—as chalk and cheese, as they say in England," Holte finished for her.

In spite of her current dejection, Poppy chuckled. "That's very apt. The two are very unalike."

He moved in a way that suggested a bow. "Courtesy of my time in Oxford."

As Poppy had wondered whenever he spoke of his education, she could not decide if this were true or not, and found herself tempted to write to Brasenose College to ask if they ever had a Canadian student named Chesterton Holte enrolled there in the decade before the Great War, but so far she had been unable to bring herself to do it; as peculiar as it was, she preferred to believe him rather than seek for confirmation—an inexplicable quirk in a crime reporter. "It's a great expression."

"I think so, too. We Canadians have our own wit, but it isn't as...deft...as the English." Holte went to the side window and looked out. "Have you thought about the matter I asked you about?"

"You mean that Warren Derrington, Louise, and Stacy were in on Madison Moncrief's death. Yes, I have—how could I not?—with Aunt Jo defending Stacy so vociferously at every turn: he's becoming the spectre at the feast even though, for all we know, he's still alive, and up to who-knows-what." She took a deep breath and let it out slowly, then said, "At first I thought it was unlikely, but your bringing up the drugs in Madison's drink rankled with me, and I can see why Louise might have been the one to do it, and then let in Stacy or Derrington, or both, to string him up from the chandelier. It still seems unlike Stacy to ruin such a fine antique, but there are parts to his character that might ignore the vandalism in favor of immediate advantage."

"Have you discussed any of this with Inspector Loring?" Holte had turned around from the window.

"No, not yet. I don't want him to go off in the wrong direction if I've made a mistake in my thinking." She studied Holte. "Do you still think it's possible?"

"No, the more I've cogitated on the case, the more I think it likely that the three of them are involved." He drifted back toward her, passing through one of the stacks of boxes without any hindrance at all.

Poppy stared at her bedroom door. "Ye gods," she whispered. "What will happen if that's true?"

"It won't be easy, that's certain," Holte said.

"How in the world can we prepare for it?"

"That's not the sort of thing you can prepare for. You won't know what to do until it happens," said Holte, making an offer of consolation.

"But I can't help but wonder." She sighed again, and turned desolate eyes on him. "It's bad enough that Stacy tried to kill me, but it's worse if he's made a habit of killing. Ye gods! That would truly be a catastrophe for Aunt Jo."

"So it would; one death might be the result of a nasty confrontation, a heat-of-the- moment thing. More than one killing suggests active malice," Holte agreed, and seeing her distress, he did his best to soften the blow his question had produced. "But you cannot hurry the law." He glanced toward the window again. "In another month or so, you should have a fine display."

"Which I won't be here to see." She heaved a frustrated sigh. "I'm going to need another box. These things are too bulky to fit in this one."

"Why not pack them in one of your suitcases?" Holte suggested.

"Because both of them are already full, and my hat box, and so is my father's old traveling trunk," said Poppy. "I've also got a laundry hamper filled— underwear and nightgowns, that sort of thing—and ready to go. I never realized how much clothing I have. I'll need to buy another chest-of-drawers when I get to Aunt Esther's."

"Does that surprise you?" Holte inquired. "That you have a great many clothes?"

"It shouldn't, but it does. It's the clothes for work that does it. I have nine suits and sixteen blouses." She stopped, and snapped her fingers. "Did I mention that I'm going to buy an auto?"

"No, you didn't. What made you decide you needed one?"

"Riding the streetcars and taxis through the summer. I ought to be in charge of my own transportation; I need to be able to move about on my assignments. Not being able to get around on my own is a real hazard, and as good as the streetcars are, they aren't what I require. I've ordered a Hudson, mostly because it's enclosed." She gave a little shake to her head. "I do have a driver's *license*, in case you were wondering—you have to have one now, you know. I got it after I came home from college, but Aunt Jo does not approve of women driving. She says such things are best left to men."

"Unless the roads have improved since I was alive, there might be some truth in that," said Holte, attempting the light touch.

Poppy turned to him, incensed at the notion. "You don't mean that! I'm not a child. If my Aunt Esther can pilot an aeroplane, I can certainly handle an auto. I'm not a total incompetent. Ye gods!"

He realized at once that he had underestimated the degree of strain the move had imposed upon her, and he said more sympathetically, "No, you're not the least incompetent. I'm aware of that. You're clever and resourceful, and very capable, but—" He broke off. "Is that Missus Flowers calling you?"

"I don't—" Poppy listened closely. "Oh. Yes." She went to the door. "She sounds worried. I suppose I ought to go downstairs." As she let herself out of her bedroom, she said quietly to him, "If you want to follow me, come along, but mind the lights. Missus Flowers will not like it if they start to flicker again." And with that, she pulled the door closed.

TWO

Missus Flowers, Josephine Dritchner's housekeeper, was pacing the entry hall nervously, wringing her hands, which was rare for her; she usually displayed a composed demeanor. Seeing Poppy starting down the stairs, she was visibly relieved. "Miss Thornton, I'm sorry to bother you when you're packing," she said quietly as she came to meet Poppy at the bottom of the staircase, "but I couldn't think of what else to do."

Poppy felt a twinge of worry. "What is it? Has Aunt Jo been at the sherry again?" Ever since her youngest son had vanished, her aunt had been tippling more frequently than Poppy had known her to do before Stacy had fled.

"Nothing so easy, although she has," said Missus Flowers said. "I know how to deal with that by now; no, she has guests."

"Guests? Who are they?" Poppy asked apprehensively; her anxiety increased when Missus Flowers did not answer at once, but began to pace again, the lace collar on her conservative, navy-blue dress slightly askew, another sign of serious upset; this time she confined her pacing to the foot of the stairs.

At last she stopped and answered, "Primrose North is here; they're in the music room." She gestured toward the corridor that led to the rear of the house. "Your aunt invited her to come for a drink yesterday afternoon. You were still out."

Poppy could not decide what might be sinister in the presence of the aged widow from across the street, but she remembered that Missus Flowers had said *guests*, and so she asked, "Who is with her? Not Nurse Perkins?" Missus North no longer ventured out without Doris Perkins' help, but the nurse would not be in the music room; her place would be in the kitchen or the servants' day room; an unhappy thought took form in her mind, but she kept it to herself, not wanting to exacerbate the situation with speculation.

"Her son," Missus Flowers wailed softly. "He accompanied her across the street, and wasn't about to leave his mother without protection, at least that was what he told me when they came to the door."

This took Poppy aback. "Denton? Not Tyler?" She almost held her breath— Denton was an Assistant District Attorney, assigned to the case of counterfeit antiques and Customs fraud that involved the absent Eustace Dritchner; Tyler managed the Norths' extensive upstate horse- farm.

"Mister Denton, I'm afraid," Missus Flowers confirmed.

"Oh, dear; no wonder Aunt Jo is at the sherry; if Denton is in one of his moods, I'll be at the sherry, too," said Poppy. She went down the last step, and was distantly aware that Maestro, the sooty household cat, had run up the stairs, tail aloft. "Denton being his usual ham-handed self, is he?"

"I'm afraid so, though it's not my place to say it." She stopped moving for a moment. "He was asking about Mister Eustace when I took in the tea-tray."

"Ye gods," Poppy said in a hushed tone.

"Mister North wants to locate Mister Eustace, and he seems to think that Missus Dritchner knows where he is." Missus Flowers resumed pacing.

"And Aunt Jo is becoming outraged that Denton is suggesting that Stacy had done anything wrong; that he is not a fugitive, but is necessarily hiding out until his good name is cleared." Poppy nodded, her worst fears realized. "Lord preserve us from righteous prosecutors! Aunt Jo must be beside herself."

"Exactly. She's said *of course* nine times now that I have heard. She may have said it more." Both Missus Flowers and Poppy knew this was a bad sign.

"Nine times? Oh, ye gods and damn!" Poppy exclaimed without apology; Aunt Jo must be seriously distressed.

Missus Flowers nodded emphatically. "I didn't know what to do, so I called you. I hope you don't mind."

Poppy shook her head. "You've done the right thing, Missus Flowers. I'll go into the music room, shall I? And see what I can do to...um...defuse the situation. You might bring in some extra refreshments, including a pot of strong coffee. While you're at it, you might dress it up with something more to eat. That would make it easier for Aunt Jo." She could see that this satisfied Missus Flowers, although refreshments had already been served.

"I'll ask Missus Boudon to make some of her clam-and-onion cream-cheese spread; we'll use the Salteens for serving it, and the butter-knife, and perhaps some pâté. I think we have some left from last night: pork and duck with ground chestnuts. You weren't here for hors d'oeuvres," she mispronounced as *horse doovers* as she always did; Poppy no longer bothered to correct her. "Missus Dritchner always likes those, and Missus North is a stickler for proper presentation, and a variety of finger-foods. Often she likes things sweet, but savory will do." With this viable plan in mind, Missus Flowers whispered a *thank you* to Poppy, and was about to cease pacing and go off to the kitchen, but stopped when Poppy asked, "By the way, where is Hawkins? Has something come up?" Usually Josephine's butler was near at hand when there were guests in the house, yet now he was apparently among the missing. "Is there a problem? I would have thought he would be keeping an eye on this situation."

Missus Flowers turned back. "He's gone to the butcher's shop to pick up an order. Their truck is being repaired, and there's a dinner—"

"—tomorrow night. I remember." Poppy took a deep breath and let it out slowly. "It's a special occasion, isn't it?"

"For Mister Galahad's birthday; he has confirmed that he and his wife will be driving in by mid-afternoon tomorrow. They're expected between two and three; dinner is at eight, drinks at seven. Cake at ten, with coffee and brandy. Mister Galahad doesn't turn forty-seven every day," Missus Flowers was keenly aware that Missus Dritchner's eldest son preferred to be called Hank, but she could not bring herself to do it.

Poppy frowned. "Who else are we expecting?" The last she had heard, it was to be a small gathering, but that had been a week ago, and Aunt Jo might have changed her mind about keeping it small.

Summoning up all her customary sang-froid, Missus Flowers spoke without any show of emotion. "Missus Dritchner is expecting fourteen guests thus far: only the Smiths have declined the invitation, having just returned from their summer in Europe. We haven't heard back from the Greenlochs...if they accept, there will be sixteen—seventeen, if we count you. Mister and Missus Pearse will be attending, which pleases your aunt, since they have been keeping to themselves this last month; something about their boy GAD. Ever since HOB died, they've tried to keep a leash on GAD, and now that he may be missing, they stay close to home, for GAD's sake. They don't want to miss any contact with him; Missus Pearse has said that she expects a telegram from him any day, and she wants to be at home when it comes. GAD—" she pronounced both sets initials as if they were words, as everyone did, and went on coolly— "should have been back from Europe by now, and at university. They didn't go to the shore as they usually do, for fear of hurricanes has been their usual reason, but it's really GAD, and Missus Pearse has said that she needs to get out of the house, which is understandable. Having a missing child is truly dreadful. Not knowing if he is alive or dead is enough to make one run mad. If one of my children had disappeared, I don't know what I would have done." She took a deep breath. "Oh, dear. There I go again. I promise I won't make any mention of GAD or the Pearses again. The rest of the guest list I think you know." She put her finger to her lips. "I apologize for babbling, and gossiping, but it is such a terrible circumstance; one cannot help but imagine the worst. It's so distressing."

Poppy gathered her thoughts. "I agree. Toby and I used to play with the Pearse children, and I was quite fond of GAD, even though he was much younger than I was."

Missus Flowers put her hand to her lips. "Then you understand. I wouldn't be talking about this if Missus Dritchner didn't carry on so about Mister Eustace being...away."

Poppy nodded once. "Neither of us can do much about that."

"No, we can't," Missus Flowers said, and changed mental gears. "Missus Boudon and I will have the house cleaned by noon tomorrow, and Hawkins will put the extra leaves in the dining room table this evening. It's coming along as planned."

"Oh." Poppy sighed, doubting now that he would have much of a chance to help her move boxes. "Well, if you will, let me know when he returns."

"Of cour—" Missus Flowers began, then stopped herself. "I'm catching it from Missus Dritchner." She resumed her walk to the kitchen.

Poppy watched her enter the swinging door, then went to the corridor that led to the rear of the house. As she went, she tried to think of how to deal with this awkward situation; she knew she could not make it obvious that she was coming to provide a distraction from Denton's attempts to pry information out of Aunt Jo, which, by the sound of it, he was surely doing. She took a moment to decide why she might interrupt Aunt Jo while she was with her guests, other than her actual one, and decided that Hawkins' chore would be a plausible enough cause to speak to Aunt Jo, since Hawkins had been tasked with carrying her boxes down to the auto and then to drive them around to Aunt Esther's house, slightly more than three miles away from Temple University, something that Poppy was certain would now be postponed. Perhaps, she told herself, it was just as well that she not try to do everything at once; making the move in easy stages would soften the reality of separation, she told herself. Reassured, she squared her shoulders and prepared to march down the central hall to the music room.

"Difficulties?" Holte asked from slightly behind and above her. "Is your aunt having problems with her guests?"

She swung around to face him. "That's what I'm going to find out. If you're coming, be quiet. Please." This last was an afterthought. She resumed her march down the corridor, doing her utmost to order her thoughts.

"As you like," said Holte, falling in a step behind her. "But only you can hear me—don't you remember?"

"I most certainly do. But Duchess is probably with them, and she can hear you. So can Maestro. Animals and babies are aware of you: you see, I remembered, and a drunken sailor saw you once." She was whispering and looking about as if afraid that someone would notice. "I don't want that poor old spaniel baying at you; Duchess isn't up to attacking you, which is good. It's bad enough when the cat hisses."

"Maestro has already greeted me; he met me at the top of the stairs and cursed me thoroughly, his hair standing out in all directions." He made a kind of amused snicker. "I think he's secretly pleased I'm back."

Poppy was almost to the music room door, so she made no rejoinder beyond putting her hand up to signal his silence. She knocked twice, and waited for her aunt to speak, mentally editing her excuse for disturbing the visit.

"Come in," called out Josephine, sounding strained.

Poppy steadied herself and opened the door, forcing herself to smile. "I'm sorry to interrupt your entertaining, Aunt Jo, but I was hoping to have Hawkins load up some of my boxes to take over to Aunt Esther's; Missus Flowers tells me he is out. Would you object if I asked his help when he returns? I know you have chores for him to do for the party, but if you could spare him for an hour, it would help me very much."

The music room was shadowy, being at the eastern end of the house, and made more so by the partially closed draperies over the four tall, narrow windows that would have provided some degree of fading afternoon light. As it was, three of the shell-sconces were lit, but they seemed to increase the shadows; one of them flickered, informing Poppy that Holte had accompanied her into the room.

"It would be inconvenient today—perhaps tomorrow, or Thursday. You'll have more boxes ready by then, of course," Josephine said in a critical tone; she was perched on the bench in front of her piano, a small plate of shortbread cookies lying on it beside her, an untouched cup of tea next to it, as well as a half-drained glass of sherry. She was wearing a very dark dress of dull- purple with a half-cape with off-black feathers for trim, four years out of style, and her badger-grey hair was done up in a sleek knot, while her shoes were black lizard, with buckled straps around her ankles; hardly Josephine's usual costume for receiving company, since—as she had complained after she had bought the ensemble—it made her look like a gloomy crow. "Come in, Poppea," she said rather grandly. "You know Primrose North, and her son Denton," she added, waving in the direction of her two guests from across the street, who were seated at a small occasional table set between two upholstered chairs.

"Yes, I do," said Poppy, coming a few steps into the room. "Good afternoon, Missus North. Hello, Denton." She had seen him fairly recently, at his office, where he had given her the news that there had been a bit of a break in the counterfeit antiques case, and had augmented this with a steady effort to pump her for any additional information concerning the whereabouts of Stacy; she could tell by her aunt's demeanor that he was doing much the same with Aunt Jo. "Do you have anything to report, or is this simply a social call?"

"Good afternoon, Poppy; it's been a while, hasn't it, since we sat down together," said Denton for his mother as well as himself, and managed what he thought was a mischievous smile. "This is a social call, but I'm afraid I have been bedeviling your aunt. She's on to all my tricks, I've discovered—too clever for me." This attempt at flattering jocularity failed dismally.

"I don't see anything amusing or commendable in taking me to task about my unfortunate son, but of course, you know what will please you better than I." Josephine's hauteur was at its most daunting, and only an aggressive prosecutor like Denton could ignore its implications. Just to make sure her disdain was obvious, she picked up her glass of sherry and took another defiant sip.

"That's against the law, you know," Denton pointed out, determined to provoke her. "I could have you arrested."

"It's a foolish law, and everyone knows it, including those bumpkins in Congress, who drink as much as anyone. Brigadier General Smedley Butler may be a brave Marine, but he has no notion of how things are done in Philadelphia: arresting people for having a convivial drink at home! Absurd! Why Bill Kendrick should have taken it into his head to hire the man to *stamp out* the use of alcohol, I cannot imagine. He's usually more sensible than that, but someone must have put the notion into his head; if I knew who that person was, I should most assuredly express my disapprobation to him. Bill Kendrick certainly didn't come by it through Gifford Pinchot." Having successfully yet obliquely reminded Denton that she was personally acquainted with the mayor and the governor, Aunt Jo reached down to replace the sherry-glass on the piano bench, then snapped her fingers; Duchess shambled out from where she had been napping next to the piano.

Primrose North took another cookie from the platter on the table beside her chair and bit into it, smiling as the cookie came apart in a buttery crumple. "This is very good shortbread; my congratulations to your cook," she remarked to no one in particular. "I'm very fond of shortbread. And strawberries."

"I'll tell my cook you liked it," said Josephine at her frostiest, smiling wanly as Duchess thrust her nose into her mistress' palm and licked it.

Feeling very much at loose ends, Poppy made an attempt to enliven the atmosphere in the room. "Missus Flowers will be bringing in coffee shortly; it will keep the afternoon warm. There will be spreads and crackers as well. She asked me to tell you." She paused, then added, "No doubt there will also be another bottle of sherry."

"That's good of her," said Josephine. "Yes; I do hope she brings the sherry as well as coffee; my bottle is nearly empty, and well she knows it." She glared at Denton, challenging him to do something about it.

"I am going to pretend I did not hear that," said Denton firmly.

"Oh, don't be such a hypocrite, Denton," Josephine admonished him. "You have hot toddies at Christmas, don't you?" She made this an accusation. "You drank Champagne at the July 4th Croquet Games, like everyone else, and you knew it cost a fortune. Eight dollars a bottle! Outrageous."

Josephine's indignation stirred Primrose North to speak up. "Yes. It was eight dollars a bottle, and Jonathan Butterworth could not stop boasting about it, though Olympia did her best to cease his gasconade. A parvenu, that man, trying to bribe his way into our set. It is unfortunate that Olympia married beneath her. No good will come of it." Since both her son and her hostess had presumed that Primrose North was not paying any attention to their cumbersome discussion, both stared at her.

Josephine recovered first. "Very true, Missus North," she declared in her most formidable tones. "The man may be excessively rich, but he owns a store. What can he expect? That we'll ignore it?" Having taken care of the lamentable Jonathan Butterworth, she now turned again to Denton. "Why did your people have to arrest Marcel Bonhomme? You know how many of us relied upon him. He was dependable and his prices were reasonable, *and* he was discreet; he conducted his business like a gentleman. Why couldn't you leave well enough alone? Stanley Miller is a feckless man, and he charges twice what Marcel did." Having spoken in defense of the man who had been the bootlegger for most of Philadelphia's upper crust since the Volstead Act had gone into effect, Josephine glared triumphantly at Denton North, and reached for the bell next to the music stand on her piano.

Poppy decided it was time to intervene. "Please don't bother to ring, Aunt Jo; Missus Boudon and Missus Flowers are working on the second tray right now, and should bring it in shortly. If you interrupt them, it will only slow them down." She waited to hear what her aunt would say.

"We'll see about that," Josephine responded.

Poppy went over to her aunt and said to her, very quietly, "Do you want the Norths to go? I can think of something to encourage them, if you like."

"Arranging for more sherry?" Denton needled, and wiped his mouth with the embroidered napkin Missus Flowers had provided.

"Of course not," Aunt Jo replied at her most imperious, then changed to what Poppy thought of as her society manners. "But so long as you're here, Poppy, make yourself useful and warm up everyone's tea."

"If that would help," said Poppy, and went to the sideboard to fetch the teapot, then dutifully refilled Primrose's and Denton's cups, noticing that the tea was not steaming any longer. As she put the teapot back on the tray on the sideboard, she heard Holte murmur, "She's in rare form, isn't she?"

"Alas," Poppy agreed, and joined in the general silence that lasted half a minute; it ended when Denton set his cup aside and sat up straighter in his upholstered chair. Here we go, thought Poppy, and went to stand near the door; she could feel the tension in the room increasing and wanted to be ready to intervene if things turned nasty.

"Missus Dritchner, I'm sorry to have to belabor the point, but it is my duty to pursue this matter, no matter how bothersome you may find it," Denton said with a sigh of ill-usage, "I can understand your desire to guard Stacy...Eustace, but you have to see that this case requires your coopera—"

"You would say that, of course," Josephine exclaimed, and took a sip of her cool tea. "This is quite dreadful," she remarked in an undervoice, and picked up the glass of sherry, taking it in hand and drinking it down.

"Missus Dritchner," Denton began again, "we are hoping to arrest Miles Overstreet within the month, and once that happens, it may not be possible for us to offer Eustace any kind of...negotiation that would spare him from prison. I'm sorry to have to tell you this, but you must understand that there is good evidence that he has broken the law." He waited in the renewed stillness that followed his remarks. When he realized that Josephine would say nothing more, he went on, "We're fairly certain that Overstreet killed Percy Knott."

"He didn't," Holte whispered to Poppy.

"So you've told me," Poppy murmured, and raised her voice. "Aunt Jo, would you mind if I join you? I don't want to intrude, so you must tell me if you prefer I leave," she fibbed. "I'm a bit worn out from packing, and some tea or coffee would be most welcome. It's been an exhausting day. As you know, I skipped lunch, and I'm peckish, and since I am at something of an impasse, I'd like to join you. Hawkins is out at the butcher's shop, and I would love a cup of tea and a snack, and I'd welcome a chance to speak with Denton," she said mendaciously.

Aunt Jo beamed benignly. "How thoughtless of me. Of course, Poppea. Draw up a chair, and one of the tables. No doubt Missus Flowers will have provided a cup for you when she brings in the second tray."

"I imagine so," said Poppy, and pulled up one of the chairs from along the wall and set it next to another of the occasional tables that had been placed about the room. As she sat down, she addressed Denton with the intention of drawing his remarks away from Aunt Jo. "I'm curious: what do you think of the trial going on in Chicago?"

Reluctantly Denton abandoned his hectoring of Josephine and said, "Leopold and Loeb? I think Darrow is taking a tremendous risk—in his situation, I would have thrown those young men on the mercy of the court rather than hoping that psychiatrists and alienists could save them. Not that they deserve it."

Poppy heard this without surprise; Denton was a prosecutor and would be expected to take such a stance. "I would have liked to cover the trial, but Lowenthal sent Martin Harris. He's the lead man for trials at the *Clarion*."

"I know the man," said Denton, not very cordially.

Josephine interrupted. "Of course you do. But why are we even talking about such a lurid case? Killing a little boy on a whim. Appalling."

Denton would not relent. "It's going to set a precedent, no matter how the trial turns out. Darrow knows it, and so does most of Chicago. I'd be willing to wager that every lawyer in the country is following it."

"And most of the reporters," Poppy said, doing her best to keep Denton's attention on that case rather than on Stacy.

In less formidable company, Denton might have used stronger language, but as it was, he chose his words as if he were appearing before a judge, and not Josephine Dritchner. "Poppy's right. The trial is more of a freak show than a court proceeding, and it can only get worse, no matter what the final outcome may be. Everyone—everyone!—has some kind of sentiment about it. The press is having a field day, and that is not making the proceedings any easier. Public opinion is running high, and the press is fueling it. More than that, reporters like Clarence Darrow, and he uses that to his advantage."

"Well, wouldn't you, in his position?" Poppy inquired. "Aren't attorneys required to represent their clients zealously within the limits of the law?"

"Touché," whispered Holte from the air on her right.

"There are those of us who believe he is pushing those limits too far," Denton informed her, his back as stiff as his face was set.

"What would you have done differently, if you were in Darrow's shoes?" Poppy was genuinely interested, and prepared to go on interrogating him. "You're a prosecutor, I know, but I am curious to find out how you, as an attorney, would have prepared a case for the defense that would differ from what Darrow is doing."

Denton cleared his throat, and said, "I wouldn't do what Darrow has done," he began.

But Poppy's question was destined to go unanswered, for before Denton could summon up a sufficiently impressive response, there was a knock on the music room door, and Missus Flowers asked to be admitted, whereupon the conversation turned to the safer topics of finger food and whether tea or coffee was the preferred drink to serve with it.

THREE

HAWKINS HAD BEEN ON ALERT FOR THE LAST HOUR, HOVERING NEAR THE FRONT door in order to be the first to greet Galahad and Cecily when they arrived. It was nearing two-thirty, and everyone in the house was on the qui vive. Missus Flowers had put a bouquet of hot-house carnations with fern fronds in the Gold Bedroom on the antique dresser, and closed the window, which had been open for six hours to air out the room. In the kitchen, Missus Boudon had interrupted her readying for the evening's dinner to remove two sheets of oatmeal cookies—Galahad's favorite—and set them to cool on the baker's rack next to the pantry door. Josephine, who had retired to her room immediately after lunch for a fortifying nap, was now seated at her vanity table, putting the last touches on her appearance, and fretting that Poppea was still at the *Clarion*, finishing her story on the process of extradition as it applied to Miles Overstreet, and would be unable to join them until an hour before they were scheduled to dine. She checked her reflection one last time, making sure there was no lip rouge on her teeth and that every strand of hair was right, then rose and signaled to Duchess to follow her downstairs; she was wholly unaware of Chesterton Holte hovering, invisible, near the ceiling, who slipped through the door after she closed it.

Downstairs, Eliza, the extra help, was just finishing using the new Electrolux to vacuum the carpet in the sitting room; the noise of the machine had driven Maestro from the place, and he now lurked outside the music room, muttering to himself.

Josephine had made her way down to the entry hall and was inspecting the condition of the telephone table and the state of the hall closet in order to assure herself that all was in order. She had not seen her oldest son for four years, and although he wrote to her weekly, it was not the same, she told herself, as seeing him face to face, to say nothing of his wife. She fingered the frame of the portrait of her mother, in glorious Gibson Girl array, that hung on the wall between the stairs and the kitchen hallway, trying to imagine what Millicent Thornton would have said about the way the world had changed since she had breathed her last shortly after the Great War had erupted in Europe; she could think of nothing that sounded right. The bang of the knocker, followed by the shrilling doorbell, shocked her out of her reverie, and she hastened to join Hawkins, rehearsing in her mind the greeting she had planned for Galahad and his new wife, whom Josephine had only met once, and that briefly.

Hawkins opened the door and stood back to allow the arrivals to enter; his face revealed nothing but polite satisfaction, but Josephine nearly stopped in her tracks as she caught sight of the tall, pleasant-faced man and the auburn-haired beauty beside him.

"Galahad!" his mother exclaimed, "what have you done?"

He bent to kiss her cheek, and then fingered his chin. "You mean the beard?" It was a neat, thin line along the sides of his jaw that joined in the middle and expanded upward into a Van Dyke; his chestnut hair had a sprinkling of white it in, as if there were drops of water left over from his morning shave.

"Of course I mean the beard," Josephine said reprovingly. "No one wears them any more, not in our circle."

Galahad gave his mother a second hug. "Don't be such a stick, Mother; yachtsmen wear them often. Rob Jennings"—by which he meant his business partner—"has worn one for years." He took a step back. "I think it's quite appropriate, now that I'm accustomed to it. Cecily talked me into it. And," he joked, "it's grown on me." His laughter was contagious; he shot his wife a covert glance of relief.

"Hank, you're impossible," the lovely Cecily reproved him, chuckling. She came up to Josephine and kissed her cheek as her husband had done; Josephine caught the faint scent of Chanel Number 5, the new fragrance that was attracting so much attention. "It's so kind of you to arrange this party for Hank. He's been sulky as a bear this last month, thinking that he's getting old. Forty-seven isn't old; by such a standard, I must be ancient," Josephine informed Galahad. "You're in the prime of life. And if you are certain that you must have a beard, who am I to say nay?" She took Galahad by the arm and drew him toward the sitting room. "Hawkins will bring your bags. I've had the Gold Room readied for you. You'll want to have a short lie- down before evening, I know. But for now, let's have a cozy chat. It's been a long time, Galahad, and I want you to tell me everything." She glanced back at Hawkins. "When you're done there, bring the sherry and the bourbon to the sitting room if you would, please." With a careless wave, she included Cecily in her original invitation. "Mind the spaniel," she added as Duchess toddled up to Galahad to sniff him, and utter a soft bark.

If this welcome perplexed Cecily, she gave no sign of it as she flashed another smile at her mother-in-law. "Would you happen to have some cognac? I think it goes well in the afternoon."

"Bring the cognac, too," Josephine ordered Hawkins, as he stepped out onto the porch to retrieve the suitcases sitting there.

"Directly, Missus Dritchner," Hawkins said as he started to maneuver the cases into his arms.

Once inside the sitting room, they chose their places—Josephine in the recently acquired maharani's chair, Galahad and Cecily on the settee. Josephine took a moment to assess Cecily's appearance, and approved of the unpressed-pleated skirt in lustrous green silk and the ecru blouse over it, both of which complimented her auburn hair and green eyes, although Josephine was a bit critical of the pearls in her necklace; they were not quite white enough, but she allowed that Cecily made a fine appearance and that the pearls were mere quibbling. She resumed her role as hostess, and asked, "How was your drive here? You must have made good time to arrive before three."

Galahad knew his mother well enough to understand what her short silence and measuring look had been about, but he indulged her by giving her the answer she sought. "We left Portland yesterday well before noon and traveled to New London where we spent the night. The roads are pretty well-kept up, so we'd been able to rattle along at thirty-five miles an hour for a significant part of the time, a great improvement on four years ago, when we rarely got above twenty-five miles an hour and had to pull over for all horse-drawn vehicles. We had a very fine dinner at The Black Sheep—we've liked it on prior occasions—and returned to our hotel at nine. We rose early, had a light breakfast, and were on the road again by eight. And here we are. Four hundred twenty-nine miles from our home."

"But Galahad, this is your home," Josephine said reproachfully.

Galahad made a quick recovery. "So it is, Mother, it is the home of the Thorntons and the Dritchners and always will be. But Cecily and I have our own home, as well, as an off-shoot of this one."

Josephine beamed at him, his possible lapse forgiven. "Yes. Here you are, home again. I wish you didn't live so far away, Galahad. It's been too long since you've—"

"I know, Mother," he said, hoping to forestall one of her outbursts. "I agree. It's time and more since we've been able to enjoy one another's company. If you want me to apologize, I will. You know how demanding my work has been these last few years; that's not an adequate excuse, but it's the best one I have. Designing yachts has become a very demanding business, and I won't ask your forgiveness for our success."

Josephine offered Galahad a tenuous smile. "You needn't. Your letters were sufficient, under the circumstances." She turned to Cecily. "How do you bear it, his long hours and days away?"

"It isn't easy," said Cecily without complaint, "but I know it is for a good cause, and doing it makes him happy, so I encourage him."

Josephine was pleasantly surprised at this generous answer; she turned her gaze on her son again. "Well, Galahad, if your wife approves, then I must do the same."

"You're a real trooper, Mother," he said, then added, "And I think you're an absolute peach to have this party for me. Cecily's right: I've been impossible about turning forty-seven, but I know the party will change that."

Holte drifted around the ceiling, wondering how Hank would deal with such an event as one of his mother's harangues so early in his stay; his way of speaking with her showed Holte that Hank had long ago learned to placate Josephine. Upon brief reflection, Holte's first impression of Hank/Galahad was that Josephine's oldest son did not like emotional scenes or dramatic effusions, but he was startled when Cecily spoke up.

"I know we're both sorry it has taken us so long to visit, Missus Dritchner, but I am most grateful that you do understand that Hank's work has been very exacting, and that is truly good of you. Many mothers would not be so sympathetic, and it is to your credit that you have not made an issue of his current venture. I'm glad that you realize that the competition in developing modern ships and aeroplanes is very high just now, and Hank has been needed. Dritchner, Jennings, and Mayberry is on the verge of great things."

"Of course, dear; I do understand," said Josephine, patting her son's hand.

"That's good of you, Mother." There was nothing overtly suggesting that Hank might have wanted to keep the distance between him and Josephine, but Holte suspected that Hank preferred to have it that way. He moved a little nearer to hear what Josephine would say to Cecily's oblique apology.

"Yes, I try to make an effort." She turned to speak to Cecily. "His letters are full of the work he has been doing with aircraft along with ships. He is very good about keeping me informed. I must confess I don't entirely understand the relationship between the two disciplines, but I gather it is an important one." Josephine gazed on her son with pride. "You are a credit to all of us."

"Thank you, Mother," said Galahad, and then hazarded more unknown territory. "How many are you expecting tonight?"

At this question, Josephine absolutely glowed with pride. "Nineteen, perhaps twenty. Missus Boudon is preparing beef and two turkeys with oyster stuffing for this evening, and Eliza will be here to help, as she is now. We have some very good Bordeaux to serve, and a passable Chenin Blanc, for those who prefer fowl to red meat; there's also a pork roast cooked in a coat of chopped cherries and served with a sweet onion relish. There will be nine dishes for the dinner, beyond the soup and salad, and not counting the cake."

"It sounds wonderful," said Cecily, trying not to over-do it after her previous eloquent commendation.

Josephine was satisfied, so she clapped her hands together, saying, "That's enough about tonight. You must tell me how the last four years have been with you, Galahad. While your letters are wonderful, there is so much more I want to know."

Galahad obliged, taking care to watch her to see how she was receiving his report. "Well, as I've said in my letters, I've branched out into the aeroplane field. Who would have thought that being a yachtsman who designed boats would lead to this? Not you, and not I, at first. But after my work with Brigadier

General William Mitchell—we call him Billy—on the demonstration bombing of the *Ostfriesland* three years ago, I've broadened out. Not that I've given up designing yachts, for I haven't, but I am including aeroplanes in the process. I haven't wanted to bore you with the specifics." He was clearly used to explaining how his transition had come about. "When I was first approached, I was reluctant to commit myself to the project that had been proposed, but the more I looked into it, the more I saw how useful I could be. They have many of the same problems to deal with, yachts and aeroplanes. Air influences both sailboats and aeroplanes, as well as currents and barometric pressure, so it is important to design both yachts and aeroplanes with these things in mind. Only last week, I was approached by William Bushnell Stout, who is starting a passenger airline—can you imagine what it would be to take an aeroplane over long distances rather than an auto or a train?—and asked me to assist him in the design of his all-metal aeroplanes. It's quite a challenge; I don't know if I'm up to it, since I have little knowledge of all-metal aeroplanes, but in that, I am hardly alone. This is new territory, and we're all beginners."

Josephine stared at him as if adoring the shrine of a saint. "How wonderful. What more can you tell me?"

For the next two hours, the three took over the sitting room, while Chesterton Holte hovered around them, picking up bits and pieces of information and family gossip that he knew could be helpful to Poppy. Over their conversation, Josephine, Galahad, and Cecily had a delicious selection of finger food: broiled baby oysters; minced ham on toast; chilled, thin-sliced beets marinated in vinegar and herbs; cubes of celery root lightly breaded and roasted in butter with diced onions; an array of berries in sweetened cream with leaves of mint atop them; chopped bacon and wilted spinach served in a pastry shell and garnished with minced parsley and shredded Parmigiano cheese; slices of apple wrapped in a blanket of Camembert cheese, slightly warmed; and a plate of three dozen oatmeal cookies. Holte tried to imagine how these three would be able to face dinner in four hours after such a repast, to say nothing of the *horse doovers* that would accompany the drinks before dinner. Even without the liquor, there was enough here to keep them satiated for the entire evening. By four-thirty, all three agreed to get ready for the evening's festivities at six and would leave the sitting room to Eliza's last-minute ministrations; Holte left them to it and went back in the direction of Poppy's room, where he found Maestro hunkered down in front of the door, staring at him balefully and muttering imprecations in what Josephine called High Cat.

"Little you know about it," Holte informed Maestro, and passed through the door into Poppy's bedroom with its stack of nine taped and marked boxes. Already the room felt empty, and Holte made his way around it carefully, thinking that it would be too easy to leave some trace of himself among all her things. When he was satisfied that all was in order, he hurried away toward the *Clarion*'s office, and sought out Poppy's usual desk, only to find she was not there. A quick sweep of the place told him she was not in the Addison Newspaper Corporation building, so he went off in the direction of the police department, to the floor where Inspector J. B. Loring had his desk, and was relieved to discover her in Loring's visitor's chair, her notebook in her hand, and her pencil working rapidly. Holte settled in on the ceiling above Poppy and Loring, his full concentration fixed upon them; he realized that the two were in the middle of a discussion.

"—it could lead to greater revelations than a simple confession. May I mention your belief that Overstreet might not be Knott's murderer?" Poppy asked, cognizant as she did that his answer might implicate Stacy in the crime more than the fragmentary evidence did now. For the last hour, Poppy and Loring had been reviewing the complications and loose ends of the Knott murder and the counterfeit antiques investigations, discussing where the two probes seemed to overlap, comparing their news and guesses with the current attempts to bring Miles Overstreet back to the United States, as well as speculating on the progress of the search for Stacy Dritchner and Warren Derrington. It took Poppy almost half an hour to gather all the information she wanted; she departed the police station and drove directly to Aunt Jo's house, fretting a little at the traffic, and arrived ten minutes earlier than she had anticipated. After informing Missus Flowers that she had arrived, Poppy went to join her aunt, cousin, and cousin-in-law in the parlor. After a round of welcoming, she said, I'm so sorry I had to be late. I was interviewing the lead investigator on Stacy's case. I'll have to write the story later tonight."

"Does it bother you, talking with the police?" Hank inquired.

"A bit, but it is part of my job," Poppy said.

"Your *job!*" Josephine said as if the word tasted vile.

Poppy ignored the outburst. "The case is stalled just now; they can't do much until they find Stacy, wherever he is."

Hank chose his words carefully. "Yes, I can see that. Stacy has managed to disappear, hasn't he?"

"It seems so unlike him, not to write to me," Josephine lamented.

"He's a fugitive, isn't he?" Hank asked. "Officially?"

"Well, he hasn't been arrested, but there is a warrant out for him," said Poppy without a trace of emotion.

"Poppea, you mustn't," her aunt rebuked her.

Hank intervened before his mother could ring peal over Poppy. "He's my brother, and I want to know what is going on with the police, since they are attempting to arrest him."

"That is wrong," Josephine insisted. "The police have been mistaken before, and they are now. Eustace would never do violence to anyone, and as to the claims of fraud, that is clearly absurd."

While Poppy knew such an inquiry discomfited Aunt Jo, Poppy was aware that there was a real possibility that Stacy was in some way connected to the killing. "Inspector Loring was most informative: he told me that in my article, I can mention that the evidence, while inconclusive, is sufficient to allow the police to continue their case against him while the District Attorney is pursuing a number of other potential leads, in spite of Overstreet appearing to be the most obvious of their suspects. Unfortunately, it's those others that have delayed the extradition for so long: the Canadians want more certainty before they hand him over to the authorities here." Loring had been tired when he had told her this, but there was a light in his eyes that revealed how happy he was to have Poppy's company, on whatever justification; the way he had looked at her still lingered in her thoughts, as she went on. "The case is by no means closed, much as Commissioner Smiley would like it to be otherwise."

"Commissioner Smiley is a sensible man," Josephine said.

"From what Loring told me, what they have would suggest a conspiracy, if there actually are others involved," Poppy told them. "If one chose to interpret the circumstances in that light."

"Conspiracy?" Josephine cried out. "Eustace would never—*never*—do anything so reprehensible." She shook her head emphatically. "Let's not discuss this any longer. I can't bear it. Truly, I can't."

So they spent their last half-hour talking about the upcoming presidential race, and debating about the plans to widen several of the roads that joined various New England cities to one another, and rancor was averted for the time being.

Up in her room, Poppy's thoughts returned to her interview with Loring; while she dressed, she reviewed the conversation they had had after he had brought her up to date on the search for Stacy. In her mind, she carefully replayed what they had said, once the matter of Stacy, Derrington, and Louise had been dealt with:

"While I am eternally grateful to your guardian angel, I'm still perplexed how he did it—revealing where you were through making my light blink in Morse code."

"I don't have a guardian angel," said Poppy emphatically, putting emphasis on the *have* and hoping to dismiss the whole matter.

She did not succeed, for Loring said, "Ordinarily, I don't believe in such things, but in this case, I am still at a loss as to how it came about. There was no thunder that night, and most phone repairmen don't climb poles in the dark. Perhaps I should leave it to Aimee Semple McPherson—it's a lot more up her alley than mine."

The very mention of the theatrical young woman preacher now flourishing in Los Angeles made Poppy blush. "I don't think it's anything like that."

"That's right. Preacher McPherson rides a motorcycle and has a huge church with a two-hundred-voice choir, nothing at all like a desk-lamp blinking Morse code," Loring said levelly.

"Oh, please, JB, don't go looking for the uncanny when it probably isn't there; the next thing you know, we'll be testing out table-tapping," said Poppy, feeling a bit abashed that she should present Holte's efforts in such a demeaning light, and went on more sensibly, "I can't explain it either, but I'm glad it happened, whatever it was."

"Okay, but you might have changed your mind if you had been there," said Loring. "It was a most peculiar thing."

Poppy rallied to Holte's defense. "If I had been there, there would have been no need for the Morse code signal."

Loring chuckled. "I can't dispute that." He went silent as a kind of conversational shrug. "And most policemen, if they stay on the job long enough, have at least one experience that isn't readily explicable by most standards, though the bulk of them are reluctant to admit it. I'd like to know how it happened, but I won't go out of my way to find an explanation. Finding out what caused it might make it worse, not better. Your aunt told me last month that she is certain it was Eustace, proving that his locking you in the basement was never intended to be a crime. The trouble with that explanation is that we know now that Stacy was on his way to New York by quarter after four, and could not have meddled with my light. What is the most perplexing is that the information was specific and accurate—not one of those vague, fortune-teller-like hints." He gave a single laugh. "Well, that's enough for today, I think. I know you have a busy schedule this week, but might you be free tomorrow? So long as you don't mind sandwiches, I'll be glad to buy you lunch."

"I'd like that," she said before she could stop herself.

"I might have some news about the whereabouts of Warren Derrington, and if it pans out, I'll tell you all about it. I wish I had more."

"Anything more about Stacy?" she asked.

"I hope so, but there's something else: I have had a case cross my desk that I'd like your help with, unofficially. You can't use it in the paper, not yet. There are matters about the case that require me to handle them...um...with circumspection, which might include working with the Department of State, something I've never had to do before." He coughed to show his discomfort. "It has to do with someone in your—"

"—social rank," she finished for him, a trace of fatigue in her tone. "So long as I can have until two to interview Neva Plowright about her sister, I would be glad to. It took me three days to talk her into letting me speak with her. She's understandably skittish about anything having to do with Louise. I might have information for you, too, but that will depend on Neva." It was not quite true but near enough that she had no reason to apologize, for anything that Neva might tell her about Louise Moncrief could be as useful to Loring as it would be to her, and she would share whatever she learned over lunch. Then a thought struck her. "This other case you mention—does it have anything to do with GAD Pearse? He's missing somewhere in Europe."

There was five seconds of silence, and then Loring said, "Yes. But please keep that to yourself."

"You're working on that? Isn't that a bit strange?" Poppy could not keep from asking,

"It is. I'm not certain what I can do from here, but the Pearses are demanding local participation in the search for their son, and I caught the assignment, since I was stationed in Europe, during the Great War." Loring coughed. "It's awkward. I don't know what the Pearses expect me to do. Mister Pearse has been a pinchpenny when it comes to providing useful information. He says he will tell us more when the time is right."

"That sounds like him."

I've asked to see GAD's original itinerary, but Mister Pearse has refused to show it to me until he's satisfied that I'm the right man for the job. If he decides I am, he'll send over a copy of it." There was aggravation in Loring's voice. "I don't know what I'm supposed to prove, with so little information to go on, and no instructions as to how the Pearses want me to proceed."

"How frustrating," said Poppy.

"I realize that Mister Pearse wants to keep his hand in; what father wouldn't want to? But considering how little I have to go on, and how inexperienced the Pearses are in this sort of thing—GAD could be in serious trouble. Taking up with refugees can have repercussions, many of them quite unpleasant."

"Do you think it could be dangerous? Would you have to go to Europe?" Poppy had a sudden and unexpected rush of anxiety.

"It might be that I'll have to travel, but let's not spread it about; bear in mind that we may be overheard, and I don't want this bruited about. If you've already heard about this case, you'll know that it's an unusual one, and I'm trying to feel my way through it. I may not have kids of my own, but I saw enough of families who lost their sons in Europe that I'm aware of how devastating it can be—not knowing makes it worse. The Pearses are trying to keep this from the general public. The family is demanding—"

"Confidentiality. I understand." She waited a second or two, then said, "If there's anything I can do to help you with that case, please let me know."

"We can talk about it later. Tomorrow."

"When we meet for lunch," Poppy affirmed. "Is there some place you'd like us to meet?"

"Do you know the Firebird Café, on Old Green Street?"

"I can find it. It sounds like one of the narrow alleys around the old docks. There's a map in the city room. I'm sure I can find Old Green Street there." She smiled at him. "I'm looking forward to it. I pick up my Hudson tomorrow morning, and I'll drive it over to the Firebird Café. This way, I'll have a chance to show it off. You can give me your opinion of it." She came close to giggling, but was able to control her impulse before it became too strong to resist. "It's dark-green, or that's what I was promised, not quite so drab as black. The seats are tan leather, front and back."

"A Hudson? And dark-green. That sounds pretty grand; grander than mine, certainly." He was pleased enough on her behalf, but there was a hesitance in him now that made it apparent to Holte that Loring had recalled the separation between their places in society, as well as their financial situations. "What made you choose it? Are you wanting to cut a dash?"

"More practicality than grandiosity, I'm afraid. I chose it because it's closed."

"That's a reasonable precaution for a woman in your line of work." He cleared his throat. "Very sensible of you."

Poppy did not bother to show resentment at the notion that she would need protection that others did not, for his remark closely matched her reason for purchasing the Hudson. "I know the way out," she assured him. "You needn't escort me. After all, I'm surrounded by policemen, so I ought to be safe, and you don't want to bring attention to what we've been talking about."

Loring couldn't argue with that. "Then I'll wish you a good evening, and look forward to seeing you tomorrow."

"I hope so. My cousin Hank is in town, and Aunt Jo is having nineteen guests—at this morning's count—to celebrate his birthday, and who knows what she might want us to do tomorrow?"

"This would be Stacy's brother? Why haven't I heard about him?" Loring could not keep from asking. "Older or younger?

"His oldest. Cosmo and Reginald both died young, so only Hank and Stacy are left." She made herself stop talking before she fell into a complicated explication of family dynamics. "Hank will be forty-seven today."

"Hank?" Loring laughed aloud. "Really? You can't tell me your aunt gave him such a commonplace name, can you?"

"He was christened Galahad; Aunt Jo was in her Arthurian phase when Hank was born. He's preferred Hank since he was five, I've been told, and I don't blame him. He's a yacht designer, sort of by accident, but he's taken to it very well. And recently, he's been helping to design aeroplanes. He lives in Maine. He was widowed in 1917, and remarried a couple of years ago. This is our first real chance to get to know his new wife. She's beautiful and has truly excellent manners, or so Aunt Jo insists."

While this answer aroused Loring's interest, he kept this in check and only asked, "Do you think he knows anything about Stacy?"

Poppy stood still. "I very much doubt it. They are son number one and son number four, and the gap between them—sixteen years—was much too wide to cross. And they're vastly different in style. Hank is upright to a fault, and dependable."

"That's reassuring," said Loring, adding, "So it would be useless to talk to Hank?"

"Go ahead, if you like, but wait until the weekend; Aunt Jo is going to keep him busy from now until all the guests leave tonight."

Loring thought for a moment, then said, "Okay. Tomorrow at the Firebird. Shall we say two-thirty?"

"I'll try," Poppy responded. "But don't fret if I'm late."

"I won't," Loring said mendaciously, then went on with a new thought. "If you have a chance, will you think about how I can deal with the Pearses? I feel at a loss, talking to them."

"Happy to." Poppy prepared to leave the police station. "Until then, JB, and thanks"

"Tomorrow." Loring waved to her as she went out the door, wholly unaware that Holte was observing his every move.

As she finished rubbing a bit of rouge into her cheeks, Poppy gave herself a last, critical stare in the mirror. She put her thoughts of Loring aside and left her room to venture down to dinner.

FOUR

THE BIRTHDAY PARTY ENDED A LITTLE PAST ONE IN THE MORNING. MOST OF THE guests departed merrily tipsy, and replete with the magnificent dinner and the superb cake that Josephine had offered them in honor of Galahad's turning forty-seven. By the time Hawkins had closed and locked the front door, the clock had struck one, and Josephine put a hand up to tuck in a stray tendril of hair that had escaped from the coronet braid on the crown of her head. Her beige wool-crepe dinner dress with midnight-blue piping still looked flawless, but her eyes were dark with fatigue.

"Well, they seemed to enjoy themselves," she said to Galahad, who was loosening his tie and unbuttoning his dinner jacket; he, too, looked tired.

"As well they should. It was a resplendent evening, Mother. Thank you, thank you, thank you. Everything was perfect."

"It was my pleasure," Josephine said, beaming with pride.

Galahad kissed his fingers in salute to her. "I'll remember this evening for the rest of my life."

Cecily, gorgeous in a backless dinner gown of apricot peau de soie, took hold of her husband's arm and bent down to remove her right high-heeled sandal, then stepped back and took the left off on her own. "Yes, Jo," she said, rubbing her left foot through her silk stocking, "it was a splendid party. I believe your guests will be praising it for weeks."

Josephine radiated her delight. "How very kind of you, Cecily. Yes, I think we can say it was a success."

Hawkins suppressed a yawn, and said, "A very grand occasion, Missus Dritchner. I'm proud to have been part of it." He paused, and added, "But if it is all the same to you, I'd like to retire. With your permission?"

"You have it, and my thanks," said Josephine, more fatigued than grand. "You needn't rise until eight. I'm going to let Missus Flowers and Missus Boudon do the same, and we'll set breakfast back to nine, and have it buffet-style for a change. That should simplify things in the kitchen." She looked at Hawkins, who was starting toward the kitchen corridor. "Hawkins, will you tell Missus Flowers and Missus Boudon of the schedule change? And inform Eliza that she may wait until ten in the morning to finish the clean-up. Thank you."

Hawkins nodded. "My pleasure, Missus Dritchner," he said, and continued on his way.

Galahad watched Hawkins, and said, "He's remarkable, isn't he? He changes so little. He's a little greyer now than he was when I was at Harvard, but otherwise, he's much the same as he was more than twenty years ago."

"It's remarkable," Josephine agreed. "It was good of him to escort Primrose North across the street. Denton made his excuses around ten, as I recall. I shall hate it when Hawkins retires. I can't imagine that anyone else could do his job half so well as he does."

Before his mother turned mawkish, Galahad changed the subject. "I had a pleasant word with Edna Blanchard. Her husband is improving."

"She always says that, and I take it to mean that he is not getting any worse," Josephine said. "It's a pity that he should have become so great an invalid, but strokes can be like that."

Galahad continued his account. "Wilbur Millard brought me up to date on the Moncrief murder. What a tangle it is; I think Hadley and Grimes has been remiss in their dealings with the police. With Louise leaving as she did, it's made for quite a scandal." As soon as he said it, he realized that he should have kept that last part to himself.

Josephine frowned again, her indignation mounting. "That woman! Of all the effrontery. Dragging Eustace's good name through the mire because she left the city about the same time Eustace did! And her husband not in the grave yet."

"It will blow over, Mother. These things always do." Galahad had put his foot on the first tread of the stairs, but stopped.

"Do we have to bring all this up again?" Josephine complained.

Hank acquiesced. "I talked for a while with Isadora Pearse—she seems exhausted—and she told me that she's worried about her son GAD. He's due back from Europe but has not returned, and she's afraid something might have happened to him. Is there anything to it? Is GAD really missing, or is she making a mountain out of a molehill?"

"Isadora is a fool, and she's obsessed with protecting GAD, and he's all she's been able to think about for the last two years; I can't blame him for running off to Europe for the summer, seeing how she's been cosseting him. If it were up to her, she wouldn't let him go farther than Constitution Hall, and even then, she would chafe," said Josephine emphatically. "She wants to wrap that boy in cotton batting because HOB died. What nonsense. Imagine if I had done that to you, when your brothers—" she glared at the parlor entrance, and changed her tone as she went on, "I don't know. There may be reason for her worries, yet no one can say for sure. One hears whispers, of course, and there are suspicions, but it's all guesses, and Isadora's constant maunderings only serve to make things worse. That boy! He's determined to save the world. If only HOB were still alive, or Auralia had been born a boy, GAD would be free to tilt at whatever windmills he chooses, but now that he's the heir, he has obligations here, not off among foreigners, in who knows what God-forsaken place, helping refugee Albanians or Armenians or some such barbarians! Just imagine if I had carried on the way that Isadora does when Stacy disappeared." She gave an emphatic shake to her head. "Isadora is far too anxious about GAD. She imagines disasters around every corner. Not that I blame her, of course. She has a more volatile nature than many women I know, and just now, she is centered on GAD, which, to my mind, explains his absence. Can you imagine a woman more given to emotional outbursts than Isadora Pearse?" Her vehemence faded. "Well, there's nothing we can do about it, except commiserate when needed. You did that, I'm sure."

"I tried," said Galahad. "And I wouldn't dismiss her concerns too readily: she may well have good cause to worry. GAD has always been a bit...odd."

"I know you sympathized with her," Josephine said fondly, and went to turn off the entry hall lights. "You two go up. I'll follow you in a minute or so; I have to find Duchess."

"She's in the parlor," said Cecily, pointing out the direction the spaniel had taken. "I saw her come in just before the Pearses left."

"Oh. Thank you, Cecily. I thought she might be in the music room; she often goes there when we have company in the house." Josephine whistled softly, hoping for Duchess to respond.

"She licked up some of the cake on a plate that was set aside on the footstool in front of the wing-backed chair," Cecily added.

"Greedy little rapscallion," Josephine said at her most indulgent. "She'll need a long walk in the morning."

"Why not call her? She's not likely to hear your whistle," Cecily suggested, starting up the stairs, her high-heeled sandals hanging by their straps from her hand. She passed her husband, but slowed her ascent. "It was a lovely evening, Jo."

"Thank you, Cecily. I believe we carried it off well." Josephine shook her head, a bit distracted. "Duchess is a bit hard of hearing these days; or she pretends to be. She's nine next month. No, I'll just have a peek in the parlor. I assume that Maestro is in the library with Poppea." This last comment was said in a faintly condemning manner as she went to the parlor door. "It's that *job* of hers." She said *job* as if it were an obscenity. "She works all hours of the day and night, and hardly ever goes to parties. She spends hours in the library, typing away, and passing her days with the most dis*rep*utable people—reporters and even criminals! It will be the ruin of her. I've tried and tried to convince her to give it up, and improve her social life, but she'll have none of it. She refuses to think of her future."

"She certainly went to this party, Mother, and she didn't begrudge any of the guests her company. I saw her make the rounds of the guests at least twice, and didn't say much about what she does at the paper." Galahad was a couple of stairs below his wife. "She was with us until midnight, Mother, and half the guests left about then."

"So they did," Josephine said, willing to make concessions on Galahad's behalf. "This is a week-night, and there were a few who plan to rise early, which we will not have to do, thank goodness. You needn't be up with the larks unless you want to be. I plan to wait an hour past my usual time." She made a sign that she was almost ready to go up to bed by snapping her fingers at the dozing Duchess, who, she found, had curled up behind the parlor's wing-backed chair; the dog shook her head, sneezed, and doddered over to Josephine, still half asleep, but attempting to wag her tail. "I'll say good night to you now and will see you in the morning."

"Sleep well, Mother, and thank you again," Galahad said, resuming his upward climb while Josephine bent down to pet her spaniel.

"Let me wish you many happy returns of your day." She straightened up and smiled. "I hope you will let me plan a better occasion for when you turn fifty. Fifty. Where do the years go—weren't you just starting out in business with Amanda?" When she realized this might be seen as a slight to Cecily, she added, "Nothing against you, my dear. But there are still times it seems like only yesterday," she amended, and took a little time to admonish her dog, "You cake thief. I don't know what I'm going to do with you." She bent down again to rub Duchess' head as a way to soften her rebuke.

Duchess wagged her tail and made a moan in pleasure, then dutifully followed Josephine up the stairs, waiting patiently while her mistress made a detour, stopped at the library door, and knocked. When she heard no response, she knocked again, a bit more loudly, and called out, "Poppea?"

"Who's there?" came Poppy's reply in a slightly distracted voice.

"Poppea, are you still in there?" Josephine spoke up firmly.

"I am," she told Aunt Jo. "I'll be going to bed shortly. It was a wonderful party. I'm sorry I had to leave when I did. A deadline is a deadline." This was not quite the truth, but near enough for both aunt and niece.

"Well, have a good night's sleep; you'll probably be up before I am, so I'll also wish you a good day," said her aunt, and did not wait for Poppy's response, for having discharged her hostess-duties, she felt ready to reward herself with quiet. She went on toward her bedroom, Duchess at her heels.

Inside the library, Poppy rolled the papers out of the Smith typewriter, put the top sheet, the carbon paper, and the onion-skin copy in established stacks on the left side of the machine, saying to Chesterton Holte as she did, "I'll tend to the rest in the morning. For now, I'm getting sleepy; I don't think well when I'm sleepy."

Holte drifted over toward her. "Three pages?"

"Perhaps not quite so many. About the arrest of Miles Overstreet in Chateauguay. That's near Montr—"

"Montreal." He did not bother to remind her that he was from Halifax in

Nova Scotia, and was familiar with Quebec.

Poppy paid no attention. "—and the disinclination of the Canadians to expedite his extradition. That means all manner of red tape, if they choose to hold onto him a while. It's more make-work than real news at this stage, but those following the case will want to see that there is progress. I hope Lowenthal keeps me on this assignment as long as he can. So I've been gleaning as much as I can turn up."

"What will Inspector Loring say? Are you going to ask him about it?" He was tweaking her a bit, but hesitated when he saw the frown-lines deepen between her brows. "What's the matter? You aren't going to tell me that he isn't singling you out for information he rarely gives out to others." Poppy went to the couch in front of the fireplace and sat down, reclining slightly on one arm, wholly unaware of how pretty she looked: she was in an evening ensemble of teal handkerchief linen that featured a cowl neckline which fell far enough to reveal the square topaz pendant her father had given her for her birthday shortly before he had left on his last trip to Europe; the long bell-sleeves broadened three inches above her wrist, revealing a simple gold bracelet. The ankle-length skirt, of the same material, had a trumpet-flare at her knees and showed off her gold Chanel shoes. Her bobbed hair was prettily waved, and even now, after a tiring evening, her face had a tranquility about it that was rare for her. "Inspector Loring is very good to me, and I know it, and it's not just because the two of you got me out of that basement. There are times I'm afraid that I'm taking advantage of him."

"Taking advantage? He offers it to you, you don't impose on him. Isn't that convenient for you?" Holte inquired. "And for him?"

"Yes and no," said Poppy. "It's awkward to have him...take our occasional meetings away from his office or mine. Some of them are in discreet places, but a few could be construed as clandestine, and that could get both of us into hot water if someone wanted to make something of them. It could be assumed that there is more to our friendship than professional concerns would require. Ye gods! If it got about that we—" She sat up, her hands gathered in her lap, the tranquility gone from her face. "If there are rumors that there is a...a romantic involvement, it throws a great deal of my work on the counterfeit antiques investigation into question, and it makes it seem to some of my...colleagues that

I offer favors to get inside information."

"But you don't, and Inspector Loring would be the first to say so," Holte observed. "He likes your information almost as much as he likes you."

"Then his coming to my defense would make thing worse," Poppy said, her shoulders tense, so that it seemed that she had left the hanger in her blouse. "His denial of any connection beyond the professional one would make almost everyone at the *Clarion* absolutely certain that there was something more than inquiries going on."

"Is the staff there really so cynical about their own colleagues?" He did his best not to sound too incredulous.

Poppy noticed that the light on the ceiling flickered. "Not about most of their male colleagues, but for female reporters, the situation is different."

"But you're not just a reporter, you are the victim in a case Loring is investigating, and the two of you have good cause to consult, particularly since the crime concerns a member of your family. Why would the other *Clarion* reporters doubt that you have good reason to speak with Loring? They know you talk to Denton North, don't they? And for the same reason. What might they disapprove of with Loring?" Holte was perplexed by her refusal to permit herself to recognize the growing attraction she and Loring felt for each other, and her explanation was even more bewildering.

"It's not the same thing," said Poppy.

He tried to keep her talking. "Why is it so wrong for you to like Inspector Loring?"

Poppy tightened her hands. "You don't understand. If I were to become involved with J.B., it would destroy my credibility as a crime reporter. I would be accused—maybe not directly, but the gossip would insinuate—of using my womanly wiles to get my story, inquiring on my back, as Harris would put it—and believe me, he would do. After that, I wouldn't even be assigned to the Society page, since my reputation would make me unacceptable to people I've known for most of my life. I'd probably end up covering committee meetings and lectures, or something equally boring and backwater, if Lowenthal kept me on at all." She did her best to stare at Holte, filmy though he appeared to be.

"Lowenthal likes you. He's not about to fire you."

"He wouldn't let liking me stand in the way of firing me if he thought the paper would be better with me gone. He has a responsibility to Addison, and he knows it. He wouldn't go to bat for me if he supposed it might cause problems for the paper." She pressed her lips together to keep herself from saying more. "First and foremost, Lowenthal is loyal to the *Clarion*, and if he thought I was damaging it, like me or not, I'd be out the door." She sighed. "It could damage Loring, as well, if his superiors found out he was sharing information with a reporter; that's frowned upon. Both of us have to be careful."

Holte still wanted to know more; he was certain that something had happened at the party to upset her, for she had that fixed manner about her that she only revealed when she was aggravated. "What disturbed you this evening?" It was a guess, but after a long career of spying, Holte had become sensitized to the undercurrents that ran through small-talk, though this time he had not caught the nicety with the barb in it.

"Nothing directly," she said, and wiped her eyes, smearing her mascara; she stared at her fingers and the dark stain left on them.

"Did your aunt say something?"

Poppy shrugged stiffly. "Nothing that she hasn't said many, many times before. Everyone knows she disapproves of my job."

"But there was something more," he insisted. "If Josephine didn't vex you, someone did; I wish you'd tell me what happened." He moved a bit nearer to Poppy. "It's not like to you to hold such things in."

Poppy got up and started to the far end of the room, to the old leather chair Maestro had occupied an hour ago. "Are you ready for bed, cat?" she asked.

Holte was right behind her, repeating his plea. "I wish you'd tell me what was said—and who said it."

"Ye gods, Holte!" She rounded on him. "Can't you leave it alone? You're making a mountain out of a molehill."

"Since you're dwelling on it, no, I can't. You're disturbed, and that troubles me." He put out his hand, wanting to rest it on her shoulder in a reassuring way, but noncorporeality made this impossible, and she felt only a cold sensation where his fingers passed through her. "Sorry," he muttered.

"I wish I could explain it to you. Most men don't understand how easily women can be dismissed—literally and figuratively—on account of obvious affection. It's bad enough that they think I got my job because of my father, rather than through my own abilities." She could feel his skepticism, and pressed on. "Before she went on her first trip to the Soviet Union, Aunt Esther and I talked about this very thing, and she told me that in the newspaper environment, I would have to be particularly discreet, for gossip travels like lightning in this profession. At the time, I didn't quite believe her, but after a year at the *Clarion*, I saw for myself that she was right. I've observed Aunt Esther's admonitions ever since."

"What do you mean?" Holte asked, paying no attention to Maestro's low growls.

"There was another female reporter working at the *Clarion* when I first got there, just over two years ago, when they were hiring to replace those on the staff who had died in the Flu epidemic. She did the science and education stories, mostly, but also covered the background on local political inquiries as well; she was good at getting to the root of issues, particularly in education. She was often talking with the principal of James K. Polk High School, the one that often wins the science fairs? You know where it is? The one with the rocketry club and the new auditorium?"

"Generally speaking. Across the street from the park with the apple orchard, about two miles from here," he said. "Not quite upper-crust, but affluent."

"Yes. That's the school. Anyway, Thelma Rhilander spent a lot of time with the principal to keep up with what the school was doing that got such excellent results, and rumors started flying that there was more than the gathering of information going on between them. Thelma ended up quitting the paper and moving to the *Sacramento Bee* to get away from all the talk. She was very angry about it, and I don't blame her."

"That sounds a little extreme," said Holte, keeping his voice level. "She didn't have to move across the country."

Poppy flung up her hands. "Yes, she did; she did. That's the point—she had to. She now covers agricultural news, and never meets with any man alone."

Holte was skeptical. "Isn't that overly cautious?"

"I wish it were. It's not. Thelma left the *Clarion* well over a year ago, and the reporters—the male reporters—still talk about her."

"Really?" Holte had the disquieting notion that perhaps Poppy was right about this. "After all this time?"

"I've heard them," Poppy agreed, her animosity undiminished. "Ye gods! You should have listened to some of the things that were said about her; when they talk about her now, and the things they said to her face, for that matter, with the condescending addition of *can't you take a joke* when Thelma protested. I wish I'd had the nerve to speak up, but if I had, I would have been subjected to the same thing. At the time, I excused myself, because I was new to the paper, but I was kidding myself." She put her hands to her face. "I know I should have said something, but I was too scared to do it." To her horror, she started to cry, saying through her sobs. "My mother was a Suffragette, and what I've done— or not done—would disappoint her. I should have stood up for my principles. I should have spoken out. I should have said something. After all, I don't need my job; I've money enough. But I *want* my job, so I said nothing. Sometimes I am such a coward, I want to just scream."

Holte watched her in consternation, feeling helpless to comfort her. "Poppy, I wish I could make it better. And for what it may be worth, I think you're braver than most men I knew when I was still alive." It was a futile admission, for when he had been alive he had seen the winks and heard the innuendos exchanged among men when they spoke about women—he had sometimes participated in the quips and double entendres—and he knew this had not changed. He moved next to her, and put his gauzy hand over hers, coming as close to a succoring touch as he was able. Although he did not wholly comprehend her dejection, he wanted to assure her that things would improve, but he could not summon up the words.

With an effort, Poppy stopped weeping. She wiped her eyes with her finger, further smearing her mascara. "Damn," she muttered, and offered no regrets for her language. "I'm sorry. I'm overtired."

"Hardly surprising. You've had a demanding day, with another one ahead of you." He did his best to let her steady herself. "And it is late."

Poppy sighed. "*And* I need to be at work by eight. As you say, I have another busy day ahead of me."

"Then you'd better get some sleep." He wafted back toward the desk. "Are you finished here?"

"I am," Poppy said, yawning. "I can't think straight any more tonight. I'll do my polish tomorrow morning at the office." Saying this reminded her that she needed to pick up a new typewriter ribbon for the Smith; the quality of the letters it produced was fading. She made her way toward Holte, then looked back at Maestro. "I should take him down to the kitchen. He has the run of it most nights; Missus Boudon doesn't want any mice to get in. The kitchen and the mud-room, where his sandbox is now, are his bailiwick. When you were here last, he was kept in the laundry."

"The mud-room makes more sense, but Missus Boudon has a point." said Holte to let her know he was listening; he pointed to Maestro. "What does he make of it?"

"He hasn't said." She went to pick up the cat, who eluded her and headed for the door, tail up and whiskers bristling. Poppy followed after him, and opened the door to allow him to depart. "He knows the way. Missus Boudon will let him in; she's still cleaning up."

"Are you certain?" Holte asked. "It's getting late, and she might want to get home and finish the work here tomorrow."

"Well, usually it takes her two hours, with Eliza's help, to get the kitchen in order after such a large party. They have it down to a routine; they're quite efficient—even Aunt Jo says so, and she has high expectations of her staff. So Hawkins will take the leaves out of the dining table in the morning, and by dinner time, you would never guess that we'd had tonight's festivities." Poppy stretched to loosen the muscles in her arms and back. "Missus Flowers should have finished gathering up plates and cups and glasses from the parlor and the dining room, and perhaps the sitting room as well. She'll be off to her cottage by now, but Missus Boudon will be here for another half hour at least. Eliza will drive her home."

"She has an auto?" Holte asked in surprise.

"It's her father's. He doesn't like her walking alone after dark." She lingered at the door. "Do you ever get tired?"

"Yes," he replied, and offered an explanation. "Staying materialized for any length of time can be exhausting; it's a matter of concentration. Noncorporeality doesn't lend itself to keeping in even marginally visible form, and after a while, it's wearing." He saw that her eyes were slightly red and the lids were puffy. "Go on. Get some rest. You look as tired as I feel. I'll see you in the morning, and I'll do my best to make sure you see me. For now, I'm evanescing; if you'll excuse me."

Poppy gave a little chuckle. "What about your trick with the lights and the phone lines? Do those wear you out, too?"

"Not as much as materialization does, but it can be fatiguing." He floated up toward the ceiling, fading away to a misty shimmer as he went.

FIVE

CORNELIUS LOWENTHAL, THE DAY CITY EDITOR OF THE *CLARION*, WAS HAVING A bad day, and it was not yet eleven, plenty of time for more disasters: Dick Gafney, his primary crime reporter, had been injured in a traffic accident the night before, had been taken to the hospital where he would be staying for at least three days, and there was no one free to cover for him, which put Lowenthal in a dicey position. He sat at his desk in his office, twirling his fingers in his thinning hair, making a curl that drooped toward his right eye; he was frowning portentously, anticipating the displeasure of the Addison Newspaper Corporation's Board of Directors if there was no coverage in this evening's edition about the robbery at the Napier's Jewelry Store which had netted the thieves about three million dollars-worth of unset stones; Napier's had been in business for over a century and was renowned for the quality of its jewelry, and its customers were numbered among most of Philadelphia's upper crust; they would want to be kept abreast of developments. Reluctantly Lowenthal got up from his swivel-chair and tromped to the door. "Thornton!"

Poppy started at this abrupt summons. "Has something happened?" she asked of the air, and expected no answer. She closed her notebook, put it and her pen in the center drawer of her desk, picked up her purse, and left her desk to make her way across the city room to Lowenthal's office. "What do you want, boss? I haven't been able to get any confirmation on when Overstreet will be brought back—"

Lowenthal indicated the chair in front of his desk that faced his own. "Sit down."

"Will do," she said, and did as she was told while trying to figure out what it was that Lowenthal wanted now; he had signed off on the story she turned in at nine, so she worried: had there been some new developments in the last hour she had not heard of?

"Is there anything popping on the counterfeit antiques, or the Knott investigation right now? Can you spare a little time for something else?" He trod back to his chair and plunked himself down in it. "By the way, that's a nice outfit. It suits you and it suits the work." The grin he attempted in order to show that he intended the pun was more of a wince, but he assumed she would understand.

Poppy groaned and gave him a thumbs up. "Thanks, boss." She brushed the whiskey- colored sleeve of her new suit, which she had chosen as much for her lunch with Inspector Loring as her interview with Neva Plowright; it had a Goudy jacket of fine worsted wool, with a fan collar and modified bell sleeves, her blouse was ivory silk with a small lace ruff at the collar and more lace around the wrists. The skirt was straight but with a deep double-pleat in the back so that she would not be hobbled when she walked. "Nothing more on Knott so far today," she said to him. "I've got a call into the District Attorney's office to find out if there's any progress on Overstreet's extradition, but as of twenty minutes ago, it's pretty much the same as yesterday. It's unlikely that there will be anything new on that front until Monday; it's Thursday, and the District Attorney's office doesn't like to have a lot of hold-overs on Fridays."

"No kidding," Lowenthal growled.

Poppy considered her editor carefully. "You do recall, don't you, that I have time off after three so I can pick up my aunt at four and tend to my moving."

Although it was obvious to Poppy that Lowenthal had forgotten, he said, "Sure, sure," and grunted, "Three o'clock? Can you stay as late as three-thirty? Could you go to police headquarters and cover the press briefing on the Napier robbery? It's at two-thirty, and should take half an hour or so—and knowing Elmer Smiley, the police won't answer many questions. If you'll write up about three column inches..." He let the request hang between them.

Taking the assignment would mean she would have to cancel her lunch with Loring, so she hesitated. "I'll need to make a couple of phone calls; I have the interview with Louise Moncrief's sister this afternoon and I don't know how long it will take." This last was a fib, since she did not want to mention her other plans to Lowenthal. "I'm hoping that she'll have something to tell us about Louise's whereabouts." That provided her with an explanation for this follow-up since it was unlikely that Neva Plowright would talk with anyone not part of the wider family circle.

"Wouldn't that be a scoop," Lowenthal said at his most dubious.

"Well, no one else is going to get her to talk. I can't promise I will, but at least I can get my foot in the door." That had been the reason Poppy had been assigned to the case when it began, and it was still true.

"Yes, I know." Lowenthal banished the scowl from his face, then leaned forward on his elbows. "You can draw out cab money, if that will make it easier," he offered, as much for his surliness as his request for extra time from her.

Poppy smiled, and pulled a key-ring from her suit-jacket's hip pocket. "I don't have to. I picked up my Hudson this morning."

"That's right. You told me a week ago, didn't you." Lowenthal snapped his fingers as a kind of minor applause. "That's a big help. Just make sure that you drive it safely—it's bad enough having Gafney in the hospital. I don't want you there, too. You know what they say about women drivers."

Although she bridled a bit, Poppy was able to respond without snapping. "I'll do my best, boss," she promised, and made up her mind to skip lunch; after last night, she would not need fuel beyond another cup of coffee.

"Then get on with it. I'll want to look at your interview notes when you get back from the press briefing. If you need information about Napier's, have one of the copy-boys get it from the morgue. Don't bother trying to come here between your interview and the briefing, just get to the central station by quarter past two, so you can get parked and inside in time." He stretched and then turned his attention to the stack of papers on his desk. "Make your calls quickly and leave here. Chop-chop." He waved her out.

Back at her desk, Poppy called Loring, hoping that he was not out of his precinct station; when the receptionist answered, Poppy gave her Loring's name and waited while she rang her through.

"Loring," he said curtly; from his tone, he, too, was having a rough day.

"Hello, JB. It's Poppy," she said.

His manner softened at once. "Good morning, and how is your day going? Tell me it's better than mine."

"I wish I could, but that would be a taradiddle, unfortunately," She took a deep breath and plunged in. "I'm going to have to postpone our lunch. There's a briefing on—"

"—the Napier robbery," he finished for her. "So Lowenthal has put you on that, has he?" He laughed once. "The stolen property guys are all over it, like ants on honey. Jewels and moneyed people always get their blood pumping. There's so much hoop-lah that every man in that division is expecting to get at least a commendation for it—when they solve it, which they believe will be quickly. I don't think it's going to be the piece of cake they're saying it will. Whoever pulled it off had it planned down to the last detail; they got in and out without fuss or notice, and that building has a night-watchman; he claims he was knocked out, but he might have simply hid, or ran off while the robbery was in progress. There might be a few fingerprints we can use, but there's hardly a scintilla of hard evidence so far, and there's no hint of where the jewelry has gone, and that suggests an inside job. No witness has come forward, either. It's going to be a bitc...riddle to unravel enough to get it before a judge. I'm glad I'm not part of it."

"May I quote you—not that you're not on it, but about how difficult the case is apt to be? All reporters will want something from any policeman who'll talk to them," she warned him, scribbling his remarks on the back of a used envelope.

"Go right ahead, so long as you don't use my name," he told her. "Are you going to be free later?"

"I doubt it. Aunt Esther is arriving at four and I'm supposed to pick her up at the station. We'll probably have dinner out, assuming her train is on time and we can get to her house before the traffic builds up, and unload her luggage. If the train's late, I hope that Missus Sassoro has something she can prepare on short notice." She hated having to speak to him this way; it sounded as if she were trying to avoid him, and she didn't want him to think that, so she changed the subject. "If you're not going to be working on the Napier robbery will you be at the briefing today?"

"Nope," said Loring. "I'm on stand-by to go to Canada to retrieve Overstreet, and I usually don't do robbery investigations anyway; that's Ned Harper's fiefdom, not mine." He hesitated. "Speaking of cases, though, there's another case pending. It's the one I want to talk to you about. I have a hunch that it's going to take up more time than I anticipated, and I'm not sure how to evaluate the...ramifications. I'd be much obliged for your help."

"Sounds intriguing," she said half-heartedly, hearing the kind of distant sound in his words that meant he was troubled; she was about to ask more, but frowned as the light above her blinked off and on twice.

"That's not the phrase I'd use," he said, the fatigue back in his tone, and Poppy was sure the distant stare was back in his eyes. He followed her example and changed the subject. "Am I right, that you're moving tomorrow?"

"You are. I'll have tomorrow off—I told you that, didn't I?—and a couple of hours this afternoon, as well as Sunday. I'll be unpacking." Poppy ran through her calendar mentally. "What about Monday? I'd be free for lunch—unless something comes up. If that won't work, I should know by Sunday what my schedule will be."

"Yes. I'll let you know on Sunday; both of us will have a good tentative agenda by then." He went quiet.

"You'll need Aunt Esther's number," she reminded him, debating with herself whether or not he wanted to discuss his perplexing case now; she decided against it. "I'll give it to you tomorrow, when I'm moving in. I have it in my book at home." While that was true, she knew the number by heart, but wanted Aunt Esther's permission before she gave it out.

"Much appreciated." He coughed gently. "If something unanticipated arises, you'll let me know, won't you?"

"Of course. Things should be a little less hectic next week," she said, reluctant to hang up.

"Okay. If you don't call me Monday, I'll phone you Tuesday unless I'm in Canada. If I have to go, I'll try to reach you before I head out."

"You can leave a message with Aunt Esther's housekeeper: her name is Miss Roth, Alexandra Roth."

Loring was silent for a second or two; Poppy surmised that he was writing down the name. "I'll do that. And you can give me the address then, too." He hesitated. "I'll cross my fingers for Monday."

"I will, too. I'm looking forward to it, and I apologize for having to postpone it. Thanks for the rain-check." She prepared to hang up. "Good luck with Overstreet." As she said it, she decided she would ask Holte if he could supply more information about Percy Knott, and a few more bits of information about Miles Overstreet; she was eager to find out anything that might lead her to Stacy, and the satisfaction of seeing him charged with her attempted murder. When she had felt the first stirrings of desire for revenge, she had been shocked, but now she was accustomed to them, and was able to relegate them to the bottom of her mental lists, but had one last thought: it was prudent to move out of Aunt Jo's house before the investigation of her case heated up again.

"Thanks, Poppy," he said, and rang off.

She sat still for over a minute, wanting to ask Holte what he thought of the conversation, but with six other reporters in the room clacking away at their typewriters, she did not want to seem completely out of her mind; she remained silent, planning to spend some time with Holte later that day, when they could talk in private. Perhaps she would learn more about the mysterious case he had alluded to, including why he felt it needed to be kept secret. With that for consolation, she prepared for her interview with Neva Plowright.

Holte drifted around the city room just below the ceiling, and found himself curious about what Poppy was going to do in the latter part of the afternoon. He considered his options, and made up his mind to join her in her Hudson when she made the drive to the Moncrief house, where Missus Plowright was staying. For the next half-hour, he watched Poppy jot questions in her notebook, sensing that she was not looking forward to the interview; small wonder, he told himself, since it would be awkward for both women. In the lobby of the Addison Newspaper Corporation building, she stopped to buy a cruller and a cup of coffee, ate both standing up, then wiped her fingers on a dish rag attached to the counter for that purpose; she winced at its well- used state but said nothing to the man behind the counter, who was known to be adverse to suggestions from customers.

When Poppy left the lobby, she had her large, patent-leather purse under her arm, and the keys to her car in her hand; in her other hand, she carried her brief-case. She walked swiftly to the alley where most of the *Clarion*'s staff who owned autos parked, all of them with their left- side tires on the narrow walkway in order to leave enough space in the street for vans and trucks to pass. Her Hudson stood out among the predominantly black autos—Fords for the most part—and she took pleasure in getting into it, proud as she was of the auto, and for once glad that she could afford such an obvious luxury. She unlocked the door, slipped inside onto the buff- colored leather front bench, and settled herself behind the wheel.

"There's a large van coming up behind you," Holte said from the rear seat. "He's not slowing down."

"Thanks. I see it in the rear-view mirror," she responded, not wanting to give him the satisfaction of knowing he had startled her. She rolled down the window, pressed the starter, adjusted the choke, counted to fifty as the engine warmed up, and engaged the clutch as she released the hand-brake, then put the Hudson into first gear. Gently depressing the accelerator, she pulled on the steering wheel before she thrust her left arm out of the window, held straight, to warn approaching traffic that she was about to come away from the curb just as the van lumbered by her. As soon as it was gone, she pulled out from her parking space and followed the larger vehicle to the corner, turned right, shifted into second gear, and headed toward the Moncrief house, driving carefully through a cluster of delivery vehicles that clogged the street.

"I haven't asked—how did you sleep last night?" Holte inquired, paying little attention to the traffic around them.

"Well enough. I woke up early, and that surprised me. I was afraid I might oversleep, even with the alarm on. Missus Boudon left a plate with a buttered muffin and two sausages, with instructions to put it in the oven at 375 for ten minutes. That would warm it up enough without burning the food, she informed me in the note she provided. I made my own coffee. It was kind of strange to be all alone in the kitchen, except for Maestro, who was complaining of hunger. I gave him a little of the leftover turkey. I guess I'd better get used to it—being alone in the morning. At least I know how to make breakfast for myself." She slowed down to pass a large delivery wagon laden with a great many burlap sacks and drawn by a quartet of large, seal- brown mules. The nearer on-side lead-mule laid back his ears and brayed when Poppy came abreast of him. "Not very well-mannered, is he?"

"Mules seldom are," Holte observed. "Doesn't your Aunt Esther have a cook?"

"She does. Missus Sassoro; but with Aunt Esther so often out of town, she has an...irregular schedule. I don't know how Missus Sassoro feels about more fixed hours. I suppose she and I will have to work something out."

Once past a wagon pulled by two sweating Percherons, Poppy picked up speed, but kept within the flow of traffic, growing more accustomed to the confusion around her. She was concentrating so intently on her driving that she did not quite hear the next question Holte asked. "Pardon me: what do you want?"

"I was asking if you were taking Allegheny or Lehigh." He sounded a bit amused. "I'd think Allegheny will get you to Riverview faster."

"I'm not going to Aunt Esther's until later—remember? I'm on my way to the Moncriefs' house, to talk to Louise's sister." Poppy's severity of expression astounded Holte. "I haven't decided how to approach her."

"It's not likely she'll be forthcoming; you'll have to deal with her indirectly," he said. "You might want to mention that this has been a difficult time for you, and for much the same reason that it has for Missus Plowright."

"Play on her sympathy, you mean?"

Holte hesitated before he spoke. "If you want to call it that."

"Spy-style?" Poppy suggested, and wished she could take the words back. "I'm sorry. I didn't intend that the way it sounded."

"I am aware of that," he said at his most reasonable. "But yes, that was what I was getting at. You'll learn more if you can avoid a direct confrontation. Let her take the lead, and choose the topics. You can make nudges, conversationally, that should get her to what you want to know."

Poppy braked at a new stop sign and watched a large truck laden with huge wheels of cheese and sacks of russet potatoes going across the intersection, followed by a taxi and an Oakland touring-car. When the way was clear, she went on, doing her best to make herself appear calm, in accord with Holte's suggestion, reminding herself that she would have to ration her energy; this was going to be a long day.

SIX

Missus Haas opened the door promptly in response to Poppy's knock. "Good afternoon, Miss Thornton. Missus Plowright is expecting you." She was dressed in black, and indicated the black wreath above the knocker; she made a dignified nod, as if to show that the household was still officially grieving. "They finally delivered the mourning decorations, two days after Missus Moncrief... left. I've had them refreshed once a week ever since, and will for the next two months. No matter what Missus Moncrief has done, her husband is still dead, and I'll make certain that we mourn him properly."

"You've done well," said Poppy, stepping into the beautiful entry-hall of the Moncriefs' house. There was black bunting over all the doors, and black-silk roses in a lilac vase next to the foot of the stairs. Black bands crossed the fronts of two old portraits. The place had an empty feeling to it, as if more than its owners were gone from it.

Missus Haas continued her recitation. "There are black ties on the draperies and around the mirrors—at least those downstairs—which will also be kept in place for another two months. Missus Moncrief's maid—you recall her? Missus Reedley?—has left, which leaves the kitchen understaffed. Missus Plowright will be doing interviews to replace her. The trouble is that this is short-term employment, and it will be difficult to find qualified help for what is likely to be only a few months; those who have applied so far are more interested in the notoriety than the running of the house." She smiled uncertainly. "I want to thank you for how well you handled your references to me and Missus Reedley in your articles. So considerate and tactful."

"I appreciated all your help," said Poppy, and noticed that Missus Haas was quite pale, and a bit thinner since the last time they had spoken; she could tell that the stress of the summer was weighing on her, so she said, "I'm sure that I'm keeping you from your work. Where is Missus Plowright? I don't want her to have to wait."

With another discreet lowering of her eyes, Missus Haas said, "She's in the back parlor; I'll show you the way."

"Thank you," said Poppy, and fell in behind Missus Haas as she went down a shadowed corridor; the walls were lined with paintings and photographs, several with small black bands across them, even the shell-shaped light sconces had black ribbons around their tops. The house was eerily silent, and there was a staleness in the air that could not be banished with open windows.

"I know I should set out some bouquets to sweeten the place," said Missus Haas, as if this lack were a serious social gaffe. "But it would look so disrespectful, and that is something I wish to avoid just now, things be as...uncertain as they are."

"Very sensible," Poppy agreed, and stopped behind Missus Haas, who was opening one of the pocket-doors in the corridor that revealed a fairly small but beautiful room, painted in periwinkle-blue, with upholstery and draperies in dull-gold. South-facing windows were sunlit, enlivening the back parlor and setting off three glass-fronted cabinets containing a large collection of Oriental porcelains, each carefully labeled; in spite of herself, Poppy was impressed; it was a gem of a room, and most likely the result of Louise's attention, who, in her own flighty way, had a deft way with decor.

Missus Haas stepped into the room, and addressed the woman in a walking-dress of deep- iris: half-mourning. She was seated at a neat, antique secretary, the desk open, and a stack of papers laid out in front of her, but looked up as Missus Haas announced, "Missus Plowright, Miss Thornton is here."

"Thank you," said Neva Plowright, gathering the pages together and setting a carnelian paperweight atop them before closing the front of the desk. That done, she turned around and held out her hand. "Miss Thornton. Thank you for coming."

"Thank you for seeing me," said Poppy, advancing and shaking Missus Plowwright's hand.

"I'm aware that this could be awkward for you," Missus Plowright said, gesturing to an overstuffed settee that stood at right angles to the window.

"Missus Haas will bring us tea shortly."

"It may be awkward for us both," said Poppy as she went to sit down. "Let me say that although my cousin may have run off with your sister, and that both of them remain unaccounted for, there are larger issues here, and those are the ones I believe we should address. We'll have to touch on Louise and Stacy, but the greater interest will focus on your brother-in-law's murder, as well as that of Percy Knott, and the impact these tragedies have had and are having upon you and your family."

Neva Plowright managed a weary smile, and left her chair at the secretary to occupy the grandmother chair next to the occasional table across from the settee. "It hasn't been an easy time."

"For any of us." Poppy took her notebook and pencil from her large purse. "If you don't mind, I'll take notes."

Neva Plowright made an automatic smile. "Go right ahead. I must admit that I am glad to have a break from gathering up information for the probate court."

"I'll be ready in a minute." While this was accurate, Poppy already knew what she wanted to ask, but she needed a little time to get a sense of what sort of person Louise's sister was, having never before had a private conversation with her. Looking at Neva Plowright, Poppy made a swift mental comparison of the two sisters: where Louise was pale-blonde, fey, and willowy, mercurial in temperament, and deliberately beautiful, Neva was more sturdily built, her dark-blonde hair in ordered waves, fashionable but not excessively stylish. Her features were less lovely than her sister's, but she was attractive in a way that had been in fashion twenty years ago. She was blessed with a disciplined manner and the demeanor of someone who would always make the effort to comport herself with dignity. Unlike Louise, Neva wore little make-up, and only a hint of violet scent. There was no suggestion of the flirtatious about her, nor any tinge of questionable conduct. No one would ever call Neva Plowright a madcap or a minx, as had often been the case with Louise. Poppy opened her notebook to an unused page and said, "I'd like to know a little about how things have been in the last month or so. I understand there have been some difficulties with Mister Moncrief's will."

"Yes, there have been, unfortunately." She folded her hands in her lap.

"Madison's attorney has been held up in discussions with Hadley and Grimes, who is claiming that Madison was part of what appears to have been a conspiracy to defraud their clients whose accounts were in his—Madison's—hands, which is blatantly untrue. There has been a threat from Hadley and Grimes to sue his estate for damages. He was rich enough to bear a reasonable settlement, if it comes to that, but I would be remiss in my duties if I failed to assist Madison's attorney in nipping that idea in the bud. Until this is straightened out, the whole estate will be in limbo."

"I've been aware of that." Poppy scribbled a few words and asked, "Has there been any progress in resolving the issues?"

"Not that I am aware of, but I am expecting to have a conference with my attorney as well as Madison's, and the representatives of Hadley and Grimes, before I return to Baltimore, very likely sometime next week. This has taken much longer than I first expected. When Louise left, I thought she would be gone for a month or so, to recover from the shock of Madison's death, but—" She unlocked her hands and attempted to smile. "I have been hoping to have some news of Louise; I've had nothing so far, and that is exacerbating the delays in settling the estate. I don't know how she wants me to proceed; I hope that my guesses will not be too far off the mark, when and if she conveys her wishes to me."

"That is a problem," Poppy said, a little taken aback that Missus Plowright, after indicating that she did not want to discuss her sister's affairs, should be so eager to bring Louise's highly irregular fortunes into their discourse.

"Shortly after she left," Missus Plowright went on as if she had not heard Poppy, "there was a new washing machine delivered to the house. Missus Haas said that Louise had ordered it before she departed for her unknown destination. But what am I to do with it? I have no authorization to sell the house or its contents at this time, and may not have it after the will is read. Both my sister and Madison had said they wanted me to be the executrix of their wills, but I have no idea if they got around to revising their wills to reflect this desire, let alone designating me officially, or providing me with instructions as to how to—" She stopped abruptly, her thoughts unfinished. "I'm sorry. I didn't mean to bring any of this up."

"Sometimes things of that nature just pop out." It was as much comfort as

Poppy thought she should give. "When will you know how things stand? If you want to say anything more on that point, that is."

"By next Tuesday at the latest, at least that's what their attorney, *Titus van Boew,* tells me." She took a handkerchief from the cuff of her sleeve and dabbed at the tears welling in her eyes. "Oh, dear. I'm sorry, Miss Thornton."

"Nothing to apologize for," said Poppy. "In your circumstances, I'd probably be hanging from the light-fixtures, and howling at the moon. Your composure is a lesson to me." She had a quick sense of Chesterton Holte drifting along the ceiling, but was uncertain if he had come in with her.

"You're very kind," said Missus Plowright.

"You certainly need this resolved," said Poppy, hoping to get their interview moving once again; she wrote Titus van Boew, doing her best to conceal her astonishment that Madison Moncrief's estate should be handled by a criminal attorney. "I trust that Mister van Boew has been available to advise you."

"Yes. He has, and I have followed his advice, although I do hate being so trammeled." She sniffed, wiped her nose, and folded her handkerchief neatly. "Where were we?"

Poppy chose her words carefully. "You were about to tell me how the current investigation has burdened your family." She held her pencil poised.

Missus Plowright nodded. "Yes; that's right." She sighed. "The worst of it is being away from my family. But the on-going public attention is troubling, and the press may not be on the doorstep hour on hour now, as they were for the first week after Madison's...death, but I hesitate to leave the house." Suddenly she turned to Poppy, her face exposing the depth of her chagrin. "I didn't mean you, Miss Thornton. You're being reasonable, and not at all intrusive. Please don't take my remarks personally."

"Oh, I won't," said Poppy. "And I can understand your feelings in regard to many of my colleagues."

"You would, wouldn't you? After what you went through," said Missus Plowright, still conscience-stricken. "I fear I'm making a hash of this."

"You're doing fine," Poppy assured her, and pressed on, "What in particular has been most difficult for you?"

Missus Plowright answered at once. "The not *knowing*. If only Louise had told me she was leaving, or sent me a letter when she arrived wherever it was, I wouldn't feel so rudderless. I have a thousand questions I want to ask her before I proceed, but all I'm left with is speculation, and that does no good. I dislike floundering, and that's all I've been able to do since she...went away. I love my sister dearly, but there are times I would like to shake her, and although I am deeply distressed by her absences, I still want to—" She stopped, chagrined.

"Understandably," said Poppy.

"And Mister North, from the District Attorney's office. That man will drive me to drink. I don't go two days without an impertinent call from him. You would think I were the criminal not that Louise or Madison could be called criminals."

"I know Denton North," said Poppy, "and I agree with you about him."

Missus Haas appeared in the doorway, a tray laden with a teapot, cups-and-saucers, a milk jug, a sugar-bowl, two folded linen napkins, and a plate of six napoleons. "Shall I put this on the table, Missus Plowright?"

Neva Plowright looked up. "If you would, please, Missus Haas." She nodded in Poppy's direction. "Do you mind if it's only napoleons?"

"Not at all. With everything that Missus Haas has to do here, I'm impressed that she has had the time"—and, she added to herself, the inclination—"to go to the French bakery."

Missus Haas shot a look of gratitude toward Poppy as she put the tray down. "I'll be in the laundry if you need anything more. You'll have to ring." She indicated the bell that sat on the small end-table next to the settee. "Shall I plan dinner for seven, Missus Plowright?"

"Whatever is convenient for you, Missus Haas," was her answer; she looked toward Poppy. "It's Assam; I'm afraid that's all we have."

"One sugar and a little milk, then, if you would," said Poppy, and wondered how well- stocked the kitchen and pantry were. If Louise had left her affairs in total disarray, which Poppy suspected she had, keeping the household running must not be easy.

While Missus Plowright poured out the tea, she said, "My husband is taking the train up this weekend. It seems an age since I've seen him, though it is only sixteen days. We've had four phone conversations while I've been here this time. I dislike the need for spending so much when the post is so reliable, but he says he misses the sound of my voice. Well, he'll be able to hear it for his entire visit." Her laugh was self-conscious, and she hurried on, "To celebrate his visit, I went to Butterworth's yesterday and bought a new dress and a hat. I don't want to look a complete hag when he arrives. Napoleon?" She held out the plate with one hand and Poppy's cup-and-saucer with the other.

Poppy put down her notebook, accepted her tea, and selected one of the elegant pastries to put on the broad sauce next to the cup. "Thank you. This looks very good."

"Oh, yes; for ordinary occasions, I am quite fond of French pastries. There is something about their flavor and texture that hints at the forbidden, and they make me feel so self- indulgent," said Missus Plowright, and poured herself some tea, adding three lumps of sugar. "I have a dreadful sweet- tooth."

"It's easy to do with such delicious pastry," said Poppy, taking a sip of the tea; it was too hot, so she set the cup-and-saucer on the end-table.

After a brief nod, Missus Haas withdrew, leaving Missus Plowright alone with Poppy and the tray of afternoon tea.

"She's been a great help, staunch, self-sufficient, and steady as a rock," Missus Plowright confided, leaning a bit forward and lowering her voice. "I know Louise thought well of her, but never said what a treasure she is. That's very like Louise; taking people for granted."

"Do you mean your sister did not appreciate Missus Haas?" Poppy asked, to be sure.

"Oh, certainly Louise undervalued Missus Haas. She is a most capable woman, reliable and trustworthy. For the most part, I can leave her to her own devices." She put two of the napoleons on her saucer with her teacup. "The few times I've had to supervise her, she complied without complaint, and has often made respectful suggestions as to how we might begin to pack up the house, and deal with general maintenance; for the most part, they have been quite sensible recommendations. She works tirelessly, and I need not bother myself about minor chores or regular tasks being done. When I am away, I don't have to worry about how she is managing without me, for she's proved to be trustworthy. She is unflagging in her dedication to Louise, being careful to preserve all confidences entrusted to her. Her good judgement is beyond reproach. I'm afraid I'd make a wretched farrago of all that has to be done on my own; Missus Haas has no such problems. I have no idea what Louise wants to keep, what she wants to store, or what she would like me to dispose of; Missus Haas has been a great help in making those kinds of decisions."

Thinking of Missus Flowers' careful handling of Aunt Jo, Poppy said, "Housekeepers always know more than we give them credit for."

Missus Plowright wiped her fingers on her napkin, glancing wistfully at the remaining napoleons. "Very true. Mister Plowright tells me that he leaves the running of the household to me, but I would be lost without Missus Carew, and I know Louise never gives a thought to all that Missus Haas does."

"I'm sure you can resolve household matters… and with Missus Haas' help, you can sort out your sister's affairs appropriately," Poppy said, convinced that Missus Plowright needed reassurance. "If you decide in ways that Louise would not like, then she should have left you instructions, shouldn't she."

This simple observation brightened Missus Plowright's mood. "Yes, she should have. You're right. But forethought is not in her nature—never was. She's been governed by her impulses since she was a baby." She picked up the second of her napoleons and bit into it, taking care to wipe her mouth with her napkin after the bite. "So good."

"So you think her departure was impetuous?" Poppy was half-expecting Missus Plowright to object to this question, and was dumbfounded when Missus Plowright laughed. "You don't think it was planned? Since she apparently left the country, that isn't something that can be done on the spur of the moment, is it?"

"Gracious, no, but I do think it was a sudden decision. She was fretting about the funeral, and having to maintain the decorum of grief, so she left. I know that some people have claimed that there was some sort of plan between Louise and your cousin, but that is so unlike Louise. For one thing, if such a plan had existed, she would have told a dozen of her friends about it, swearing them to secrecy, naturally; half of Philadelphia would have known about it in a week."

Poppy waited while Missus Plowright finished her napoleon, then asked, "Has Mister Eastley been any help to you? I've assumed he would be, for Louise's sake." Julian Eastley had been Louise's frequent companion during her marriage to Madison Moncrief, and although Eastley was devoted to her, there was never a whisper of scandal about his idolatry. "He adored your sister, just adored her."

Missus Plowright took a sip of tea, then shook her head. "No, he has not been helpful; he said it was too painful to be here, in this house. He's gone back to his place on Godwin Lane. I haven't seen hide nor hair of him in weeks. He didn't come to Madison's funeral, though he did send a memorial wreath to the church. He hasn't phoned the house in over a month, and I am just as glad that he has not, for I wouldn't know what to say to him." She had another sip. "I know he is reckoned to be a great hero—and he may well have been, in the Great War—but his conduct has left me with a very poor opinion of him."

Poppy was surprised to hear this, but did her best to conceal her reaction to this news. "How unlike him."

"Missus Haas told me that he phoned once when I was home in Baltimore. She thought he might be drunk, because he was weeping. I suppose I ought to feel sympathy for him, but given his behavior, I can't."

"If he has behaved so poorly, there is no reason to sympathize," Poppy assured her. "Have you had other visitors?"

Missus Plowright nodded. "Your aunt has been kind enough to call twice, to commiserate with me on the lack of information we both have had from our missing kin. Then Isme Greenloch has visited once, but she seemed to be searching for some shreds of gossip rather than to provide support to me, not that I blame her for her curiosity. The same with Eulalle Kinnon, although she only phoned; I'm sure the operator listened to everything we said, and no doubt told her friends. I had a very nice note from Fernald and Bernadette Stanton, but they have not come by. Isadora Pearse sent a note, but said that she would be unable to call. I can understand her reluctance, given the situation with her son; seeing me would likely be a reminder of the missing."

Poppy could think of nothing to say, so she once again changed the subject. "How much longer do you plan to be here?"

"On this visit? I think I will have to be here until the end of next week. I'll have to consult with Mister van Boew, but I trust he will understand my desire to return to my family, at least until there is some progress on Madison's estate. I have obligations at home, you know." She took a third napoleon from the plate. "I'll probably ruin my appetite for dinner, but I can't resist them. I hope you don't mind."

"They are excellent," Poppy agreed, even though she had done little more than taste her own. "You've had a great deal to contend with, Missus Plowright."

"That I have, but someone has to do it, and as I am the eldest, the responsibility falls to me." She said this without any trace of self-pity, which Poppy attributed to what was probably a life-long pattern with the sisters. "But I will be glad when it's over."

"With good reason, it seems to me; to have your brother-in-law killed and then your sister vanishes—that's a lot to bear," said Poppy, and drank the rest of her tea, preparing to make her excuses. "If you hear anything about your sister, will you let me know? I don't mean for the paper; we're still looking for my cousin, and Louise might know where he's gone."

"Certainly. You seem intelligent; you will know what to reveal, and what to keep private." Missus Plowright took a sip of tea, clearly buying time while she made up her mind how to go on. "I spoke with Rudy before I left Baltimore, and he hasn't heard anything from Louise, either. He's in Florida, you know."

"Rudy?" Poppy asked, trying to remember who that was.

"Our brother. Well. Half-brother. Our mother was married twice. Rudolph Norman Beech. I don't suppose you've met him. When Louise went away, I thought that perhaps she had gone to Rudy, but she had not." Missus Plowright sighed. "They were very close as children, but that...faded when Rudy was sent off to school in the sixth grade; he'd had tutors before that."

"Did he have any idea where she might have gone?"

"He said that in her last letter, she told him that she wanted to travel. She had said something about South America—she didn't want to go back to Europe until it had recovered from the Great War, according to Rudy. But she might have changed her mind; the last time she and I spoke, she was thinking about Australia."

This coincided with what Poppy had heard from others. "Australia, or South America. That doesn't narrow it down much, does it?"

Missus Plowright gave a little shrug. "And she might not be in either place. It depends on whatever whim she had."

Poppy closed her notebook and put it back in her purse. "I'm sorry, but I have another commitment in twenty minutes. I want to thank you for being so forthcoming, and for receiving me so graciously. I will make every effort to be circumspect in what I write, and will see to it that you have a copy of the *Clarion* in which my story on our meeting occurs. And if I learn anything that may be of use to you, I will notify you of it promptly." She did her best to smile. "I trust you and your husband will have a pleasant reunion this weekend."

"I'd be grateful for that." Missus Plowright held out her hand. "It was kind of you to visit me, Miss Thornton. I had reservations about talking to you, but I can see now that I had no cause for concern. You are aware of how to manage delicate matters like this one, particularly since a member of your family seems to be directly involved, along with my sister." She set down her unfinished napoleon. "If I learn anything more that might be useful to you, I will pass it on to you, and hope that it benefits us both."

Poppy made her farewells and left the house without encountering the redoubtable Missus Haas on her way. As she drove toward the police station, she felt more perplexed than ever about Stacy and Louise Moncrief—so much so that she was disappointed when Chesterton Holte did not make his presence known, if he were with her; she wanted his opinion on what had just transpired, so that she could make up her mind about all that Neva Plowright had told her, and what Poppy surmised she had withheld.

SEVEN

THE PRESS BRIEFING HAD BEEN LATE IN STARTING, BUT HAD BEEN COMPARATIVELY short, and had consisted of Commissioner Elmer Smiley introducing the men who were investigating the robbery, starting with Inspector Ned Harper, who was in charge of the case; Harper, in turn, introduced the four men working under him, all of whom promised speedy results without admitting that so far, they had no leads and no clues as to the culprits' identities. They spoke with enthusiasm about fingerprints and two footprints, but evaded questions about progress in identifying either; Poppy duly copied down their various remarks, and left the briefing as soon as it ended. Back at the paper she had handed her notes to Lowenthal after writing a quick summary of her meeting with Missus Plowright and those she had taken at the briefing; she had left the building at quarter to four, unlocked the right-rear door of her auto before getting behind the wheel, then drove as rapidly as possible to the train station, where she caught sight of Aunt Esther waiting on the curb, two suitcases and a trunk at her side.

Esther Thornton resembled her sister Josephine Dritchner to the extent that she had the same badger-grey hair and was much the same height and build, and the same shape of nose, but in demeanor and style, she was much more like their brother, Poppy's late father—hale at seventy-two, inquisitive, clever, and capable—and seeing her gave Poppy a brief but intense pang of sorrow.

From behind her, Chesterton Holte said, "She is very like him, isn't she." He had known Beresford Oliver Thornton for less than a day, but his recollection of Poppy's father was acute; they had met over lunch at an inn near Liège, had spent a pleasant hour comparing their impressions of the progress of the Great War and sharing tales about their homes—Thornton's in Philadelphia, Holte's in Halifax, Nova Scotia—and by the end of the afternoon, both of them were dead.

Aware now that he was with her, Poppy looked into the rear-view mirror and saw only a shimmer that might have been a reflection of sunlight. "In many ways," she responded, jockeying for access to the curb.

"I can see how your Aunt Jo might not approve of your Aunt Esther," Holte remarked with a trace of amusement in his tone. "Between them, they must have driven their parents to madness, being so opposite."

"I suppose so." Poppy was concentrating on maneuvering around a taxi, and said nothing more to Holte as she finally pulled up about two feet beyond where her aunt stood; she put the Hudson in neutral and set the brake. "So sorry I'm late, Aunt Esther; I had work to finish at the paper," she exclaimed as she leaned over to open the passenger door.

Esther said something that Poppy could not hear over the honking of a black sedan passing on her left. Esther signaled to a porter, who came promptly to assist her. "Put the trunk in the...trunk, and the suitcases on the back seat, please," she said, handing him a very generous dollar tip. "Is there a key for the trunk of your auto? I suppose you keep it locked—if you'll provide the key?" she asked as she pulled the passenger door wide and held out her hand for it. "It won't take long to load."

Poppy fumbled to get it off of her key-chain, then offered it to Aunt Esther. "Here. The rear door is open on your side." She thought she heard Holte chuckle, but with the clamor of the train station all around her, she could not be sure.

The porter got the trunk open and shoved Aunt Esther's trunk inside, then slammed the lid down and locked it before coming to put the suitcases in the back and to return the key to Aunt Esther. He touched the brim of his cap and closed the door, then went to help a middle-aged man get his luggage out of the auto behind Poppy's Hudson; Esther waved to him.

"How was your journey?" Poppy asked as she signaled with her arm to pull away from the curb.

Esther removed her modified trilby and set it on the seat beside her. "Most of it was wretched. I wish now that I had kept with my original plan and returned to America via the Pacific instead of coming back through the Soviet

Union and Europe to cross the Atlantic. We had squalls three days out of Southampton." She made a sound between a laugh and a snort. "Soviet Union. Now there's an irony for you. It would be difficult to find a self-proclaimed country that is more divisive." She ran her fingers through her jaw-length hair and removed her glasses to clean them with a pale-blue linen handkerchief. "If the Ottoman Empire hadn't gone the way of the Dodo, some Soviet ambitions might have been better-focused in dealing with their own people than they are now. And with Lenin dead, the men in power are at one another's throats, and the Russian people are paying the price."

"In what way?" Poppy asked, a dawning notion of preparing an independent article on what her aunt had observed, forming in her thoughts. "What is happening to the people?"

A Dodge Brothers Model 9 went by them, speeding through the crowd at more than thirty miles an hour, swerving in and out of the slower-moving vehicles, accompanied by hoots and shouts from the vehicles around it.

"That's a foolish fellow," Aunt Esther remarked, keeping track of the Model 9's erratic progress along the street. "He's not going to go much faster than if he keeps to the speed of those around him, and he is risking an accident, going in and out of traffic like that."

"He's not the only one on the road who drives recklessly," said Poppy, pointing out a model A Ford that was weaving through lanes ahead of them.

"That's no excuse," Aunt Esther said, for once sounding very much like her sister Josephine. "They're being irresponsible."

"This from a woman who flies aeroplanes." Poppy fell in behind a delivery van, and settled into a steady twenty miles an hour. The afternoon sun glinted off the radiator cap at the front of the hood, forcing Poppy to squint in order to see anything beyond shine. "About the Soviet Union?"

Aunt Esther made an irritated gesture. "Oh. Yes." She thought for half a minute, and then answered Poppy's question. "For one thing, the Soviets could have done something to stop the slaughter of the Armenians, had they not been squabbling internally, back when the damage was being done. If the Soviets had taken the time to put pressure on the Ottomans, then the worst abuses might have been prevented, and perhaps the Ottoman Empire would not have fallen so abruptly. Those poor people were killed by the thousands, and no one seemed to mind, or to notice, and the Great War is no excuse for that lack. The few Armenians who escaped the massacre have been left to wander all around eastern Europe, or parts of the Middle East, where there is little acceptance of Orthodox Christians. I saw a group of them in Vienna: they were called Living Spectres by their leader, having no work, no homes, and no prospects of either. The Armenian Orthodox priest who looked after them, a fanatic of sorts, told them that their suffering would bring them glory in Paradise, for they would wear the crowns of martyrs. I believe his name was Ahram Avaikian, and his people venerated him for saving their lives. They had taken a vow of pacifism, which is understandable, considering what had happened to so many of their people—it was that or open rebellion, and they were in no position to undertake armed conflict. They were housed in hovels and survived on bits of charity provided by the Austrians, who are having troubles of their own. I have a couple of photographs I took of the camp where about a hundred Armenians were living in conditions that would embarrass a Hottentot; I was hoping to have the National Geographic Society run an article about the plight of Armenian refugees, but I haven't been able to convince them of the significance of the crisis, which just goes to show you how appalling their situation has become." She shook her head. "There are times I am embarrassed to be a human being."

"Would you like me to speak to my editor about an article from you?" Poppy ventured.

"On the Armenians? Certainly. But I doubt he'll be interested. If the National Geographic Society won't run such a piece, I doubt the *Clarion* would, either. But don't let me discourage you. I'd be pleased to find out I was wrong." She gazed out the window. "It's strange. I rarely get homesick until I return here, and then it hits me that I've missed this place. While I'm away, it rarely crosses my mind."

"Anywhere in particular you'd like to see?" Poppy asked, wanting to show her pleasure in her aunt's company. "I could drive you by."

"Not yet. Give me a day or two, and I'll have pangs for those parts of the city that have changed since I left, like those lakes you told me the city would be draining." Esther smoothed the front of her pewter-colored jacket. "I must be quite bedraggled."

"You look wonderful," said Poppy, adding diplomatically, "But your skirt is a little wrinkled."

"A little?" she scoffed. "I appreciate your kindness, if not your candor. I need to do something about my appearance before I step out in public. Is there a beauty shop that will take me on short notice, I wonder? I wouldn't blame anyone for thinking I had traveled in steerage."

"Would you like to go home, Aunt Esther?"

"Home, yes, if you don't mind. You're going in the right direction."

"I did assume," said Poppy.

"With good reason. We'll set Galliard to unloading—he knows we're coming. I sent the staff a telegram last night, so they could prepare for my arrival. We can get my things out of this auto, and set my employees to work, and I'll change clothes." Esther sniffed her sleeve and made a face. "I feel as if I've been wearing these for an age. I can't wait to shed them, and to get out of my stays. I suppose I should invest in a few of those new brassieres they're selling now; so much more comfortable than corsets, they tell me." She leaned against the back of the seat, her eyes closing a little. "Then I want to have a drink, and after that, a good meal somewhere pleasant, and when we get back from dining, I plan to soak in the tub until my fingers pucker."

"Will you want to be up for breakfast?" Poppy asked, doing her best to work out how to respond to her aunt.

Esther sat up. "Naturally I'll want breakfast. I'll have Missus Sassoro serve it at seven-thirty, if she's willing to arrive so early; only Miss Roth lives in, as I suppose you know better than I at this point." She took a deep breath, exhaled, and said, "Good gracious, Poppy, I'm not such a ninny that five months of travel leaves me worn to the bone."

"I didn't suppose you were," said Poppy. "But you've covered—what is it?— well over ten thousand miles in the last two months; and from what your letters have described, not all those miles were easy ones."

Aunt Esther laughed again. "Don't imagine me such a hot-house flower that I need to indulge myself in fainting fits, if that's what's bothering you. I recover reasonably quickly, even at my age." She reached over to pat Poppy's arm. "Not that I don't appreciate your concerns, because I do, but I'm not used to coddling myself. Neither are you, I gather."

"I'm nowhere near as adventuresome as you are," Poppy said, a bit wistfully.

"That's not what my sister says," Aunt Esther told her.

"She's written to you?" Poppy asked, puzzled. "When did she do that?"

"In mid-June, I think. The letter caught up with me in Vienna, toward the end of July. I spent six days, doing research, and I found more than a dozen letters waiting for me when I arrived, four from you, and two from Jo among them; she asked me if I might consider having you live with me, since you were making such a fuss about Stacy's so-called prank."

Poppy was taken aback. "Aunt Jo never said anything about that to me. I assumed the idea was yours."

Esther could see Poppy stiffen, and continued more companionably. "When I read Jo's letters, I decided it would be a fine solution to the animosity that plainly was developing between the two of you. I'm capable of reading between the lines, especially when the lines are Jo's. She insists that you made too much of what she called Eustace's escapade, saying that no one could have foreseen that he would be unable to return to set you free which, she insisted in her second letter, he had every intention of doing. She's never going to understand what a weasel Stacy is, but I could tell from the first that he had his mother mesmerized, and still does. Only Jo could think that locking you in a warehouse basement was intended to be a joke."

"I was tied to a chair, as well," Poppy said.

"Jo believes you exaggerated your danger, so I thought I could defuse the situation by providing you a bolt-hole, and I'm pleased to have you in my house. It wants more regular occupation than I can provide, and you are not going to be traipsing about the world, as I do. The staff is a good one, and attentive; there's no question of them being irresponsible. They manage the place very well when I'm gone, but it's not the same as having someone in residence to maintain the place properly. You're one of the family, and you understand how I like things done. I know you'll do your usual capable duty, and guard my house from neglect or anything untoward." Esther clapped her hands twice, as if seeking the attention of all Philadelphia. "There. I've said it. You're helping me as much as I am you."

"Well, however it came about, I'm looking forward to living in your house. It is...cozier than Aunt Jo's." Poppy felt nonplussed by what Aunt Esther had revealed, and wondered what Holte made of it, assuming he was still in the auto.

"That's good, because I'm looking forward to having you with me. I'll be glad of your company," she reiterated with gusto.

A bit unsure of herself, Poppy tried to hide her confusion with practical information, "That's reassuring, because I've already moved fourteen boxes over from Aunt Jo's to your house. I'm in the larger bedroom on the second floor, as you recommended to me. I like it—all the trees around it, and so much light."

"You can have the study, if you like. It's too small to be useful for entertaining, and in any case, I use the front parlor for guests, and the sitting room for myself in the evening, but that's—" She stopped speaking as a clamor of horns announced a minor accident ahead on the road; slewing around in her seat, she peered out the rear window. "Goodness, how long has the traffic been this bad?"

"Not as long as you might think. The last two years have seen the largest increase, almost all of it automobiles and trucks. There's talk of widening some of the streets, but nothing much has come of it so far." She held her arm out the window, angled up to indicate a right-hand turn, and endured the aggravated honk from a taxi two autos behind them. "We should be at your door in another ten minutes, barring mishaps."

"At least the roads have been improved," said Aunt Esther. "Missus Sassoro can probably put together a bit of finger-food to help us stave off hunger until we can decide where we want to dine."

"Would you rather stop now?" Poppy asked. "If you're hungry, we could get a sandwich or two at Louie's."

"No reason to do that, but it's kind of you to offer." She pinched the bridge of her nose. "I should make an appointment with Doctor Sawyer I need a new pair of reading glasses. The ones I have now are three years old, and my eyes have aged more than I'd like to admit. I should attend to it sooner than later." She squinted at a couple on the sidewalk. "Gracious! Have skirts really gotten so short?"

"Is your need urgent? For new glasses?" Poppy slowed down behind a delivery wagon drawn by four Fjord ponies with hogged, two-tone manes and braided, two-toned tails.

"Somewhat. I have a fair amount of writing I need to do in the next couple of weeks, and I don't want a constant headache. Having my hair done is as much vanity as necessity. I'm beginning to look like the leaves for a bonfire." She watched a group of school- children accompanied by two harried adults make their way across the intersection ahead. "Things seem so...so normal, don't they? The fashions have changed a bit—the skirts, for example, and so many young women with short hair: I don't mean you, Poppy; your hair is modern but not extreme. But the children still look like children, and the delivery wagons are pretty much unchanged. The autos are more interesting than they were when I left."

"Unchanged compared to what?" Poppy sensed Holte behind her once more, and resisted the urge to speak to him.

"Compared to the Soviet Union, and a good portion of Europe, where damage is still obvious from the Great War and the Revolution, as well as the Flu." Aunt Esther glanced around the street now that they were nearing her neighborhood. "They finally took down the Black Crow?" She pointed to a space between buildings, like a missing tooth in a smile, where a century- old tavern had stood.

"Last autumn; about two weeks after you left. The city declined to make it a landmark, so the owners sold it. The buyers say there's going to be a department store there by next summer, like the ones in New York City. They're taking Gimbels as their model." Poppy positioned herself for another right turn.

"That's a good plan, I suppose, if the city doesn't load the design up with requirements. With Prohibition, the Black Crow would not have been able to keep its doors open for very long in any case." She took a last look at the place where the tavern had been. "Does anyone know yet how foolish it is to outlaw alcohol? The government has created a whole new area of crime, more fools they."

"I hate to say it, but you sound like Aunt Jo." Poppy turned into the side-street and started up a gentle rise toward a cluster of trees that crowned it.

Aunt Esther shrugged philosophically. "I suppose she and I have to agree on a few things." She coughed once. "Incidentally, is there really a police inspector you're sweet on, or is Jo being a snob again?"

Poppy's chuckle did not quite come off. "There is an inspector, yes, but Aunt Jo is worried about nothing. I like him well enough, but I have my work to consider." She held her arm out once more, bent down along the side of door, indicating that she was slowing down in preparation to pulling over. "I do like the setting here. You're high enough up to have a view of the river, and the neighborhood is pretty."

"I agree," said Aunt Esther. "It's good to be home. Park in the driveway for now, so Galliard can unload the trunk."

EIGHT

On Friday the move went more smoothly than either Aunt Jo or Aunt Esther had anticipated, or that Poppy had hoped for. Half of Saturday and all of Sunday, Poppy had busied herself with unpacking and arranging, assisted by Miss Roth, so that by that evening, as she was sitting in the parlor with Aunt Esther, enjoying a companionable glass of cognac and a plate of spiced lamb with mint jelly in pastry shells, she felt deeply satisfied, even though her arms ached and she was slightly featherbrained with fatigue.

"All in all, a most satisfactory day," Aunt Esther pronounced as she put her feet up on the rotund leather poof in front of the sofa.

"I hope so," said Poppy, lifting her gaze from the plate of appetizers.

Aunt Esther poured out a second tot of cognac into her bell-shaped glass, and said, "I gather you're almost settled in." The parlor was on the north side of the house, and by now was darkening with the coming of sundown. Aunt Esther had done her version of dressing for dinner by donning a long skirt of iris-blue wool crepe and a long-sleeved sweater in a slightly lighter shade, which she had ornamented with a strand of high-quality pearls. She smiled over the rim of her glass. "Cheers."

"I think I am, for the most part, settled in," said Poppy, noticing that the newly lit table- lamp was flickering. "I've got almost all my clothes put away, my bed is made, my luggage is in the back of the garage, and my Hudson is protecting it for the moment. I'll need to install some bookcases in the drawing room, if it's all right with you." She said this tentatively, glancing at her aunt as she said this.

"It certainly is all right with me. I'm always happy to see more books in the house. Talk to Galliard about what you want done, and he'll get to it this week. In the meantime, feel free to make use of any of my books you like. A goodly number are in the study." Aunt Esther scowled at the lamp. "September lightning," she accused the wavering lamp-bulb, then went on, "Now that you're in, would you like to have a small gathering of your friends and colleagues around, to make your move official? I was thinking that Friday evening might be a good time for a buffet. Nothing elaborate, so no one will have to dress excessively, but genial: dinner jackets optional, and the same for long skirts. It will cover an occasion for my return, as well, so don't think that you're imposing upon me, for you're not. I'll ask Jo, if that's acceptable to you. She might not come, but it would be a politic gesture. Think it over. You could invite your editor and your police inspector if you'd enjoy having them here."

Poppy had put on a dinner-dress of ochre linen; its simple V-neck and dropped waist were fashionable enough, but almost casual; Aunt Esther might not mind it, but Aunt Jo most certainly would; she would need something grander for Friday. Poppy smiled. "You want to check them out, do you? Lowenthal and Loring?" She cocked her head. "It could be a nice way to mark the transition. But if you're going to invite Aunt Jo, you should probably include Hank and Cecily—they'll be here until the sixteenth—and one or two of her other friends, or she'll have to stay away. You know what she's like."

"Sadly, I do know. Yet I'd love to see Hank, and meet his new wife. I've liked him since he was in short-pants. I hope he hasn't turned out like Tobias has." Aunt Jo paused. "Your brother was such an engaging child, and he's damned impossible now."

"So he is," said Poppy sadly, unshocked by her aunt's language.

"Then we shan't invite him to the party. He's become such a stuffed shirt, he probably wouldn't enjoy it, anyway." Aunt Esther nodded, and took another sip of cognac as if to summon up her courage. "Would you mind if I included Benedict Stephanson among the guests? He's a very old friend."

"It's your party and your house," said Poppy. "If you want Judge Stephanson here, by all means, invite him. I won't protest."

"You may, if you like. The party is mostly for you, and that gives you veto power." She turned toward the door as Miss Roth approached. "Is anything wrong?"

"No, not exactly. Mister Hawkins is here. He has something for Miss Poppy."

Miss Roth's face revealed nothing as to what that might be.

"I must have forgotten something at Aunt Jo's," Poppy said, feeling apologetic. "I'll just go get it." She put her glass aside and stood up. "If you'll excuse me?"

"Go on," said Aunt Esther. "Thank you, Miss Roth," she added.

Miss Roth fell in next to Poppy as she left the parlor. "The side entrance, Miss Poppy."

"Thank you," said Poppy, and turned toward the sitting room reserved for the staff; there was a door between that and the kitchen, which led out into the kitchen-garden.

Standing just inside it, Hawkins held a large cardboard box with small holes cut into it in his arms; a battery of loud feline complaints came from inside it. "Miss Thornton," he said unhappily.

Poppy stared. "Ye gods! Is that—"

"—the cat?" he finished for her. "Yes. Missus Dritchner says you had better take him; he's done nothing but scratch and yowl since you left." He held out the box. "I have his sand in the auto."

Miss Roth stood very still, her face impassive. "Do you want me to take...it up to your room, Miss Poppy?"

Recovering herself a little, Poppy shook her head. "I'd better do it. Maestro doesn't know you, and he's...in a strange place." She grabbed the box. "If you'll tell Mister Hawkins where you want to put Maestro's sand? I'd recommend the upstairs bathroom, but my aunt might prefer a different arrangement." She could feel Maestro shift inside the box, and caught a glimpse of a black nose thrust up to one of the small holes. "I'll close the door at the top of the stairs, to keep him confined until he's used to the place."

"Thank you, Miss Thornton. I'll just go get his bag of sand," said Hawkins, and opened the door to step outside.

"I'll tend to this," Miss Roth said to Poppy. "If you will take the..." she faltered, trying to decide what to call the cat.

"His name is Maestro. He is a former tom, so you needn't worry about his behavior too much." That was not quite candid, and she knew it, but she would explain about the cat's temperament later. "I'll take him up now, and get a bowl of milk for him before my aunt and I sit down to dinner, if you'll ask Missus Sassoro to get it ready for him."

"Very good, Miss Poppy." Miss Roth turned her attention to the garden door.

Satisfied that the competent Miss Roth would handle matters, Poppy made for the stairs, listening to Maestro's proclaiming his displeasure. "What on earth am I to do with you, Maestro?" she asked as she hurried up the stairs. As she reached the top, she hooked the door with her foot and jerked it closed behind her. "You'll have to stay up here for a day or two," she informed Maestro as she set the box on the hallway runner and opened the top.

Maestro laid back his ears and hissed fulsomely, his baleful stare directed at a dim spot in the air hovering in the open door of Poppy's bedroom.

"Hello, cat," said Chesterton Holte as Maestro slid out of the box and made for the safety under Poppy's bed.

"Why did Aunt Jo send him over?" Poppy asked Holte.

"Revenge?" Holte suggested mischievously.

Poppy resisted the urge to make a sharp rejoinder. "I believe you two can amuse each other while I go back to the parlor," she said with exaggerated courtesy. "I'll make sure he has—"

"—a bowl of milk in a short while," Holte said, drifting upward.

"Yes; I thought you were listening," said Poppy, and opened the door at the top of the stairs. "Don't bedevil the cat while I'm gone."

"That will depend on the cat more than me," Holte remarked as Poppy started down the stairs after making certain that the door was fully closed.

"So now you have Jo's cat," Aunt Esther said by way of greeting as Poppy came back into the parlor. "Miss Roth told me."

"I hope you don't mind," said Poppy. "Or Miss Roth, for that matter. He's not such a bad creature."

"If you want him, there's no reason you can't keep him, so far as I'm concerned. After all, I'll be gone in a few weeks, and you'll have the house to yourself until after New Year's, and the cat will provide you a little company while I'm boating up the Amazon, not that I expect you to live like a hermit." She chuckled. "He's not much of a chaperon, is he? But you're twenty-five now, aren't you? So that shouldn't be an issue."

"Born May 27th, 1899, so I turned twenty-five this year," Poppy said, trying to contain her chagrin.

"Yes; I remember. Oliver was beside himself with delight." Esther sounded a bit wistful, but did not belabor it. "Don't let me become maudlin about his death, will you?"

"Not if you don't want to." Poppy sat down, picked up her glass, and drank down the last bit of cognac. "I'll bear that in mind."

"I asked Miss Roth to have Missus Sassoro gather up some scraps of lamb for...him?"

"Thanks. Yes; him. Maestro will be glad of something to eat," said Poppy. "I'll keep him upstairs for a week or so; that way he won't be underfoot at the party."

"That's probably wise," Aunt Esther said. "And speaking of the party, how many guests would you like to have?"

"For a buffet? You know better than I how many can be in this house without crowding, and what your staff can accommodate. What would you like?"

"I've been thinking about that while you were dealing with...Maestro." Aunt Esther gave a decisive nod. "Shall we say twenty guests or so? Perhaps a few more, making allowances for spouses. Missus Sassoro will have an opportunity to shine; she doesn't get that very often with me. I'll ask her to arrange for more help for the party so she won't have to pay attention to anything more than cooking. Miss Roth can work out the plans in the next day or two. I'll have Galliard get in touch with Enrico Ruscelli, to arrange for the wine and booze; he's Galliard's usual legger. Supposed to have premium goods."

"Italian?" Poppy guessed from the name.

"Second generation American, but with many relatives back in Genoa, so he has access to all the French wines and spirits as well as the Italian ones." Esther tapped the bottle of cognac. "This is some of what he imports; I think you'd agree it's top quality."

"It is good," Poppy agreed. "You said a buffet—how extensive will it be?"

"I'll have to speak to Missus Sassoro about it. She understands these things better than I, and she'll be able to supply a good number of side- dishes and a great deal of finger-food; no one need go hungry. I won't have to concern myself with them, but we don't want it to look shabby. I think a crown roast of pork might be nice, and perhaps a rack of lamb. I'm fond of lamb." She paused and made a face. "I've had camel, in the Middle East, which I don't like, and dog in Manchuria, which bothers me—it has nothing to do with the taste or texture; it's the idea of dog that I dislike."

"Then let's not have any," Poppy said, and saw her aunt smile.

"I'll let you know what Missus Sassoro recommends," said Aunt Esther.

"Will you invite anyone from the National Geographic Society?" Poppy asked, trying to imagine how large an event Aunt Esther really had in mind.

"I suppose I should. It will make for an interesting mix, don't you think? Elliott Wickman ought to be invited, and Professor Timms; he'll bring that dreadful wife of his, but it can't be helped." She shot another disapproving look at the flickering lamp. "I suppose I'll have to have that repaired."

"Shall I screw the bulb in more tightly?" Poppy offered.

Aunt Esther's frown remained in place. "I'll ask Miss Roth to replace the bulb."

Poppy resisted the urge to apologize for Chesterton Holte's usual disruption of electric light, not wanting to broach the subject of his haunting. "It may be the weather; the evening is fairly humid."

The light stuttered again.

"So it is," Aunt Esther agreed, eyeing the lamp with suspicion. "But I don't want the light going out during the party. I'll ask Miss Roth to get a new bulb for it. And something brighter for the porch-light; it's as gloomy as an abandoned tomb with the one we have now." She took a long sip of cognac, her intense stare indicating she was lost in thought. Then her gaze shifted to the appetizers on the china plate. "Have another canapé. Dinner won't be served for twenty minutes at least, and with all you've been doing today, you must be famished."

Obediently Poppy reached for another of the lamb-filled pastry shells. "These are very good. I don't think I've had anything like them before."

"I got the recipe in Greece, on my way toward the Soviet Union. It was easier to come in through the southern route than from central Europe, and I did my best to make the most of it." Aunt Esther grinned at the memory. "I collected about a dozen new dishes on the trip. I think I may have Missus Sassoro make the cheese fritters that the Greeks offer with bread in the evening. They serve it all with some devilish twice-distilled plum brandy that they pour for their guests as a welcoming libation, which they offer along with a saucer of salt and a pinch of bread."

"Are all your new recipes Greek?" Poppy inquired, fairly certain that Aunt Esther would enjoy telling her about her most recent journey; she bit the lamb and pastry-shell in two, chewing discreetly.

"Four of them are. The rest are from farther east, and not just the usual fare from those places. I came upon some interesting dishes in the Caspian region: there's a very nice pork roast stuffed with onions and figs and mushrooms; they slather almond-butter all over it before it's roasted, to keep the meat from drying out. They serve it with cracked wheat or rice seasoned with garlic and coriander. And I have a salmon dish from Siberia."

The combination of flavors for the pork was unfamiliar to Poppy, but she said, "That might be a good choice for Friday. And it might be wise to have some fish. Perhaps your Siberian salmon?"

But Aunt Esther shook her head. "We don't have easy access to the spices for that one; Missus Sassoro will have to go into New York City, to where the Russians have their groceries. Don't worry. Missus Sassoro does a nice baked cod in cheese sauce with tarragon." Aunt Esther said. "It ought to please the more serious Christians among us."

Poppy was startled to hear Aunt Esther speak so nonchalantly about the religious observances of many of their friends and family. "You can't not have fish on Friday, Aunt Esther," she said.

Aunt Esther tasted her cognac. "That's the trouble with my travels," she said as if admitting to improper behavior. "Not everyone everywhere conducts their religions as many of us do here. I get out of the habit of fish on Friday for High Church Episcopalians and the occasional Catholics I entertain. It's good of you to remind me."

"Missus Sassoro would speak up if I said nothing." Poppy said, all the while thinking of the number of dining traditions Aunt Esther must have encountered on her journeys: that was another possibility for an article for the *Clarion*.

"She most certainly would, good Catholic that she is." Aunt Esther had more of the lamb appetizers, licking her fingers rather than using the linen napkin Miss Roth had provided for her use. They sat in companionable silence while they finished up the lamb canapés, then spent the next ten minutes talking about Aunt Esther's next trip, and were still discussing it when Miss Roth announced that dinner was served; they went to the dining room and sat down to a meal that began with Scottish soup, then roasted chicken, mashed potatoes, and asparagus with mayonnaise, finished off with a vanilla custard. When they got up from the table, Aunt Esther announced her intention to retire for the night.

"You may do as you wish," she told Poppy, "but I know you'll be up early, and you've had a busy day."

"You're right—I'm tired. Will I see you in the morning?" Poppy stifled a yawn and started toward the stairs.

Aunt Esther shrugged. "Perhaps. I may sleep in."

Since Aunt Esther said nothing more, Poppy said, "Well, good night, then."

"Yes," said Esther, going toward the corridor to the rear of the house where she had her bedroom and study. "Good night."

NINE

BY NOON THE FOLLOWING DAY POPPY WAS ON HER WAY TO A LUNCH WITH Inspector Loring, bound for the Blind Pig Grill, which was half-way between Loring's precinct station and the Addison Newspaper Corporation building; the place had been a compromise, hurriedly agreed upon when Loring had phoned her an hour ago, requesting her to join him without more explanation than that. Poppy drove through the streets, half-listening to Chesterton Holte, whose voice came from the back seat, relating something he had learned in the dimension of ghosts the night before.

"—and Percy Knott remembers that he had a phone call the night he was killed, one from your cousin. About authenticating an antique."

"You've said something about this already," Poppy reminded him, as she turned left toward the old Franklin Building. "And it was about the dispute between Warren and Stacy, wasn't it?"

"From what Knott is remembering, it probably was." It was a careful answer. "His memory is far from complete."

There was a blast of horns a short way ahead; Poppy slowed down. "Do you have any idea why Stacy would be telling Knott anything about his business with Warren Derrington? He usually plays his cards close to the chest."

Holte gave a grim laugh. "Knott thinks that perhaps it didn't actually have anything to do with business; Knott now thinks it is likely that Stacy was setting him up to be murdered. He is fairly certain that Stacy was worried about their importing business, and wanted Knott taken out of the picture. By Derrington, probably, but possibly Stacy. It may sound a bit convoluted, but at least Knott is remembering, bit by bit. The actual murder is very hard to recall, for all of us."

"Stacy killed him?" Poppy repeated, to be sure she had heard Holte clearly above the blare of the traffic that was occasionally pierced by a loud shrill of a police whistle; she disliked the idea that her cousin was willing to kill, because that would confirm that he had intended to do away with Poppy when he had locked her in the room in the Mayes Brothers' basement warehouse, an idea she still disliked thinking about. "What reason would Stacy have to murder Knott?"

Holte had a ready answer, "What reason did Stacy have to attempt to kill you?"

Poppy swallowed against the sudden tightness in her throat. "I don't know, and I've thought about it many times."

"Hardly surprising," said Holte.

"All right; giving Knott the benefit of the doubt, is he certain that it was Stacy who called him?"

"That's what he said. He's not completely positive, but he thinks it's probable—it's Stacy or Derrington, and he's inclined to think it was Stacy, and not simply because of the phone call. He told me that he now believes that at the time he had assumed that the bad blood between your cousin and Warren Derrington had somehow been resolved, and that they were planning to continue in their business venture together. At least, that's the way he recalls at present; he knows he might have got it wrong, which is why he wants to confront Derrington, to see if any of this can be confirmed, but hasn't been able to locate him."

"But ghosts often forget things, don't they," Poppy said. "You told me that."

"True enough, but they often remember, as well, given time, and at present, it isn't helpful to have to wait; I'm aware of that," Holte said, and added, "I didn't remember that I had been the cause of your father's death until I'd been in the dimension of ghosts for almost five years, more or less, time being—"

"—less well-defined than it is when you are corporeal," Poppy said, a bit impatiently as she double-clutched into second gear.

"Yes; it takes time to accustom oneself to being noncorporeal, and five years is not an unusually long time to do that, all things considered. I didn't remember a lot of things about my life and death until about five years had passed. Then it came back to me—even the parts I would rather have forgot." A suggestion of an outline of a tall, lean man glimmered in her rear- view mirror.

"So we may have to wait five years to find out who killed Madison Moncrief and Percy Knott?" Poppy asked, unanticipated distress washing through her.

"Possibly, if your inspector friend doesn't find out first." He moved a little, as if settling down on the rear seat. "A very dogged fellow, Inspector Loring."

"And smart," Poppy added.

"Being an officer in a war requires that combination, if one is going to survive," said Holte.

"What about being a spy?" Poppy asked before she could stop herself.

"Both those things are necessary," Holte said without a trace of emotion. "And so is sneakiness. And guile." He went silent. "When I was alive, I took pride in the latter two."

Thinking in for penny, in for pound, Poppy pursued her inquiry. "And now? What do you think of your sneakiness and guile?"

"Now I accept what happened pragmatically, which is why I am haunting you: I am responsible for your father's death, and I want to balance the books. I did what I deemed was necessary at the time, which is what I am doing now, as well."

"Um," she said. "Necessary. That makes it sound like a nasty chore."

"That's putting too harsh a purpose on it, not that I wouldn't do it if it had been less...satisfying...than it has become." He paused, then went on. "Yet working with you is turning out to be more...more engaging than I thought it would be." He was a bit more visible, as if his admission had provided a surge in his manifestation.

"Why?" she asked.

"For a number of reasons, I suspect," he said, more obliquely. "You're not a typical privileged young lady—that's no surprise to you. My value to you is more than a matter of providing what your father can no longer provide; you have proved to be a most unusual young woman, doing unusual work: those factors together have fired my curiosity."

Poppy saw the Blind Pig three blocks ahead, and she said, "Keep an eye out for a parking place, would you. The curbs looks pretty full."

"Isn't there a parking lot?" Holte asked.

"A small one, and it fills up rapidly at lunch time."

"If that's what you want," he said, and inspected the spaces along the street as Poppy made her way more slowly toward the Blind Pig, paying little attention to the honks and shouts around her.

"There's one mid-block ahead. You'll have about a block to walk." Holte said suddenly. "Just ahead of the Ford."

"I see it," Poppy told him. "Thanks. Let's hope no one gets to it before we do." She kept a wary eye on a Cord that was two cars ahead of them, the driver going as slowly as Poppy.

"If you lose that one, turn left at the next corner and go over to Founders' Green. The parking isn't difficult around there, in spite of the construction under way." Holte spoke confidently, for he had recently made it his business to acquaint himself with Philadelphia. "It's a bit of a walk, but not too demanding."

"Aren't you the savvy one?" she asked lightly. "Next you'll be telling me where to get fuel most cheaply."

"That would be at Gordon's Garage and Livery," Holte said drily.

The Cord inched past the parking place, and Poppy sighed as she moved into position to back into the space. She put the Hudson in reverse and backed in next to the curb; it was a tight fit but not too impossible. After she put the gear in neutral and set the hand-brake, she picked up her large purse and got out of her auto, being careful to open the door when there was no vehicle immediately beside her. She locked the door quickly and went around the front of the auto to reach the sidewalk. Striding briskly, she was at the Blind Pig Grill in short order, and as she stepped through the door, she saw that Inspector Loring was waiting for her on the bench next to the mahogany reception desk. He was wearing a tweed sport-coat over a white cotton shirt, a dark-brown bow-tie and dark-brown slacks, making him look more professorial than inspector- like. His eyes were tired, and Poppy found herself wondering what had happened that had kept him up at nights.

"You're here," he said as he rose to greet her.

"I am. And you're here before me; I didn't notice your auto—you must be in the lot." He nodded while she went on, "By the way, I like how you're dressed today: you look spiffy." Listening to herself, she mentally chided herself for sounding so inane. "What have you got to tell me?

"Once we're seated. They're setting up a booth for us now."

"A booth. This must be a very important meeting." She grinned at him, wanting to show her enthusiasm.

"It is. And I am relying on you to keep my confidence," he said, trying to smile but not succeeding.

A waiter, resplendent in a blue-and-white coat of Revolution-era design over a standard white shirt and black trousers, approached, menus in hand. "If you will follow me? Your booth should be ready." Without waiting to see if Poppy and Loring were behind him, he set off through the maze of round tables in front of the long, polished bar, making his way toward the bank of curtained booths along the far wall, each one with a number on the left-hand side of the curtain. He stopped at number 11, and pulled its curtain back to allow the two to enter. "I will return in five minutes to take your orders."

"Thanks," said Loring as he stood aside for Poppy. "Bring us some coffee when you come, if you would."

"Yes, sir," said the waiter with a supercilious smirk, revealing his assumption for their reason to want privacy, and let the curtain close behind him.

The booth was small but not cramped; the oak-paneled walls that defined it went almost to the ceiling, the curtain was canvas-backed velveteen, there was a brass coat-rack in one corner, and an oval cherry-wood table with four chairs placed around it. Salt and pepper shakers stood at the center of the table, along with a sugar bowl and a creamer; two sconced lamps provided illumination. Loring held out the nearest of the chairs for Poppy, then took the one next to hers.

"So what is this about?" Poppy asked as soon as Loring was seated. "Does it have anything to do with Overstreet? Has he agreed to testify regarding Derrington and Stacy?"

"Sorry, no. I still don't know when I'll be off to Montreal in Quebec to take charge of him." He made a motion of dismissal. "This is a more...delicate matter. Very hush-hush."

"Oh? Are we going to be talking about GAD Pearse?" Poppy was mystified. She opened her purse and took out her pencil and notebook. "Do you mind if I keep notes?"

"If they aren't too specific, and only for your private use," he said. "At least for now."

"Ye gods," she said.

"Yes." Loring picked up his menu and glanced through it. "Order anything you want."

"Thanks," she said, recognizing this maneuver for the distraction it was. "Anything you recommend?"

"The mussels are good, and so is the osso bucco. The hasenpfeffer is quite nice. The beet- and-cabbage salad isn't bad, either." He shrugged. "It depends on how hungry you are."

"Um-hum," she said, reading quickly through the dishes offered. "What are you having?"

"The Flemish Stew," he said quickly, glancing at his wristwatch. "As soon as we order, I'll tell you what's going on. I don't want to be overheard when we get down to business."

"Are you really worried about that—being overheard?"

"Yes. The booth helps, but someone outside the curtain might be listening and offer what he hears to one of the yellower papers, which would compromise..." His voice faltered. "Indulge me in this, okay? You know how insistent the Pearses can be. For now, tell me about work, or how you like your new living arrangement, or what you found out from Missus Plowright."

"Let me see," Poppy said, doing her best to conceal her disappointment at being put off. "Work is still on the routine side, and probably will be until we find out where Stacy has gone; my new living arrangements seem fairly good, but I'll know more when I'm used to them; and Neva Plowright is perplexed and confused, judging from the answers she provided. I can't say I blame her. Louise left a mess for her."

"This has got to be a rough time for her," said Loring.

"It seems likely." Poppy resigned herself to the short wait to find out more, and thinking this was as good a time as any, she summoned up her courage and asked, "Are you busy this Friday evening?"

"I don't know. Why?"

One of the sconce lights blinked rapidly three times, then resumed its soft shining.

"Aunt Esther is having a buffet-dinner party, and I was wondering if you might like to come? Nothing terribly fancy," she added before he had a chance to talk. "She wants to make my move to her house official, and she's going to have a few of her colleagues join us as well, to mark her return from the Soviet Union."

"Friends and family sort of thing?"

"Friends and colleagues is more like it. I'm not expecting much family."

"I see," he said, and stared at the sconce that had flickered as if daring it to blink again.

"My cousin Hank and his wife will probably be there. He's going to be in town a while longer."

"What about Missus Dritchner?"

"Aunt Jo's been invited," Poppy told him, being scrupulously correct. "She hasn't accepted or declined yet."

Loring considered this. "I gather I'm the sole policeman," he said.

"Probably. Esther's asking Cornelius Lowenthal, and his wife. Also Judge Benedict Stephanson, who's an old friend of Esther's, and possibly Denton North and his mother, and a few of her colleagues from the National Geographic Society. My old friend Mildred Fairchild and her husband Humphrey will be with us, and Arnold Schultz, who used to be at the Department of State; he retired last year, and now does some lecturing." She almost held her breath waiting for Loring to respond.

"They're from a higher rung up the ladder than I am, by the sound of it," said Loring.

"It won't matter; Aunt Esther has a very eclectic group of friends—she once invited a union organizer to Thanksgiving, and another time had a famous dancer at the table—and I'm getting more inclusive, thanks to people like you," said Poppy, her courage deserting her as soon as she had spoken. "We won't be doing jewels and furs, and no one is planning to dance. I don't think you'd be uncomfortable, but it's up to you."

He put down his menu. "Okay. If I don't have to be in Canada, I'll come to your aunt's party. I have to admit, I'd like to meet her."

Poppy was so startled by his acceptance that all she could say was "Fine. I'll tell her. It'll be at six-thirty for seven."

There was a soft tap on the door-frame and the waiter pulled back the curtain. "Would you like to order now?" he inquired, setting down a tray with two cups of hot coffee on it.

"Yes," said Loring as he saw Poppy nod.

The waiter readied his pencil over his order-pad, scowling as the light blinked again.

Poppy ignored the light, saying, "I'll have the scallops with bacon and spinach."

Loring ordered the Flemish Stew, a kind of pot roast with carrots, onions, and potatoes, cooked in secretly imported dark beer; he sat back in his chair while the waiter wrote it down and left them alone. "It'll take about twenty minutes to get the food, and that's enough time."

"Ye gods," she murmured.

"Are you ready?" He looked down at her notebook as if expecting it to open on its own. "And keep in mind, nothing with specific names."

Poppy had put a lump of sugar in her coffee, and was reaching for the creamer. "So what is this all about? I'm filled with curiosity." She poured a little bit of cream into her coffee, and wished she had a spoon to stir it; she picked up her pencil and prepared to write. "Who, what, where, why, and how?"

"It's awkward," he said.

"So you've told me," Poppy said by way of encouragement. "Care to enlarge on it?"

The waiter knocked on the door frame, then stepped into the booth with flatware and linen napkins, which he put into place with the quick efficiency of long practice. He nodded once and withdrew.

Loring glared at the curtain. "Damn it," he muttered, adding a conscientious "Sorry," by way of apology for his language.

"You haven't said anything significant yet, even if he tried to eavesdrop," Poppy told him. "Give him half a minute to get to the kitchen and then tell me."

"You're right," Loring conceded, adjusting the position of his fork. "It's a habit I picked up during the Great War, not letting anyone eavesdrop."

"Are you keeping track of the Napier robbery?" Poppy guessed, to keep Loring talking. "Have you been assigned to the case?"

"No. Robbery is handling it, so I'm not involved. It's still Harper's game." He coughed nervously. "If the robbers had killed someone, I'd be working it."

"Oh?" She quickly recalled everything that had been in the *Clarion* during the previous week. "Something political turning up, then?"

"Not directly, no, at least I don't think so. Nothing about the coming election, anyway, or any of the races." He rubbed his chin. "It may have something to do with the international situation."

"You mean it has something to do with Stacy as well as GAD?" Poppy asked, excited and repelled at once.

"Not that I know of," said Loring.

Poppy leaned toward him. "Then what?"

TEN

"You know the Pearse family, don't you? You know them fairly well." It was not a completely unexpected question, but Poppy could tell that Loring was uneasy about asking it, which puzzled her.

"A bit, yes. Sherman and Isadora were friends of my father's. When I was a child, my father took Toby and me to their house to have Sunday dinners with the Pearse family from time to time. Why? That was years ago."

"Gameal Augustus Darius, called GAD? Did you spend much time with him?"

"Yes, during our visits, I did. I knew his oldest sister, Auralia, somewhat—she's a few years younger than I am—and his late brother, HOB. Auralia is Cassandra Auralia Thalia; she refuses to answer to CAT, which she loathes." She suddenly realized what was going on. "Do you have news about GAD? Has something's happened to him."

Loring nodded unhappily. "Pearse was in to report his son missing, as I mentioned, and filled me and two other senior officers in on what he knows about his son's situation, but asked that the information not be released to the public, or the Federal Bureau of Investigation, to avoid press attention, so the whole matter is unofficial, as I've said. There's no paperwork on file anywhere. Pearse doesn't want people prying into his family affairs. But his wife is afraid that GAD has been kidnapped, which is a possibility, though there's been no real hint of that yet, beyond her dread. Pearse himself is afraid of being barraged by all kinds of claims for money to reveal where GAD is, and what has happened to him if knowledge of GAD's being missing becomes public, not without cause: the man's worth ten million if he's worth a dime. He'd be barraged with demands for money, either offering information or the return of

GAD. Pearse is asking us to maintain his privacy until we know more."

"Thus you talk to a reporter?" Poppy asked with a suggestion of a laugh.

"No, thus I talk to a friend of the Pearses, who understands Mister Pearse's reticence." He put his elbows on the table and leaned on his hands. "You know if there are secrets in that family, and you can do some snooping if you catch a scent. I'm not interested in scandal, only in things that might have something to do with GAD's being missing." He stared into his coffee cup. "And if you decide to do any spying, I hope, you will report to me if you discover anything useful. Later on, you'll have an inside story on the case."

"If anything comes of it," Poppy added in as neutral a tone as she could achieve.

Loring shrugged awkwardly. "It's the best I can offer."

"The same bargain as the one we've made for you to continue telling me, sub rosa, about what you have found out about the Moncrief and Knott murders?" She considered this for a few seconds, then nodded. "All right. You've been a great help to me before and it's only fair that I help you where I can. But if the family goes public with their worries, you'll let me use whatever you find out."

He looked directly at her. "Deal; and if you can pass on anything you might pick up from your invisible friend...?" He let the suggestion hang in the air.

Poppy gave an exasperated sigh. "I don't *have* an invisible friend," she reminded him, and inwardly chided herself with the thought that while she had been truthful, she had said nothing about the ghost of a Canadian spy who was helping her in various ways. "I'm not aware of any secrets in the Pearse family, beyond the usual gossip. But I'll make some inquiries among my...acquaintances—discreet inquiries—to see what's what."

"Okay," Loring said, and visibly relaxed.

Poppy regarded him for a moment or two, then asked, "What have you learned so far? So I can start snooping." She did not want to use the word *spying*, thinking that Holte might be annoyed.

He took a sip of his coffee and put the cup aside. "According to Pearse, GAD went to Europe in the second week of June, and had reservations to return the third week in August. When he left, he told his parents that he would be going into Eastern Europe. He mentioned Vienna and Buda-Pest as places he expected to visit before returning on the 28th of August. Throughout July, he sent home letters weekly, the last two coming from Vienna. In his final letter, he declared his intention to spend the rest of his time in Vienna doing what he could to help the Armenian refugees there—he was distressed at their plight, and the state of their living conditions, as well as the lack of indignation that the Europeans felt for them—and believed that someone should do something about it, so he decided he wanted to be useful before he—"

"Aunt Esther said something about the Armenians. She spent a few days in Vienna on her way home, and was able to see the conditions in which they were living, which she thought outrageous; she may do an editorial essay for the *Clarion* about the Armenians," Poppy interjected. "I'll have a word with her tonight, to see if there's any light she can shed on where GAD might be."

"That's a good place to start; better than anything we have here; the reporting from Eastern Europe is...sketchy, so if you can provide some solid facts, I'd be grateful," Loring approved, and took another sip of coffee. "Anyway, he was scheduled to leave from England over two weeks ago, but a telegram from the White Star Line informed his family the day the ship—I forget its name—sailed, that GAD was not aboard, and that he had made no other reservations, at least not with the White Star Line. They've made inquiries with other shipping lines, but there is no mention of him among their passengers; in fact, from what we can turn up, he never made it to England. This is quite upsetting to his family, as you may suppose."

"I don't need to suppose—I've heard Missus Pearse expostulate on the matter," said Poppy, thinking back on Hank's birthday party.

"Then you know that she is certain that something dreadful has happened to GAD." Loring saw her nod. "She's very worried." He rubbed his chin. "That's pretty much all I know."

Poppy thought a moment, then answered carefully, "I know that Missus Pearse has been clamorous in expressing her worries to anyone who will listen, and that her fears grows worse with each retelling. She was at Aunt Jo's dinner-party last week, and belabored the guests who would listen with her dreads and dismay at GAD's absence. I think she's in a panic, but I wouldn't say so to her face, and she's fueling it by describing her imaginings." Poppy sat back in her chair, her pencil dawdling over an empty notebook page. "I've also heard rumors that the reason the Pearses let their son travel is that he has been courting a young woman they don't approve of here in Philadelphia, and they hoped, if he got away for a time, the infatuation would blow over."

"I hadn't heard that," said Loring. "Do you happen to know who she is?" He shot a disapproving glance at the nearer sconce as it went off, then back on at once. "If that happens again, I'll ask for a pair of candles."

"It's working fine now," she said, and before she could stop herself, she added, "It's not blinking Morse code—that's something."

Loring scowled. "Okay. No candles." He tapped his fingers on the table. "So tell me who the unsuitable young lady is."

Poppy could feel herself blush, worried that Chesterton Holte might be up to mischief, and testing the depth of her knowledge. "Merrinelle Butterworth, or so Isadora Pearse claims. I don't know it for a fact, but before she was worried that GAD went missing, she was horrified at the prospect of having Merrinelle Butterworth for a daughter-in-law. The Pearses are wealthier than the Butterworths, and that's saying something, and Old Money besides. Isadora has no intention of letting GAD marry beneath him. She once was in favor of his journey, hoping that it would put an end to GAD's crush on Merrinelle." Poppy felt a rush of chagrin. "I'm sorry. That sounded awful."

Loring chuckled. "Well, at least Miss Butterworth can't be called a fortune-hunter. The Butterworths are doing quite well for themselves. Their department store is probably the most successful in the city."

Poppy achieved a smile. "Not even Missus Pearse could make that claim, although she's certain that Merrinelle wants to advance herself socially. Isadora's main objections to the Butterworths is that the family is still making its money through business, not inherited investments and land. The thought of a nouveau riche bride in the family was more than she could endure. She might not feel that way now."

Loring fell into a brief, thoughtful silence before going on. "Mister Pearse was quick to warn us about his wife's tendency to bruit GAD's dangers about. He has persuaded her not to go to the press with her fears, and for now, she is in agreement with her husband, but he told us that he doesn't know how long he will be able to keep her from announcing GAD's disappearance to the world at large." He had more coffee. "I'm supposed to call on her tomorrow and explain what the police can do to search for him—which isn't very much, to be honest about it—and that for our work to succeed, her continued silence is necessary."

"Since he's apparently in Europe, I wouldn't think there is much anyone can do from here."

Loring shook his head. "If we don't make this an active investigation, there's almost nothing anyone can do, and that includes the Department of State. But during the Great War, I made some contacts among various police forces, and I'll be writing to the men I know, those still in active service, and a few retired, to find out if they have any recommendations for how I might pursue this... non-case."

"Is that why you were included by Mister Pearse? That you have foreign connections?" Thinking of Sherman Pearse, Poppy decided it was likely the reason.

"I think so. Most of my job in the Great War was..." He faltered, looking away from her. "Was graves' registration—finding and identifying the dead, and that included bodies that did not obviously belong to any specific army, mostly parts of bodies." His eyes turned ancient again, fixed on memories rather than this sunny but breezy afternoon.

Poppy took this in, and had to resist the urge to ask him if he knew anything about the death of her father. America had not entered the Great War yet when B. O. Thornton had been killed, so Loring would not know anything about it. "That's pretty demanding work."

"Yes, it is," he said bluntly. "But, as Commissioner Smiley said during our meeting with the Pearses, I have contacts no one else does, and I know how to keep my mouth shut." He offered a tentative smile. "And so do you."

"That won't be easy if things get out of hand," said Poppy, frowning. "Because Isadora Pearse is overwrought about GAD, he drives all other considerations from her mind. So far, she has kept her outbursts to her friends, not those beyond her group. If she decides she should make a public announcement, she will, and no one, including her husband, can stop her." She reached for her coffee and tasted it; she found it cooler than she liked, but knew that was her own fault; she could have sipped it while they talked instead of taking insubstantial notes. "She's not going to lose another son if she can help it."

"I understand that." He unrolled his napkin and dropped it in his lap. "Can you tell me anything about GAD? Mister Pearse said a lot about him, but I think it would be useful to get your take on the boy."

Poppy thought this over, and finally said, "I don't know how useful it might be, but our families used to be on good terms. We spent a fair amount of time together when I was young, and if you think that would help..."

"It would give me some notion about GAD from someone other than his parents; you may know things about him that neither his father nor mother do." Loring studied her. "That is, if you think it's a good idea."

"I understand what you're after," she responded. "The thing is, I don't know him very well. I haven't seen him for almost three years, and that last time was a month or so after HOB—their eldest—died, which hit GAD hard; he may have changed since then, but if you like, I'll find out what his friends are saying about him now. At that last meeting, he was just getting used to his brother's death."

"I'll bear it in mind; it's possible that loss did change him to a degree, but you're observant, and at least you're not one of his immediate family; you have a clearer view of him," Loring said, a wry quirk to his mouth. "I would like your opinion of him. Tell me anything you think might help me be able to get a real fix on him."

"I don't see him the way his family does, it's true," she said, and ruminated briefly. "All right. This is what I noticed about him." She stared into the distance of memories, trying to recall the boy she had known. "He was adventurous as a boy, always getting into things: climbing trees, running into streams, going up in tall buildings, that kind of thing. He did most of those things alone. He has a sympathetic streak, too, and that meant that every abandoned kitten, every injured rabbit, every fallen baby bird, every hapless puppy that came his way ended up in his room, much to the consternation of the rest of his family. When he thought something was unfair, he would rail at it, and upbraid his brothers and sisters for not being as upset as he." She paused, trying to summon up her memories of him as she had seen him the summer before she went to college—he was a little older, some of his character emerging more clearly than before he went to preparatory school. "He's athletic, but doesn't go in for team sports: he is an outdoors sort of man; he camps, and hikes, and canoes, and sails; every now and then he fishes. He told me once that nature restored his soul. He doesn't hunt, but I'm told he's a crack shot. He was talking about becoming a naturalist when he was younger—back then, he admired the work of John Muir, and President Roosevelt, for all the old Rough Rider had done to preserve nature, and said that he wanted to follow in their footsteps—and he still might do something of the sort now. It wouldn't surprise me if that's what he's up to in Europe."

"Then you would believe that he might take on the misfortunes of displaced Armenians," said Loring.

"I'll put it this way: he has always sympathized with those who are less fortunate than he is. His father was not pleased, for although he praises charity, he doesn't approve of needing it," said Poppy, and lapsed into a brief silence. "You should talk to his sister Genevieve—Genevieve Yolande Guinevere—GYG, called Gigi within the family. She's the most like him of them all, and if you can speak with her privately, she may tell you things she would never tell her parents. In fact, I think you should speak to all the children alone, if that's possible."

"I'll have to talk to everyone in the family eventually," he said, not pleased at the prospect. "I'll ask Mister Pearse if I can do this in private, and soon."

"Tatiana—Tatiana Roxanna Augusta, and the family added *La La* to TRA—won't want to help you; if she tells you anything, it isn't likely to be the whole truth. She's secretive and she likes to mislead; if she smirks, it means she thinks she's getting away with something. A few years ago, she got into trouble for *borrowing* Auralia's pearl necklace. She and Auralia don't get along very well—never have. The twins, Felix and Berengaria—they call her Gari rather than Barengaria Eleanor Morgana or BEM—should be about twelve, as I recall, and they stick together; other than that, I haven't much to say about them. I don't know how reliable they are in regard to GAD. Felix is Felix Alexander Darius. Not called FAD, just Felix. "

"Twins often do stick together," said Loring. "Either that, or each resents the other."

"You might want to see them together when you go to interview the children," Poppy said, recalling the twins' shyness when alone. "They're fairly cooperative, or they were a couple of years ago. They may not be now."

"What about Auralia?" Loring asked after looking through his notes.

"She's married, and lives in Connecticut with her husband, William Mikkelsohn. She's just twenty-three, if I remember correctly, and he's about twenty- eight; they married last year, at the end of January. I think she's pretty ambitious, and Mikkelsohn is from a political family; one of his forbearers signed the Declaration of Independence, and Auralia never lets anyone forget it. When I saw her at school, she was hard-working and eager for success, which for her meant a good marriage to a man interested in politics, so she's succeeded so far. At school, she was in charge of the Committee for Public Health. They raised money for families unable to afford medical care during the Flu. She managed to convince the dean to establish a clinic for mothers with young children in one of the old buildings on campus."

"That sounds commendable," said Loring.

"Oh, it was. Auralia garnered all manner of praise for what she did, and she deserved it, in a way. But I think Auralia would like to be in charge of almost anything if it had political worth. She has her mind on the long game, not immediate advantage. And I know from experience, she would not let you forget the things she has done." Poppy blinked at her own audacity. "I'm sorry. I shouldn't have said it that way."

"You said it just fine." Loring gave an amused single laugh. "Then, do you think it might be worthwhile for me to talk to her?"

Poppy was about to answer when the waiter appeared with a plate of rolls and butter. He did a quick survey of their cups. "I'll bring you more coffee. Your meals should be ready in about ten minutes. Sorry for the delay. There's a private party in the banquet room, and that is slowing down things in the kitchen." Then he withdrew, taking care to make sure the curtain was completely closed.

Loring was silent for several seconds, then said, "Let's wait until he brings the coffee. We can have a little more privacy after he's gone."

Poppy nodded. "It's never easy when there's an interruption." She drank what was left in her cup and then made a few hasty notes. "Would you like to talk to Aunt Esther? About the Armenians? You could do it Friday night."

Loring stared around the booth. "Why don't you ask her if she would like to talk with me? A party might not be a good setting. Could we arrange another time for that?"

Poppy saw his point. "If that's what you'd prefer, I'll do it, of course. She said she has some photographs of the group near Vienna; I'm sure she'll show them to you." She sketched a star next to where she had written *Esther – Armenians – GAD – Loring*, so that it could be a more emphatic reminder to bring it up with her aunt that evening. "Is there anything more you'd like me to arrange for you with her?"

"Not that occurs to me," he said, closing the file in front of him and cocking his head in the direction of the curtain as the waiter came back, a large silver-plated coffee-pot in one hand, and small paper napkins in the other. As he refilled their cups, he set down the napkins. "Will you want anything else to drink? We have an array of sodas, and milk. Or, if you prefer, we have tomato juice, orange juice, and apple juice. The tomato juice is canned, the orange juice is fresh, and the apple juice is in glass bottles. Your order should be out in five minutes or so. I can bring you an appetizer, if you like."

"I don't think so," said Loring, and nodded to Poppy. "Would you like anything? More coffee? A glass of water? Juice?"

"A glass of water when you bring the food." Had she been at home, she would have told Missus Sassoro to bring her a glass of Sauvignon Blanc, but knew better than to do it here, in the presence of a police officer, even so accommodating a one as Inspector J.B. Loring. "So long as you keep the coffee coming."

"Very good," said the waiter. "And you, sir?"

"Water when the food comes would be fine," Loring said.

"Very good," the waiter repeated, and slipped back through the curtain.

"Now, where were we?" Loring asked rhetorically, taking a roll from the basket and setting it on his butter plate. "Weren't you about to tell me more about whom else you know who might be able to tell you something about GAD?"

"Was I?" Poppy asked, then tried to resume her train of thought. "Humphrey Fairchild knows the Pearses quite well, and he and Mildred will be at the party on Friday. You needn't worry about talking to them there."

"You mentioned them." He thought. "If it looks as if he could provide anything useful, I'll make an appointment to meet with him privately. We're agreed, aren't we? That clandestine discussions don't usually go well at parties."

Poppy was convinced he was right, so she only said, "I'll introduce you. Mildred will probably pester you for information about Louise Moncrief."

"She's the one who called the police when you went missing, isn't she?" Loring asked.

"Yes, bless her. She's expecting, so they probably won't stay late—she needs her rest." Poppy heard steps approaching. "I think lunch is here," she said just as the waiter drew the curtain back; their conversation was once again abandoned.

ELEVEN

CHESTERTON HOLTE WAS A FILMY BLUR IN THE LATE AFTERNOON SUNLIGHT THAT flooded Poppy's room, more like a flaw in the three tall windows than an actual presence. He watched as Poppy sat down on the edge of her bed to take off her shoes. On the end of the bed, Maestro raised his head to give a half-hearted hiss before curling himself into a tighter knot and going back to sleep. "Your Inspector Loring is in a difficult spot," he said as he drifted toward the chaise lounge next to the new chest-of-drawers standing against the north wall.

"He is," said Poppy, sounding a bit distracted.

"Would you like me to make some inquiries?" Holte offered.

"In the dimension of ghosts, or nearer to home?" Poppy countered, and immediately added, "I apologize. I meant in the dimension of ghosts. Don't take offence at what I'm saying. My feet are killing me."

"I thought they might be, since you're rubbing them before you remove your hose."

"I'm not going to remove them. I want to get out my new low-heeled pumps, after I dress for dinner. There's no reason for anything fancier than they are." She smoothed the bedspread in a slightly distracted way, her thoughts in a jumble; Maestro raised his head to stare at her, then dropped it back on his pile of paws.

"That isn't for almost three hours," Holte observed.

"I know. But we'll have a drink together before we sit down to eat," Poppy said, stretching, "and that will be in about an hour and a half. Aunt Esther has been busy today, and she'll want to talk about it. She has an appointment with Lowenthal tomorrow, to discuss some articles on her travels. No doubt she'll want some pointers on how to approach him." She gave a little sigh and took a handkerchief from the nearer night-stand drawer, using it to wipe her face carefully, so as not to smear her mascara.

"When do you expect your Aunt Esther to arrive this evening?" Holte asked. "And does Miss Roth know when that will be?"

"I suppose she does." Poppy stared down at her feet. "I wish you were corporeal enough to manage a foot rub."

"My apologies," said Holte, thinking that even something so minor as that would be a most welcome reminder of the advantages of having bodies. "About the housekeeper?"

"Miss Roth has worked for Aunt Esther for nearly ten years. She started out as a maid and eventually became housekeeper. That was at the end of the Flu, I believe, when trained help was as hard to find as trained anyone. She's lived in for four years; her quarters are at the back of the house, facing the garden with a patio." She started to stand, but changed her mind. "If you don't mind, I'm going to lie here for a bit."

"You were up late last night," said Holte.

"Ye gods!" Poppy exclaimed, straightening up in an effort to seem more indignant. "Don't tell me you were watching me?"

"No more than usual," was his oblique answer.

Poppy lay back, her left arm behind her head to serve as a pillow. "How comforting," she muttered.

Holte sank an inch or two into the chair. "Your lunch with Inspector Loring appears to have been a success. Did you know about graves' registration?"

Poppy shook her head slowly. "No. I thought he was probably in intelligence— he hasn't volunteered much about his activities until today. But a lot of soldiers don't say much about what happened to them."

"The same thing is true among the ghosts. If it takes them longer to remember, that means they need more time to go on to the next stage. Most of what they don't remember is what they are trying to forget. Unpleasant things."

Poppy gave a crack of laughter. "Does that include you?"

"It looks that way to me," he said, more solemnly than he had intended.

She heard the somberness in his answer, and nodded slowly, taking the time to consider what it might mean. Staring up at the ceiling, she thought about what might have happened to her father, and she found her recollections of him so overwhelming that she very nearly wept. After a few minutes, she said, "I'd better get changed."

"Don't worry, Poppy; it isn't as hard to do as you might imagine. There isn't much else to do in the dimension of ghosts but remember." He had deliberately lightened his tone, and he was rewarded with her rueful smile.

"What about you? You are spending a lot of time here. Is that slowing you down in going on?" Poppy asked as she got up and went to her closet to bring out her dinner ensemble: a drop-waisted dress with an ankle-length skirt in dusty-rose silk twill, neat but not girlish. She carried this back to the bed and dropped it onto the narrow, upholstered chest at the foot.

"One of the main reasons we ghosts remember is to allow us to balance the books. We can't, or don't, go on until we do, and to that, we have to come to terms with our lives." He rose out of the chair to half-way to the ceiling.

She looked around for his ephemeral presence, and finally saw his shimmer on the level with the tops of the windows. "Do you know how much longer your...book-balancing is likely to take?"

Holte did something not quite visible that was probably a dismissive wave with his non-existent hand. "Not yet. I'm still dredging up memories, trying to find the balance-point. I don't have any notion of how long it will take me to go on. But I'm trying to talk about the things I can remember a little more: the Bastins warned me that refusing to speak could make it more difficult for me. Their son won't say anything about the Great War, and he's in a madhouse."

"Can ghosts go mad?" Poppy asked him, at once curious and abhorred by the idea.

"Not the way the living can, or none that I have seen or know of ever heard of that happening. Maybe if they were mad to begin with, in life, they might hold onto the madness for a time. Ghosts can become...less connected to their lives, and then it can take them decades to move on. I've seen the ghost of a young lieutenant in the Confederate Army who still cannot bear to consider what happened to him and his men at Gettysburg. I've been told by others that he was one of the junior officers with Pickett, but he can neither confirm nor deny that."

"He's been in the dimension of ghosts for fifty years?" Poppy exclaimed. "Ye gods!"

"He's not the only one, but taking so long is rare." He paused, then said in a more subdued manner, "I think Poindexter may have gone on."

Poppy was startled by this news. "But from what I understood, he had not remembered who killed him, or even why."

Holte moved up from the chaise horizontally. "I'm not aware that he did, but he may have put it behind him, let it go, thought about other things. Some ghosts do that. Maybe he was not as disappointed at having his life end as it did as Moncrief, or Knott is. Maybe he simply decided to let it go. Many of us do, when it is too painful to grasp the truth."

"Ghosts can do that?"

"A few can. Sibyl seems to have done it. I haven't been able to find her in the dimensions of ghosts for a while. I can understand why she might want to put her life behind her." The mention of his dead wife made Holte uncomfortable, making him fade in and out like a weak projector light at the flickers.

"I'm sorry?" Poppy said in a rush of sympathy. "Is that the appropriate comment?"

Holte swung around and slid toward her, now seven feet off the floor and almost horizontal to the ceiling. "I wish I knew." He dropped down from the height as if sliding down a waterfall feet first. "Is there anything that I can do to help you? About the Pearse boy?"

"I don't know. Since it's not a family matter..." She motioned him to turn around, then unbuttoned her suit-jacket. As she removed it, a possibility occurred to her. "Maybe you could find out if GAD is still alive? If he'd dead, someone in the dimension of ghosts should be able to help you find him. And if he has died, where we might look for his remains. Would you do that?"

"If you like." He floated down two more feet. "Would you like me to find out if there is any news about Stacy?"

She was surprised to discover that part of her had no wish to know, but that impulse was quickly overshadowed by her desire to make him answer for what he had done to her. "If you can do it without too much trouble. There's no reason for you to spend all your time looking for my reprehensible cousin." While she continued changing clothes, she said, "I'd so like to put that all behind me, but until Stacy is located, I can't. And neither can the law."

"True enough, about the law." Holte hung an arms-length away from

Maestro, and was rewarded with a warning hiss. "He doesn't try to attack me anymore," he remarked, a bit wistfully.

Poppy shrugged. "He knows it won't do any good."

"Clever cat," said Holte, and swooped away from the disgruntled animal.

Poppy watched this as she removed her skirt. "I'm beginning to think you *like* aggravating Maestro," she said to Holte.

"Well, I prefer it to being ignored." He slipped into a small alcove with a bay window at the end of the room. "You have a very nice view of the garden."

Poppy slid her dinner dress over her head and shimmied it down her body until it hung properly. "That's better," she announced. "But I'll have to comb my hair again."

"Then you're dressed?" Holte inquired.

"I am: you may turn around." She curtsied a little. "You see? Not too formal, but not office-appropriate, either."

"Don't tell me that Aunt Esther bothers about that; she hardly seems the type," Holte said, a bit stunned by this news.

"Oh, no, she doesn't care if you think of changing for dinner as a matter of propriety. But after knocking about the world as she does, she likes to indulge in the niceties of society, and this is one way she can do it. It's a reminder that's she's at home instead of in Morocco, or Siberia, or Peru." Poppy went to her vanity table and inspected her reflection; she picked up her boar's bristle brush and went to work on the froth of short curls, going on while she brought her hair into order. "I need to go to Hannah's Beauty Box in a week or so. This is getting a bit too fly-away."

"Isn't that the fashion? Fly-away hair?" Holte watched while Poppy coaxed her hair into more ordered waves.

"In a way, it is, but it can't be wild. A little recklessness is fashionable, but wholesale riot is not." She stared into the mirror, looking for flaws. After a minute, she nodded. "This will do."

"You're satisfied?" Holte asked her.

"Yes. Is there a reason I shouldn't be?" she countered as she got up from the vanity table and went to fetch her more comfortable shoes: Louis XIV heels and ankle straps, maroon leather. She sat back on the bed to put them on. "I like to present a reasonable appearance, if only for myself."

"I think you look quite charming, but I'm not conversant with the current styles." He slid toward the window. "I'll be back later."

"Meaning in a few hours, or next month?" Poppy smiled at him.

"Probably tomorrow. There are some things I'll check on, and I'll give you a report on what I find out. Have a pleasant dinner." His faint image vanished like thin fog in the morning wind.

Poppy watched the air where he had been, then left the room, taking care to leave the bathroom door across the hall open for Maestro's convenience. She shut the door at the top of the stairs and made her way down to the parlor, where she found Esther sitting at the phone table in the entry-hall alcove, deep in conversation with someone involved with the coming party; it was clear that Esther had changed into dinner-clothes—a smart ensemble of a long, olive-green, trumpet skirt in linen topped by a linen jacket with a print of tropical leaves on it that Poppy had not seen before. Poppy waved, and saw Aunt Esther wave back while she continued her discussion.

"There is a door on the side of the house, near the kitchen garden. There's a shed to the right of the raised beds. I'll arrange to have the door left open. My man-of-all-work will help you, if you will give me an hour when you will arrive on Thursday night." Esther pointed to her lapel brooch, which contained a watch, indicating she would not be long.

Poppy sat down on the couch, and sniffed the air: there was beef in the oven—that much was obvious—and some kind of sauce just forming up. Beyond that, an aroma of scalloped potatoes mixed with the beef. It would be a very good, but unusually ordinary dinner, she thought. She saw Aunt Esther take a cigarette from the box on the phone table, and light up using a kitchen-match from the slide on the bottom of the box. The odor of tobacco burgeoned in the parlor.

"Yes. I'll have that amount ready for you, in cash...One hundred twenty-nine dollars, to be handed over upon delivery...I've always had the full amount, and I will now...Very good. Thank you." Aunt Esther hung up. "Well, at least we'll have reasonable drinks. Most of what I'm getting are French wines, along with a few of the better Italian ones. I already have brandy and scotch on hand, and may be able to get some rum. I wish I could get some good English gin, but at least I have a fair amount of port on hand. Miss Roth will be picking up groceries for the party later today. If there's anything you want specially, please let her know. Missus Sassoro will begin preparations tomorrow." She came over to the couch and sat on the end opposite Poppy. "There's always so much to plan for."

"Would you like some help?" Poppy offered.

"Goodness, no, unless you want to give some," said Aunt Esther. "I'm enjoying myself, including the complaining."

Poppy laughed. "Then go right ahead. I wouldn't dream of interfering with your pleasure."

Miss Roth appeared, her manner politely efficient as usual, carrying a tray with a bottle of cognac on it, two small balloon glasses, a basket of Winesap apples, and a paring knife on it. She set it down on the side-table and said, "Dinner will be ready in eighty minutes. Missus Sassoro is marinating the pork shoulder in vinegar and maple syrup. I should be finished tending to the sitting room by noon tomorrow."

"Just the way I like pork served." Esther smiled her approval. "Was she able to find some chard?"

"At the Italian market, yes, though she says it's a little past its prime. She said the string beans looked particularly good, and asked me to pick some up tomorrow; she'll make a side-dish for the party. She'll serve them with bacon and slivered almonds." Alexandra Roth made a sweep of her arm that took in the whole room. "I'll clean in here tomorrow afternoon. You may want to take your drinks in the grape arbor tomorrow afternoon; I'd like to close this room off until Friday afternoon."

"That sounds nice," Poppy interjected. "Drinks in the grape arbor."

"Weather permitting; I can tell it's on the turn, and we may want to stay indoors," said Esther, and turned to Miss Roth. "We should be able to find some place that won't interfere with your cleaning."

"Thank you. You're such a reasonable employer." Miss Roth chortled, enjoying a joke with herself.

"How are we going on party strategies?" Esther asked. "I don't like to leave anything to the last minute if it can be helped."

Miss Roth was prepared for the question. "I've interviewed six waiters, and selected two for the party. They're ordered to be here by five, ready to work.

You know one of them from the dinner last Thanksgiving: Howard Dale. The other is new—a young fellow named Abner Bridges."

Esther thought a moment. "Is Dale the one with the blond moustache? There's a birthmark on his left hand?"

"Yes," said Miss Roth, who, if she were surprised by Esther's recalling the man, showed no sign of it.

"Oh, good. He's quite reliable, as I recall, and not at all officious." She sat back on the couch, indicating that Miss Roth could go. When she did not leave, Esther asked, "Is there anything else?"

"Well, Galliard tells me that the creeping juniper along the walkway ought to be pruned back. With so many coming on Friday, he's afraid someone might trip. I would recommend it, as well."

"It *is* a little woodsy out there," Poppy agreed. "Hawkins mentioned it to me while I was moving in. We brought the two large trunks up the front, the driveway being too steep for him to bring them in the side."

"Then by all means, tell him to take care of it." Esther said, with a wave of her cigarette that gave Poppy the unnerving sense that Chesterton Holte might be hovering somewhere in the room; she dismissed the notion, reminding herself that he was in the dimension of ghosts.

Emboldened by Esther's implied permission, Miss Roth went on, "We're going to need another block of ice for the cooler. The refrigerator is almost as full as it can get, and Missus Sassoro needs to keep—"

"Yes, yes," Esther interrupted impatiently. "Order the ice first thing in the morning. You know what's needed. And have Galliard cut the flowers for three good bouquets, one for the dining room, one for the entry-hall, and one for this room. I rely on all of you to attend to it. You needn't wait for my permission." She glanced at Poppy. "If you must consult someone, my niece will be here when I'm gone; she'll know what to do. But ordinary maintenance I leave to you, and Missus Sassoro, and Galliard—I don't want you pestering Miss Thornton about it. But I want you to regard her as my lieutenant, and give her your full attention."

"Yes, Ma'am," said Miss Roth, and left Aunt Esther and Poppy to their drinks and apples.

As soon as she was sure that Miss Roth was in the kitchen, Aunt Esther said,

"The three of them are wonderful—Roth, and Sassoro, and Galliard—but like all staff, they tend to let things slide a bit when I'm not here. You will be my deputy. I know you're familiar with how a household is to be run. I'll say this to Josephine's credit: she knows how to hold household."

"That she does," Poppy agreed, not completely favorably.

Aunt Esther caught her tone, and chuckled. "Well, yes," she conceded, "Jo is trying to live in 1910, not 1924, and she is fighting the future with all she's got, but when it comes to running her home, she's really quite good at it. Even Max said so, and he rarely noticed such things." Her face grew forlorn. "Ah, Max."

The mention of her Uncle Maximilian—missing now for eleven years since he went off to the South Pacific to study the natives—saddened Poppy; her father had been very close with his older brother, and this reminder made her feel sad. "I'll give you that," she told her aunt, then added impulsively, "Do you miss him?"

"Of course I do. Your father and I were planning to do a search of the islands on Max's itinerary and collaborate on a book about it, no matter how it turned out. But the Great War came along, and then Oliver died…" Esther stopped. "If I had to lose another brother, I'd just as soon it were Regis. Max had spirit—may still have it if he's alive. Once Cordelia died, Regis was worse than a badger with a sore tooth; acting as if his wife had died to disaccommodate him, and now, he's no credit to old age." Regis was the oldest member of Esther's generation, a retired railroad president and breeder of champion show-dogs, now living in western Pennsylvania in the care of two nurses.

"I remember Uncle Max. I liked him. He was fun."

"Yes, he was." Satisfied with this exchange, Esther reached for the cognac and one of the glasses. "One finger or two?" she asked Poppy, withdrawing the corked lid.

Poppy sighed. "Better make it one. I still have work to do tonight."

"One it is," said Aunt Esther, and set to pouring.

TWELVE

SLIPPING INTO THE DIMENSION OF GHOSTS, CHESTERTON HOLTE FOUND HIMSELF more disoriented than he had ever been before. The greyish nothingness of the place was somehow more mystifying, the numberless ghosts caught in its invisible tides more restless than when Holte had left. He moved through the churning masses, searching for Madison Moncrief, in the hope of learning something from him; he hoped that Moncrief would be willing to assist him. At last, after a timeless drifting, he came upon Moncrief in an energetic helix, and addressed him in the silent manner of ghosts. *"Moncrief, are you the only one around?"*

Moncrief changed the direction of his motion and said, *"Oh. It's you."*

"What's happened?" Holte asked, meaning the sudden influx of ghosts. *"What brought them here?"*

"Something happened in French Indo-China, or maybe Batavia. Something natural, I gather. Probably a flood, by the look of them. Perhaps a tidal wave or a typhoon. Anyway, something drastic." Moncrief sounded very disinterested. *"There are thousands of them."*

Holte did not bother to question Moncrief's voiceless tone, but asked, *"Where're Poindexter and Knott?"*

"Elsewhere," Moncrief replied. *"Knott is looking for Overstreet; he thinks that Miles knows where Derrington has gone, and you know how determined he is to confront Derrington. He's as determined now as he was just after he arrived here."* He faded a bit. *"I think you were right, and Poindexter has gone on. He hasn't been around for quite a while."*

"Knott's still looking for Overstreet? I assumed he'd found Miles, but you say not?" Holte was astonished. *"Isn't Overstreet in Canada, near Montreal? Hasn't he been arrested?"*

"Not any more, according to Knott." Moncrief said, turning slowly at the edge of

a vortex of ghosts.

"But..." Holte faltered, recalling what Loring had told Poppy. *"I understand he's scheduled for extradition. It's being arranged."*

Moncrief had started to drift away, but changed his mind. *"I hope he is going to be sent back into the US. Then Knott can find him, and we'll have that settled. All this slipping in and out of the world of the living is beginning to annoy me."* He considered what he said, and added *"I don't mean you, Holte. It's Knott who's doing it."* There was the hint of a sigh in this. *"He's bent on revenge."*

"So you've said, and who can blame him," Holte muttered, then reminded himself of the purpose of his visit. *"Do you happen to remember a young man named Gameal Augustus Darius Pearse?"*

Moncrief was perplexed by the question. *"GAD? Yes, I knew GAD, not well, of course, but his family was part of our set. We attended a lot of the same functions, though GAD was just entering the adult world when I was killed. Kind of a strange one, GAD, seemed to me—a bit of a loner, more interested in plants and animals than politics. You know the type, don't you? Too bad that HOB died when he did."*

"Have you happened to run into HOB here?" It was unlikely, Holte knew.

The other ghosts circling around them in the crowded emptiness made a non-sound that was somewhere between a wail and a whimper, a reminder that everyone here was trying to come to terms with the lives they had led; to be asked to recall more than what each was wrestling with was a burden that most were eager to avoid.

"Once or twice," said Moncrief, astonishing Holte. *"Why?"*

"Did he say anything about GAD?"

Moncrief mulled this over. *"I don't think so. What's going on with GAD?"*

Holte decided to be blunt. *"He's missing."*

Now it was Moncrief's turn to be surprised. *"Missing? How?"*

"That's what I'm trying to find out. You're sure he isn't here?" Holte felt Moncrief shrink back, and realized that he would have to soften his approach. *"His family wants to find him, if he's still alive, and bury him, if he's dead."*

"I didn't know you have books to balance with the Pearses," said Moncrief, intrigued; he moved nearer to Holte.

"I don't, not with them," Holte told him.

Moncrief fluctuated at the edge of a minor swirl. *"Has this something to do with that Thornton woman? The one who's a reporter? Oliver's girl?"*

"Indirectly, yes, it does." Holte prepared to explain himself, but for once, Moncrief took Holte's answer at face value. *"I want to settle the matter."*

"And you want to do it by finding GAD?"

"If I can. If he's still alive, that could make it harder to do." He tried not to sound too cynical, but was worried that he might have done so.

"Well, all I can say is that I haven't seen GAD here—but I might not; I haven't been looking for him. I told you we weren't all that close." Moncrief drifted sideways. *"Where did he disappear?"*

"Somewhere in Europe, they think, but he could be in Russia or Algeria, for all I know." Holte gave Moncrief a short while to absorb all this.

"Then you've got a lot of places to look. That'll keep you busy." He faltered. *"Would you like me to look around for him, just in case?"*

Holte did the equivalent of nodding. *"If you would. That's kind of you."*

"I'll try to remember. If I do, I'll tell you next time you're here." When a little more time had passed, Moncrief asked, *"How are things at Hadley and Grimes? Do you know if the government is investigating them yet? Or have the police been scared away from the case? Poindexter was sure that the investigation had been sabotaged."*

"The federal government and the Philadelphia District Attorney are on it," said Holte, trying to determine where this might be leading.

"Good." And again, *"Good."* Another, more silent, silence fell between Moncrief and Holte. Finally Moncrief wondered, *"Is there any news of Louise?"*

"I'm sorry, Moncrief. Nothing so far."

Moncrief began to drift again. *"That's too bad. If you find out anything about her, will you let me know?"*

Holte was more baffled than he had been by the question about Hadley and Grimes, but he managed to summon up a response. *"Yes. Of course. I'll let you know."*

"Thanks. I'll let you know if I find out anything about GAD—you can remind me." By now, Moncrief was caught up in the swirl of ghosts, fading into their general confluence.

Frustrated by Moncrief's departure, Holte allowed himself to drift through the dimension of ghosts, hoping to recognize even one of them. When that did not happen, he recollected his pledge to Poppy, and aligned himself to slip back into the world of the living, the beginnings of an idea forming in his mind. He began to materialize outside of Poppy's bedroom window. It was very late at night, he realized, and debated with himself as to whether or not he should enter her room and wake her. He was fairly certain it was still Wednesday night, so he moved through the window, and did his best to make her bedside lamp blink, to no avail. He slid toward the end of the bed, and found Maestro glaring at him, a low, musical growl just beginning to get louder.

At this sound, Poppy came half-awake. "Maestro? What's wrong?" she mumbled.

"I bother him," said Holte, apologetically. "I said I'd be back soon."

Poppy blinked and shoved herself up on her elbow. "What time is it?"

"I don't know," said Holte, and flitted across the room to her alarm clock. "Three seventeen."

"Ye gods," Poppy groaned. "Why did you wake me up at this hour? Is the house on fire?"

Holte ignored her sarcasm. "I've come back from the dimension—"

"—of ghosts. Yes. All right," she finished for him, now almost fully awake. "What did you find out?"

Holte drifted down to the floor and appeared to be sitting cross-legged about four inches above the carpet. "I talked to Moncrief. He doesn't believe that GAD is dead, but he'll look around for him." If he remembers, Holte added to himself. "By the way, he doesn't seem to think that Overstreet is still in Canada, but he's not certain."

"Why not?" Poppy asked, her curiosity fully engaged; was it possible that Loring had left to escort Overstreet back to Philadelphia without telling her? She frowned in dismay, and immediately chided herself inwardly for such a reaction.

"Because Knott seems to be unable to find him there. He thinks Overstreet knows where Derrington has gone, and since he's almost certain that Derrington murdered him, Knott wants to have a word or two with him. But to do that, he has to find him." Holte rose a little way into the air, turning more filmy as he went.

"And Knott hasn't been able to find him?" Poppy reached for a pillow to lean on. "I thought ghosts could find anyone."

Holte sighed. "If we know how to define the person we're looking for, we can, but there are a lot of people on earth, and sorting through them takes time and patience, if you don't know where to start. Knott has lost his place to start."

"Not completely," said Poppy, giving voice to her thoughts. "He knows where Overstreet *was*, and surely that's a place to start." She reached over and turned on her bedside lamp; she blinked in the brightness. "It's that following-a-scent kind of thing, isn't it?"

"Yes." Holte studied her for a few seconds, and then recalled a lapse. "I'm sorry. I forgot to ask about Stacy."

Although she gave a short, irritated sigh, Poppy said, "It doesn't matter."

"Yes, it does. I said I would do it, and I didn't, so I owe you an apology. The next time I go to the dimension of ghosts, I'll see if I can find out anything about him—anything useful." Then he changed his tone, proceeding more cautiously, uncertain how to present his idea. "Something occurred to me as I was coming back here, something from my life. It might be helpful in the search for GAD."

"What is that?" She tried to cover a yawn, but did not succeed. "Sorry. I'm interested, but I'm also still sleepy."

"Do you want to go back to sleep?" Holte asked.

"Not now. My mind's racing its engines—that is the phrase, isn't it? Racing its engines?"

"Among the fast set with autos, yes, it is," Holte answered, amused.

Poppy blinked and stretched. "There. Now I'm ready. Carry on."

Holte steadied himself in the air, and began as if submitting a report. "There's a man in London. He's out of the Service now, but when I knew him, he was my—I suppose you'd call him my co-ordinator—when I was working on the Continent. Since he retired, he's been running a kind of search bureau: he specializes in locating displaced persons, finding them for families and such. He's in his late fifties now, but still capable and committed to his work." He paused, trying to decide how to go on. "He was known as N.Cubed when we were working together. His last name is Blessing."

Poppy gave a snort of disbelief. "A co-ordinator of spies, called Blessing?"

Holte was able not to laugh. "It's worse than that: N.Cubed stands for Noel Nicholas Naman. I should warn you that he has almost no sense of humor about his name, or any part of it."

"Was he born at Christmas? That might account for it—his parents wanting to commemorate their son emphatically," said Poppy, half seriously. "I suppose if he could survive school with that name, he can survive anything."

"I have no idea when his birthday is. I never dared to ask." He took a short moment to get focused again. "He knows how to locate people, and has had a good number of successes. The government still enlists his help from time to time. I understand his prices are reasonable, and he gives good value for money." He went silent again. "If you like, I can go to London and get his address, if you think it might be of use."

"For Inspector Loring?" she suggested.

"And perhaps the Pearses. It could be a place to start."

Poppy reached out to open the drawer in her night-stand and took out a pencil and a pad of paper. "Tell me if I have this right: Noel Nicholas Naman Blessing, in London?" She was scribbling as she spoke.

"You do. I think he's somewhere near the Courts, but I don't know for certain." He rose a few inches higher. "Do you want me to look?"

"Not yet. The *Clarion* should have a London telephone directory in the reference library. If he isn't listed, then perhaps I may take advantage of your kind offer." She closed her notebook and put it back in the night-stand drawer, along with her pencil. "Does he work alone, or does he have a staff?"

Holte waited while she readied herself to take notes, then launched into his account of Blessing. "He has a staff of sorts, most of them in Europe, but he often handles his searches himself. He speaks five languages, including Czech and Hungarian, so you can see how this would help him locate missing persons."

Poppy thought about this, then asked, "How do you know so much about him now? Unless you have books to balance with him?"

Holte had a spurt of panic, which carried him to the far side of the room; he realized he had not given her credit for her skill at making deductions. "Yes. I did want to balance the books with him. He was the first person I contacted, when I remembered enough to work it out." He drifted back in her direction. "You were the second, in case you're curious. The Bastins are third."

Poppy mulled this over as she attempted to ward off sleep. "What had you done that needed balancing with Mister Blessing?" She steeled herself for his answer.

"It's the nature of the business, owing people," said Holte, sounding exhausted, as if the memories were a demanding weight upon him, noncorporeal though he was. "Blessing had given me orders, very strict orders, and I...neglected to follow them."

"You disobeyed orders?" She was troubled by the implications of his admission. "That doesn't sound like you."

"I improvised." He became marginally more visible so that he and Poppy could have the illusion of looking one another in the eyes. "My contact did not reach me at the time and place that had been arranged, but there was a need to get some papers to the...it doesn't matter now which company wanted what I carried." Now that he was telling her, it seemed impossible to stop. "Suffice it to say, they were English and at the Front. In the trenches. I could not find a way to reach them, and in my attempt to do so, I exposed a whole network of spies, which ruined our chances to assist the soldiers in their fighting, and they suffered heavy losses. But that wasn't the sum of it: I hadn't realized that N.Cubed had a back-up plan—although I should have inferred it—and had I remained where I was, where the failed contact was to take place, another of N.Cubed's network would have found me, and completed the delivery, so the network would have remained in place, and the men in the trenches wouldn't have been so badly depleted. N.Cubed took full responsibility for the loss, and four months later, I was dead, so I could not make it up to him—until I remembered."

Poppy's expression had grown somber as she listened to Holte. "How... dreadful. For all of you."

It took Holte a little time to come up with a response. "In the weeks immediately after the network was exposed, I tried to think of it as fortunes of war, something that could not have been avoided, and that was not my fault, but all along, I was certain that I had been too precipitous, that I should have remained in position, waiting for orders. But with the fighting getting worse, I was afraid that my contact might have been taken prisoner, and that could have meant that I was no longer safe. I panicked, though I didn't believe I had, at the time. I made for the coast and was taken aboard a Dutch fishing boat, and carried across the Channel to Plymouth. Blessing was distressed, but he blamed my unknown back-up more than he blamed me, which only made it worse. I was kept in England for a fortnight, where I was safe."

"Strange, to think of being a spy and being safe," Poppy remarked, trying to offer him a bit of sympathy.

"It is, isn't it," Holte observed. He moved a little higher in the air. "I've kept you awake long enough. Turn out your light and go back to sleep. I'll see you in the morning, on your drive in to the paper."

He had almost disappeared when Poppy called out, "Wait!"

Holte hung against the ceiling. "What is it?"

Now that he had halted for her, Poppy had to order her thoughts. "It's none of my business, I know, but how many other books of yours need balancing?"

"More than I'd like to admit," he said, and vanished through the ceiling, leaving Poppy to cogitate on all he had told her.

THIRTEEN

THERE WAS A MESSAGE SLIP WAITING ON POPPY'S DESK BY THE TIME SHE REACHED
the *Clarion* on Thursday morning. She recognized the number as Loring's, and
so sat down and called the phone bank of the paper and asked to be connected
to Loring's number at the police department. Little as she wanted to admit it,
she was worried that Loring might be turning down her invitation to her party.

The operator came on the line. "You're connected to Inspector Loring, Miss
Thornton."

"Thank you," Poppy said as the operator completed the contact.

"Thanks for calling back," said Loring. "I was about to go out but I wanted
to be sure I reached you early today."

Poppy began to think about what Holte had told her, and she did her best
not to hold her breath. "Has anything come up?"

"Indirectly, yes." He coughed and lowered his voice. "We had a call yesterday
evening from the Mounties, saying that Miles Overstreet escaped while being
brought to the British Army Detention Center at Montreal. There is a manhunt
on for him now."

"A manhunt? Surely they don't think he's dangerous, do they?" She spoke
almost by rote, and made herself add, "How did it happen?"

"The escort was held up at a drawbridge, and apparently a yacht that was
passing below the bridge shot up at the Mounties and while they ducked and
hid, Overstreet flung himself out of the rear of the touring car, and jumped
into the river, where someone from the yacht picked him up and hauled him
aboard before turning around and going downstream, raising their sails as they
went. At least that's what Captain Joiner told me this morning."

"Was it planned, or serendipity?" Poppy asked, reaching for a notepad and a pencil.

"I don't know—not yet. It seems to be a coincidence; I don't believe in them. Captain Joiner has promised to keep me abreast of their investigation. He'll make another report to me tomorrow. In the meantime, the Canadians have alerted the American Coast Guard with a description of the boat in question. Or should I call it a ship?" He sighed. "I wish it weren't such a big ocean."

"Small wonder," said Poppy by way of commiseration.

After a brief pause, Loring said, "It means that, barring the unexpected, I should be able to be with you tomorrow night. And thank you again for your invitation." He lowered his voice. "If there are any...complications, I'll let you know as soon as I learn of them."

"Much appreciated," said Poppy. "I hope we do see you."

"So do I," Loring admitted before he hung up the phone.

Poppy sat still at her desk, staring at her scribbled notes, a distant expression in her eyes. After the greater part of a minute, she rose, and taking her notebook in hand, went to Cornelius Lowenthal's office, and tapped on the door.

"Come in, and this better be good," Lowenthal growled from inside.

Poppy took hold of the doorknob and pushed. "It's Poppy, boss," she said as she came in. "I just talked to Inspector Loring, and he tells me that Miles Overstreet has escaped from the Mounties and is probably on the run."

Lowenthal's scowl faded to a wolfish smile. "Overstreet escaped? Can you get confirmation on this?"

"I think so. Inspector Loring gave me the name of a Mountie I should be able to use. I'll get right on it, if you want me to pursue the story?" The doubt in her voice was more because she was remembering what Holte had told her, and realized that this would not be a source that Lowenthal would approve. "The Mountie should be able to give me information. Is it all right for me to call him?" She glanced at the name in her notebook. "It's a Captain Joiner, and I'd guess he's in the Montreal department. If he isn't, I'd assume they could tell me where he is posted."

Lowenthal's smile became crocodilian. "I knew you had a nose for this kind of work, Thornton. Go right ahead. If anyone upstairs asks about the cost of the calls, you send 'em to me." He pulled at his thinning, curly hair. "I'd like something by two this afternoon, so I can place it well."

Poppy did her best to conceal her delight. "I'll get right on it, boss," she pledged.

"Damn right you will. Chop-chop." Offering no apology for swearing, he made a shooing gesture to dismiss her. "Get back to me as soon as you have confirmation."

Back at her desk, Poppy picked up her phone and told the operator to connect her with the Montreal office of the Royal Canadian Mounted Police, thinking as she did, that Holte would be pleased that she used the full title. "I want to talk to a Captain Joiner. If he's not assigned to that office, see if they can tell you where he is."

"Is this urgent, Miss Thornton?" asked the operator.

"Yes," said Poppy, and tapped the eraser on her pencil on her notebook. "If you need permission, check with Lowenthal."

"All right. Please stay on the line and I will connect you as soon as I have reached Captain Joiner for you." The operator had a sing-song delivery and a tone worthy of a schoolmarm.

"Thanks," said Poppy, and went back to bouncing her eraser on her notebook while she formed questions in her mind.

"I have Captain Joiner for you, Miss Thornton," the operator informed her some four minutes later. "Go ahead, Captain."

Captain Joiner had a deep, soothing voice that bordered on the soporific. "Good morning to you, Miss Thornton," he said. "Inspector Loring told me you might call me about Overstreet."

"How perceptive of him," she responded in as cordial a tone as she could muster. "I'm a reporter with the *Philadelphia Clarion*, and I have been following a case in which Miles Overstreet was deeply involved."

"I understand that," said Captain Joiner.

"Then you'll understand my need for confirmation on what has occurred before I can go to press," she said crisply, readying her pencil to write. "He was being transported by which agency?"

"I'm afraid we were handling the transfer, the Royal Canadian Mounted Police," Joiner said, a note of chagrin in his voice.

Poppy had already decided on using the direct approach. "How much can you tell me about it?"

"Rather a lot, I'm sorry to say," the captain admitted. "I was in charge of the escort. I was in the lead auto, and three of us had got over the bridge when the alert sounded and the midsection began to turn, leaving Overstreet in the transport vehicle on the midsection. That seemed safe enough, because the midsection was isolated, so there was no way he could get away, or so we thought."

"So let me get this pictured in my mind," said Poppy. "You were on the rear section of the bridge, and therefore connected to land, and Overstreet was in his transportation was on the middle part of the bridge that had rotated to let river traffic through? What about the leading part of the escort?" She began to sketch the situation on the edge of her desk blotter. "Were there vehicles stopped behind you?"

"A few; the rear auto had its siren on, so there was no pile-up of vehicles immediately behind us. The front of the escort was on the far side of the bridge, and connected to land, just as I and my men were. I and a few others had got out of our autos to see what was going on in the river, to get some idea of how long we might have to wait. A few minutes later, there was a flurry of shots that came, we presumed, from the embankment behind us, and we took cover, which is fairly standard procedure in these circumstances. There was a rifleman in the second lead car, and he was busy trying to locate the origin of the shots."

"How do you mean that the bridge turned?" Poppy asked. "Will you describe how that works, please?"

Captain Joiner was silent for a second or two, then began, taking care to provide details. "The bridge is in three sections. The midsection sits on a column that pivots. The alarm is supposed to provide time for all vehicles to get off the midsection before it is turned, but in this case, only the transport vehicle was on the midsection when the turn began. The turn is ninety degrees, and the roadway in the midsection aligns with the flow of the river, allowing marine traffic passage on either side of the column. We find that this speeds up the movement of ships on that busy stretch of the river, and returns road travel to its normal flow more quickly than the standard drawbridge does."

"I take it, then, that it was not the La Salle Bridge, because of the railroad bridge next to it? The turning mechanism probably would be too broad for that arrangement," Poppy said, pleased now that she had taken the opportunity to look at Aunt Esther's atlas before she had come in to work that morning.

"No, you're right, Miss Thornton," said Captain Joiner, a quality of new-found respect in his tone. "For safety reasons, we went along to the Pont Champlain. That turns out to have been a mistake."

"How long before the transfer was that decision made?" Poppy almost held her breath for the answer.

"The day before. We had to make changes in our arrangements, but there was nothing unusual in that."

"Did you ever determine where the shots had come from?"

"Alas, we did not," he confessed. "I wondered at some point if they had come from the yacht, but that sounds unlikely, and in these instances, you do clutch at straws, don't you?"

"I would think so," said Poppy, writing hurriedly.

"The rifleman told me that he thought it was someone shooting—illegally— at the geese that were about; after the first shot, the geese took to the air, which would account for the upward angle of the bullets." He paused, and added, "There are those who hunt out of season."

"Can you tell me anything more about the incident?" Poppy asked.

"Well, the bridge began to rotate, and those of us ahead of the midsection did not at first realize what was happening, and by the time we did, there was no way to stop it, for the mischief was already done." The chagrin was back in his voice. "I must admit that I paid very little attention to the yacht—it was a very handsome yawl, about fifty feet, I'd say, and perhaps fifteen or slightly more abeam, brightwork polished, decks clean, the engine humming along like a first-class generator, sails properly furled, quite yar as the sailors say— for I was expecting a larger vessel to be coming, not that solitary craft; it was the height of the masts that made the rotation of the bridge necessary. After the shots were fired, I allowed myself to be distracted by the yacht's passage, fearing that it might also be in danger, but then heard the siren on the transport vehicle go off, and saw that the door on the rear of the transport was lifted all the way up, and the passenger door in the front was coming open. Because of the open door, I could not clearly see what was going on, but I did see a man fall from the midsection of the bridge into the river, not far from the yacht."

"The Saint Lawrence?" Poppy asked, just to be certain.

"Yes. The Rivière des Prairies is on the other side of the city, in the west." He cleared his throat. "At first I did not notice any potential connection between Overstreet and the yacht, and there might not have been one, but the boat turned back, perhaps for altruistic reasons rather than any plan, and took Overstreet from the river."

"Does this yacht have a name?" Poppy was writing rapidly now, striving to keep ahead of what Captain Joiner was saying.

"It was *Belle Helene*, and it flew an American flag, which may or may not be significant. We're trying to trace it to its home port, but so far, we have had no luck; it's early days yet."

"I gather the American Coast Guard is looking for the yacht? Do you think they could help you, by arranging some kind of mutual search?" It was an obvious question, but one that Lowenthal would want included in her report.

"I hope so, but I have to tell you that we saw no home port on her stern, and there was no port medallion on her mainmast flag, or none that I could work out. That was what was most troubling about the rescue of Overstreet. It suggested that the yacht was not there by happenstance, and that there was a surreptitious purpose to its presence. Some of my men disagree with me, but the whole thing is too coincidental for my taste."

"That's a possibility, that it was a set-up," Poppy allowed, thinking of Loring's comments about coincidences.

"We have sent word to the Royal Navy about this, in case the yacht is bound eastward, or toward the Caribbean. The Atlantic is a big ocean, but the Royal Navy might get lucky, or your Coast Guard."

"Does that mean the *Belle Helene* is an ocean-going craft, and not just a coaster?" Poppy was writing even more rapidly now, and her concentration was increasing.

"It had that appearance," said Joiner, very carefully. "But many private boats that operate in the Saint Lawrence are ocean-going, whether they need to be or not."

"I'll be sure to mention that," said Poppy, taking great satisfaction in having Holte's account confirmed. "Is there anything you'd like to add?"

"Not at this time, no, since it would have to be entirely speculation."

Poppy was satisfied. "Then thank you so much, Captain Joiner. You've been most helpful."

"You will benefit us as well, Miss Thornton. Your report will alert many persons out sailing to be aware of the *Belle Helene* and to report her if she is sighted." He sounded sincere enough, but there was still a note of worry that Poppy could hear.

"The *Clarion* is glad to be of any help we can, Captain," she declared.

"We're grateful for any assistance you can render." He sounded sincere, which reminded Poppy to ask one more thing.

"May I quote you, by name? And if you are willing to be quoted, will you spell your first and last names, and confirm your rank?"

"You may quote me. My first name is Peregrine, like the falcon, and my last is Joiner, like a carpenter. My rank is Captain in the Royal Canadian Mounted Police. If you would send me a clipping from whatever article or articles you publish on this case, I would be much obliged. I am in the Montreal office." This had the sound of something he had said many times before.

"I'll do that," Poppy told him, and added, "Thank you for talking with me on what must be a very busy day for you."

"It is my privilege," he told her, and hung up.

For the next hour Poppy roughed out her story, and by the time she went to lunch, she was confident of making her two o'clock deadline. On impulse, she took her car and drove to the Seagull Café, that overlooked a private boat club on the Delaware, where she occupied herself with watching the boats passing the broad windows that faced the river until her fish chowder arrived, along with a basket of cornbread and a mug of strong, black tea. Taking a little time to think about it, she was fairly certain that the *Belle Helene* would not come here to any New England port, nor to any port this side of Havana, not with the Coast Guard looking for her. The same might be true of England and Europe, given that the Royal Navy was also on alert, which left points farther south to be explored. The Mediterranean seemed unlikely—too closely watched, and with the British controlling Gibraltar, the risk would be tremendous. Would the *Belle Helene* make for the Caribbean Islands not under British control, or the Azores, farther east and south? The yawl could hold along the coast of South America, or Africa, for that matter. Perhaps she should ask Hank about it—he should know. By the time she had finished her lunch, Poppy had also decided how to present her story, and she was returning to the *Clarion* in a much more positive frame of mind than she had had when she left. As she drove back to the Addison Newspaper Building, she was whistling, beginning to think that finding the *Belle Helene* could help re-energize the Moncrief investigation; she would have to thank Loring for the tip.

Lowenthal was waiting for her when she walked in. "Well?"

"Give me fifteen minutes and I'll have what you want," she said, heading for her desk; she could feel the eyes of the eight other reporters in the room upon her, and so she moved at a brisker pace.

"You have two sources for the story?" His demeanor was unusually edgy as he followed her to her desk.

"Yes boss and I can quote both of them," she said, sitting down and reaching for two sheets of paper and a carbon. "Why? Are you getting grief about this?"

"You might say so," Lowenthal said, his gaze shifting around the room. "Just bear in mind that we can't afford an error on this one. Our bosses upstairs reminded me that we don't want any grief from the law. The District Attorney requires accuracy in anything we print about anything having to do with Moncrief and Knott."

"He's anticipating the trial already?" Poppy asked.

"It looks like it; he's confident, he says, that when Overstreet is caught, he'll give up all he knows, and that will lead to Derrington and your cousin," said Lowenthal, suddenly aware that he had the full attention of everyone in the city room. "I had a call from his office not half an hour ago, ten minutes after I heard from upstairs, and I was told that if anything we printed corrupted the case, he would take action against us, freedom of the press be damned. And that is an exact quote."

Poppy rolled the sheets into the platen and prepared to type. "I got it."

"Make sure you keep it in mind," Lowenthal told her, then turned and made his way back to his office, pausing at the door to call for Dick Gafney to bring him the latest on the Napier robbery investigation.

Gafney, one arm in a sling, glowered through a haze of cigarette smoke and mumbled a reply.

"Ten minutes!" Lowenthal barked.

"Tough on you, Thornton," said Jim Franks, who covered sports; he was grinning at Poppy's discomfort. "Better get cracking."

"You, too, Franks," she said, refusing to be distracted by him. She began to type, taking care to make sure she spelled Captain Joiner's name correctly, aware that she would have to answer for even a minor mistake in the story. She was half way through the report when the lamp above her desk flickered.

"Not now," Poppy whispered as she hit the carriage return with more force than usual.

"Thirty-one Museum Street, Westminster," said Holte from immediately behind her left shoulder.

Poppy stopped typing. "What?"

"N.Cubed's business address. Thirty-one Museum Street, Westminster."

It took Poppy a moment to realize what he was telling her; she felt a rush of chagrin that she had not gone to the paper's library to look it up herself. She reached for a pencil and scribbled the address in her notebook, doing her best to make it appear that she was fact-checking rather than adding something about an entirely different story. "London, England?"

"Yes." Holte could feel her stress, and added, "Finish what you're doing. I'll talk to you later."

"Thanks," she muttered, and went back to work on the Overstreet article. In twelve minutes she was through; she pulled the papers out of the typewriter and went toward Lowenthal's office, trying to reread what she had written as she went. Not bad for a rush job, she decided, and knocked on his door, knowing that the eyes of her colleagues were still trained on her.

"Come in," Lowenthal barked, and looked up as Poppy obeyed. "Have you?"

"Done," Poppy said, and put the top sheet down on his desk.

"Good. Gafney still isn't done with his." Lowenthal picked it up and skimmed through it. "I may trim out a sentence or two, but otherwise, it does the job."

"Thank goodness." Poppy sat down in the chair across the desk from Lowenthal. "Do you want me to stay on it boss?"

"For a day or two, yes. If there's no more news, we'll talk about it on Monday. I'll want you to have a word or two with your inspector. And make sure you check in with the Mounties first thing Monday." He began to read the page more closely. "You sure quoting Inspector Loring is all right with him?"

"Yes. He's known to be on this investigation, and he's not about to say anything that could compromise prosecution of the case." Although she said this more forcefully than she planned, she was certain that Loring would not object to her account of Overstreet's escape—or, she thought, she would owe him an apology, a notion that made her ill at ease.

"Anything wrong?" Lowenthal asked, peering closely at her.

"Not really. I just wish I'd had more time to polish the story." It was near enough to the truth that she did not feel she had been dishonest.

"It's enough for now. You can do something slicker if there's a follow-up to Overstreet's get away—I won't put too much of a rush on you," said Lowenthal. "If they catch Overstreet in the next week or so I'll put your report above the fold."

"Be sure to include a reminder to send Captain Joiner a clipping. His contact address is with the notes. As to a slot above the fold, I'll hold you to that boss," she said with a wavering smile.

Lowenthal nodded as a sign of surety. "You'll deserve it if you can see it through."

"Oh I can," said Poppy. "I have my own interests in this story."

"That's what I mean about *if*," Lowenthal said, "After what you've been though, you may lose your...perspective. You're supposed to keep your objectivity in this field, and it might not be possible for you to do that. If that happens, let me know." He coughed. "I'd say the same thing if you were a man, so don't think I'm underestimating you."

Poppy shook her head adamantly. "I've got to see this through."

"Fine with me, but you can change your mind; I won't think any the less of you, if you do." He did his best to achieve a reassuring smile, then pointed to the door. "Out. I got work to do."

FOURTEEN

Poppy had stopped off at the beauty parlor on her way home, and she waited until she was at Aunt Esther's house to phone Loring at his flat. It took him nine rings to answer, and she wondered what she had interrupted, but controlled her impulse to question him. "I have an address that may help you in the Pearse investigation," she began after they had a brief exchange of pleasantries.

"Unofficial investigation," he reminded her.

"Yes, of course."

"What kind of address?" He sounded preoccupied.

Driving home, she had worked out an explanation that would not reveal who supplied the information, and now she delivered it as smoothly as she could. "I spoke to a...colleague of my father's. I didn't mention any names, if course, but I explained that there was a missing person who might be in Europe, and this...colleague, told me that there is a man in London, who used to be part of the intelligence operations during the Great War, who now works as an investigator locating missing and displaced persons, and he might be willing to take on the case."

Loring was paying attention now, his tone dubious but polite. "Who is this fellow? Not the one who told you, the man he recommended, in London."

"The name is N. N. N. Blessing—that's three Ns—and his address is thirty-one Museum Street, Westminster, London. You might want to tell the Pearses about him."

"Will they be at your party?"

"I don't know," Poppy said. "Aunt Esther hasn't shown me the guest list yet. She's been busy."

"Then I suppose I should call them—the Pearses—to show them I'm doing something, at least. I know Missus Pearse is getting anxious. She wants this in the papers as much as Mister Pearse does not." He paused. "Will you give me the information again? All of it?"

"Certainly," she said, and repeated Blessing's name and address.

Loring read it back to her, then added, "This colleague of your father's, is he reliable? The one who recommended this Blessing fellow?"

"Very," said Poppy, and realized that her conviction might sound too confident. "He helped me to find out what happened to my father, so I trust any recommendation he might offer."

"Okay," said Loring. "I'll see what the Pearses want to do. Thanks for the lead though."

"My pleasure," said Poppy, and felt herself start to blush. "And thanks for the help on the Overstreet escape."

"Glad to do it." He went silent for a second or two. "Will it be in tonight's edition?"

"Yes," she said. "Page two, but above the fold."

"That's great. So I'll see you tomorrow evening." He seemed ready to hang up, but asked, "Do I need to dress up? I should warn you that I don't own a dinner jacket."

"I think a good suit would do; this isn't the Opera Ball. You could come in a sports jacket and I doubt Aunt Esther would mind. It's going to be a diverse lot, from what Aunt Esther has said," she said, and once again wondered who would be coming. "She and I will be in dinner dresses. I think Aunt Jo will be here with Hank and his wife Cecily, and they'll be in proper dinner-dress, but Cornelius and Eunice Lowenthal, and a couple of her colleagues from the National Geographic Society will be there, too. You'll fit in as well as any of them."

"That ought to be interesting; quite a mixed crowd," Loring said, sardonically amused.

"Then you see what I mean about what to wear."

"I do," he said, and hung up on a chuckle.

Poppy put the receiver back in its cradle and then picked up her new brief-case, her purse, and her hat before hurrying upstairs. She opened the door at the top of the stairs carefully, to ensure that Maestro did not escape; the cat was not at the top of the stairs, but was crouched, waiting, just inside her bedroom door, and leaped out to wrap himself around her ankle, purring and growling at once.

"Let go you monster. You'll ruin my stockings. They're silk, and more expensive than a week of chopped chicken-and-fish for you. Let go." She put down what she carried and bent to disengage him.

As Maestro retreated, sulking, to the corner of her bed, Chesterton Holte spoke up from near the ceiling. "I gather all went well."

Poppy refused to be startled. "If you mean passing on the address, I think it did. I waited until I got here to phone Loring. The operators at the newspaper are notorious for listening in on conversations."

"So you've told me." He came slowly down from the ceiling, becoming a bit more clearly defined on the way; when Maestro hissed at him, Holte turned to the cat. "Same to you old boy."

"He's still not pleased with his move. Give him some time and he'll quiet down." Poppy went over to the bed. "Yes, I've told Loring. I don't know how much use he'll make of it, but do you think I should send a note to N.Cubed Blessing, informing that he might receive contact from the Pearses, or from Loring?"

"No, not yet; no reason to; for the time being, you needn't be directly involved," said Holte, settling into his usual place three inches above the seat of the side-chair between the chest-of-drawers and her vanity table. "Let's see if anything comes of it first. For all we know, the Pearses won't want to use N.Cubed services."

"I'm assuming you listened in on my conversation with Captain Joiner?" She bent to take off her shoes and stopped as she looked at the ruins of her stockings. "Ye gods, these are a total loss."

"Yes, I did listen in," Holte admitted without apology. "Very direct fellow, Peregrine Joiner. I'm pleased he was so cooperative."

"And with very nice manners, too; not like some policemen I've talked to," Poppy observed. "Must be a Canadian trait."

Holte did something that suggested a partial bow. "By policemen, in this instance I gather you don't mean Inspector Loring."

"That would be most ungracious of me," Poppy conceded.

"I like to think you're more generous than that, particularly since he is so fond of you," Holte rejoined, "You needn't protest it; it's obvious that his fascination has not faded through the summer." He made a gesture with his barely visible hand and strove to change the subject. "Where is your estimable Aunt Esther? I thought she would be here ahead of you."

"I assume that she is out with Miss Roth, doing the last-minute shopping for tomorrow, since both Miss Roth and Mister Galliard are missing, as is the auto. I can tell by the aroma that Missus Sassoro is in the kitchen. From the scent, we're having veal tonight." A thought suddenly struck her. "Can you smell any of her cooking?"

"No. I can't smell anything. I don't hear the way you do, either. And you know I can't actually touch anything. Senses get...diffuse, once you lack a body to have them with." There was a note of nostalgia in this admission.

"Do you miss it—any of it?" she could not keep from asking.

"Yes and no," he answered, and became slightly more misty than he had been. "But it's one of the things we forget, in time."

"You're being deliberately vague," she told him.

"I am aren't I?" He swung toward the ceiling again. "All right, I'll try to explain. I don't actually speak. I don't have a mouth or vocal chords any more. You can hear me because my obligation to you allows you to receive my thoughts, and because of this link, I can hear you clearly."

"Sort of like a radio tuning in on a station?" she asked.

He dropped down once more. "It's a good enough analogy. Animals are not so tightly tuned as living adult humans are. Babies receive almost everything."

She was studying his filmy presence intently. "Do I see you because of that tuning?"

"In part. As you know, keeping the semblance of a living appearance has some demands for ghosts. It's tiring to manifest the way I'm doing now, for you, who can pick up my presence. For those who can't, the best I can manage is kind of mist and a sound like the echo of a moan." He returned to the chair. "So what can you tell me about tomorrow night? Is there any reason I should... attend?"

Poppy cocked her head. "Is there any reason you shouldn't?"

Holte made a noise that was almost a chuckle. "I'll make an effort then. Just promise me you'll keep your infernal cat up here, closed in."

"I'll do it whether you're here or not," said Poppy. "Maestro isn't comfortable at parties."

"Yes," said Holte, glancing over at the cat, who pointedly ignored him, his ears remaining fixed forward as if he had heard nothing. "I've realized that."

Poppy bent down and picked her purse up off the floor. As she opened it, she said, "I really ought to get him some toys. Give him something harmless to kill."

"Didn't they send along some from the Dritchner house?"

"A couple, none of his favorites." She took out her checkbook and opened it. "I wonder if Galliard would be willing to plant catnip for him. I'll be letting him out by Monday, and catnip would delight him." She thought a bit, and added, "It might bring too many neighborhood cats to the house, but Maestro would like it."

"Always a problem, having catnip in the yard. What about a window-box, over there?" He pointed to the tall windows that faced the side of the lot. "You might get the occasional cat on the roof, but the catnip would be all Maestro's."

She would have tossed one of her pillows at him if she had thought it would have done any good. "At Aunt Jo's house, she refused to let the Jeffries plant any; Aunt Esther isn't such a stickler, and I'll suggest a window-box."

"Speaking of your aunts, has your Aunt Esther had an interview with Lowenthal yet, about that proposed article about the Living Spectres?" Holte asked, as if he wanted to prolong their discussion.

"I don't think so, no. Neither of them has mentioned it." She fussed with her purse and took out her compact. "My face needs attention."

Holte made what could be a resigned sigh. "I know you have to change and take care of your hair—I like the new cut, by the way—but I'm curious about Aunt Esther."

"I don't know if she has an appointment; I pretty sure she hasn't spoken to Lowenthal. I'm surprised that you don't know that," she said, glad that she had persuaded Renee at Hannah's Beauty Box to give up her four-thirty departure to restore Poppy's coiffeur. "You're at the *Clarion* almost as much as I am, and you have access to all the phone conversations."

"I don't spend all my time hanging around the *Clarion*," he told her.

"That's right. You often go into the dimension of ghosts." She hesitated, then plowed on, "Have you any news from there?"

"No, but I hope to have some soon," said Holte, then added, "I'll probably go there on Saturday for an extended period. That's your half-day at the paper, isn't it?"

"Yes. This Saturday, I'll be working in the afternoon rather than the morning, to make allowances for tomorrow evening." She stood up. "Not that I'm a prude, but I need to unfasten my hose from my garter-belt, and I'm still not used to you watching me undress."

Holte rose out of the chair toward the ceiling. "I'll be back in a little while. I need to talk to Knott. It shouldn't take long." He passed through the ceiling and *slipped* into the dimension of ghosts, leaving Poppy alone with Maestro.

Once she was sure that Holte had gone, Poppy unfastened her skirt and let it drop to the floor, then removed her jacket and blouse, taking the time to loosely fold them and set them next to her pillows. After tugging her slip over her head, she unfastened the garters from her garter- belt and let her ruined silk stockings slide down her legs. Kicking these away from her, she looked over at Maestro. "I should be very angry with you, you know. These hose cost almost a dollar." She sank back onto the side of the bed, and leaned over to pick up her skirt and lay it on the side of her bed. "But you have no appreciation about the cost of things, do you?"

Maestro opened one eye, then yawned.

"It's all very well for you to take such a cavalier attitude, but in future I'd be grateful if you would leave my hose alone." Satisfied with her admonition to the cat, she reached down for the stockings and knotted them together before dropping them in the wastebasket beside the night-stand. "I'm going to put on a new pair. If you'd be good enough to leave them as is?" Without waiting for a response from Maestro, she got up and went to her chest-of-drawers and removed a new pair of stockings. Taking care to keep the seams straight, she drew on the left one first, fastened it to the garter-belt, then did the same with the right, all the while trying to decide what to wear for dinner. "Aunt Esther probably wouldn't mind if I wore riding britches and a barn-jacket," she mused aloud, then selected an ankle-length skirt of rosy-mauve wool crepe, and then a long blouse of polished linen the color of ripe Santa Rosa plums. On impulse, she added a multi-colored silk scarf, which she knotted loosely around her neck. She was just putting on a pair of low-heeled black shoes when she heard the side-door open on the ground floor.

"Poppy! We're back!" Aunt Esther caroled out.

"Good evening, Aunt Esther," Poppy answered loudly enough to be heard downstairs. She went to her vanity table, refreshed her lipstick, and ran a comb through her hair, all the while trying to decide if she liked the slightly shorter length. Without reaching a decision, she went out of the room and, taking care to secure the door at the top of the stairs, went down to the study, where she found Esther in the act of pouring out a dollop of cognac into one of the little balloon glasses.

Hearing Poppy arrive, Esther turned toward her. "Can I get you a drink? I like that ensemble you're wearing." Esther herself remained in her walking suit, a handsome jacket with long peplums over a below-the-calf pleated skirt, all in a warm, light-grey. Her blouse was Prussian blue, as were her ankle-strap shoes.

"Whatever you're having is fine with me," said Poppy, dropping into the side-chair at the end of the coffee-table. "Thanks for the compliment."

"Hardly a compliment, just an observation; I suppose I ought to apologize for not changing for dinner, but since it's just you and me, I didn't think it would matter," said Esther, reaching for another of the small balloon glasses. "How was your day?"

"How was yours?" Poppy riposted with a fencing gesture from her finger.

"Oh, no; you first," Esther insisted, handing the second glass of cognac to her. "I need to gather my thoughts."

Poppy lifted her glass in a perfunctory toast to her aunt. "Mine was about usual; I did a squib on an auction fraud—it may be one of the counterfeit antiques that Knott and Denton North have talked about—and then I did a short column on the current state of the hunt for Miles Overstreet—he's escaped, by the way, so I had nothing very much to tell, except that he got away on a yacht, and that the Royal Navy as well as the Coast Guard is looking for him; it's under my own by-line again, which is very kind of Lowenthal. After I turned the story in, I had a kind of tea in the cafeteria this afternoon, spent a little time on the phone trying to learn more about Overstreet. And I got my hair cut."

"Um," said Aunt Esther, giving her niece's hair careful scrutiny. "Very nice. I thought that you had a bit too much curl in the back. This is much neater." She sat down and took a sip of cognac. "Miles Overstreet is the young man who used to work for Percy Knott? He fled after Percy was murdered?"

"He's the one," Poppy confirmed.

"That complicates matters. How unfortunate. I don't suppose anyone knows where he's gone." Aunt Esther stared at the silent radio on the high-boy next to the fireplace as if she expected it to express an opinion; after a second or two, she shook her head. "There isn't much either of us can do about it, is there? Is there a hunt on for him?" Since this was clearly a rhetorical question, Poppy said nothing. Suddenly Esther stifled a yawn, covering it with her left hand. "Oh, drat. I'll have to plan a nap for tomorrow afternoon, otherwise I may doze off in front of our guests—most negligent for a hostess."

"You? Doze off?" Poppy marveled. "Never."

"You'd be surprised," said Esther. "I haven't the stamina I had twenty years ago. Still, I like to think that I can still run with the best of them; it only takes a little more effort." She toasted the air, and took a long, slow slip. "Better. Much better."

Poppy joined in her toast, then asked, "Do we have a final count on company for tomorrow?"

Esther looked around, meeting Poppy's inquisitive gaze. "Didn't I tell you this morning?" She saw Poppy shake her head. "Well, I intended to. As of last evening, there will be twenty-six of us, counting you and me. I've told Miss Roth to use the Italian china, the set with the rose- wreaths on the rims of the plates. We have thirty-two of those settings, thank goodness. And the Baroque sterling; it goes well with the china." She had another sip of cognac. "I wish I'd thought to bring some schnapps back from Vienna while I was there. I'd have had to smuggle it in, of course, but it would have been a nice touch for tomorrow."

"Can't your bootlegger Ruscelli get you any?" Poppy asked.

"Probably, but it's ever so expensive, and it's also not a sure thing that the quality would be up to the standards I would like." She took a deep breath. "I found some very good cheeses at a little market on Fulton; Missus Sassoro will do a tray of them, with soda crackers. That, along with an array of Belgian chocolates, should be an adequate dessert, don't you think?"

"It sounds expensive," said Poppy, a bit dubiously.

"It is, but it's nice to be able to spend my money on something other than travel." She laughed softly. "I'll be off again soon, and I want to make the most of my time here with you."

Poppy did not know if she should be wary or grateful, so she only said, "Thanks," and had more of her cognac. "Do you have a date for when you'll leave?"

"Not a firm one yet; I'm negotiating with the National Geographic Society on particulars, and they are taking their time about responding. I'm hoping that I will have a firm departure date in three weeks at the latest, which means I'll probably be away through the end of the year. My guess is they'll make up their minds by the end of the month, which puts us into October—four weeks at the most, I hope—and then I'm on my way to Central and South America, including a journey up the Amazon. Winter in the Amazon. It should be fascinating. I've been to the mouth, of course, but never penetrated beyond Brazil. This time I'm going all the way to Iquitos, which is in Peru."

"Quite a distance," said Poppy, who knew some kind of response was required of her. All the while she was thinking that Iquitos struck a chord with her, and wished she could remember what it was.

"I've been curious about the place for years, but never had the opportunity to go there. They say it's quite civilized for a city in the middle of the jungle; we—that's the editorial we—shall see," Esther said, and looked up as Miss Roth brought in a small tray of broiled crab legs wrapped in Chinese pickled ginger. "Thank you, Miss Roth."

"Dinner will be on the table in half an hour," Miss Roth announced. "I'm needed in the kitchen."

"Of course you are," Esther agreed. "There's still a lot to do for tomorrow night."

"That there is," said Miss Roth, and withdrew.

"Thank you," Esther called after her, then gave her attention to Poppy. "So tell me about this escape. I want to be au courant for the party."

FIFTEEN

THE DIMENSION OF GHOSTS WAS MORE ACTIVE THAN USUAL, AND IT TOOK Chesterton Holte more time than he had anticipated to find Madison Moncrief among the energetic swirls that were ghostly existence. When he finally approached Moncrief, Holte was surprised to find an unfamiliar ghost with him, and so he hesitated as he approached.

"Moncrief? It's Holte," he said in his non-voice.

"So it is," said Moncrief, sounding a bit restored by Holte's greeting. *"How long are you back for this time?"*

"Not long. I have a few things I'd like to find out."

Moncrief did what passed for a sigh among ghosts. *"Haven't we all?"*

Holte glanced at the newcomer again, and saw that he had the stupefied stare that those just recently dead had when their death had been unanticipated. *"Who is this?"*

"This is Julian Eastley," said Moncrief. *"He was a hero in the Great War, but it took a lot out of him. He used to do some speaking about the fighting, for civic clubs and the like, and he had an inheritance, so he didn't need to work, which was just as well. After the war, he didn't have a head for business, though he did before it. He used to hang on Louise's lead-strings; if he were a boy, we'd call it puppy love, but in his case, he said it was devotion. Always around the house, and never any worry to me. He hasn't been here very long; I suppose you can tell. He hasn't been able to remember anything of what killed him, not yet, anyway."*

"I can see that," said Holte. *"What led up to——?"*

Eastley directed his attention toward Holte. *"Do I know you? Can you tell me where I am? I can't seem to recognize it..."*

Moncrief responded before Holte could provide an answer. *"I've told him several times, but he's still in shock. You don't have to tell him he's dead if you don't want to.*

It won't stick."

Holte signaled his understanding to Moncrief, and asked Eastley, *"What are the last things you remember before you arrived here?"*

The question seemed to confuse Eastley, and he could not bring himself to answer for a short while. *"It all seems so...remote, like something I dreamed...a long time ago..."* He faltered, then steadied himself and went on, *"I had been in my house...I share it with my uncle now, you know? A tidy little place with a partial view of Independence Hall...Well, enough of that. I decided to go out for a drive...you know, to restore my equilibrium? I have to do that when the megrims are on me."* He did something that implied an apology, then resumed his narrative. *"I drove westward out of Philadelphia and had gone through Columbia—dreadful roads they have in that part of the county—and was approaching York. It was late in the afternoon, and I was thinking about turning back after dining at York, you know, as one does. I find driving at night soothing. I had my flask with me, and was taking a nip now and then, I remember that; it helped me to keep steady, and it almost made up for the roads, and it kept the Black Dogs away. Can't drive well when the Black Dogs are on me. Anyway, there was sun at my back, and when the rear-view mirror flashed, I had trouble seeing what lay ahead. There was a bad patch on a curve, I recall that much. It went around a hillock and the curve tightened toward the far end. The rear-view mirror caught a brilliant ray that dazzled me. I think I might have swerved."* He stopped abruptly, floundering for a better explanation of what happened. *"There might have been someone coming up behind me, too fast, on that curve. I believe I thought I should go faster or pull over and let him pass, and then the mirror flashed..."* He stopped again. *"And now I'm here, wherever that may be, and I have no remembrance of how that came about."*

"I think you crashed your auto, Eastley, that's what I think," said Moncrief with the patience of frequent repetition.

"That sounds likely," Holte seconded. *"Poor fellow."*

"How do you mean, crashed my auto? That's absurd," said Eastley, offended by the possibility.

"You'll figure it out, in time," said Holte, trying to console Eastley. *"When you do, I'd like to know what you do remember."*

"So would I," said Moncrief, and abruptly changed the subject. *"Do you have any new ideas about what's become of Louise, Holte? Eastley hasn't been able to tell me anything about her."*

Before Eastley could summon up an answer, Holte said, *"No, I don't."*

"She's still missing?" Moncrief was sounding alarmed now.

"Yes; I'm sorry," said Holte. *"So are Stacy Dritchner and Warren Derrington, for that matter,"* said Holte. *"They haven't cropped up here, have they?"*

"No," said Moncrief, downcast at the lack of information about his wife, now his widow. *"Not that I know of."*

"What do you mean, linking Louise's disappearance to Derrington's and Dritchner's? There was disgusting gossip about a connection between them during the summer, the nasty innuendos were sickening. Utter nonsense, I call it," Eastley said, coming staunchly to Louise's defense.

Now it was Moncrief's turn to bristle. *"You can't deny that they were all close friends. It was Stacy who introduced me to Louise. Can't thank him enough for that. I remember that he said at the time that he thought she would be a perfect wife for me, and that she was already taken with me. I couldn't believe my good fortune—a bang-up girl like that."*

"You were a most fortunate fellow, Moncrief," Eastley declared.

"I wish I knew where she is. Not to haunt her, you understand nothing like that. But I would like to look in on her, now and again; I miss her. I didn't know what it would be like, not to have her about." Moncrief pondered for a short time. *"If you learn anything more about her, Holte, you must tell me. I'll feel better when I know she's all right."*

"If you will tell me what you learn, if you learn anything, about her whereabouts. If you remember." Holte looked around at the swirls and flow of the ghosts. *"Any more groups of newcomers?"*

"Just another group of Armenians. I thought we'd seen the last of them, but apparently not. This lot starved to death." Moncrief was disinterested in them. *"Have you made any progress in discovering who killed me?"*

Holte answered this carefully. *"I may have a lead to follow up. I'll let you know if it goes anywhere."*

"Much appreciated," said Moncrief in a display of automatic good manners.

Eastley swirled around, staring in the eyeless manner of ghosts. *"That's right: you're dead, aren't you? How did I come to forget that?"*

"You'll figure it out, Julian, in time," said Moncrief with ironic sympathy.

Holte realized that he had gained as much information as he could, so he addressed Moncrief. *"When Knott gets back, will you tell him I'd like to speak with him?"*

"If I remember, I will." Moncrief was being drawn back into the maelstrom of

ghosts. *"You know how that goes, don't you, Holte?"*

"Do you know where he has gone?" Holte persisted, trying to persuade Moncrief to make an effort to bear these things in mind. *"I need to talk with him."*

"Not that I'm aware of; he didn't tell me where he was going, the last time I saw him," Moncrief murmured, losing definition.

Holte became more insistent. *"Anything, Moncrief. Anything you can recall."*

"...don't know. Something about a boat..." and saying that, he vanished, Eastley following him into the spiraling grey mist.

Left to his own devices, Holte decided to return to the world of the living, and *slipped* back into Aunt Esther's house in Philadelphia, where it was about four in the morning. He rose from the pantry, where he had arrived, and materialized in Poppy's room, where Maestro woke, sprang up, and greeted him with a low, musical growl. "I'm not going to do anything to her," he explained to the cat. "I can't; and even if I could, I wouldn't."

Maestro was unimpressed; he turned his back on Holte and flipped his tail twice before he settled back into a curl on the end of the bed.

Holte moved away from Poppy's bed to settle in the chair, sinking into it about an inch before he folded his arms and took on the sketchy appearance of someone napping, had there been anyone in the room who could see him besides the sleeping Poppy. It would be morning soon, he reminded himself, and he would be able to speak with her before she went off to the *Clarion*. He let his thoughts drift where they might and after a time, came back to the association of Stacy, Derrington, and Louise. There was something about it that rankled: Holte had some time before reached the conclusion that theirs was not the coincidence of acquaintance that so often happened to members of the same group, but something more—the question was what. He was still lost in contemplation when the alarm on Poppy's night-stand jangled and brought him out of his reverie.

Poppy turned over in bed while Maestro took cover under it. She reached out, pushed down the toggle on the alarm clock, and was rewarded with silence. After a stretch and a yawn, she sat up and rubbed her eyes. "Ye gods," she said as she caught sight of Holte. "How long have you been here?"

"Not very long," he answered. "Perhaps an hour." He drifted toward her. "You're going in early to work, are you?"

"Yes. I'll be coming home at three. Lowenthal arranged that for me. He's going to leave early as well, to get ready for tonight, but he'll get into work at the usual hour." Her chuckle ended on a second yawn. "So let me get up, will you?"

"I'm not stopping you," he said, even as he moved back.

She lifted the comforter and sheet, and swung her legs out from under. "What a beastly hour to be awake," she said sourly, and got to her feet.

"Will you have any time to lie down before this evening?" Holte asked.

"I hope so, but I'm not counting on it." Poppy turned away from him. "I need to have a little time to myself, if you don't mind. Say fifteen minutes?"

"I'll have a look around the house."

"Thank you," said Poppy, and went to her closet to take out her apple-green suit with the dark-blue piping on the seams. She laid this on the bed, then went across the hall to the bathroom to get ready for her day.

Holte was waiting for her when she came down to the kitchen. "There's a plate of chopped meat in the refrigerator," he informed her as she filled the basket in the percolator with coffee grounds.

"That's for Maestro. I'll take it up to him before I leave for work. He thinks he's starving." She selected a mug and set it on the central table, and then went to take two slices of bread from the open loaf in the bread-bin. "The milkman is due this morning, so there's going to be fresh cream. I wish I could stay for it, but the bottle of it that we have isn't too old. He's going to leave three pounds of butter—Missus Sassoro says we'll need two for tonight, and Aunt Esther relies on her to know those kinds of things." She put the slices of bread in each side of the toaster and depressed the switch to turn it on. "Cramer's is the dairy we use here. Aunt Jo uses van Hooten's—it's been around longer than Cramer's; Aunt Jo thinks that Amish make the best dairy farmers."

Holte realized that she was talking as much to wake up as to provide him any specific information, but he listened on the chance that she might want him to respond to something she said. So when she took the butter-plate from the refrigerator, he asked, "Are you expecting a busy day today?"

"Who knows? Fridays are either very slow or very busy. So far today doesn't look to be too hectic, but it's too soon to tell. There's supposed to be some sort of political rally at Independence Hall this morning, but that's not my bailiwick;

Foster covers those events." She took a plate from the crockery cupboard and set it on the table next to the mug, then put the percolator on the stove and got out a match to start the nearest burner. "I'm hoping we might have some more information from Canada on Overstreet, but it might be too soon." She took a butter-knife from the silverware drawer. "I'm thinking of contacting the Coast Guard about the *Belle Helene*. I'd like to know who owns her."

"Will you be talking to your Inspector today?"

Poppy reminded herself not to rise to such obvious provocation, and said, "Since he's coming this evening, I suppose I will."

Holte mimed a fencer's salute. "Sa-sa," he approved. "What else is happening at the *Clarion*?"

"Aside from the Napier investigation? There's a Mayoral Committee being formed to investigate corruption in city government and Lowenthal's sending two reporters to cover the announcements. Again, not my cup of tea. There is a delegation from Holland expected at the Maritime Commission this morning, which is Norton's beat. There's an exhibition of medieval art at the museum, which Anders covers; I don't know how he stands it. And there's a boxing match that the sports desk will cover. I don't know anything about boxing; tennis perhaps, and sailing, and croquet, and equestrian contests, but not boxing or wrestling, for that matter." She went to check the toaster. "Another minute or two," she said as she carefully turned each slice of bread around so it would be toasted on each side.

"How long do you think Lowenthal will keep you on the Overstreet story?" Holte hovered near the stove, looking like a badly faded sepia print.

"As long as something newsworthy is happening." She reached for the butter-dish and began to make curls in the butter for her toast. "Since I'm going in before Lowenthal arrives, Matthew Pike might have an assignment for me. I hope he doesn't bother." Just the mention of the night city editor of the *Clarion* made Poppy uneasy; Pike was known to disapprove of women taking jobs that were, in his view, the rightful domain of men, and she had clashed with him more than once during the summer.

"What sort of assignment?" Holte asked.

"Probably a rewrite or two. That's his style. It's a way to keep me in my place." She glanced at the percolator; the water in it was beginning to thrill and soon the rich aroma of coffee would pervade the kitchen, which, to Poppy, was the official beginning of her day; she got the cream out of the refrigerator and poured a dollop into her mug. "I really need my coffee this morning."

"At this hour, I'm not surprised." Holte drifted toward the pantry door. "Your aunt is hiring extra help for the evening?"

"Yes, a couple of waiters, and Missus Sassoro wants to have a scullion in the kitchen, so Aunt Jo has arranged for one. They'll be here until midnight, and then the household will be on its own. Knowing Aunt Esther, she'll take charge of the kitchen after Missus Sassoro goes home, unless she had made other arrangements with her staff, in which case, I don't know." The percolator was bubbling and the aroma of coffee was now much stronger. "Almost ready," she said.

"Are you going to stay in the kitchen?"

"In the breakfast-nook," said Poppy, pointing in the direction of an arched doorway that at present had closed pocket-doors. "It faces east, not that that matters at this hour; the sun won't be up for a little less than an hour." She went to the stove and picked up the percolator with a pot-holder and brought it back to the central table and poured out the fragrant, dark liquid into her mug, watching it turn a dark tan as she did.

"Speaking of the time, when does Missus Sassoro arrive?"

"Quarter to seven. Her husband drops her off on his way to work and picks her up at eight-thirty. Tonight it will be later, of course; closer to eleven or midnight is my guess, or maybe later, and she won't be expected back until noon tomorrow. Why so curious?" She went to remove the toast and to turn off the toaster.

"I'm just trying to get the rhythm of this place," said Holte.

"Um," she said, busying herself with spreading butter on her toast.

"And Aunt Esther? When does she rise?"

"You are being nosy," Poppy said by way of rebuke before answering him. "She's usually up a little before seven. Is this more rhythm?"

"Yes, in part," said Holte.

"The schedules are less fixed here than they were at Aunt Jo's; you'll find the household beat a syncopated one, I'm afraid," Poppy said as she picked up her coffee mug and went to open the pocket-doors. "I'm not going to bother to raise the blinds," she informed him as she turned on the light in the ceiling of the small room that was dominated by a large, oval table with six chairs set around it, and with a sugar-bowl and salt and pepper shakers in its center. There was a narrow cupboard angled into one corner, and a painting of Guernsey cows grazing in a field on one wall. Poppy pulled out a chair and set down the mug, then went back for her plate of toast. "Nothing so grand as Aunt Jo's breakfast room, but I like it; it's cozy." She sat down and began to nibble on the toast. "I'm beginning to wake up. I'll be fine when I get behind the wheel."

Holte came into the room and sat, apparently crossed-legged, on the table opposite Poppy. "Do you mind if I come along with you to work?"

"You'll probably do it anyway, so why should I mind?" She added sugar to her creamed coffee.

"Just trying to be polite," said Holte cordially, and changed the subject. "Is there anything more on that missing boy? The Pearse—"

"You mean GAD?" Poppy asked, and went on before Holte could confirm it. "Not that Loring has mentioned, and there's still nothing in the papers. You can probably thank the Napier robbery for that."

Holte made a kind of nod. "What do you think happened to him, really?"

Poppy tried an experimental sip at her coffee and set the mug down again. "Not yet," she said to the air; then she looked at the shimmer that was Holte. "Since you haven't come across him in the dimension of ghosts, I'd say that either he has taken off on some adventure of his own—which he has done before—or he has been kidnapped, which doesn't seem likely. His oldest sister is more likely to want to be rid of him than the Europeans are. "

"Why would he not be a target in Europe?" asked Holte.

Poppy considered her answer, and finally said, "An American on his own in Europe may be a rarity, but GAD doesn't go in for high living nor draws attention to himself, so it doesn't mean that a lone American is rich, and an object of exploitation, only that he is inquisitive, so not worth the effort. Or so it seems to me."

"Do you think most Europeans understand that?" Holte leaned forward to hear her. "The last bunch of Americans they experienced were soldiers."

"I couldn't say what they understand," said Poppy as she finished her first piece of toast and reached for her coffee mug. "You probably know more about that than I do."

Holte circled the breakfast-nook. "What did you mean about his older sister?"

"Is this another one of those are Stacy and Derrington and Louise in it together questions? I was making a wise-crack—obviously not very well—about how disappointed Auralia is about GAD being the heir, when her husband is so much more suited to the position, at least in Auralia's mind. I don't know William Mikkelsohn well enough to have a view of his beliefs in the matter." She started on her second piece of toast.

"Auralia is the one you don't like, isn't she?" said Holte. "She's the one you warned Loring about: Auralia and Tatiana."

Poppy swallowed her bit of toast and sighed. "We don't get along, Auralia and I. To give the devil her due, it's a pity that she couldn't be the heir—she has a real talent for running things, including the Pearse's fortune." She paused. "And don't ask me about Tatiana. She may be sneaky and secretive, but she likes GAD."

"And fourteen is a bit young to be organizing an overseas kidnapping," Holte conceded.

"Being a spy, you would know such things," said Poppy lightly, and took another bite of toast.

"Yes, I would." He sounded a bit affronted, and Poppy realized that she had overstepped with him.

"Another witticism goes astray," she admitted. "I didn't mean to insult you, or to slight you. It's early, and I'm a bit cross. Apologies for my sharp tongue."

Holte made a gesture of acceptance. "And to make it worse, you have Matthew Pike to deal with when you get to work on Saturday."

"You understand, don't you? You're right: I'm borrowing trouble." She took the last of the toast and washed it down with the rest of her coffee. "Ye gods, but I'm ready for tonight's party. I need to unwind."

"Then I hope you make the most of it," said Holte in a rush of sympathy.

"So do I," said Poppy, and got up from the table, gathered her plate and her mug together and went back into the kitchen to place them in the sink before retrieving the plate of chopped meat from the refrigerator and bearing it off to Maestro.

SIXTEEN

IT HAD TURNED OUT TO BE A SLOW DAY FOR NEWS—THERE HAD BEEN A FIRE IN some old row-houses that was quickly put out, two men had been arrested at the political rally, and a college football demonstration game had been postponed due to rain—so Lowenthal had let Poppy go at quarter to three, coming out of his office to her desk saying, "You have a lot to do before your guests arrive, so hop to it. Chop-chop."

"Thanks, boss," said Poppy, startled but relieved; she put her desk perfunctorily in order and gathered up her purse and her brief-case. "I'll see you later."

"Looking forward to it," he called out to her as she left the city room, a couple of wolf- whistles echoing behind her. She hurried to the alley where she had parked her Hudson, got in, and headed off toward Aunt Esther's house. As soon as she arrived, she parked in her usual spot and hotfooted it up to the door, letting herself in with her key, crying "Hello; it's me," as she stepped inside.

"I'm glad you're here," Aunt Esther called out to Poppy as she came into the entry-hall. "I need to run out to the legger again—we're short on the Champagne—and I need someone to sign for the chocolates and pastries, and Miss Roth is on an errand, so it has to be you." She paused. "Be careful; Galliard brought down the spare chairs from the attic a couple hours ago, and I still haven't set them all about the room yet. Same for the four occasional tables."

"Where are you?" Poppy wondered aloud.

"In the dining room. I'm putting out the cups and saucers; I was going to do the plates next, but I'll let you tend to it if you're willing. I shouldn't be gone more than a half hour. I've phoned ahead; they'll be ready for me." She smiled as Poppy came into the dining room, and indicated the stacks of Italian china that was waiting on the china cabinet, about to be set on the long, oaken table. "In stacks of eight, in clusters; leave room for silver and napkins between the clusters. Dinner plates at this end, salad plates in the middle, and the shallow dessert bowls at the far end. Put out all thirty-two of each of them; we may have a few extras turn up. You'll find the reserves in the crockery-pantry on the next-to-bottom shelf. Miss Roth will take care of the glasses and the silverware when she gets back. It shouldn't take you more than twenty minutes to attend to this, and it will be a world of help."

Poppy laid her purse and brief-case on the nearest chair and went to the glass-fronted hutch where the good china was stored. "You've done the cups and saucers I see. So I'll start with the salad plates? Or the dessert bowls? Four stacks of eight is what you want?"

"Yes, whichever you like. The serving platters will go on the side-board behind you—the waiters will take care of what goes in them—and the desserts will be put out after the main meal is removed." She took off the apron she was wearing and draped it over another chair. "You won't need this; I've been washing carrots and radishes in the kitchen to give Missus Sassoro a hand."

"I thought this was going to be a finger-food event," said Poppy, trying to decide whether to do the salad plates or the dessert bowls first.

"I thought so too at first, but then I reconsidered. This is going to be a proper celebration, and I don't want it to look skimpy, so I decided that something more substantial would be needed. Not that there won't be finger-food, but there will be more to it than that." She looked around the room. "Well, you should be able to handle everything. Missus Sassoro is in the pantry at the moment. If you need some help, go into the kitchen and tap on the pantry door. I should warn you that the kitchen is getting hot." With that, Esther strode out of the dining room, going toward the coat-closet between the dining room and the entry-hall, where she kept her purse. "I'll be back in twenty minutes, thirty at the most. Miss Roth should be here by then."

"That's good to know," said Poppy. "I'll get right to this," she added as she heard the front door close. "Salad plates, I guess," she said, and began her work.

As Aunt Esther had promised, she was back in a just over twenty minutes announcing, "My auto is in the garage and the trunk is locked. Galliard can bring the cases in later. How are you doing?" She peeked in the door. "Oh, very good."

"I finished up five minutes ago; the pastries and chocolates are in the kitchen," Poppy reported, "and I am going to go and lie down for half an hour, and then I'll have a short bath and dress."

"Is Miss Roth back yet?" Esther inquired.

"Not yet. Missus Sassoro says Miss Roth will be here no later than five. That gives her an hour and a half before any of the guests arrive." Poppy came around the table and approached her aunt. "Have you had a nap yet?"

"Oh, yes; I lay down immediately after lunch, and didn't get up until two-thirty. I'm quite refreshed." She flicked her fingers at Poppy. "Shoo. Go have a nap. I'll see you at around five- thirty. You'd best take the evening food up to your cat now. You won't have time later, and he'll start complaining."

"Good idea; and I can bring down his morning plate after I dress and...gild the lily." She kissed the air near Aunt Esther's cheek, then hastened off to the kitchen where Missus Sassoro was just putting a large baking-tray of stuffed pastry shells into the oven; her face was red from heat and effort. "The cat's dinner is...?" Poppy asked.

"In the refrigerator, top shelf. I gave him some of the trimmings from the ducks, and some of the left-over pot-roast from last night." She shut the oven door and rounded on Poppy. "Take it now. I'll need the space in a little while. I'll put his breakfast together before I leave tonight, so he won't have to go hungry."

"Thanks," said Poppy, and retrieved the plate. "He's going to love this."

"So long as he doesn't get used to the duck, that's grand," said Missus Sassoro, going to lift the damp cloth over a large bowl of rising dough; she punched it down as Poppy left the room.

This time, Maestro was waiting right beyond the door at the top of the stairs, his eyes alight, and his intention to escape obvious.

"Oh, no you don't," said Poppy, bending down to push him back with the hand that held her purse and brief-case, the treasure of duck-trimmings and pot-roast held aloft. "Come into the bathroom, and have a taste of your bribe."

Maestro uttered imprecations at Poppy, but his dinner proved more irresistible than the opportunity to explore the rest of the house; he backed up, his full attention on the plate in her right hand.

Poppy kicked the door closed behind her, and went into the bathroom, taking care not to step on the cat, who was twining himself around her legs. She bent down, set her purse and brief- case aside, picked up the used plate from the morning, and set down the duck-trimmings. "There you go," she said, rubbing his head as he bent to eat as if he had not had a meal in days. She set the used plate in the sink, picked up her purse and brief-case, and left Maestro to dine. In her bedroom, she stripped down to her slip, removed her silk stockings, and took her bathrobe from the closet and wrapped herself in it, set her alarm, then stretched out on her bed; she almost expected to find Holte watching her from some odd corner of the room, but there was no sign of him, and in less than ten minutes, she was asleep.

She roused herself shortly before the alarm sounded, and turned off the ringer. After taking a little time to stretch, she got up and went to the closet, removing the dress she had chosen for the evening: a long-sleeved, cowl-necked, drop-waisted evening dress with a tulip- skirt in mulberry-colored silk that reached just below her calves. It had cost her over seventy dollars, but she told herself that it was worth every penny. Leaving it on the hook on the outside of her closet door, she undressed completely then donned her bathrobe again and went across to the bathroom where she found Maestro curled up on the fresh towel next to the sink. "Wretch," she said fondly, and put the plug in the bathtub drain and turned on the hot water. "It would serve you right if I gave you a bath," she warned him.

Maestro opened one eye, then closed it, sniffing as he did.

Poppy resisted the urge to throw her washcloth at him, removed her bathrobe, turned on the cold water and got into the rapidly filling tub. Lying back, she felt the warmth take her and was tempted to nod off again; the aromas wafting up from the kitchen reminded her of the purpose of this afternoon indulgence. She reached for the soap—Pears—and began dutifully to wash, taking care not to get her hair wet, for there would not be time for it to dry before the guests arrived. When she had soaped and rinsed, she left the tub, pulled the plug, and removed Maestro from his place on her towel. He protested; she scratched his ruff by way of showing regret for her lack of courtesy, and then set about drying off, planning which of her new brassieres she would wear tonight, and what scent she would use.

Twenty minutes later and ten minutes early she was downstairs, smelling of rose-and- jasmine, her small amethyst earrings complimenting her dress without ostentation. She found Aunt Esther in the drawing room, in a spruce-green, ankle-length ensemble of peau de soie; she had on gold bracelets and an Art Nouveau brooch of gold and tourmaline in a lotus design; she had done her hair up in a bun and fixed it in place with a pair of inlaid chopsticks.

"I'm glad you're early," said Aunt Esther, taking a critical look at her niece. "Just the right note. That color becomes you."

"I agree," said Poppy. "And your dress is very flattering."

Aunt Esther chortled. "What you mean is that it isn't bad for an old lady like me." She held up her hand. "No, don't. I appreciate the sentiment, you don't have to apologize for it; I know what I see in the mirror, and I know I'm not a fair young thing anymore, though I'm glad you tried to let me think so."

"Old needn't mean ugly," said Poppy, thinking back to her mother's mother, who had remained an attractive women to the last.

"No—but often it can," said Aunt Esther, adding, "Judge Stephanson is going to arrive in about half an hour; I asked him to come early."

There was a loud clatter from the dining room and a male voice called out, "Nothing's broken; just a little trouble positioning the platters!"

"That's the new waiter," Esther explained. "They both arrived here an hour ago, and between Missus Sassoro and Miss Roth, they've been working hard ever since. They're the ones who organized the extra chairs and tables. We should be ready well in advance of the company. Incidentally, Miss Roth has changed for the evening; a very nice dress of dark-blue polished cotton; she'll be on door-duty." She went to the high-boy at the end of the sofa. "Would you like a splash of cognac? I'm going to pour myself a little brandy."

"I'll have brandy with you," said Poppy. "But just a little."

"Marvelous," said Aunt Esther, and set out two small snifters. "We'll do the inspection in ten minutes, if that will do for you?" She opened the bottle and poured out a little more than a tablespoonful for each of them. "By the way, Langton Timms is bringing Beatrice; I knew he would. Do your best not to pay her much attention. She's a bit...overdone."

"I think you warned me about her before," said Poppy, taking the proffered snifter.

"She's always trying to generate male admiration, like a shark after chum. She has a taste for well-set-up young men. You might want to warn Inspector Loring." She touched the rim of her snifter to Poppy's. "I don't like speaking ill of other women, but one must draw the line somewhere."

"Amen to that," Poppy responded.

"Eulalie Kinnon phoned in regrets this morning, well after you left. And you know that Isme Greenloch declined as well. Eulalie claimed she had forgotten a prior engagement, but I suspect that Josephine told her about the mixed company we're going to have, so she thought it better to stay home. Fernald and Bernadette Stanton are still going to be here, and Josephine with Hank and Cecily, so we won't be completely without the upper-crust. And the Fairchilds will be here, too. We're covered for high-class guests. And Sherman and Isadora Pearse have said they'll be here, which is a pleasant surprise." She sipped her brandy.

"Does it bother you that Missus Kinnon is giving us the cold shoulder?" Poppy asked, a little startled that this should bother her.

"Not really. I've known Eulalie a long time, and I was hoping she might come because of that, but—" She shrugged. "Archibald Wyman will be here— you know him. His wife is visiting family in Maine, so he'll be alone. The Lowenthals are coming, of course, and Inspector Loring. I can't wait to see what they think of all this. Elliott Wickman will be here, but he plans to leave early; he's taking the train to Chicago in the morning."

Poppy understood that Aunt Esther was reviewing her guest list aloud rather than reminding her niece about them, so she sipped her brandy and half-listened to what her aunt was saying. She heard the clock in the study chime six, and a few minutes later, the doorbell rang. Poppy sat up, and Esther smoothed the front of her long jacket; Miss Roth appeared and went to open to admit Judge Stephanson, saying, "The ladies are in the sitting room, Your Honor, if you would care to join them?"

Esther stopped her cataloging of the evening's company, and called out, "Good evening, Benedict. Come join us." She stood up and held out her hands in welcome to the distinguished, white-haired man in a dinner jacket who came into the drawing room holding a small bouquet of yellow roses.

"Good evening, ladies," he said, and thrust out his bouquet. "By the way, the rain is slacking off."

"How thoughtful of you," Esther exclaimed, and signaled to Miss Roth who was a few steps behind the judge. "These in water, if you would."

Stephanson handed to bouquet to Miss Roth, then took Esther's hands in his and beamed down at her. "How lovely to see you my dear," he murmured, and bent to kiss her cheek. "I've missed you."

"You're looking fit as ever, Ben," Esther remarked, not quite blushing, and keeping hold of his hands for a little longer than courtesy required. "Please have a seat." She nodded toward Poppy. "You remember my niece, Poppy Thornton?"

Poppy had risen from her chair, and now she held out her right hand. "Good evening, Your Honor," she said.

"How could I forget you?" Stephanson asked as he shook Poppy's hand, his style the gallant manner of a generation past. "I've been following your reporting on the antiquities scandal all summer, Miss Thornton. You're a most enterprising journalist."

This unexpected compliment startled Poppy, and it took her a little time to summon up an appropriate response. "It's gratifying to know that someone is paying attention to what has been going on. Thank you so much."

Esther had gone to the high-boy and asked, "What can I pour for you, Ben?"

"You wouldn't happen to have any single-malt Scotch, would you?" He was about to request something else, but Esther smiled.

"Yes. I have two bottles. How many fingers?"

"Two, if you would," said His Honor, and watched while Esther took a square, three- inch-deep glass from the high-boy, and then removed a bottle with a simple label: Tarrisers. "I hope this will do," she said as she removed the stopper and started to pour. "I forgot to ask: do you want ice?"

"It's lovely the way it is," said Stephanson. "How do you manage to have that uncommon label among your other offerings—and don't tell me. I'm not supposed to know such things—I may be retired, but I'm still an officer of the court."

Esther handed him the glass and put the Scotch back inside the high-boy.

"You're being cautious." She picked up her small snifter and lifted it in his direction. "Confusion to our enemies, may they all rot in hell."

"Truly," said Stephanson, and drank. That done, he fixed his pale-blue eyes on Esther. "Is this going to be one of your hodge-podge evenings, my dear? I know how you like to mix people and professions and classes."

"You make it sound like a chemistry experiment," Esther protested. "It's not that, I promise you. This is a shared party, in part for my being back from Europe and the Soviet Union, and in part for my delight in having my niece move into my house." She added a little more brandy to her glass. "She and I have varied interests, so that will be reflected in the guests."

"Another chemistry experiment," said Stephanson, grinning. "I hope there are no fisticuffs."

"Oh, I wouldn't think there would be," said Poppy.

Knowing what was expected of him, Stephanson asked, "Why not?"

"Because everyone is too fond of Aunt Esther to behave so badly," said Poppy; she was beginning to feel less edgy about the evening and wondered if Holte was observing the start of the festivities. As an afterthought, she added, "And if guests should come to blows, there will be a police inspector here to control them."

As if in response to her thoughts, the sconce-light over the high-boy flickered.

"Not another light-bulb going," Esther said, exasperated. "We just replaced three of them not two days ago."

"But not this one, I'm guessing," Stephanson pointed out.

"No; not this one." Esther sighed. "Well, if it fails, we'll have to bring a pair of candelabras into the room. I must ask Miss Roth to make sure we have some ready. Excuse me," she said, and hastened off to the kitchen.

Left alone with Poppy, Stephanson did his smooth best to strike up polite conversation. "How are you enjoying your new home, Miss P. M. Thornton?"

"Oh, Poppy, please," she said. "I'm still getting used to it, of course, but I'm liking it very well, thank you."

"What do you think of the neighborhood?" Stephanson pursued with determined courtesy. "I trust you're learning your way around."

"I like it. We have a professor and his family on one side, and a civil engineer on the other. I haven't met the neighbors behind us yet." She paused. "But I suppose you know that."

"Yes; fine people, both families." He waited a moment, then went on, "Hagen Kristman is a colleague of mine, now that I'm teaching. I like to think that your aunt introducing us some dozen years ago helped me in securing the position I have now."

"She introduced you?" Poppy asked, then answered her own question. "Of course she did; how like her."

Stephanson nodded. "She's always willing to extend herself. And speaking of extending herself, Esther told me that you have a cat," he said.

"That I do, not by plan; he more or less followed me here," Poppy told him, not wanting to get into a discussion of family politics with more guests sure to arrive shortly. "His name is Maestro, and my Aunt Josephine sent him over to join me when I moved from her house, saying he missed me. He's confined upstairs for tonight. I'm afraid he isn't very sociable."

"Not many cats are," Stephanson allowed, taking another sip. After a second or two, he asked, "Do you enjoy working at the *Clarion?*"

"Not always. The demands of the work can be grueling, and often it's difficult to see a story through to the end. But I do get great satisfaction out of covering crime; I feel that when I cover a crime, I'm helping to bring the miscreant to justice, and to alert the public to danger," except, she added to herself, when I am the object of the offense; she lobbed the conversational ball back at him. "Now that you're off the bench, what do you do to fill your time?"

"I teach, as I've mentioned: three pre-law seniors' classes a week on Constitutional law," he said. "And I'm trying my hand at gardening. I haven't much to show for my efforts, or not yet, but I'm liking it more than I feared I would. I don't want to end up one of those doddering old men, pottering about in a confusion of plants. At present, I'm attempting to get three apple trees growing."

"That must be challenging," said Poppy. "The classes, not the gardening."

"I'd say quite the reverse; the young men in my classes are pretty well prepared for law school, and my main job is to review the fine points. Having spent thirty-two years on the bench, I can do it almost automatically. Gardening, on the other hand, is completely new territory for me."

"That doesn't seem—" Poppy began, only to be interrupted by Aunt Esther's return to the sitting room.

"Any failure of light-bulbs will be off-set by candles. I have it all arranged."
She picked up her abandoned snifter and drank down what remained of its
contents. "Let them come. We're ready for them."

SEVENTEEN

Fernald and Bernadette Stanton were the first to arrive, on the stroke of six-thirty. He was in a dark-blue business suit; she was in a short, ivory-taffeta evening gown strewn with beads and sequins. They turned their coats over to Miss Roth and came into the drawing room with great enthusiasm. By the time Esther had got their drinks, Primrose North and her son Denton were at the door, and shortly after them, Mildred and Humphrey Fairchild joined the party; they moved from the sitting room into the larger parlor where they were more comfortable.

"Oh, Poppy!" Mildred cried merrily, "What a delightful house." She came to offer an awkward hug, her six-month state of expectation interfering with their greeting hug. "And where is your Aunt Esther?"

"Right here," said Esther, from her place next to the high-boy. "Good to see you, Mildred. And you, Humphrey."

"It is a delightful house," said Poppy, catching a little of Mildred's speech cadences from her; Poppy indicated the couch. "Sit down, Milly, please, and tell me how you are."

"You can see how I am," Mildred answered with a laugh. "Humphrey can tell you that I'm doing very well. But I can't wait for November. The doctor thinks I'm likely to have something more than turkey this Thanksgiving." She held her hand up to take her husband's. "Humphrey has been a prince through all this, an absolute prince."

Humphrey Fairchild, a large, florid man with thinning, fair hair, and a self-satisfied expression, just thirty, beamed at Mildred. "You're an angel, Milly." He turned to Poppy. "I can't tell you, Miss Thornton, how many times I have thanked my lucky stars that I married Milly." He half-bowed in the direction of his wife. "What would you like to drink?"

"I don't know." She took a moment to think, and in that moment, Professor Langton Timms and his wife Beatrice came through the door; Beatrice's energetic greeting drowned out Mildred's answer, and she had to repeat, "I think a little brandy, with soda—we'll be having wine with dinner, and I don't want to get tipsy. Top-heavy as I am, I need to keep my balance." She laughed, and Humphrey chuckled.

Before Poppy could go to get her drink, Mildred detained her. "Oh, Poppy, did you see the dreadful story in the *Tattler*—not that I read the *Tattler*—but still?"

"What dreadful story?" Poppy asked, pausing in her mission to get Mildred her drink.

"The one they've published about the Butterworth girl? She claims that she and GAD Pearse are engaged, and that he's been missing since July, and that his family is doing nothing to find him."

Poppy stopped. "No, I haven't seen that," she said, a cold feeling going through her that was nothing like Holte's non-touch. She would have to pick up the *Tattler* in the morning and see what damage had been done. "You stay here, Humphrey; I'll fetch Mildred's brandy-and- soda."

"Well, do you think there's anything to it?" Mildred looked from Poppy to her husband.

"Surely not," said Humphrey. "You can't put any stock in what the *Tattler* prints. Last month, they claimed that there were Russian refugees escaping into Alaska. That's hardly responsible reportage, is it Poppy?"

Poppy gave no response, but continued on to the high-boy, and saw that Aunt Esther had opened the pocket-doors between the parlor and the sitting room. "Milly would like a bit of brandy with soda, if you have any to spare."

"I can manage that; I have a little of everything, including port and sherry," said Esther, "but I'll save the more expensive bottle of sherry for Jo."

"That's probably wise," said Poppy.

A few seconds later there was another flurry of excitement as more company came into the sitting room from the entry-hall. Leading the group, Beatrice Timms was resplendent in a rustling gown of dark-red taffeta with cap-sleeves and a scalloped hem, and smelling of Attar of Roses; she headed straight for

Judge Stephanson, her husband trailing behind her. "Your Honor! How nice to see you again!"

Poppy watched this encounter, and very nearly dropped the brandy-and-soda she was carrying to Humphrey and Mildred. She glanced back quickly at Aunt Esther, and saw her brows come together in a frown that was quickly banished. "I'll just take this to Milly," Poppy said, and did.

Beatrice moved in nearer to Stephanson, a smile fixed on her rouged lips. "I was hoping you might be here tonight Your Honor, knowing you and Miss Thornton are such good friends."

Stephanson took a step back, and assumed a more formal manner. "Good evening, Missus Timms." He made a point of looking past her to Langton Timms. "And good evening to you Professor. A pleasure to see you."

"And you, Judge," said Timms, shaking Stephanson's hand.

The next ten minutes was a clamor of new guests coming into the parlor, among them Cornelius and Eunice Lowenthal, he in a dinner jacket that strained around his barrel chest, she in a beautifully made dress of lavender faille. Poppy excused herself from Mildred's side and went to introduce the Lowenthals to the rest of the company.

"You look very nice," Poppy's boss said to her, clearly out of his depth in this crowd. "Good of your aunt to throw you this party."

"It's also for her," said Poppy, pulling the Lowenthals out of the way as Howard Dale made his way through the parlor with a tray of broiled clams on toothpicks to offer to the increasing number of guests. "What would you like to drink? I'll go pour it myself if you would like to find a place to sit."

"Scotch or Bourbon. No ice," Lowenthal said.

"Lemonade, if you have it," said Eunice.

"I'll ask my aunt, but I believe we have some in the refrigerator." Poppy motioned to Stephanson, and was relieved to see him start toward her. She introduced the judge to her editor and his wife, and then said, "I'm going to get them some refreshments, and they're new here. Would you mind—"

"My pleasure," said Stephanson, and proceeded to engage the Lowenthals in easy small-talk, beginning with, "I often read the *Clarion*, and wondered how you manage to bring out a paper every day, without fail, as you do? It must be very demanding work. How do you manage to accomplish that, day in and day out?"

Lowenthal warmed to his favorite subject. "It's a real scrum sometimes. I could tell you stories of the near misses we've had, Your Honor."

"I'm all ears," said the judge, and sat down next to Lowenthal; Missus Lowenthal sat down on the ottoman next to the occasional table where she could listen to her husband.

Lowenthal all but preened. "It can be a near thing, I can tell you," and he launched into the tale of one of his favorite incidents.

Making her way through the gathering, Poppy encountered the new waiter, Abner Bridges, near the kitchen door. "Would you be good enough to bring in the pitcher of lemonade? One of the guests has asked for it."

"Just as soon as I hand around these deviled eggs," he said and continued on toward the parlor.

Poppy shook her head and was about to go into the sitting room when the doorbell sounded.

Miss Roth, standing in the entry-hall, was waving to attract Poppy's attention, and as soon as she caught Poppy's eye, she motioned to her to come. "Your guest is here," she informed Poppy as she approached.

Poppy took a moment to decide who Miss Roth meant, and then smiled as she saw Inspector Loring standing in the doorway; he was in his best dark suit with a somber black bow-tie in front of the well-starched collar on a very good white shirt. "Oh, Loring," Poppy said as she took his hand. "I'm so glad you're here. Come in, come in." She tugged him in the direction of the parlor, toward Esther, who was still at her station by the high-boy. "Aunt Esther, may I introduce Inspector J. B. Loring?"

Aunt Esther smiled and held out her hand to Loring. "You certainly may, Poppy. How very nice to meet you, Inspector. I must tell you that I've been looking forward to welcoming you to this house ever since I came home." As they shook hands, she added, "And let me offer you my belated thanks for all you are doing to bring my odious nephew to justice for his treatment of my niece, and anything else he may have done. I'm glad you're not letting the matter drop."

For a moment Loring looked nonplused, but he recovered himself enough to say, "No thanks needed."

"No," said Aunt Esther with a quick, wicked half-smile. "I didn't think so." Then she indicated the array of bottles before her. "What's your pleasure?"

"Do you happen to have any rum among all that contraband?" he asked.

"Jamaican rum, coming up. Do you want ice?"

Loring nodded. "Yes, please." While Esther poured out his drink, he looked around the room. "Quite a do you're having."

"I certainly hope so; that was my intention," said Esther, and handed him a glass with just over two fingers of dark rum in its depths. "I hope you'll enjoy yourself this evening, Inspector; feel free to help yourself to the contraband. If there is anything else you'd like, don't hesitate to ask. If I'm busy, I'm sure Poppy can assist you."

The light over the high-boy flickered once more, and Poppy was almost certain that she heard a quiet, ghostly snicker in her left ear.

Loring noticed the faltering light as well, and glanced at Poppy. "Morse code, do you think?"

To her dismay, Poppy flushed. "More likely an old bulb," she said, and drank down the last of her brandy. "Come; I'll introduce you around." She slipped her arm through his and led him about the room. "I should warn you: Aunt Esther will be keeping an eye on you."

"And why is that?" he asked.

"Because you're my friend," Poppy said, wholly unaware of the faint smile that softened his mouth.

Beatrice Timms' eyes lit up at the sight of Loring, and she sashayed over to him. "Tell me, Miss Poppy, who is this handsome man?" She made a poutful smirk at Loring while continuing to speak to Poppy. "How do you come to know him? I don't think I've seen him before. Are you keeping him for yourself?"

"He's with the police." Poppy saw Beatrice Timms blink. "Inspector Loring, this is Beatrice Timms. Missus Timms, may I present Inspector Loring."

"I had no idea that a policeman could be so handsome," Beatrice cooed. "I'm drinking shouldn't you arrest me?"

Professor Timms came up to pull his wife away; he exchanged a hurried handshake with Loring, then directed Beatrice's attention to the platter of chopped mushrooms in cream-sauce in pastry shells that Howard Dale was just handing around. "Sorry," he said to no one in particular as he watched his wife go after the waiter.

"No reason to be," said Loring, and let Poppy move him along.

By ten minutes to seven almost all the guests had assembled, and the buzz of conversation had risen to a roar. The waiters continued to circulate, offering an astonishing variety of finger-foods to the guests; Esther continued to pour drinks while she conversed with her company. She was exchanging pleasantries with Archibald Wyman when there was a barely audible ring from the doorbell, and Miss Roth went to answer it.

"Are we late?" Hank Dritchner asked as he came in, bearing box of chocolates for his aunt and hostess. He was in a very neat dinner-jacket and formal trousers, but he was overshadowed by Cecily, who wore a damask dinner-dress the golden-orange of persimmons, set off with a long pearl necklace and matching earrings. She handed her fox wrap to Miss Roth, and made way for Josephine, who was rigged out as formidably as if she were going to opening night at the Metropolitan Opera in New York: her hair was done up in an elaborate knot and secured with a jeweled comb and a spray of dull-red feathers; she had on a three-tiered diamond-and- topaz collar, and a gown of dull-gold satin with heavy embroidery in the same color on the hem and sleeves that almost glowed. Josephine looked around the guests with an air of hauteur that made Poppy want to rebuke her for such bad manners.

The lamp on the high-boy blinked twice; Poppy decided it was a kind of wink from Holte.

Esther went toward them as the sound of conversation drifted to silence at this splendid entrance. "Very nearly, Hank. Good evening, Josephine," she said crisply to her sister. "You're here just under the wire. Only the Pearses haven't arrived. Everyone else is here. I've put dinner back for ten minutes, but we'll have to start then, whether Sherman and Isadora are here or not." She then addressed Cecily. "I'm Esther Thornton, Hank's aunt. I'm very happy to meet you at last." She indicated the way into the parlor, and started back toward the high-boy. "If you would like a drink before dinner, now's the time."

Cecily looked around, and said, "A pleasure to meet you, too. I see we're overdressed. I'm sorry. I was told this would be a more formal occasion than I see it is." She held out her hand to Esther. "I hope you won't hold it against me."

Poppy saw the entry-hall light blink, and nodded in agreement; she decided to accompany the near-last of the visitors back into the parlor.

Josephine was standing ramrod straight. "I hope you have some sherry, Esther, and that it is not too common."

"Since I knew you would be here, I ordered some especially," Esther told her sister, a bit too sweetly. "Come into the drawing room and let me pour some for you." She led the way through her guests, making occasional introductions, back to the high-boy, where she produced a bottle of the best sherry that Ruscelli was able to secure. "Will this suit you?" she asked Josephine, showing her the label. "Portuguese, you see, the seal is still in place on the cork, so there has been no fiddling with it."

Josephine studied it, squinting for want of glasses, and made her pronouncement. "Better than I expected from you, Esther. I'll have some."

Gradually, other conversations resumed, but not to the level they had been before.

About five minutes past the hour and Miss Roth again answered the doorbell, admitting Sherman and Isadora Pearse; she took their coats and mentioned that the dinner was about to be served.

"I'm sorry we're late," Isadora said in a soft voice as she entered the parlor and made her way to Esther's side; her manner was carefully subdued, and she moved as if in an unpleasant dream, or a wholly unfamiliar place.

"We had matters at home to attend to," Sherman added as he joined his wife and hostess. "It couldn't be helped."

"No harm done," said Esther. "Can I get you something to drink, or would you prefer to wait for the wine we'll be having at dinner?"

"I think I'll wait," said Isadora just as Sherman asked for Scotch.

"Very good," said Esther, and looked over at her niece. "Poppy, will you go tell Missus Sassoro we're ready to dine?"

"Certainly," said Poppy, and hurried off to do this.

In the conversational lapse, Josephine came over to Esther, nodded to the Pearses, and said, "This is quite an unusual occasion, Esther."

Taking care not to display rancor to match her sister's, Esther said, "You're too kind." She took Jo's almost empty glass and poured out more than three ounces of the antique-gold liquid sherry into it. Handing this to Josephine, she added, "How fortuitous. The sherry nearly matches your gown."

"Thank you," said Josephine at her frostiest. She glanced at the Pearses. "I've heard about GAD. How difficult for you. I know what you're going through: my Eustace is still missing. You must be beside yourselves. I know I am consumed with worry for my youngest." She made an apologetic gesture. "GAD's not your youngest, but still."

"It hasn't been easy," said Sherman in a tone that made it clear that he did not want to talk about it.

"Certainly not," said Josephine grandly. "It's a parent's duty to look after children, no matter how old they may become. To have a child gone and not know to where, is a pain that there are no words to describe." She came closer to Isadora. "Like you, I have endured the waiting, and all the uncertainties."

Esther watched this with dismay. "This is hardly the occasion to compare scars, Jo," she said as calmly as she could.

"But I haven't seen Isadora for months," said Josephine indignantly. "And I sympathize with her uncertainly so keenly."

The conversation in the room had quieted; the other guests were watching this exchange with a mixture of curiosity and alarm.

Josephine went on without apology. "Just think of what Sherman and Isadora are subjected to. Most everyone here can only imagine, but I understand. I can comprehend their pain. When your child is missing, possibly in danger, or worse; it eats at you, doesn't it. I know it eats at me."

"Jo, you're not helping," said Esther quietly.

It was as if Josephine had not heard her older sister. "It wrings my heart to spend day after day, longing for a word, a simple reassurance that Eustace is alive, that I—"

"Stop it!" Isadora shrieked. "Don't say another word!" In the next breath, she was weeping. "Don't you dare speak."

There was a startled silence, and a few of the guests did their best not to stare at the Pearses, although they did begin to whisper.

Isadora glared at Josephine. "I came here tonight to get away from my worries, not to grovel in them. Now you've brought them all back! I can't bear it!"

Aunt Esther recovered her composure quickly. "Poppy, will you take over for me? I'm going to take Isadora to my room, so she can lie down for a while. The dinner will be out in a minute or two, and you can supervise the buffet." Saying that, she went to Isadora, who was leaning on her husband's arm. "If you'll come with me Isadora, I'll get you a cold compress for your face."

"Thank you, Esther," Isadora managed to say as Esther guided her out of the parlor, leaving Josephine standing, incensed and nonplused, by the high-boy.

In the next instant, conversation erupted throughout the room, everyone trying to talk about anything other than what had just happened in front of them.

Making her way to the high-boy, Poppy said, "What may I pour for you Mister Pearse?"

He shook his head. "I think I'd better go to my wife. She...hasn't been quite herself since GAD..." His voice trailed off and he turned to follow after Esther.

"What a...display!" Josephine exclaimed, preparing to break into a diatribe, only to be interrupted by Mildred.

"Missus Dritchner," Mildred spoke up, "won't you take a seat on the couch? Then you and I can have a comfortable coze. I'm sorry that my condition does not allow me the luxury of standing. I realize that you've been having a difficult time, but this may not be the place for commiseration; that needs more privacy, don't you think? Please. Sit down with me." She patted the cushion next to her. "We all need to unwind a bit, don't we?"

For once, Poppy felt deeply grateful to Mildred, and decided she would have to do something nice for her in the coming days. She poured out a small glass of cognac and took as sip as Hank came up to her. "You can't blame Missus Pearse. She has had a terrible time about GAD."

The noise of conversation grew louder, sharp and brittle as glass.

"You're handling this well. I'll speak with my mother in the morning," said Hank to Poppy. "And you needn't show me around. I can introduce myself to anyone I don't know." He held out his hand to Cecily, who had come to his side, his fingers interlacing with hers. "Let's do a quick reconnoiter darling; you have your drink. I'll collect a refill in a minute or two." He moved off through the crowd, taking the time to greet some of his acquaintances, and to introduce his wife. As Poppy watched them, she saw Hank approach Loring, and had to resist the desire to eavesdrop on their conversation.

"Thornton," a voice sounded a bit behind her.

She turned and found herself facing Cornelius Lowenthal. "Yes, boss?" she replied, dreading what he might say next.

"I take it that nothing about this will be in the papers? I mean what happened with your aunt and Missus Pearse." He sounded as if he spoke in jest, but there was a kindness in his question that surprised her. "It's not the kind of news we like to run. That's more for the *Tattler*."

"Well, I'm certainly not going to put it there," said Poppy.

"Nor will I," said Lowenthal, and changed the subject. "That guy who arrived next to last? The one with the beard? Who is he and what does he do? I think I know him from somewhere, but I can't place him."

"That's my cousin, Galahad Dritchner; everyone but his mother calls him Hank. He designs yachts and aeroplanes. He and his wife live in Maine." She saw Lowenthal nod in the way he did when he had put things together.

"Aha. Yes. We did a story on his company, sometime early last year. I didn't make the Dritchner connection back then, you still being fairly new to the paper, and me not familiar with your Aunt Josephine."

"And I was still covering the society page, and garden parties," Poppy added.

Lowenthal ignored the barb. "Is he Stacy's brother?"

This question surprised Poppy. "His oldest. Why?"

"Think you could get information out of him? Something to add to your on-going assignment. Not that I expect you to pump him or anything like that, but he might give you a lead you can use in a follow-up story. Having the personal touch should be useful. An interview, or some such. Not tonight, but maybe some time in the next day or so? Think about, won't you?" He held up his glass. "Your aunt Esther serves first class booze."

"So she does," Poppy agreed. "But about Galahad; he hasn't been in touch with Stacy for some time; he and Stacy don't get along very well."

"Oh. Pity with two *t*s." He gave a hitch to his shoulders. "Thought it might be worth a try," he added, and made his way back to his wife, who was now sitting demurely on one of the extra chairs, next to Bernadette Stanton; the two women appeared to be having a lively discussion about the finger-food.

Poppy watched them for a moment, then took a quick step sideways as Abner Bridges came through with a pitcher of lemonade, which he set on the high-boy among the bottles and glasses.

"Quite an evening, at least so far," Holte remarked from a place beside and above her. "Your aunt is every bit as eclectic as you told me she'd be."

"Ye gods, Holte," she muttered.

"I didn't mean to startle you." It was as much of an apology as he was prepared to give. "What a...diverse group."

"That it is," Poppy said, and started to move away from him.

He drifted after her. "They're getting ready to bring the food out of the kitchen."

"I know. Thank goodness. It's almost seven-fifteen. Missus Sassoro is probably beside herself." She glanced about to be sure no one was paying attention to her, and noticed Loring watching her from a place by the nearer of two bookcases. She smiled in his direction. It was tempting to think that he might have noticed or heard things that she could glean from him later, but not tonight, with so many people thronging the house. She looked away from Holte and let her gaze shift around the room.

As if this were an invitation, Loring came toward her, one of the pastry-shells-with- mushrooms in his fingers. "I want to thank you for asking me to come, although I almost begged off. I was afraid it would be one of those stiff, hoity-toity gatherings that I would expect from your Aunt Josephine, all formal and elite." He ducked his head and lowered his voice. "Not the needling of Missus Pearse, of course. But you were right about your Aunt Esther and Aunt Josephine—chalk and cheese."

Poppy giggled. "Have you met everyone?"

"Not everyone. I've met Judge Stephanson a couple of times before, when he was still on the bench, and I know Doctor Wyman, in the line of work. I had a few words with Franklin Grimes; not quite what I expected."

"He's not like most of his family."

"That's what makes him interesting to me," Loring said.

"Snooping?" Poppy suggested.

A rattle of pots came from the dining room, augmented by a range of intensified aromas; the evening meal was being moved from the kitchen to the waiting platters in the dining room.

"Unsuccessfully," Loring admitted. "Is he really so disinterested in the family business as he claims to be?"

"I think so. Second son, and all that." Poppy more felt than heard Holte make a non- sound very like a titter of amusement; she ignored him.

"By the way," Loring said as if as if something had just occurred to him, "does Missus Timms go after every man in the room, or just ones she hasn't met until now?"

"I don't know; tonight is my first exposure. A few days ago Aunt Esther said Missus Timms is like a shark after chum: it's more a question of quantity than quality." She disliked the catty tone of her remark, but had to admit that it was more accurate than she had expected. "No offense Loring."

"None taken. I'll rely on you to protect me from her," he said teasingly.

Before she could answer, the dinner-gong sounded, and the guests moved in the direction of the dining room, some of them leaving their cocktail glasses on the various tables in the parlor and sitting room, in anticipation of the wine to come.

EIGHTEEN

Poppy did not waken until almost nine the following morning; she stretched and glanced toward the windows, and encountered an ominous stare from Maestro, who interrupted his grooming to let Poppy know he was not pleased. "Don't fret, cat," she said fondly. "Between your late-night snack last night and left-overs for the next few days, you won't be going hungry. Not that you ever have," she added affectionately.

Maestro was unimpressed with this assurance, and offered another loud reprimand for her laxness.

"All right, all right, I'll get up and bring you something to eat." She threw back her comforter and sheet and swung her feet to the floor. "Missus Sassoro should be here by now. I'll bet she has a plate made up for you already." Rising, she went to the closet for her bathrobe, pulled it on, and stopped in the bathroom on her way down to the kitchen, claimed her slippers, and headed for the stairs.

"Good morning, Miss Poppy," said Missus Sassoro as Poppy came into the kitchen; it was almost restored to normal but for three large roasting pans sitting on the drainboard. "It was a fine gathering, last night."

"Ye gods, I should hope so, with all the wonderful food you supplied," said Poppy. "I was wondering if you had anything for Maestro? He's been asking."

Missus Sassoro grinned. "He'll like his breakfast—more duck, and a slice of glazed pork along with a little of the grilled cod. There wasn't any lamb left, or I would have given him some of that, too. His plate's in the refrigerator, on the top shelf, wrapped in wax paper."

Poppy made a gesture of thanks. "Sounds perfect."

"Will you be wanting breakfast?" Missus Sassoro asked as she put a tray of scones into the oven to bake.

"In forty minutes or so," Poppy told her while she retrieved the cat's meal from the refrigerator. "I'm going to rise slowly today."

"A sore head?" the cook ventured.

"No, just the product of a very long day yesterday." Poppy thought for a second. "Will the scones be ready by then? And might I have two of them with butter and raspberry preserves? Along with my coffee?"

Missus Sassoro nodded. "Of course. Missus Thornton has already asked for the scones, and a cheese omelette in her room; I was planning to start with Miss Roth's oatmeal as soon as I finish the dishes."

"Do you know when she's going to be up? Aunt Esther, not Miss Roth." Poppy asked, recalling that she thought Aunt Esther had looked weary by the end of the evening.

"She said before ten, and if she wasn't, that I or Miss Roth should go and wake her." Missus Sassoro said, glancing at the kitchen clock.

"So she's in good hands. I'll see you in forty minutes or so." Saying that, she went out of the kitchen and through the entry-hall to the stairs.

Maestro met her at the top of the stairs, exclaiming insistently for the treat he was to have, and wreathed around her legs as she carried the laden plate into the bathroom and set it on the floor. "There you go. It's probably better than you deserve, no matter what you think," she scolded fondly, then refilled his water-bowl before returning to her bedroom and pulling open her closet door again. "What to wear today?" she asked herself.

"The mauve suit with the short jacket would be nice; you could wear it to the latest briefing on the Napier robbery, which is coming up," said Chesterton Holte from somewhere near the ceiling. "And that pale-pink blouse would set it off well."

Poppy rounded on him, seeing him as a bright smudge next to the central light fixture. "I should have known," she said.

"Yes, you should have," he agreed, dropping down to her eye-level. "I assumed you would want to discuss last night's festivities before you go off to work."

She took out the mauve suit and studied it. Holte was right, she decided. "What did you want to say about the party?"

He became a little more distinct. "On the whole, I thought it went well."

"But——?" she said for him.

"Your Aunt Josephine really out-did herself: she can be quite a piece of work when she wants to be. And Aunt Esther was right about Missus Timms. I wonder whatever possessed him to marry her?"

"I have no idea. Perhaps she wasn't so...florid when he did." Poppy hung the suit on the outer hook of the closet door, and then went back inside to look for the blouse.

"Whatever possessed Josephine to take after Missus Pearse that way?" Holte asked, while Poppy sorted through her blouses.

"I wish I knew. That was deplorable behavior." Poppy took the pale pink blouse off the hanger and stepped out of the closet.

"Do you think the Pearses have reason to worry about GAD?" Holte asked her.

"It doesn't matter what I think: they're worried," said Poppy.

"All right. But is Missus Pearse really making too much of things?" Holte persisted.

"I don't know. She has been trying to keep GAD enveloped in cotton batting since HOB died, but that doesn't mean that she's exaggerating her distress." She glanced toward the window. "It looks fairly cool out," she remarked while she took the suit down.

"I can't tell, but I'd think that's likely; there are clouds building up."

"I'll keep rain in mind," Poppy said.

He lingered at the closet door. "Another thing?"

"Yes?" Poppy said cautiously.

"What was Mildred Fairchild telling you about the *Tattler*? And pray enlighten me what is the *Tattler*?"

"It's a weekly gossip sheet, the very best of yellow journalism." Her sarcastic tone underscored her back-handed compliment. "You know the kind of thing—tales about all manner of misbehavior, and rumored misbehavior of celebrities, officials, sport champions, and so forth, the more lurid the better."

"That's what I supposed, given the name," said Holte, moving toward Poppy while she set the suit out on her bed. "They must have had a field day with Moncrief's murder. Or Knott's, for that matter."

"I didn't bother to read it to find out; I'd guess you're right," said Poppy. "But I know they hung around the story for a month or so." She put the blouse on top of the suit. "I'm going to have a short bath, and then we can resume this analysis—if it's all right with you?"

"Whatever suits you," he said at his most courtly.

At this, Poppy laughed, then went across the hall to the bathroom, where Maestro had finished about half his meal. "Saving some for later?" she asked him as she turned on the hot water, and then the cold.

Maestro murred at her, and jumped onto the toilet seat, his steady gaze fixed on her.

"You needn't guard me; I'm not going to drown," said Poppy as she removed her bathrobe and nightgown, hanging them on the towel-rack before getting into the tub and sitting down in the rising water. When the water was high enough, she turned off the taps and lay back, letting the warmth sink into her; the dull ache in her lower back gradually faded, and the tension eased. She sighed with pleasure and closed her eyes, letting herself luxuriate. After a few minutes, she sat up and grabbed her soap and washcloth and began with her face and neck, working her way down her body. She had reached her waist when something that had been lurking in the back of her mind suddenly surfaced. "Ye gods!" she blurted out. "The *Tattler*. Merrinelle Butterworth. I should have said something to Loring last night. It's going to be a—" She did not say scandal, as if silence could keep it from happening. Hurriedly she rinsed off and pulled the plug, scrambling out of the tub, snatching her bathrobe from the towel-rack, and tugging it on. She bolted out of the bathroom and down the stairs, pausing only to make sure the door was closed to keep Maestro confined upstairs. In the entry-hall, she went to the phone alcove and picked up the receiver, telling the operator Inspector Loring's number, and waiting, breathing a little fast, and trying to marshal her thoughts without too many self-recriminations.

"Loring," said his familiar voice in her ear.

"Hello, Inspector, it's—"

"Poppy. I recognize your voice. What's on your mind? Have you recovered from last night?"

"I've mostly recovered. But there is something I should have told you last night. It slipped my mind in all the confusion." She felt horribly contrite, and so hurried on to make a quick confession of the whole. "Mildred Fairchild mentioned an article or interview in the *Tattler*. You must know what it is. Well, there's a story in the most recent issue about Merrinelle Butterworth, Jonathan Butterworth's oldest daughter. In it, Mildred says, Merrinelle not only claims to be GAD's fiancée, but that he has disappeared, and the family isn't pursuing the matter. The Pearses won't like that when they find out about it."

Loring cursed quietly, then said, "Sorry. I didn't mean to offend you."

"You didn't. I happen to agree."

"Well, do you think any of it's true? The *Tattler* isn't famous for its accuracy, as the police have reason to know." He waited for her response.

"I know that Merrinelle has told people before that GAD is her intended', but whether that is his intention as well as hers, I don't know." Poppy took a deep breath and hurried on, "Isadora has said that it's unthinkable that he should form such a connection, but that doesn't mean he hasn't; GAD goes his own way in most things."

"So you've said," Loring interjected.

Poppy felt a chill through her robe and realized that Holte had come downstairs from her room. "I don't know what the family, or you, can do about this, but I thought you should know, and I apologize again for not informing you sooner." She paused. "I'm planning to pick up a copy of the *Tattler* on my way in to work. I'll have a better idea of how bad the story is after I've read what they've published."

There was a brief silence on the other end of the line, then Loring said, "This is your half- day, isn't it?"

"Yes. I'm doing the afternoon instead of the morning, but I'll be going in around ten- thirty." She took a deep breath. "Lowenthal arranged it."

"Interesting fellow, your boss," Loring observed, but did not enlarge on his meaning. In a different tone, he went on, "Would you be adverse to me stopping by in the evening, around seven? We could talk about this in more depth. You can show me the *Tattler* story and give me your take on it. You know what kind of coverage the *Tattler* is after, and you can tell me why they're running this story. I'll have a chance to check out some of the particulars and, by then, I should have more from the Pearses—I'm not looking forward to that. Missus

Pearse is not going to be happy, no matter what. She wants public attention, but she wants it to be carefully managed, not the kind this article is apt to bring about, and who can blame her."

"She'll be mortified," Poppy agreed. "What a mess."

"That it is," Loring said slowly, and then went on more briskly. "So. I might as well get to it. Thank you for calling. I'm rather glad you waited to tell me until this morning. I'm not sure I would have paid that much attention last night. There was so much going on."

"That's nice of you to say," Poppy responded, despondency coming over her without warning. "I feel as if I've let you down."

"What?" He gave a kind of laugh. "No such thing. You've done me a great favor, and I hope I can repay it in some way. I'll see you tonight." And with that, he hung up.

Poppy hung up as well, and made her way back up the stairs, despondent and cold. Once she was in her room, she got out of her bathrobe and let it drop to the floor, then sat on the bed, trying to sort out why she had botched telling him about the article when she had first heard about it. She decided that it was because she had not yet seen the article, and couldn't inform Loring with anything more than second hand information, all the while admitting to herself that this was exactly what she had ended up doing. Although this was readily explainable, she had an uneasy feeling that she was dodging an issue in allowing herself to be persuaded so facilely.

Standing up, she began the routine of dressing, doing her best to put the whole episode out of her mind. She had got as far as her slip and silk stockings when Holte addressed her from the far corner of the room.

"You haven't done anything very dreadful; word of a spy—and believe me when I say that I understand what dreadful is. The damage had already been done when you learned about it, and you made it possible for Loring to prepare to talk with the Pearses rather than being blind- sided by them—as you say, they aren't going to be pleased. At least now, he'll be able to take the high road." As he spoke, Maestro bounced sideways into the room, fur puffed out in all directions, his tail like a bottle-brush.

Poppy clapped her hands at the cat. "You can't scare a ghost, Maestro. You should know that by now." Secretly, she was glad of the diversion Maestro's presence provided. She opened the zipper in the left-hand-side seam in order to step into the skirt. "Why do you say that, Holte?"

"Because you're castigating yourself needlessly," he said at his most reasonable. "You've no reason to do it, not from my perspective."

"That's kind of you," she said in patent disbelief.

He drifted a little nearer. "If you feel compelled to apologize to someone, apologize to Cornelius Lowenthal. You did not let him know that there was a potential big story he could get on before other papers. Of course, he would have sent you out to the nearest newsstand to get a copy, and then would have ordered you to go to the study and cobble together an inch or two of material, which you would then have had to confirm with the Pearses, and wouldn't that have made for a better party?" This last bit of ironic advice had the effect of pulling her up short.

"I can only tell you that you're probably right," she said, summoning up the remnants of her dignity, "but I still think I should have informed Loring last night."

"Give the poor man a break. He was having fun, which I wager he doesn't do often."

"You're very likely right about that," said Poppy, doing her utmost to restore her equanimity.

"You do realize that he came because he likes you," Holte said. "He likes being in your company."

"So you tell me," Poppy snapped, and then stopped, her manner becoming less caustic. "I beg your pardon: I seem to be in a beastly frame of mind this morning. I shouldn't have spoken so bluntly. I think I may have got over-tired last night; it was a demanding evening. I didn't fall asleep until sometime after three."

"And you were up before the crack of dawn yesterday." He moved nearer to her. "Don't be so demanding of yourself. You're blowing your minor errors way out of proportion."

"I can't afford not to," said Poppy, continuing to dress. She wished now that she had remained in bed a little longer.

"Because you are convinced that you have to hold yourself to a high standard—no, to a higher standard, because you have something to prove—I understand that. But you are expecting far more from yourself than you expect of others, and that puts you at a disadvantage. If you're willing to extend the benefit of the doubt to others, you should do the same for yourself. Please believe me." He swooped over to the end of her bed and gave the appearance of sitting on it.

Maestro hissed and scooted under the bed.

Poppy paid little attention to the cat, and kept her focus on Holte. "I should be off to the paper shortly; right after breakfast."

"You don't have to arrive until noon, you know," Holte reminded her. "It wouldn't hurt you to take advantage of that; spend a little time with your aunt. You can review the party, and catch up on the gossip."

"I want to get into the paper early."

"To show that an evening of socializing won't flatten you?" He did the ghostly equivalent of a laugh. "If Lowenthal isn't bothered by this, you shouldn't be."

"Harris and Gafney will use it to make hay, joking and speculating on oh, everything." Still in her stockinged feet, but otherwise fully dressed, Poppy went to her vanity table and began to inspect her face; she saw dull-blue circles under her eyes, and sighed. She had some foundation in her cosmetics drawer, and wondered if she should resort to putting it on to mask them—powder alone wouldn't be enough. Taking her ivory comb in hand she began to put her hair in order; thanks to the recent cut, it fell into style quickly, and that gave her a moment of hope.

"Stay in a bit longer. Trust me, you need a little time to shore up your reserves. You and Esther can have a little time to confer on last night, and it would be a useful thing to do," Holte persisted.

Poppy nodded as she opened the little box, rubbed the minuscule brush in the damp, dark-brown color, and applied the mascara to her lashes. The dullness she felt continued to nag at her until she did a quick review of the date, and realized what was happening, something that she was reluctant to explain to Holte. Ghost he might be, but she supposed he had the usual male disgust of female ailments. But finally she remarked, "I shouldn't mention this, but my Monthlies are about to start, and that always puts me out of curl." Just making such an admission to a man, no matter how noncorporeal, upset her, and she could feel color rising in her face.

Holte digested this and said, "I remember that Sybil used to become weepy when hers were on her."

"Thank goodness I've been spared that; not that my shrewishness is much better," said Poppy, inspecting her face as she applied a dot of rouge to each of her cheeks and began to blend it into her skin. "My mother used to tell me to take an aspirin or two and ignore it. At least we have pads now instead of rags." This bold admission took her by surprise. "I know I shouldn't talk about such Women's Matters with men. I'm sorry. I was taught better than this." She swung around on her chair and faced Holte's pale outline. "Why do I tell you such things? You would probably rather that I change the subject."

Holte took a few seconds to answer. "I suppose you have to tell someone, and I'm available. You can talk to Maestro, but I think you want a more developed answer than a meow or a purr." He went nearer. "Your week has been trying. I can see that. Not just the party, though it has demanded a lot of you."

"That's no excuse."

"No, but it is an explanation." He leaned back and rose into the air, now fully horizontal. "When I was alive, I thought that women made too much of what their bodies do. But being a ghost, I can see that everyone with a body has demands made on them by bodies: hunger, thirst, fatigue, illness and injury, the need to be active, the need for sleep, and many other things. One of the burdens of being alive is maintaining your body."

"How philosophical you are this mor—" She broke off. "I'm sorry. Pay no attention to me." She moved around to face her mirror.

When he spoke again, his voice was quiet. "Don't fret, Poppy. You're allowed the occasional stumble."

She shook her head. "No, Holte, that's the problem: I'm not."

Holte was about to argue the point, but saw that it was neither the time nor the place to offer his opinion. He waved in her direction and wafted out the window.

NINETEEN

AUNT ESTHER WAS IN THE BREAKFAST-NOOK, A CUP OF HOT, BLACK COFFEE IN front of her. This morning she was dressed in a tan barn-coat, a shirt of brown cotton, and a pair of sturdy canvas slacks of the same color; she wore mucking-boots on her feet. She looked up as Poppy came in and took the chair opposite her aunt's. "I see you're going in early."

"I think it's best that I do," Poppy said, and smiled at Missus Sassoro as she set down a plate with three buttered scones and a small tub of raspberry preserves. "Thank you."

"You're welcome, I'm sure, Miss Poppy. I'll have your coffee in two shakes of a lamb's tail." She stepped back into the kitchen.

"Well, while you're out, I thought I would go to the nursery and select some new plants for the garden," Esther announced. "Galliard will handle the digging, but I will do the planting."

"What kind of plants did you have in mind," Poppy wondered while she spread raspberry preserves on the top scone.

"I thought some herbs for the side-garden would be nice; fresh herbs are so much better than the dried ones, aren't they? I had some there a couple of years ago, but what with one thing and another, they didn't thrive. I was gone most of the time, and Miss Roth has no talent for gardening. Galliard doesn't mind vegetable gardening, but isn't fond of the more decorative sort, beyond trimming and pruning." She took a spoon and stirred her coffee. "Also, I'd like to get a tree or two for the back of the garden, against the fence. That part of the garden could use a little something extra. A willow or a couple of birches, I was thinking."

"Which part of the back garden?" Poppy asked.

"In the northwest corner. It doesn't get a lot of sun, and the creeping juniper there now is looking bedraggled." She took up one of her own scones and bit the narrow end off of it. "It's not a Devon Cream Tea, quite, but close enough for breakfast."

"What would make it a Devon Cream Tea?" Poppy inquired, moving her plate a little so that Missus Sassoro could set down Poppy's mug of coffee and a pretty little creamer.

"Clotted cream and four p.m.," said Esther. "Also the south coast of England would be nice."

"Surely there's a dairy in the vicinity that makes clotted cream," said Poppy.

"No doubt, but I'm not going to spend my time driving about looking for it," said Esther. "I'm just wishing, not expecting. I wouldn't mind a large glass of Russian tea out of a samovar, either, but I'm not eager to go back to the Soviet Union to get it."

"Do you think you'll go back to Rus—the Soviet Union again?"

"Probably not," Esther said, and picked up her scone. "Emphatically not to Siberia. The weather is too unendurable. Baking in summer and well below freezing in winter." She sighed. "There is one thing I'd like to explore over there: when I was flying, I saw a huge swath of fallen trees, all looking to have gone down from the same point. It was near a place called Tunguska. I asked about it, but no one would tell me anything, so naturally, I am very curious."

"A bomb, do you think?" Poppy asked, her own interest piqued.

"Not any kind of bomb I've ever heard of. There were miles and miles of downed trees, the whole landscape was blasted." She waved the matter away. "I should be thinking about the Amazon, not Siberia."

"I think you might want to concentrate on the back garden for today," Poppy recommended before she shook her head and took a bite of her first scone. Some of the butter that had soaked into the triangular bread leaked out and ran down her chin; she took her napkin and wiped away the butter, leaving a faint smear behind. "I'll have to repowder before I leave," she said, chewing. "These preserves are excellent—not too sweet."

"I agree," said Aunt Esther. "I can't abide saccharin compotes of any kind."

"You like chutney," Poppy pointed out. "Some of those are very sweet."

"And made to go with heavily spiced foods, not a bland scone or a pancake," said Esther, and sipped her coffee.

Poppy swallowed, added a little cream to her coffee, and then stirred a single spoonful of sugar to it, her thoughts in a jumble. To fill the silence between her and Aunt Esther, Poppy asked, "How do you rate last night's party?"

Esther considered her answer and said, "All in all, I'd give it seven out of ten. It would have been better if Langton had not brought Beatrice, but she is his wife, so I couldn't very well ask him to come on his own, since the company was mixed. I'm sorry Elliott Wickman had to leave early; he and Archibald Wyman were having a grand time discussing bizarre methods of execution."

"But aside from Beatrice Timms, what is your assessment of the company in general?" Poppy asked, judiciously sipping her coffee.

"In general, I think the lamb was a great success. Most of the guests got along—with the exception of Beatrice, and Josephine would not get off her high horse. The way she behaved to Isadora Pearse was beastly." She sighed briefly. "She can be so difficult, my sister. Rigging herself out that way! And then speaking only to those she already knew; I could have strangled her for the way she treated Eunice Lowenthal. If I hadn't seen her pull such a trick in the past, I would have been completely flummoxed, but I still can't excuse her for being so...so brattish. You'd think she were sixteen again." She drank more coffee. "I was worried that she might decide to...but I hoped that Hank could talk her out of..." Her words drifted off. About ten seconds later she said, "Speaking of Hank, I saw your Inspector Loring in deep conversation with him, between dinner and dessert. They were in the sitting room. Did you happen to notice?"

Poppy frowned. "No, I didn't. I stayed in the parlor and dining room for the most part. Milly and I were reminiscing about our years in secondary school and college. Why on earth would Loring want to talk to Hank?" Immediately the answer sprang up in her mind. "Stacy. Of course."

"I assume so," Esther said. "But I had the impression that Loring was asking Hank about his business, as well."

"I didn't know that Loring was interested in boats. Or aeroplanes," she appended.

"Perhaps your Inspector is more adept at small-talk than you give him credit for," Esther suggested.

"You may be right," said Poppy, and took another, more careful, bite of her scone, pondering the mystery that was J. B. Loring.

By the time Poppy got up from the table, Aunt Esther had been gone for ten minutes, and Poppy was beginning to feel that she ought to be on her way. She wanted to get to the *Clarion* while Lowenthal was still there. She hurried up to her room to repair the damage of breakfast, to give Maestro his plate of food for the day, and to put on a little scent before she left. Half- expecting to hear Holte comment on the morning, she took a little longer than usual to check the contents of her purse and her brief-case, but did not notice him anywhere.

In her Hudson, she threaded her way through morning delivery vehicles and the worsening weather, going toward the Addison Newspaper Corporation building and the parking place in the alley next to it that she was coming to think of as hers. She stopped at the newsstand outside the main entrance and bought a copy of the *Tattler*, which she folded and shoved into her purse before going through the imposing doors and up the stairs, hoping that she would have a little time to read the story in the *Tattler* before she got down to work.

The city room was as busy as it was on weekdays; most of the desks were occupied, the copy-boys were busy working their way from the composing room to the city room, answering summons from both places; cigarette smoke hung in the air. Poppy jostled her way to her desk, a little surprised that Holte had not accompanied her in her auto, and was not now lurking in a light-fixture. She took off her coat and hung it over the back of the chair, then sat down and pulled out the *Tattler* , preparing to look through it for the distressing story from Merrinelle Butterworth. It was on page 4, below the fold, for which Poppy was grateful; had it been on the front page, there would have been an uproar before now. At least, Poppy thought, the *Tattler* publishes on Thursday and distributes on Friday morning, which meant that there had not been much time for the story to take hold. With real trepidation, Poppy began to read:

This reporter has learned from Merrinelle Butterworth, daughter of Jonathan and Olympia Butterworth, that her fiancé, G.A.D. Pearse, who spent the summer in Europe and was scheduled to return two weeks ago, has been missing since the end of July. The scion of the Pearse family, G.A.D. will inherit the control of the Pearse fortune upon the death of his father. Miss Butterworth reports that so far, the parents have made no effort to locate their missing son, and have not engaged the police in opening an inquiry into his

disappearance, or if they have engaged private parties, she has not been informed of it.

Merrinelle Butterworth, the oldest daughter of mercantile tycoon Jonathan Rhodes

Butterworth, and who is a sophomore at the Mount Delos Women's College, has told

this reporter that she fears for her fiancé's life and that she believes his family's inactivity

in efforts to find him is a possible indication of collusion with foreign interests. Miss

Butterworth says she wants to alert the public to this most distressing development, and

to urge those in a position to do so, to press for thorough investigation.

"Heaven alone knows what happened to him," Miss Butterworth said to this reporter.

"If I don't act on this, who knows who will?"

Poppy went through the story twice, then picked up the *Tattler* and made for Lowenthal's office, rehearsing in her mind what she would tell him. She knocked on his door, and when he called out, "Come in," she did.

Cornelius Lowenthal sat behind his desk, his hair already twirled and twisted into small corkscrews over his forehead; he showed no ill effects from the previous night. He was on the phone, deeply engrossed in a dispute; he motioned to Poppy to sit down even as he bellowed, "No, that isn't sufficient, and you damned well know it! Get the whole story, with confirmation, or drop it now!" He slammed the receiver back into the hook on the candlestick telephone. Panting a little, he gave his attention to Poppy. "Well?"

"I think there may be something to this," Poppy said, handing the *Tattler* to Lowenthal. "Page 4, third column, below the fold."

With a snort of impatience, Lowenthal opened the paper and looked. "I repeat: well?"

"I know something about it. The Pearses are good friends of my Aunt Jo—"

"What a grande dame she is," Lowenthal interjected.

"She can be," Poppy said, and continued in a rush. "Her...outburst...last night was not remarkable; she is distressed at Stacy's absence, and Isadora Pearse has been quite vocal about her missing son; it was a very awkward moment, and I know that it's going to lead to gossip." She paused, working out how to continue. "Sherman Pearse has insisted that they keep the story away from the public because he's afraid of extortionists coming after him with false information and ransom demands that would make finding GAD impossible."

"Not an unreasonable stance," Lowenthal allowed. "How many people would you say know about this?"

"Perhaps a hundred," said Poppy. "Double that if you count the servants, but they tend to keep family troubles inside the house."

"Yes. Those women at the Moncrief house, they did their best to keep out of public attention. You think you could get some of the same from the Pearse servants?"

"No, I don't think so. The Pearses are very private and wouldn't tolerate that kind of intrusion; any servant caught telling tales outside the door would be fired in an instant and given no reference. But it is a real case; the police know about it, and most of the Pearses' circle, as I told you. Would you like me to run with it? Just to see what I can learn that's solid?"

Lowenthal mulled this over. "Tell you what: check it out and report to me on Monday morning about what you've learned. I'll decide then." He tapped his desk-blotter with his fingers. "Anything more on the Moncrief or Knott stories?"

"Nothing worth two inches in Tuesday's edition."

Lowenthal nodded. "By the way, your Aunt Esther is coming in on Wednesday to talk about an editorial piece on the Armenians. Now that woman I like."

As compared to Aunt Jo, Poppy added silently to herself. "I hope you can work something out. She's pretty much caught up in the refugees' plight."

"Plight," Lowenthal repeated as if tasting the word. "Good way to put it. Keep it in mind for later, in case your aunt wants your help on her piece—assuming I agree to run it. I don't want it to read like a term paper. Our readers like simple, declarative sentences, not complex paragraphs." He was about to dismiss her. "By the way, the wife and I had a good time at your party—better than either of us was expecting. And the food was very good. The drink, too. Tell your aunt thanks for us, will you?"

"I'll be happy to, boss," she said, astonished at his favorable comments.

"Right-o then. See what you can turn up on the...Pearse story." He pointed to his door. "Chop-chop."

"I'm on it, boss," she said as she claimed the copy of the *Tattler* and left Lowenthal's office. Back at her desk, she sat down and tried to make up her mind whether to call the Pearses directly or to try to phone the Butterworths first. After a little cogitation, she chose the Pearses, telling herself that this would be easier, because she knew them, but had only met the Butterworths in passing. She got her notebook out of her purse and looked up the Pearses' phone number, then gave it to the operator.

"Pearse residence," said their butler, an estimable man named Elliston. "To whom would you like to speak?" he inquired in a deep, plummy voice that reminded Poppy of warm jam.

"Either Mister or Missus Pearse, or Miss Genevieve, if her parents aren't available."

"Very good. Whom shall I say is calling?"

"Poppea Thornton, Josephine Dritchner's niece," said Poppy, squirming at the necessity of such formality.

"If you will wait a moment, Miss Thornton, I'll see if any of those three are home." Elliston put the receiver down and went in search of them.

Poppy took up a pencil and started to doodle; she ended up drawing intersecting circles, and wondered in the process what she was telling herself. After about two minutes, Elliston returned.

"Missus Pearse wishes me to inform you that she will call you on Monday, at your place of business, in the morning, to schedule an interview."

"Monday morning" said Poppy, making a note of it on her blotter. "Thank you, Elliston."

"You are most welcome Miss Thornton," he said, and hung up.

Poppy repeated Monday morning several times to herself, to fix the time in her mind, and then bit the bullet and called the Butterworths.

"I'm sorry Miss Thornton," the operator told her. "That line is busy. If you could call again later."

Girding her metaphorical loins to the prospect of frustration, Poppy was about to call Aunt Jo, when one of the copy-boys came by and handed her a note; it was from Gentry in Vital Statistics, saying Call me. Puzzled, Poppy picked up the phone, lifted the receiver and depressed the hook twice to get the PBX board in the basement that handled the in-house calls. "Extension 348, Rob Gentry, please."

"Calling," said the operator in an adenoidal tone.

Poppy heard the three rings on the other end, and then Gentry picked up his receiver. "Vital Statistics."

"Rob? Poppy Thornton here. I just got your note. What's going on?"

He hesitated a moment—Poppy assumed to look through the vast pile of paper on his desk—then said, "I got a call about an hour ago from York, notifying me that they had a fatal car wreck near the town, and they have confirmation on the driver."

"I gather he's dead, if they called you," Poppy said.

"Good guess," said Gentry sardonically. "I thought it might have something to do with those stories you've been on about Madison Moncrief's murder?"

Poppy's curiosity increased tenfold. "Why do you say that?"

"You've mentioned this guy in a few of your stories." Gentry's Carolina drawl got stronger. "About the Moncrief murder. This guy was part of all the fuss, kind of a family friend. You interviewed him in June."

"What guy? What happened?" Poppy demanded, although she had a degree of certainty that she knew whom Gentry meant.

"Julian Eastley? That hero fellow? He crashed his car a couple nights ago, about four miles west of town. Went off the road on a sharp turn and dropped into a small ravine and then went into a creek, according to the police report. They didn't find him until late yesterday, and it took until this morning to get a positive identification on him. The police think his car might have been side-swiped—there's extensive damage to the left side of his auto that can't be accounted for by going down the ravine, unless it rolled over twice, which it might have done. I thought I should let you know before you read it in the paper." His chuckle was grim and quite humorless.

"They're sure it's Eastley," Poppy said.

"They found his driver's license in his wallet. There was an empty flask in the car, by the way."

"That's not surprising," said Poppy, who knew a number of people who liked to have a nip now and then while driving. "What else?"

"That's all I have so far," said Gentry. "I'll let you know if I hear anything more. There's going to be an autopsy."

Poppy gave herself a mental shake and said, "Thanks, Rob. I owe you one."

"See you don't forget," said Gentry, and hung up.

After Poppy hung up, she sat and stared into space for nearly three minutes, then took a pen and began to scribble in her notebook. She would have to ask Holte a number of questions when next she saw him. Satisfied that she had enough information to consult when they did talk, she picked up the phone and made another futile attempt to make contact with the Butterworth household, and was annoyed when she again encountered a busy signal. An hour later she finally reached the butler, a very dignified individual named Trodling.

"Missus Butterworth asks that you call again at three this afternoon, Miss Thornton," he informed Poppy after checking with Missus Butterworth.

"Thank you, Trodling," said Poppy, hoping that this was not just a delay, but an actual engagement. At least she was making a little progress, she told herself, and spent the next ten minutes organizing her notes.

Shortly before she left, she called Loring and left a message to him to phone her at home after four—she had some information to pass on to him. Feeling virtuous for a change, she rang the operator again and asked if she could find a number for Rudolph N. Beech, living somewhere in Florida.

"I'll try," said the operator, sounding exasperated. "I'll try the cities first."

"Good. I'll be here until two; if you can't turn something up in that time, I'll take another crack at it on Monday."

"I'll let you know what I find at or before two Miss Thornton," the operator assured her.

"Thank you," said Poppy, and went back to trying to work out where Eastley's death fit into the picture—if it fit at all.

TWENTY

Poppy was back at Aunt Esther's house by two-thirty; she went up to her room to change out of her working clothes and to put on something more comfortable. She was just donning one of her two pairs of slacks—the bronze wool ones—when Holte, resembling a wisp of fog, came through the ceiling. "There you are," she said, making it almost an accusation. She buttoned her slacks and pulled on a cream-colored fisherman's sweater over it, then ran her fingers through her hair to restore a little neatness to it.

"Yes," said Holte. "Was it a difficult day?"

"It was a bedeviling one," she said. "I spent most of the time on the phone with people who didn't want to talk to me. I'm doing a follow-up on the *Tattler* piece. I'm supposed to call Olympia Butterworth at three. She's the only one who might tell me something." Just saying this made her want to jump up and down in vexation; it had taken nine attempts to get through to Jonathan Butterworth, who was at the office, and when she did, he declined to talk to her about the *Tattler* story. She had also had a difficult talk with Neva Plowright, who was dismayed to learn of Julian Eastley's death but had nothing useful to say about it except that it was sad. "He was so devoted to Louise," was the most she was willing to tell Poppy.

"I had to agree with that," Poppy said, trying to get a fix on Holte as he sailed around the room.

"That doesn't sound enjoyable."

"Far from it," Poppy agreed. "And speaking of that, did you know that Julian Eastley had died in an auto crash?"

To her bewilderment, he answered, "Yes."

"And you didn't say anything to me?" She considered upbraiding him, but waited to hear what he would say.

"You were deep in preparing for the party, and I didn't think it was urgent."

Her burgeoning indignation gave was to stupefaction. "Something like this, so close to the Moncrief investigation, and you thought it could wait?"

"Yes." He drifted over toward her. "He doesn't remember much about it— doesn't even know that he's dead. Moncrief has been trying to break the news to him gently. So far, he hasn't been able to get through to him."

"That's just..." She could find no word to express her annoyance.

"It's not easy when you're first dead," Holte said by way of explanation. "Particularly if you died...unexpectedly."

"So you've told me." She began to pace the room. "Have you learned anything useful from him? I'm assuming you've spoken to him."

"Only that he thinks that perhaps his auto crashed, but he isn't sure. When I asked him what the last thing that he remembers was, he was vague. He said the sun was in his eyes and that perhaps there was a car trying to get around him on a tight turn, or that there was a flash in his rear-view mirror. For someone accidentally dead, he has a good recollection of how it happened: he knows he was in his auto, which is more than many can do. That's pretty much the extent of what he remembers." He took a moment to slide over toward her vanity table, and then became more discernable.

"Is there any reason to suspect foul play?" she asked. "Does he think he was forced off the road?"

"Not that I'm aware of," Holte said cautiously. "He is certain something interfered with his sight."

"So he ran off the road and crashed? Does he remember his auto going down a defile into the creek?"

"No—did it?" Holte said with amazement.

"According to Rob Gentry in Vital Statistics. It'll be in Monday's obituary column." Poppy flung up her hands. "Just another part of the puzzle, I guess."

"Would you like me to speak to Eastley again?" Holte offered, trying to find some way to ease her distress.

"Do you think it would do any good?" She stopped moving and turned to face him.

"I think it might," he answered. "It can't hurt."

Poppy nodded slowly. "You're right. Give it a try when you're next in the dimension of ghosts. Ye gods, why not?"

He went a little closer to her. "What else is troubling you?"

"It's Overstreet, and Derrington, and Louise, and Stacy, of course. What else is there? Lowenthal wants more information, and I'm trying to dig some up for him. I tried to find Louise's half-brother today, but no luck. There's no news on Overstreet, and nothing on Stacy and Derrington, or Louise. I'm running out of people to talk to."

"That's hardly your fault," Holte pointed out.

"Don't tell Lowenthal that; he'll laugh you out of his office." She stopped. "Sorry. I'm being beastly again. Don't worry, I'll be myself again in the next few days. Until then, accept a standing apology from me." After glancing at her alarm clock, she reached for her brief-case and took out her notebook. "I better go down to the phone. It's almost time to call Olympia Butterworth."

"Shall I come with you?" Holte asked, keeping up with her as she went to the stairs.

"If you like."

He floated down beside her. "You didn't close the door at the top of the stairs."

"No; Maestro is having his first day out in the house. Monday he'll be allowed outside, weather permitting. He's probably in the kitchen, or looking for phantom mice in the pantry." Abruptly she turned to him. "Are there phantom mice?"

"Not that I'm aware of," he said, trying not to laugh.

"And a good thing too," said Poppy.

"What does the staff think of having a cat about?" Holte asked as Poppy resumed her descent.

"As far as I know, they don't mind."

"Do you know what Maestro thinks of the staff?" he said, to amuse her.

She chuckled. "I'm sure he'll let me know when it suits him."

"I hope they will all get along," said Holte, and slid up toward the ceiling while Poppy sat down in the telephone alcove off the entry-hall. Holte made himself comfortable away from the lights.

She gave the operator the Butterworths' phone number from memory and listened to the rings on the far end; after six of them, she was about to hang up when she heard Trodling say, "Butterworth residence: to whom would you like to speak?"

"To Missus Butterworth, please. This is Poppea Thornton, calling as she asked." It was a bit of an exaggeration, since Poppy was fairly certain that Olympia Butterworth did not want to speak to the press at all.

"Of course, Miss Thornton. I'll bring her to the telephone. Please hang on for a few minutes." The butler's genial tone was not what Poppy was expecting, and she realized that she might have misread the cool request that had prompted her to call. She used the time waiting for Missus Butterworth to arrive to review all that the article in the *Tattler* had revealed, and to put her questions into a less emphatic tone. She had got to her fourth question and was rewording it when she heard someone pick up the receiver.

"Miss Thornton?" The sound of Missus Butterworth's voice jarred Poppy out of her ruminations.

"Missus Butterworth, yes, this is Poppea Thornton. You wanted me to phone you at three."

"Yes. I'm sorry I was unable to speak with you earlier; I had luncheon guests and could not leave them to take your questions; you know how such occasions are." She clicked her tongue. "I could not have spared more than ten minutes to you. And I am sure you must have questions." This last was a bit more pointed than her explanation was.

"I do, and I'm afraid I may be the first of many wanting to speak with you."

"No doubt," Missus Butterworth said drily. "But you're Josephine Dritchner's niece, and you know to keep the line. I must tell you at first that I am not at all persuaded that GAD has any formal agreement with my daughter no matter what the story in that dreadful rag had to say. I'm afraid that Merrinelle is a very impulsive girl, with a romantic disposition, and nothing would please her more than to be the heroine in Romeo and Juliet, but with a happier ending, in which she becomes the heroine and gains admiration from all involved. She has always inclined to the theatrical, and never more than now." She sighed. "I trust you will not put that observation in anything you decide to write about this unpleasant business. My daughter has a yen for attention."

The carrot and the stick, thought Poppy before she launched into her first question. "Was Merrinelle actually seeing GAD before the summer?"

"Oh, yes. He visited here a number of times. His mother and I were friends in school, and I was always glad to see GAD. I realize that Isadora believes— as many others do—that I married beneath my station when I wed Mister Butterworth, and I have never held that against her, but I do occasionally miss the friends of my youth. Meeting their children from time to time has been a great consolation." Her voice was strong, but Poppy detected a note of sadness in it. "Seeing GAD was a way for me to recall many pleasant years."

"I can only imagine what that must be like for you, Missus Butterworth," said Poppy, making two curt notes, and editing her next question in her mind. "Can you tell me when you became aware that GAD was missing?"

"Yes," said Missus Butterworth. "It was late in July—around the 27th or 28th—and Merrinelle had not received a letter in more than a week. Up to that time, he had written twice a week at least. At first, I saw nothing worrisome in this—the boy was traveling, and in such distant places that I assumed it was the fault of the post. Trains and ships and all that. Naturally, I read all his letters to Merrinelle and I can assure you that there was nothing improper in them. I told my daughter that she had no reason to worry, but Merrinelle was quite the Tragedy Jane, all full of the most minatory ideas of his fate, each more fantastic than the last. Her father and I poo-pooed her fears at first, but when mid-August came and went and there was nothing more, not even a note or a card saying that he was returning to England to take ship for home, I began to be uneasy. So long a silence is very unlike GAD. Until then, he had been punctilious in keeping Merrinelle informed of his plans, and told her about his travels in great detail. I took the liberty of sending a note to Isadora, asking if she had any news of him."

"What did she say?"

Missus Butterworth hesitated before she answered. "She did not reply to me, which I took as an indication that she was as apprehensive as I was."

Poppy scribbled down as much of all Missus Butterworth said as she could. "Was that letter, the one in July, the last communication of any kind that Merrinelle had with GAD?"

"Yes. I wasn't entirely sure at first, as you may surmise; Merrinelle is not above creating a grand scenario for herself, especially where GAD is concerned, but I'm satisfied that there were no clandestine letters between them, and that Merrinelle had not undertaken to write to him privately." She paused, as if expecting another question, then decided to explain. "Trodling brings in the mail every day, and I see every letter that comes into the house."

Poppy nodded to herself: Olympia Butterworth, like Aunt Jo, was another member of the old school when it came to raising daughters, although Poppy had to admit that with a girl as excitable as Merrinelle seemed to be, the precautions her mother had taken might have been sensible. She recalled her purpose, and said to Missus Butterworth, "I apologize; I'm taking notes so that I don't misquote you."

"A sensible precaution," Missus Butterworth approved. "So far your questions have been unexceptionable."

"Thank you," said Poppy, more out of good manners than truth. "Can you tell me what GAD said to Merrinelle in his last letter?"

Missus Butterworth thought about this briefly. "He was leaving Vienna to join a group of refugees in a kind of encampment somewhere northeast of Vienna. He mentioned the name of the place, but I can't call it to mind just now. He had hopes of doing a book about them—the Living Spectres, as they call themselves—upon his return. He was upset that there had been so little attention paid to their fate, what with the Great War and all, and he wanted the world to learn how horridly the Armenians had been treated. So many of them were killed, you see, by the Ottoman Turks, apparently because they remained faithful to their Armenian Orthodox Church, since some of the same treatment was meted out to a few Greek Orthodox as well, but not on the order of magnitude of what was done to the Armenians, almost a decade ago. Now that the Ottoman Empire is officially ending, I expected that there would be more information about the Armenians, but that has not been the case, and GAD was most distressed. The Living Spectres are in dire straits. They aren't violent people, GAD told us. Their demonstrations are orderly and silent. They seek only a place to live in safety. GAD is doing what he can to advocate for them, to bring their predicament to the attention of Europe. Merrinelle had expressed a desire to join him, to assist him in his work with the Avaikian group, but, as you may conceive, her father and I discouraged such notions at once. The poor girl sulked for days."

"That must have been a difficult time for you," said Poppy, still scribbling. "I know that girls her age can be very...fixed in their—"

"Nothing that we haven't gone through with her in the past, on a lesser scale, of course. But this was more troubling, because the long wait for her to receive GAD's next letter became disheartening for all of us, and I began to share my daughter's fear that something may have befallen GAD beyond the usual hazards of foreign travel."

"Would you be willing to tell me your impression of GAD, as a young man? Did you find him sensible, or likeable, or what?"

At this, Missus Butterworth's voice warmed. "You know him, don't you? He is charming in an odd way; a bit shy and thoughtful, not like the ramshackle young men one sees about town all too often these days. He has a pleasant manner and a good understanding about the world, in the larger sense. I'm afraid that Mister Butterworth would not agree with me on that point: he found GAD a bit too much the idealist for his taste, but he had nothing against the boy. He told GAD to his face that he was ill-prepared to shoulder the responsibilities of the Pearse fortune, and to his credit, GAD agreed with him. That improved Mister Butterworth's opinion of GAD no end. I do hope nothing has happened to him, whether or not his intentions toward Merrinelle are serious."

Still taking notes, Poppy asked, "What do you think has happened to GAD? Do you have any particular view about it?"

"On the one hand, I wish I knew, but on the other, I'm afraid of what I might learn." She cleared her throat. "I hope this lack of communication is nothing that he is directly responsible for, that he has become too isolated to be able to send letters home, but I realize it could be that much worse than anything that has ha—"

Poppy heard Missus Butterworth's voice break, and said, "I do understand, Missus Butterworth. I won't keep you; I know this has been an imposition on you, and I'm grateful that you were willing to talk to me. I hope that you hear something from GAD before more time goes by. I know his mother is deeply distressed." She cursed silently as the point of her pencil broke. At least, she told herself, it waited until now to do it. She would have to organize and type up her notes for Lowenthal in any case. She sighed. It as a small consolation for a minor annoyance, but she was glad to have it.

"You've been most respectful," said Missus Butterworth. "I'm afraid we won't have your level of courtesy from all the press in the coming days."

"Sadly, you're very likely right." said Poppy, and heard Missus Butterworth hang up without a farewell. She replaced the receiver on its hook and sat for a few minutes, her mind almost blank. Then she stood up and went to the kitchen, where she found Missus Sassoro preparing a half-dozen potatoes for boiling.

"Afternoon, Miss Poppy," said the cook, wiping her hands on the dish-towel and turning on the water in the sink. "I'm doing a small turkey—it's in the oven now—and making mashed potatoes. I always add some milk to the water—it improves the flavor, to my mind. The left-over turkey will be a nice cold supper tomorrow, with enough for the cat, when I'm off. And there's lettuce for a salad."

"I thought we'd be having left-overs tonight," said Poppy, thinking of all the bowls and platters in the refrigerator.

"Don't worry about that, Miss; there's plenty of them to go around for a few days; I don't want you to get tired of them. I'll be putting out the sweet onion relish and some of the chopped spinach tonight, as a condiment and a side-dish. Tomorrow, as I said, you're on your own." There was a minuscule hesitation. "Mister Sassoro and I will be taking our children to the flickers, after church."

"I should think that Aunt Esther and I can manage to put together a couple of sandwiches, and reheat the Lima beans in your absence." said Poppy, perplexed by the way Missus Sassoro had told her about her Sunday plans. "Can you spare a moment to make me a cup of black tea? I can put the kettle on, if you'd rather continue with supper." As she said this, she realized that she would never have made such an offer to Missus Boudon: Aunt Jo's cook would be scandalized at this suggestion, and would be deeply affronted by the implication that she could not handle all her duties in the kitchen.

"Nothing to it. I'll attend to it right now." She removed the pot from the sink, poured in milk from the glass bottle on the central table, placed the peeled potatoes in the pot of milky water and carried it to the stove where she put it down on one of the front burners, then picked up the large water kettle on the rear burner. "Just as I thought. It wants refilling." She took it to the sink, removed the lid, and turned on the cold-water tap. "It's not good for the kettle to go dry," she remarked as she carried the kettle back to the stove and put it back on the rear burner. Taking a match from the box and lighting it, she set it first to the front burner, then to the rear, standing back as each burner whooshed into a ring of small, blue flames. "There you are. I'll have a pot ready for you in ten minutes; as I recall, you prefer the Assam. Would you want anything more with that, or is tea all you'd like?"

"If you have any of your excellent pound cake left, a slice of that would be nice. I'll be in the study. I still have some work to do."

"Yes, Miss Poppy." She was about to go on to the next stage of her cooking when she snapped her fingers. "Oh, by the way, I found your cat in the pantry not half an hour ago; he was investigating a likely mouse-hole under the storage shelves. I left him to it, but I'm sure he'll come out for turkey-trimmings."

"I'd say that's a safe bet," said Poppy, and excused herself.

In the study, she sat down at the writing table and paused to sharpen her pencil with the rotary sharpener attached to it, then she took the cover off the Remington typewriter she had purchased the week before she had moved. She had to admit that she missed Aunt Jo's Smith, but there was no doubt that the Remington had crisper action and a lighter carriage-return, and she knew that, in time, she would become accustomed to her new machine. She looked at the wall-clock, reminding herself that Loring would be stopping by later, and that she should phone him to be certain that was still his plan. Satisfied that her schedule was set, she opened her notebook on the left side of the typewriter, took up a sheet of standard bond, a sheet of carbon paper, and a sheet of onion-skin, stacked them together, inserted them in the platen, and began to type. She was well into her notes when Missus Sassoro came in with a mug of tea and a slice of pound cake on a dessert plate. Poppy nodded her thanks but kept on typing, and her aunt's cook, used to this kind of concentration from Esther, left Poppy to her tasks.

TWENTY-ONE

It was eight-thirty by the time Loring arrived; he looked harried as he came into the entry-hall to Poppy's welcome, his eyes had that ancient appearance they had had when they had first met at the Moncriefs' house the day that Madison's body had been discovered; his tie was loose, his hair fell over his brow, and his jaw was showing a stubble-shadow.

"I'm glad you're here at last. If you'll go into the sitting room?" Poppy said, gesturing to the right of the entry-hall. "I'll have Missus Sassoro bring in something to drink—coffee, if you'd like, or there's still some stronger fare available after last night. She's staying until nine tonight."

"That would be one way of destroying evidence that you're breaking the law, making me an accessory after the fact. Not that I mind." He chuckled. "Where is your aunt, by the way? I'd like to thank her for her hospitality."

"She's out in the garden," said Poppy. "She and Galliard have done some planting today, and she wants to have a last look at the three young birches they put in this afternoon. She went out with a flashlight about half an hour ago. I'm sure she'll be back in before you leave."

"What about your housekeeper? Or isn't she on door-duty tonight?"

"Miss Roth is having dinner with her sister and her family tonight. We don't expect her until after ten." She smiled as she opened the pocket-doors leading into the sitting room. "Sit any place you want."

"I like that wing-back chair," he said, and went to it.

"Make yourself comfortable. I'll be back in just a moment; I want to tell Missus Sassoro what you'd like, but you haven't actually told me."

"Nothing much for me." He thought for a second or two, then said, "Maybe a cup of coffee and a little of that very good rum I had last night."

"I'll let her know about the coffee, and see if she can come up with a little something solid as well." Poppy went off to the kitchen to tell Missus Sassoro what Loring wanted, and added that she would like some hot chocolate; the night had turned chilly, and hot chocolate seemed the right way to keep warm. "Are there any of those marvelous tartlets left over from last night? Would you include them, along with the coffee and hot chocolate, please?"

"Right away, Miss Poppy," Missus Sassoro promised. "Just so you know, I've got some fruit pastries in the cooler that will do for your breakfast tomorrow, and you can choose among the left-overs for your dinner. My husband will be by to pick me up in twenty minutes; he doesn't like to be kept waiting, so I won't linger to bring the tray back to the kitchen when you're through with it."

"I think we can manage it. Have a pleasant Sunday," Poppy told her, and went back to the sitting room, saying as she sat down again, "I thought you must have dined by now, so I didn't ask for anything too substantial."

"You mean, to sop up the booze?"

"And to be hospitable." Poppy sat down on the settee that was at right angles to the wing- back chair.

The light in the floor-lamp flickered twice.

"Another light-bulb problem?" Loring asked.

"It's probably due to the weather," said Poppy mendaciously. "It's supposed to rain tonight."

"So I've heard, but you know how unreliable weather reports can be," Loring said, and shifted his place in the chair so that he was able to face her. "I understand that you talked to Missus Butterworth today."

"Yes, I did," said Poppy, settling down to business.

"How did that go?" He pinched the bridge of his nose, a sure sign of fatigue for him.

"Well enough, all things considered," said Poppy. "She seemed candid to me, and though she didn't have much to contribute to the hunt for GAD, she helped clarify a little about her daughter's relationship with him, as she understands it."

"That must have been informative. I'm supposed to have a talk with Miss Merrinelle Butterworth tomorrow. Eleven a.m. at the Butterworth's house. Any suggestions?"

"About Missus Butterworth or her daughter?" Poppy asked.

"Both, if you can. I'm still a little uncertain as to why they asked me to come tomorrow." He studied her face while she summoned up a response.

"You mean on a Sunday?" Poppy marveled. "I wouldn't have thought... They must be extremely worried. All the attention that Merrinelle's getting isn't any more welcome to the Butterworths than it is to the Pearses." Either that, she thought, or the Butterworths were hoping to lessen their daughter's histrionics.

"I gather the family is expecting that the press will not be out in force until Monday," said Loring. "That, and they want to be able to say that the police are officially involved. Mister Pearse told me that he doesn't want the Federal Bureau of Investigation brought into this—he thinks they're too greedy for publicity, and is afraid that might endanger GAD, if he has been kidnapped and hasn't instead gotten in deeper with the Living Spectres, which is what Mister Pearse believes is the case. He authorized me to expand my inquiries to Europe, and I hope to give him some news on that front come Monday or Tuesday." He coughed once, diplomatically. "I've sent a telegram to that investigator in London you told me about: Blessing. I hope to hear back from him shortly. If he'll take on the search, I think it might be possible to keep this under wraps a little while longer. I know that would be a welcome change to the Pearses, and the Butterworths, as well."

"What about the *Tattler*?" Poppy asked.

"Well it is the *Old Colonial Tattler*, isn't it?" he asked, using the paper's full name. "Nobody takes anything in it too seriously, particularly if it is from an excitable young lady like Merrinelle Butterworth. They ran the story on page four, didn't they? And not on the front page, above the fold." He shook his head. "You see? I've learned that from you." He did a partial smile. "I think both families will be able to ride it out, especially if Isadora Pearse doesn't get the bit in her teeth. I don't know if she can restrain herself—she's distraught, and no wonder, but it wouldn't be wise for her to dignify Merrinelle's melodramatic performance."

"Does she really still want to tell the world about her fears for her son? Do you think she'll insist on responding to the *Tattler* piece? I trust she has better sense. The last thing that's needed now is a press carnival." Poppy had to resist the urge to take notes, all the while aware that Isadora Pearse had been willing for weeks to tell anyone who would listen about her fears for GAD. "I'll be talking to her on Monday morning," she added, and heard the garden-door open and shut, followed by the tramp of mucking-boots. "Aunt Esther's back inside."

"Is she going to join us?" Loring asked.

"That's up to her. She doesn't think that I need a chaperone at my advanced age, and you a policeman, at that, but she may want to say hello."

"I'd like to see her again," said Loring.

Poppy wondered what Holte was making of all this—so different from Aunt Jo's house—and decided to ask him later; she returned to the matter of the Pearses. "Are you expecting to have to talk Missus Pearse out of countering what Merrinelle Butterworth told the *Tattler*?"

"No; I assume her husband will do that. It is, as you point out, in their best interests to have as little flame in this particular fire as possible, and I hope Missus Pearse knows it, which means downplaying the story, not screaming it in headlines. Miss Butterworth's interview is going to end up ignored, unless the Pearses make a cause out of it. Then there'll be problems, and the FBI will try to horn in on what we're doing. As much as they like the spotlight, in this kind of case, it tends to muddy the waters." Thinking aloud, Loring stood up and took a turn about the room. "I know the government in Washington wants to keep a closer watch on foreigners in the country, in case they're spying, or up to no good in some other way, but I think they should tell the FBI to leave police-work to the police. Besides, GAD is somewhere in Europe, and the FBI can't operate outside of the United States."

"Then you're anticipating a territorial dispute with them?" It was more than a guess, and Poppy was not astounded by Loring's answer.

"If they get wind of it, you bet I am. That's one of the reasons I wired that Blessing fellow. He can go where the FBI cannot, and it would give the Pearses' a good reason to decline their aid, if they offer it." Stopping next to the glass-fronted bookcase, he scanned the titles on the spines of the volumes inside. "Your aunt has very eclectic tastes, doesn't she?"

"Yes, she does," said Poppy.

"Have you read any of these?" He sounded genuinely curious.

"Not these specifically, but I have a couple of selections from her library up in my room. One is on the new discoveries in Egypt; another is on the history of the Silk Road in Asia. She's been along a stretch of it herself, you know."

"No, I didn't, but I'm not surprised to hear it," he admitted. "Quite an intrepid woman, from what Doctor Wickman told me last night. I did enjoy meeting him. It's unfortunate that he had to leave early; he's a great source of information, and he thinks so clearly. I was very much impressed. He told me that he thought your aunt should be a member of the Explorers Club, but that they—"

"—wouldn't hear of it," she finished for him. "I agree with Doctor Wickman."

Missus Sassoro appeared in the doorway, with a large tray in her hands. There were two mugs and a large cup on it, along with three plates of various flavors of fruit tarts, a large pot of coffee, and a smaller one of chocolate, along with three forks, three spoons, and three napkins. She put it down on the coffee table in front of the love-seat, saying as she did. "Miss Thornton will be with you shortly. She is in her room, changing out of her boots and trousers; she doesn't want to track mud all over the place." She studied the contents of the tray, making sure it was all correct. "There's sugar in the breakfast-nook, and cream in the refrigerator, if you should need it, or I can bring it in now. "

"Thank you, if you would please," said Loring. "I didn't think I was hungry, but this is changing my mind."

"It will be good to see Aunt Esther as soon as she's ready," said Poppy. "Thank you for this, Missus Sassoro. I'll take the tray back to the kitchen before I go up to bed."

Missus Sassoro nodded. "Incidentally, your cat is in the kitchen, having his dinner, so don't let him tell you that he hasn't eaten later on. I'll see you on Monday morning, Miss Poppy."

"Have a pleasant Sunday, Missus Sassoro." Poppy glanced toward the kitchen. "Could you leave the kitchen door ajar, so Maestro can roam, if he wants to?"

"I will," said Missus Sassoro in approving tones; with a duck of her head, she departed.

As soon as she was out of earshot, Loring said, "She's an excellent cook, if last night was any example of her talents."

"She is," Poppy agreed. "Her husband is a lucky man; I hope he knows it."

Loring lifted one brow. "Is there any reason to think he doesn't?"

"Not really, but I've gotten the feeling that there is some tension between them, you know how you do, from time to time?" Poppy shrugged. "I haven't been here long enough to be sure about it, but I notice a hesitation when she's mentioned him, and there's a tightness in her voice when asked about him; it's not there when she mentions her children, so I can't help but wonder if there's trouble between her and her husband. He's works at the roundhouse in the mole, directing trains to their tracks. It's dangerous work, which might explain why she sounds nervous when he comes up, but I can't help but think it's more than that. Do you understand?"

"Oh, yes. Police depend on those kinds of feelings. Sometimes they're wrong, but often they're right, and we ignore them at our peril." He came back to his chair and sat down. "Should we wait for your aunt?"

If this were Aunt Jo's house, Poppy would have said yes at once, but now she faltered. "I suppose so."

"Well, you needn't; I'm here," said Aunt Esther from the doorway; she had on a calf- length pleated skirt with a cashmere sweater over it; her shoes were low-heeled with ankle-straps. "Poppy, I nearly tripped over your dratted cat on my way down the hall. I think he may have gone to ground in my closet." She came in and held out her hand to Loring, who had risen from his chair. "Good to see you again, Inspector. I hope I find you in fine fettle."

"As fine as can be expected in my job," said Loring, getting to his feet again. "Thank you so much for that wonderful buffet last night, and the fascinating company. I enjoyed myself tremendously."

"I'm pleased to hear it," said Esther, pulling up a side-chair from its place against the wall, gesturing to Loring—who had taken a step toward her to help—to stay where he was. "Sit down, Inspector. About the party: it came off quite well for the most part, I think, aside from Jo and Isadora's little set-to. I am generally pleased. All things considered." She pursed her lips to show her reservations about the considered things. "I trust you will be willing to come again? For a less hectic event?"

"I'd be delighted," said Loring.

Poppy intercepted what she guessed was a half-smile from Loring. "Missus

Sassoro left this for us, Aunt Esther. After all you've been doing in the garden, I believe you're ready for a snack."

"And a little brandy," she said, and went over to the chest next to the glass-fronted bookcase. She opened it and took out a bottle of brandy, then glanced at Poppy. "Not all the bottles are in the pantry, or in the high-boy in the parlor. I have some here. And you, Inspector, would you like some rum?"

"Rum would be most welcome," said Loring.

"Poppy? Cognac?"

"Yes, please, Aunt Esther." She suddenly worried that she should not have changed into her slacks, since her aunt had put on a skirt, but it was too late to run upstairs now, and it would make what was beginning to be a clumsy moment even more awkward. She made up her mind to brazen it out. "How are the baby birches?"

"Secured to growing stakes and the fence. They've been watered and given fertilizer which is why I changed; I smelled like a midden." Esther brought out the appropriate bottles and then went back into the chest for glasses. "Give me half a minute and we should be ready."

"You needn't hurry on my account," said Loring.

"Nor on mine," said Poppy, as Esther emerged with glassware in hand. "We've been talking about the London investigator who may be working on finding GAD."

Esther gave a quick, approving smile. "That's the first sensible thing I've heard about GAD being missing. How very pragmatic." She was concentrating on her pouring, but remarked, rather distantly, "Your mother did a marvelous job teaching you manners, Inspector. I'm most impressed. My congratulations to her. I'd wager a fair sum that your conduct is not typical of most policemen." She gave an impish smile.

"I'd tell her if she were still alive. I've found good manners can be helpful in my work. You're right: not all my fellow-policemen agree with me." He waited for her to hand him his glass. "Thank you Miss Thornton."

"I gather you and Poppy are sharing information again, not all of it about GAD," Esther said, as she handed a glass with a fair amount of cognac in it to her niece. "I won't stay with you for very long; I have work of my own to do. But I'll admit that I'm glad you've come by, Inspector. Stay as long as it suits you to stay, and have whatever refreshment you like."

"It's your house," Poppy said, no indication of resentment in her voice. "If you want to use this room after we have our snacks, Loring and I will go elsewhere; the breakfast nook would be a good place."

"No, no," said Esther, settling into her chair, her feathers unruffled. "This is a comfortable room for guests; you stay here. I need to spend some time going through notes in my journal. I want to be prepared when I present my information on the Armenian refugees to Mister Lowenthal. He strikes me as the kind of man who cares about preparedness. My memory is holding up pretty well for my age, but I like to refresh myself on details." She lifted her glass. "To our happy futures," she said.

"Amen," said Loring.

Poppy echoed her aunt's sentiments and tasted her cognac; she saw that Loring had sipped his rum, and said, "Three spirits in one room." She meant it as nothing more than a witticism, but Loring responded promptly.

"Don't you include your invisible friend? Make it four spirits." He lifted his glass. "Whatever you are, if you're here, you're included in my toast."

"Ye gods, Loring!" Poppy exclaimed, almost dropping her glass. "I wish you wouldn't talk nonsense."

Loring gave a single laugh. "Well, I have to call it something, and you don't like guardian angel; invisible friend will have to do."

"I'm not a three-year-old, Loring," Poppy said, aggravated by his antics. "You don't have to humor me."

"What are you talking about?" Esther demanded, trying to decide whether or not to be offended by this line of talk.

"You mean you hadn't noticed?" Loring asked Esther. "Strange things happen with the lights when Poppy's around—and once in a while, they flash Morse code when she isn't around, for which I am most grateful."

"So am I," Poppy interjected, hoping to end this line of talk.

Loring did not take her hint; he continued to speak to Esther. "I don't know whether you've noticed, but she comes by information that no one but the dead should know, and has yet to tell me her source." He looked over at Poppy. "I don't mind how you get your leads, but I wish you would be more open with me."

Poppy gulped. "My source is confidential," she said.

"I understand that," said Loring. "But you can't expect me not to be curious, or to turn a blind eye to blinking lights."

"Shall you and I have a little coffee, Inspector?" Esther suggested, leaning toward the tray to pick up the coffee pot. "It goes well with rum."

"Thank you, yes, I will," he said to Esther, then turned back to Poppy. "Okay. I don't know how you do it, but I can't help notice what's going on. I thought at first it was some kind of parlor trick, but no longer. When it stopped during the summer, I decided it was over, but it's happening again." He almost looked abashed for being so direct. "I'm supposed to be observant, just as you are Poppy."

Poppy took a second sip of cognac to buy a little time to think. "I think you're making too much of it Loring. But I won't tell you not to do your job."

"You should drink your chocolate, Poppy," her aunt recommended, not wanting to get pulled into Poppy's and Loring's dispute. "It's getting cold."

"You don't need to provide interference for me Aunt Esther," Poppy said, even while she dutifully reached for the smaller pot.

"I'm not doing that, I am trying to create a genial atmosphere for our snacks. You may resume your altercation once I've gone to my room, but for now, I'd like it if you would call a halt to your disagreements."

"Thank you Aunt Esther." Glad of this reprieve in spite of herself, Poppy poured out hot chocolate into the big cup, the set the smaller pot on the tray. "What a good idea; it is getting chilly in here."

"All right," said Loring, "I'll table this for now, but bear in mind that I'm alert to what goes on around you." His smile was warm, and his eyes hovered on her while she lifted up her cup of rich chocolate.

"Tartlet?" Esther offered, holding out a plate of them to Loring. "The darker ones are blueberry, the lighter are quince. The orange ones are apricot."

"Thank you Miss Thornton," he said, and took one off the plate and bit it in half, saying around the pastry, "This is excellent."

"I should hope so," said Esther with feeling.

Poppy moved her glass of cognac a little farther out on the edge of the table in order to have more room for her cup; the seductive aroma of the tartlets carried a warmth of their own to her, or that was how Poppy accounted for the flush that spread over her face. "How much more do we have to go over Loring?"

He accepted this return to business without any show of discomfort. "I have a couple of questions about Eastley, and I'd like your advice on how to handle the press, now that the GAD investigation is coming out in the open."

"I'll do what I can; and—" She stopped as she heard Holte whisper, "I'll try to be more careful around him."

"And what?" Loring prompted.

Poppy gave herself a little shake. "And I hope it all goes the way you want." She had a first sip of her tea and was pleased to find it warm enough but not too hot.

"Thank you," said Loring, then slyly added, "But I'd like to know what you were really going to tell me."

"For heaven's sake, you two," Esther said in exasperation as she poured her brandy into her coffee. "Let it go for now. Enjoy the drink and fodder; leave the fencing for later." She selected a quince tartlet and bit into it. "Have some more of these. I don't want them going to waste."

Loring gave Esther a sheepish look. "You're right, Miss Thornton. I'm sorry." He held up one hand. "Truce."

"Fine with me," Poppy chimed in.

"Then have something to eat," Esther enjoined them triumphantly. "You can wrangle later."

Obediently, Poppy selected an apricot tartlet, and, having finished his first, Loring chose a second, and began to eat.

"There, you see? Much more pleasant." Esther drank a little of her brandy-laced coffee and smiled at her companions, satisfied with her peace-making.

TWENTY-TWO

WHAT HAD BEEN DRIZZLE ON SATURDAY TURNED TO SERIOUS RAIN ON SUNDAY. AS the day went on, the wind rose, relentlessly spattering drops against the windows of Esther's house and lashing away at the three new birches in the back garden. Esther herself had gone with Judge Stephanson to an early afternoon concert featuring a small chamber orchestra playing Baroque music —"Including, ironically enough," she told Poppy over their improvised breakfast, "Handel's *Water* Music"—and would not return until she had had dinner with him. "Heat up as much of anything left over that you like, and help yourself to the remaining wine and spirits. I doubt I'll be in much before nine."

Although she had not made any plans to go out on this day, Poppy found herself pacing the halls like a caged animal, unable to light anywhere and concentrate. On her third circuit of the ground floor, she noticed a shimmer in the air in front of the study. She stopped and stared at the elongated oval of shine, shrugged her shoulders, and stepped into the study, closing the door behind her. "What is it?" she asked of the air.

"I'll be going into the dimension of ghosts this evening. Is there anything you would like me to ask about? Anyone you want me to talk to?" He became a bit more defined.

"If you can find out if there is anything suspicious about Eastley's death, I'd like to know about it. If it was just a foolish accident, then I won't waste my time on it." She thought a moment. "I'd also like to know anything you can find out about what Knott is up to these days."

"All right, but why Knott?" Holte asked, mildly amused at his inadvertent joke.

"Because Knott is looking for Derrington; isn't that what you've told me?"

Poppy said, thinking it the obvious response, "and he might have a lead on what has happened to Warren. It's like trying to untie a...knot, isn't it? You need to find an end to the cord, and that's what I hope Knott is. If he's located Derrington, then perhaps we can find Louise and Stacy through him."

"That's a logical trail," Holte agreed. "I'll do my best."

She sat down at the desk. "I can't ask any more than that, can I?"

Holte floated nearer to her. "Don't fret, Poppy. I can deal with Loring, if it comes to that. I'm honored that you would come to my defense, but you needn't."

"I should have realized that he would continue to try to account for how you notified him of where Stacy had confined me. He isn't going to believe ostensible explanations, is he?"

"No," said Holte, coming so near to her that the edge of the desk appeared to cut him in half just below the waist. "But don't let that worry you; he's only trying to show you how interested he is in you; it's his manner of flirting. He's not actually all that concerned about me, but he knows that something strange is going on."

"I ought to have seen that before now." She shook her head and stared at the place where there was a pale bit of air, about a foot from where she sat. "It's the weather that's getting me down, that and my Monthlies. If they hadn't come together, I wouldn't be in this horrid frame of mind."

"The rain will pass, and so will the other," Holte said. "Why not take the rest of the day off and read, or listen to the radio? Or you could raid the kitchen for high tea and pour yourself a glass of whatever you like. You're entitled to take a little time off on the day of rest."

"I guess I could do some research. Aunt Esther must have a book on the end of the Ottoman Empire somewhere in her library, where I can find out more about the Armenians." She sighed. "I hate it when I droop around like this. I should buck up."

"Not for me," said Holte. "Have a hot toddy and put your feet on a pillow. Read something that isn't connected to work," he encouraged her. "I saw a copy of The Marsden Case in the drawing room bookshelves."

"I'm not all that wild about Ford Madox Ford. But you're right, there are a number of good novels on the shelves in there. I think she's got This Side of

Paradise. I haven't picked that up yet, and I hear Fitzgerald is worth reading."
She rose from her chair. "You're right; I need to shake off these Black Dogs."

"You'll feel better, doing something pleasurable," said Holte at his most
encouraging.

"I hope you're right." She opened the door to find Maestro crouched down
to sniff at the sill. "Move, cat, I don't want to trip over you."

A low growl rumbled in Maestro's throat; he stared beyond Poppy and hissed.

Rather than reprimand him again for his bad behavior, she bent down and
picked him up. "Come along to the kitchen and I'll slice you some left-over
turkey while I make a fresh pot of coffee; I'll put a little brandy in it, as Aunt
Esther did last evening. At least I'll be doing something useful," she added to
Holte. "Maybe I'll call Hank and ask him about the *Belle Helene*. He might have
some suggestions for finding her."

Holte watched her go, keenly aware of the frustration she was experiencing.
The search for Stacy, Warren Derrington, and Louise had bogged down two
months ago, and now resolution of the mysteries that surrounded their absence
seemed likely to go on for a long time, and while the GAD case took her mind
off the more personal investigation, Poppy could not let go of it. He was willing
to do what he could do to bring the missing trio before a jury so that Poppy
would be free of it at last, but that was becoming increasingly difficult. He made
another circuit of the house, then *slipped* into the swirling, invisible dimension
of ghosts, moving through the vortexes of energy that provided the ghosts a
place to assemble.

After an indeterminate length of time in which Holte passed through
whirlpools of ghosts, he came upon Madison Moncrief, once more in the
company of Julian Eastley, riding the circulating energy around a group of
New Guinea natives who had succumbed to parasite infestations. As Holte
approached them, Moncrief was the first of the two to look about.

"*Holte? Is that you?*" Moncrief greeted him with what would have been a wave
had he possessed a body with hands to perform it. "*What brings you back here?
Don't try to fob me off. I don't believe that you're here on a lark.*"

"*No, it's not a lark; when is it ever that? How have you two been doing?*" Holte drifted
up to the two of them. "*Getting better, Eastley?*" he asked the glum presence that
was Eastley.

"I can hardly tell," Eastley replied. *"Whatever this place is, it's nothing like I thought the afterlife would be, and I'll warrant I'm not the only one here who feels that way."*

"No argument there," Holte conceded. *"As I remember it took me almost a year before I—"*

"And it takes some others far longer," Moncrief interrupted, making a non-gesture for silence in Holte's direction.

"Is this place ever going to change? Is it always like this?" Eastley complained.

"Sometimes it's less active and sometimes more, but that's about the extent of it," Holte told him. *"You may get used to it, in time."*

"How can anyone get used to...nothingness?" Eastley cried in his non-voice.

"Don't encourage him, Holte. He's been difficult enough without anyone egging him on." Moncrief drifted a short distance away. *"What is it you want this time?"*

"Have you seen Knott anywhere?" Holte asked as bluntly as he could.

"Not for a while now, I don't think. He may have stopped by, oh, a little while ago, but I can't be sure about that. Like you, he comes and goes." Moncrief did the equivalent of sighing. *"You know how it is here—no way to tell time. No sun, no moon, no hunger or thirst, no beard to shave, no weather. It all runs by in a kind of grey, misty blur. Occasionally there's an increase in activity, but it doesn't last long. I am beginning to understand how boring this place really is."*

"Boring is the word for it," Eastley seconded.

"Do you know where Knott has gone? Specifically?" Holte persisted.

"If he told me, I don't remember what he said," Moncrief said, sounding deeply fatigued.

"Nor I, but I don't know the fellow," said Eastley. *"Perhaps somewhere in the Caribbean?"*

Holte paid attention. *"What makes you say that?"*

Eastley made a hitch of his noncorporeal shoulders. *"He—Knott—said that he thought Derrington might be meeting up with Louise in Jamaica, or Cuba, or Santo Domingo, or some such place. I remembered it because he hoped to find Louise as well as Derrington. I miss Louise."*

"Yes," said Moncrief with exaggerated patience. *"I know."*

"Has he had any luck with finding any of them yet?" Holte was finding it difficult to concentrate, and began to wonder how much time had passed in worldly terms since he had entered the dimension of ghosts.

"Not that I know of," said Moncrief. *"If he comes back, I'll try to ask him, assuming*

it crosses my mind to do so."

Holte was tempted to try to learn more from Moncrief and Eastley, but understood that they were not going to be able to tell him anything useful. *"You might mention that I've been here, and I'd like to talk to him. If you remember."*

"That I will," said Moncrief, already fading back into the invisible swirl of ghosts, Eastley following after him.

Holte hung in the crowded, noisy silence and nothingness, his thoughts becoming more disordered as he wafted along the rim of the energetic vortex that had developed as the ghosts from New Guinea became more distraught; their shared anguish was increasing steadily, and Holte was being drawn in to their torment. Finally he was able to shift to a less turbulent part of the dimension of ghosts, and found himself in the company of a group of Danish sailors whose ship had gone down off Bermuda in a fierce squall.

"It was tossing ships about like matchboxes," said one of the ghosts; since there was no language, only thought, Holte had no trouble understanding him. *"Our steamer's ridden out heavy seas before, but this was a bitch of a hurricane. Never seen anything like it in all my years at sea. We might as well have been a kite without a tail or a tether. Waves rising up like mountains, pounding down on us. Pumps working like Hercules to keep the water out of the cargo holds. The hull moaning and screaming like damned souls. The storm put us on our beam- ends, and we couldn't right ourselves. Something amidship broke and down we went, cargo and all. So here we are."*

"Sorry to hear it," Holte said automatically. "When did this happen?"

"Two weeks, maybe. Or a week. I can't really tell. The storm wasn't fierce when it finally made landfall on Georgia, but for those of us out near Bermuda, it was hellish. There's another one building up, I hear, bigger than the one that took us down. Not a good time to be in the western Atlantic."

"Were there any attempts made to rescue you?" Holte inquired.

"Not that I know of, but it wasn't safe for rescuers any more than it was safe for us." He swung around in the whorl of energy that was developing nearby. *"The owners'll be out a lot of money, but that's the risk you take, with the sea."* His voice began to garble, and he quickly wafted away from Holte.

"Wait!" Holte cried voicelessly.

The ghost of the sailor stopped. *"What is it?"*

"Have you found any newcomers here off of pleasure boats—any yachts—in the hurricane

that's bearing down on Jamaica, or Cuba?"

The sailor shook his noncorporeal head. *"Not bloody likely. Nothing smaller than a steamer could ride out the hurricane we went through, and the one brewing tops it. A yacht hadn't a chance in the one that took us down, and less than that in the one that's building up. They'll be lucky if anything washes up on any shore."* He drifted to the edge of the vortex once more and was gone.

Holte hung in place, his thoughts racing. If the *Belle Helene* had been caught in the storm, that could mean that Miles Overstreet was now among the ghosts. He moved more quickly through the dim masses, hoping against hope that he could locate Overstreet among all the others. Finally, after an incalculably long hunt, he came upon Overstreet, floating confusedly in the agitation around him as other victims of the hurricane arrived in the dimension of ghosts. Holte moved nearer to him, and hung just out of reach, not wanting to add to Overstreet's apparent perturbation.

"WhereamIwhereamIwhereamIwhereamI," he was muttering, so disoriented that he could not negotiate the streams and eddies that made up the dimension of ghosts.

"Overstreet!" Holte cried out.

"WhereamIwhereamIwhe—" He stopped. *"Who are you? Where am I?"*

Holte approached him carefully, knowing how skittish the newly arrived ghost could be; Holte himself had been edgy for quite a while when he had first entered the dimension of ghosts. *"You're Miles Overstreet, assistant to Percy Knott,"* he said again, more calmly. *"You don't know me. I'm Chesterton Holte. I'm Canadian. I died in 1916, in Belgium. German soldiers shot me, and I ended up here."*

Overstreet spiraled—not a good sign in new ghosts—and struggled to order his thoughts. *"Where am I?"*

"I'll get to that in a moment," said Holte. *"Can you tell me the last thing you remember, before you—"*

"I was on the deck of a yacht. The Belle Helene.*"* Now that he was talking, he could not seem to stop. *"Nice boat. Nelson Hadley keeps it in Cuba, at his family's vacation home, for the most part...It's registered somewhere in Massachusetts...I think that's what he told me...He told me that he likes to do the Bermuda run...when we were coming south from Canada...going along with the coast just over the horizon...We were making good time, they said...the boat was heeled over and the sails were humming...I was told it was*

a fast boat, and Nelson likes to push it...when he's bringing in booze...and other things... Quentin arranges those....Nelson told me...He's Quentin's cousin...I think he told me...They work together....Nelson said...He and Quentin bring in...goods. They like sailing together... What was I saying?...Oh, yes. It was a lovely day, all brisk and warm...the seas were running a little high...enough of a swell to worry Quentin...But it was Nelson who was at the helm... There were dolphins swimming along beside us, and...Quentin Hadley was bringing me a drink..." He began to fade, turning in a tightening circle. *"I think that's...what it was..."*

"Do you remember a hurricane at all?" Holte said with urgency, wanting to keep Overstreet focused for a little while longer.

"A hurricane?....No. Nothing like that. Clear skies and a steady breeze...I...fell down just after Hadley reached me...it was the damnedest thing...One moment I was standing up, the next...I was on the deck...I can remember watching the deck turn red...Then I was here." He went quiet once more. *"Where am I? What happened to the boat? Where is Quentin Hadley? Where am I? Where am I? WhereamI, whereamI, whereamI—"*

"You're in the dimension of ghosts. You died, Overstreet." And, Holte added to himself, not because of a storm; there was something else that happened, and it was not an accident, not with the deck running red.

"Died?" he echoed, as if he did not understand the word.

"I'm afraid so," said Holte, sliding a little nearer to Overstreet. *"I'd guess that Quentin shot or stabbed you."*

"Can't be...that's ridiculous...Why would anyone kill me?" Overstreet muttered. *"I'm supposed to meet Warren Derrington...in Havana...tomorrow. We have an...appointment. It's arranged...Quentin wired him...in Cuba, or Jamaica...Somewhere in one of those places... He's expecting me...I have to be there."*

"You won't be able to, not now," Holte said by way of consolation.

"Why not? Where am I?" He shuddered, twisted, and blew away on the force of the churning ghosts around him.

Holte waited a short while to see if Overstreet would return, then *slipped* back into the world of the living, into the London, Museum Street office of N. N. Blessing. He kept to the far side of the inner room, marveling at the stacks of files piled on top of every surface; it reminded him of the stratigraphy of rocks. There was a light set atop the roll-top of the desk, now on to dispel the gloom of a foggy morning; Blessing himself was busy rummaging through a stack of loose papers spread out on his desk-blotter, muttering to himself. After waiting a few minutes, Holte manifested himself a bit more clearly and moved toward Blessing.

"N.Cubed," he said, and saw Blessing start; as he glanced up, Holte noticed that Blessing looked very much the way Holte remembered him: fairly average in height and build, his red- brown hair a bit greyer, his features a little more deeply hewn so that his aquiline nose seemed to stand out from his face more sharply than had been the case two years ago; his manner was still professorial and self-contained. He was wearing a tweed jacket over a navy-blue roll-top pullover, his slacks were a muted brown, and his Jodhpur boots were polished and buffed. Anywhere but this office, he might be mistaken for a country squire, but here he was plainly an investigator.

"You!" Blessing exclaimed, and let the papers fall where they might. "What the devil are you doing here, Holte? When you left, I thought we'd settled things. Was I mistaken, or did you not tell me that we'd completed the balancing?" He put on his glasses and squinted at the filmy shape on the other side of his roll-top desk.

Holte had risen about two feet into the air to be more easily seen over the desk, and said, "Yes, our business is settled, and I appreciate how handily you dealt with my help. But I have other books to balance, and it may be that you could help me with one of them. I'm afraid it's a bit complicated."

Blessing very nearly laughed at that. "When isn't it complicated with you?" He sat back in his chair. "All right. Tell me what this is about."

"A case: I'd like to think that this will interest you. It will be useful to many, if you do." He did not wait for Blessing to respond, but went on, "You had a wire a few days ago from an American police inspector."

"Yes," said Blessing, fully regaining his self-composure. "From Philadelphia. Lothian, Lawton, some name of that sort."

"That's the one; it's Loring, by the way," Holte confirmed, his manifestation growing a bit more visible. "I wonder if you would do me the favor of accepting the case? It's likely to mean a trip to Europe, around Vienna, from what limited information we have. If you don't want to go there yourself, you surely have colleagues there who could do the footwork for you. The case may be connected to the Living Spectres group near Vienna."

"Armenians, aren't they?" Blessing asked.

"Refugees," Holte confirmed.

"I imagine that it's connected to one of your book-balancing activities?" Blessing inquired, now that he had a chance to get a question in.

"Yes. Not anyone directly part of the problem, but one for whom it would be an advantage if the case can be resolved, one way or another, and discreetly." Holte paused, studying Blessing to try to assess how he was taking all this. "There is a good fee in this case, the family involved is wealthy."

"Nice of you to mention that, old boy," said Blessing with a touch of irony. "Not that it matters to you."

"Tell me if you're willing to do it, or if I shall have to look elsewhere. I'd much prefer you to an unknown." Holte's voice was steady and he made no attempt to press Blessing beyond what he had done already. "It concerns a missing young man, an American, last heard from over a month ago, from Vienna, who is——"

"Don't fret, Holte. I'll wire Inspector Loring before I go home tonight; how's that?" He gave a one-sided smile and made a note to himself on the back of an envelope lying beside his desk blotter. "And if there is traveling to be done, I'll do it myself. I can accomplish more without having to deal with my usual agents—those who are still in the business—and I haven't been into Eastern Europe in over a year. It'll be good for me."

"I'm most appreciative," said Holte.

Blessing set his pencil aside, then asked, "Anything else I can do for you?"

"As a matter of fact, there is," said Holte, and almost vanished with chagrin. "Will you tell me what day and date it is?"

This time Blessing actually laughed. "It's Tuesday, September 16th, 1924. Not quite ten a.m. Why: did you lose track of time again?"

"Fortunately, not as much as I thought I might have done," said Holte, and moved nearer to the ceiling.

"Is that it?" Blessing asked as Holte continued to fade.

"Yes. Thanks."

"Will you be back?" Blessing raised his voice to be heard.

"I don't know; it's possible; it depends on how this case turns out," Holte answered, his voice hardly more than a whisper as he went through the ceiling and out through the floor above. He moved away, using the speed of ghosts to race ahead of the day into the garden at the back of Esther's house. It was still raining, and dawn was still an hour or more away. He rose up the side of the house and slid into Poppy's room, where he was greeted by Maestro's hiss. "Hello, cat," said Holte, and glanced at Poppy's alarm clock: 5:48, a little less than an hour before she would be waking up. Holte floated up to the ceiling and gave himself over to thinking about all he had learned. Why had Quentin Hadley killed Miles Overstreet? For surely that was what had happened. Did Hadley rescue Overstreet only to kill him? Why go to the bother? Overstreet could have been left to drown in Montreal, so there must have been a reason why Hadley had saved him and then killed him? Had killing Overstreet been an alternate solution to whatever Hadley had in mind? Was Overstreet in possession of something, some information that Hadley needed, and if so, what was it? Had Derrington been in on the murder, or was he a potential victim? And was Derrington in Cuba now? Or Jamaica? If he wasn't there, where had he gone? How long had he been there? Had anyone been with him, such as Stacy or Louise? Was Derrington still there—in Cuba or Jamaica—or was he somewhere else? If he had been in Cuba, was he there or was he gone? How badly had the hurricane damaged Cuba, or had it struck there at all? Was Stacy or Louise in on any of this? And if they were, to what extent? He continued to turn these questions over in his mind, waiting for Poppy to wake up.

TWENTY-THREE

WHEN THE ALARM CLOCK JANGLED ITS UNMUSICAL BELLS POPPY REACHED FOR the toggle and turned it off, then lay back, not wholly awake. After five minutes or so, she shoved herself into a sitting position and rubbed her eyes, peering about the half-lit room. She yawned, looked toward the foot of the bed where Maestro was curled, but awake. "Hello, Maestro," she said, and stretched. "It's awfully early for getting up." As if to demonstrate this, she reached for her alarm clock and began to wind it.

"But it's part of the job," said Holte from his place on the far side of the room. "Or so you tell me."

She put the clock back on her night-stand and stared in his direction. "How good to see you again. I thought you had gone for the week when I didn't encounter you yesterday."

"I had some arrangements to attend to," he told her. "I wanted to get them in progress as early as possible."

"How did they go?" she asked, as she slid her feet into her slippers and stood up, yawning again with the effort.

Maestro yowled once and hissed in Holte's direction.

"Same to you, cat," he rejoined as Maestro went under the bed, then Holte drifted across the room toward Poppy's vanity table. "In general, it went well. Not that I found out everything I was hoping to, but I have some information to pass on to you that you might want to tell Loring about, assuming that you can find a way to explain how you came by it."

"Ye gods, that sounds sinister," she said, not wholly in jest.

"First, Miles Overstreet is dead. I'm fairly certain that Quentin Hadley killed him while he was on Hadley's cousin's yacht, the *Belle Helene*."

Poppy turned and stared at him. "What did you say?" She could not believe that she had heard him correctly.

"I thought that might catch your attention," Holte said. "Overstreet was taken aboard the *Belle Helene* after he had jumped—"

"—from the bridge. Yes, I know. But you're telling me that Quentin Hadley was on board the *Belle Helene?*"

"Yes. Apparently it's Quentin's cousin Nelson's boat. I haven't got many details, but I gather the boat's home is at the Hadley estate in Cuba, and it's registered somewhere in Massachusetts. Another apparently: Nelson brings booze to the U. S. in it from time to time, and maybe some other smuggled items. That's for starters. I'll tell you more when you're done dressing." Holte stayed in the bedroom while Poppy went across the hall. He spent the waiting time looking out the window into the cloudy early morning.

Maestro returned from under the bed and took up his usual place at its foot; he pointedly ignored Holte.

Poppy returned, frowning. "You know this because of...?"

"Because Overstreet told me. He's still trying to work through the shock of being dead, so he was a bit scattered in his reporting, but he told me that he was on the boat with Nelson and Quentin somewhere out east of the Carolinas, by my calculations, when, I infer, Quentin killed him, and, I would guess, threw him to the sharks."

"Ye gods," Poppy murmured, horrified. "And you believe him?"

Maestro jumped down from the bed, turned his back on Holte, flipped his upright tail twice, and bolted from the room and down the stairs.

"I do." Holte became slightly more visible. "He can't remember many of the details, which in ghosts is not unusual. It's going to take some time for him to recall the final events, the same way that Eastley can't yet remember driving off the road and into a ravine. From what I was able to ascertain from Overstreet—which wasn't much—he had not anticipated any trouble with the Hadleys, and he accepted their offer to save him without any hint that there could be trouble. I've deduced that Overstreet assumed that they did it because it would be to their advantage, keeping him under their thumbs, as it were, and so he never had reason to doubt their motives; whatever was going on with them, they were in it together, which must have been why Overstreet was glad of the rescue.

He's a little scattered in his mind about the actual events, but logically there is no other way to account for Overstreet's death. I gather Overstreet knew something that could be damaging to the Hadleys—I hope he can remember what it was—and that was reassuring to him. By the sound of it, Overstreet believed that he had no reason to suppose that he would be disposed of in that way. I very much doubt that he thought his rescue was a trap, even when it was closing on him."

"But what would Overstreet be doing with the Hadleys?"

"Overstreet's handled business for Knott, including his business with the Hadleys; they'd worked out some kind of Customs fiddle together, would be my guess, and I reckon that Knott was part of the arrangement. It probably has something to do with the counterfeit antiques business that your old neighbor Denton North is investigating," said Holte. "Which would tie Overstreet to Stacy's and Derrington's business. Quite a cozy little club. They've been able to work invisibly for some time, though that may be ending. I'm beginning to think that we've underestimated the extent of their activities, and I'm convinced that Hadley and Grimes are in it up to their necks. Or some other part of their anatomy."

Poppy tossed her head. "Don't be cheeky," she admonished him.

"I'm not. From what little I could glean from what Overstreet told me, he was expecting to join up with Derrington in Cuba, or Jamaica; what Overstreet thought would happen after that, I have no idea, but it does mean that we have a place we can begin looking." Holte shifted toward the side-windows, and became a transparent outline against the increasing morning light. "Why would he think that his employer's accountants would go to the trouble of spiriting him out of Canada only to...um...do him in en route to Cuba? All I've come up with is that there was something the Hadleys, or Derrington, wanted to get from Overstreet before they killed him, otherwise, why bother?"

"It does sound unlikely." Poppy sighed. "Just when I thought this was getting simpler, it's getting more complicated. Are we ever going to be able to figure out for sure who killed Moncrief and Knott, and perhaps even Poindexter?" She looked at her alarm clock. "Ten to seven. Where does the time go?" With that, she stood up. "I'm going to take a short bath and then go down to breakfast. I want to be out of here by seven-thirty, and that means I'd like you to give me a little privacy."

"I understand. I'll make a circuit of the house while you're in the tub, and then I'll ride with you in your auto as far as the paper. We can talk more then." He moved up and out, into the soggy fingers of dawn.

Poppy took a moment to gather her thoughts and her bathrobe, then went across the hall to the bathroom. She no longer fed Maestro there, although there was a bowl of water set out for him. She called Maestro softly and heard a sound of pots in the kitchen; apparently Maestro had gone to plead with Missus Sassoro for his breakfast. Leaving the door open, Poppy undressed and hung her nightgown under her bathrobe on the hook on the back of the door. She shivered in the cold air, and thought about buying a heater for the bathroom.

As she filled the tub with water, she took the time to take out her Lyons Dental Powder and brush her teeth, standing nude over the sink, goose-flesh rising on her exposed skin. The dentifrice container was getting low, and she thought she should stop by a drug store to pick up another on her way home. Then she made sure her Pears soap was in the soap-dish and got into the bathtub, her washcloth in her hand. She lay back in the steamy water and wished briefly that she could luxuriate in the warmth for an hour or so, but abandoned that hope, sat up and lathered her washcloth, reminding herself that this was going to be another busy day: Missus Pearse had postponed their interview one day, and she would have to be underway to their house no later than nine-thirty.

Twenty minutes later she was dressed and in the breakfast-nook, devouring the waffles Missus Sassoro had made; this was a rare treat, and Poppy was glad to have such an unexpected delicacy on a day that threatened to be more demanding that usual: since the Pearses had granted Poppy an interview a day later than planned, Lowenthal was all but salivating at the prospect. Poppy was bothered by the feeling that Pearses might cancel again, and would continue such delaying tactics until they were in a better position to manage what was said in the paper. But since other papers had picked up on the story, something had to be done. Thus far, only Poppy had been invited to speak with them, a concession that might change at any moment; this anxiety stayed with her through her dressing and her venture into the kitchen. She had drunk her coffee and was just eating the last bit of waffle with maple syrup and whipped cream when Aunt Esther came into the breakfast-nook in a skirt and sweater and sat down.

"You're in a hurry, aren't you?" she asked, noticing how quickly Poppy gulped down the last of her coffee.

"Sorry, Aunt Esther. Lowenthal wants me in before eight. He's not going to let the opportunity to get the Pearses' story slip through his fingers." Poppy did her best to smile. "I suppose you'll still be seeing him at one. I should be back from the interview by then, and I hope we can have a little time to talk when you're through."

"I'd like that," said Esther. "I'm sorry; I was up half the night with a sore ankle. I think I might have strained it during the planting. I came down rather hard while Galliard and I were putting the last of the birches into their hole. Galliard said that at my age, I have no business doing such strenuous work. Have you ever heard anything so absurd in your life?"

"Do you think you should see the doctor?" Poppy asked, her concern cutting through all other considerations.

Aunt Esther sniffed in disapproval. "You're as bad as Galliard is."

But Poppy would not be put off. "If you need some time to recover, I know Lowenthal will postpone your meeting if you have a medical emergency." She regarded her aunt with a suggestion of worry, but knew better than to urge her.

"No. It's not that bad. Not only did I twist it planting the birches, I slipped while carrying a flat of winter vegetables into the green-house, for the raised beds there, and its southern exposure; the walkway stones were wet and I wasn't paying attention." She rubbed her eyes. "Galliard took over for me. We'll have cabbages and onions and Swedish potatoes from December to the end of March."

"When you'll be in the Amazonian jungle," Poppy pointed out. "If your ankle can hold out until you have to leave."

"Nothing to worry about." Esther reassured her niece. "Galliard will look after the plants and will see that Missus Sassoro has the produce when it's ready."

"Good of him," said Poppy automatically. After a large sip of coffee, she added, "If you change your mind about seeing your doctor, make sure you call Miss Stotter at the *Clarion*. She's Lowenthal's secretary, and a very reliable women."

"Miss Stotter. I'll remember, but I won't need it," said Esther, and raised her voice. "Missus Sassoro, I'll have four waffles instead of two. I find I'm hungry this morning."

"Whatever suits you," Missus Sassoro answered at her most unflappable. "Your coffee is almost ready."

Poppy set down her napkin and rose from her chair. "Until sometime around one-thirty then. I hope it all goes well."

Esther smiled. "I've put together a portfolio of my photographs of the Living Spectres; if that doesn't persuade him to let me do a piece for him, I can't imagine what will. Have a good interview. Don't let Isadora wear you out."

"I'll try not to," said Poppy, and went to retrieve her purse, her brief-case, her raincoat, and her umbrella, just in case the weather forecast was right.

Miss Roth let Poppy out of the front door. "When do you expect to return?" she asked as Poppy started down the stairs.

"Six, six-thirty. If I'm going to be later, I'll phone you to let you know."

"Very good," said Miss Roth, and closed the door.

Poppy got into her Hudson and started off for the Addison Newspaper Corporation building, her concentration fixed on the road. The morning sky was hazy, but there were high clouds blowing like streamers across it; studying the western horizon, Poppy was fairly sure that the Weather Service was right about the possibility of rain by evening. As if to confirm this, a spatter of droplets struck the windshield; she toggled on the wipers and turned on her headlights. A paperboy at the corner was hawking the *Tribune*; Poppy glanced at the headline and saw nothing about the Pearse case above the fold on the front page. She allowed herself to feel a bit less harried.

"How much do you plan to tell Loring about Overstreet and Derrington?" Holte asked from the empty place on the seat beside her.

Poppy had just entered the street at the foot of Aunt Esther's long cul-de-sac, where the newspaper stand was. "Will you please announce yourself, for a change?"

"As you like. I'm here. How much do you—"

"—plan to tell Loring. I haven't made up my mind," she informed Holte. "Ask me after I do the interview with the Pearses. I should have decided by then."

"I'd like to know as soon as you do," he said.

"Very well; you can eavesdrop when I talk to him—not that I could stop you—and we can compare notes afterward," she said, edging around a delivery van pulled by four Clydesdales, their red coats as dark as mahogany, their white manes and tails a muted silver-grey in the beginning of morning mizzle. "But let me keep my mind on driving for now, if you don't mind."

Holte took a moment to think about this. "All right. It is not easy to deal with traffic in weather like this. The road looks slick, and that's a hazard. Find your parking place and I'll accompany you to your desk."

Poppy found that idea disconcerting, but she accepted it as a sensible trade for his company during the morning commute. "It should take me another fifteen minutes to get to the *Clarion*. I'll see you then."

"Fifteen minutes," he said, and hoped he would not be too far off the mark. "You'll park in the usual place? In the alley."

"Yes, if no one takes it before I get there. I won't be the only one looking for a spot this morning." She leaned on the horn to warn a Packard pulling into traffic not to cut her off from her right-hand turn. "Whatever you're going to do in the meantime, don't expose yourself to any babies or household pets. Or parrots."

"I'll do my best," he promised, and went ahead of her to the paper, trying to decide how Poppy's knowledge of Overstreet's death could be explained.

While Holte mulled over this predicament, Poppy continued on through the thickening parade of autos, trucks, delivery wagons, and bicycles; she did her best to keep her wits about her, but, being tired, the task seemed more demanding than it did on most mornings. After four blocks, she discovered the cause of the unusual slow-down: a streetcar had slammed into an old White Steamer, effectively blocking the intersection in both directions; two harried policemen in foul weather gear stood in the middle of the street, directing traffic around the mess. Poppy noticed an ambulance at the side of the opposite street, and realized that the crash had been worse than she had first supposed. She resigned herself to arriving late as she edged her way forward in the pack. When she reached the alley, her regular spot had been taken and she had to find a parking place almost a block away. Not a good omen for the day, she told herself as she hurried along the sidewalk, trying to keep her umbrella at the right angle for her to stay dry. As she crossed the alley, a Ford went by, splashing her ankles as it passed. "Ye gods," she muttered, hoping this was not another omen for the day.

Rushing into the city room, she paused at Lowenthal's office door and knocked. "Sorry, boss," she said. "There was an acci—"

"An accident on the streetcar line. Not unusual in bad weather. I've got Vance out covering it. You're not the only one late this morning." He studied her. "What have you got for me?"

"I have some questions for the Pearses ready. And I have a follow-up story on Merrinelle Butterworth; the one you told me to do yesterday when the Pearses canceled. She's a bit dramatic about her life, like something out of the flickers, so I talked to a couple of her friends, and tried to find out how they saw her claims. Would you like me to hand my notes over now?" Then, as an afterthought, she said, "I called Missus Plowright yesterday; she gave me the phone number for Rudy Beech—her half-brother—in Florida; he may know something about where Louise Moncrief is. I'm planning on trying to reach him this afternoon, assuming the lines aren't down due to Hurricane Sylvia. That's what the Weather Service is calling it."

"So the AP wire says. They expect it to be a heavy blow." He motioned her to come in and pointed to the visitor's chair. "Let me have what you've got. How soon do you need to leave for the Pearses interview?"

"Forty-five minutes, if traffic is still backed up," she told him as she sat down and opened her brief-case. "This also has my notes on my interview with Miss Butterworth, brief as it was. She didn't like the questions I asked, since they were mostly about GAD and not about her, and after a while, she became petulant. Quite discouraging. Her mother's right about her: she likes being the center of attention. She said that talking about GAD upset her—no doubt true, but that wasn't the heart of the matter." While this was direct enough as a statement, it was also a ploy to explain why her notes on her interview with Merrinelle were scant.

"Typical for a girl her age." Lowenthal took the two files she held out, opened, and skimmed them. "What's she like, other than self-centered?"

"She's pretty in a baby-faced way; about my height; short, light-brown hair;

big, cerulean eyes; more of a bust than is fashionable, which she likes males to notice. She's more intelligent than she pretends to be, and she is mesmerized by glamour. She says she wants to be in moving pictures. I don't know how that fits in with marrying GAD, but that doesn't seem to bother her." Poppy saw Lowenthal nod. "If she grows out of her penchant for dramatics, she could be a very interesting adult, but just now, that's a big if."

"I know the type," he said, handing the files back to Poppy. "You can work these up later, as you need them, once you have the Pearses' take on things." He rubbed his forehead to get the curl he had been worrying back in place.

"Yes, boss," she said, and got up.

"Your aunt will be in later," he said as Poppy made for the door. "One o'clock."

"I know," Poppy said.

"You think there's anything worthwhile in her article? Does it read right for our subscribers?" He asked as if it had just occurred to him, but Poppy was certain that he had had it in mind since she arrived at the office.

"I don't know. She didn't show what she'd written to me." Poppy studied him, trying to determine what he wanted to know. "But there may be a connection to GAD Pearse being missing. Remember, he had expressed concern about the Living Spectres in his last two letters to Merrinelle."

Lowenthal nodded once. "Maybe a sidebar, then." He pointed to the door. "Get to work. Chop-chop."

Poppy said, "Yes, boss," again, and made for her desk, noticing that about a third of the other desks were unoccupied. That accident must still be interfering with traffic, she thought as she took her place at her desk. She looked up as the ceiling light flickered, and nodded once to show she understood.

Dick Gafney, who was smoking his third cigarette of the morning, peered through his halo of fumes to catch Poppy's attention. "The Pearses and the Butterworths. Don't you move in high circles?"

"If you say so, Gafney," she answered, preparing her usual sandwich of bond, carbon, and onion-skin paper.

"You have any leads on the Pearse story? If you ask me, the boy's been kidnapped and is probably dead by now." He coughed a little.

"He may be," Poppy said, doing her best not to get upset by Gafney.

"Make the most of it, honey-girl. Since you like the crime desk. Do you want to show us how tough you are?" His laughter was cut short by the shrilling of his telephone, and he abandoned this needling of Poppy to take the call.

"He's a fool, and he's jealous," said Holte in her ear.

"I know," Poppy whispered. "But that doesn't mean I have to like what he does." And with that, she rolled her papers into the platen and began to pound the keys, taking out her annoyance on the typewriter.

TWENTY-FOUR

Elliston, the Pearses' very self-contained butler, had shown Poppy into the conservatory at the back of the Pearse mansion, a century-old structure of white-painted cast iron and glass that had recently been expanded and now not only had a fine display of mature palms and other semi- tropical plants, but had a sitting area with a service closet where water, tea, and coffee could be had, as well as other, less legal, potables.

Isadora and Sherman Pearse were waiting on the upholstered couch in the sitting area; Isadora, in a morning dress of dull-purple faille with a small ruff of lavender lace, barely acknowledged Poppy's presence. Sherman was dressed for business in a conservative, beautifully tailored suit of charcoal-grey English worsted that had been made in Saville Row; his shirt was pristine white linen, and his tie Prussian-blue silk. He rose to greet Poppy, and spoke to her as if he had not known her when she was growing up. "Thank you for coming Miss Thornton. Please join us." He pointed to one of three occasional chairs. "I apologize for the delay in seeing you; it couldn't be helped."

Tempted as she was to ask what had happened to cause that delay, Poppy held her tongue as she sat down and took her notebook from her purse, and then searched its depths for a pencil, finding it in with her ten-dollar emergency bill. "I hope you won't mind if I take notes. I've found that it helps minimize errors in reporting."

"I'd prefer you did; it saves confusion later; it's always wise to keep notes, don't you think?" Mister Pearse approved. "May I offer you some refreshment? Tea? Coffee?" Before Poppy could answer, Mister Pearse raised his voice. "Elliston, would you ask Huntsman to come out here?" He gave Poppy a self-assured look that narrowly missed being smug.

From near the door, Elliston replied, "Of course, Mister Pearse."

"It's been a long time since I've seen you, Miss Thornton, aside from the evening at your Aunt Esther's," Mister Pearse said, by way of courtesy. "You were at the gathering we hosted shortly after HOB's funeral, as I recall?"

"Yes, I was," said Poppy. "It was a sad occasion."

Mister Pearse waved his hand, dismissing that unhappy day to the past. "We're hoping to avoid another such."

"I hope you can avoid it, too," Poppy said, knowing that this reiteration was expected of her. "The loss of any child must be unendurable."

"HOB was our shining hope," said Mister Pearse. "And now we may lose our second son to adventurism. Adventurism!"

"Sherman," his wife murmured, putting her hand on his arm. "Must you? You told me you wouldn't."

"I'm afraid to say," Mister Pearse began in a tone that suggested the reverse, "that I hold your Uncle Maximilian partly responsible for this situation."

"Mister Pearse, please; this is not to the point," said his wife with a fidgety nod in Poppy's direction. "There's no reason to dwell on—"

Mister Pearse cut in ruthlessly. "If Maximilian hadn't told GAD stories about his travels, or given him that letter that President Roosevelt sent to your uncle, I've no doubt that GAD would have settled down by now, and not gone tramping across Europe, in the company of the scaff and raff of the Ottoman Empire." He sat straighter. "By the way, I don't suppose you've heard anything more about Maximilian?"

"Not in years," Poppy said, striving to keep her temper in check; she had not expected such an outburst.

"Serves him right, going off like that. If he is still alive, no doubt he has a wife with a bone in her nose and a passel of half-breed brats, unless the natives did him a favor and boiled him in a pot." Mister Pearse looked away. "I'm sorry. I'm very much on edge. We all are. But that doesn't change what your Maximilian did to turn GAD's interests to—"

"That's enough, Mister Pearse," said Missus Pearse, and turned toward Poppy. "Pardon my husband. When he is worried, he's bellicose."

"Since you and your husband are seeking to find GAD, and I am in a position to help, I would like to think we can work in concert," said Poppy in the most reasonable tone she could produce.

"Help?" Mister Pearse shook his head. "By spreading rumors and gossip about?"

"Miss Thornton is more discreet than that, Sherman," Missus Pearse said in a softly correcting voice. "She knows GAD. She won't expose him to greater danger than he is in already."

"I'm prepared to do what I can to help you on avoiding undue publicity," Poppy said, taking as professional a stance as she could. "Your interview ought to help get the ball rolling."

"GAD will be pleased to know you're helping us Miss Thornton," Missus Pearse said, paying no attention to the warning glance her husband shot her. "When he was younger, he had the most dreadful crush on you, you know."

Poppy nearly dropped her pencil, she was so taken aback. "No," she admitted a trifle unsteadily. "I didn't know."

"My dear," said Mister Pearse in a firm voice, "that has nothing to do with this meeting."

"It would, for GAD," his mother insisted.

"Shall we get on with it?" Poppy suggested, not wanting to be pulled away from the purpose of her visit.

But Mister Pearse was not to be rushed. "I understand you've been living with your Aunt Josephine Dritchner," he went on in a sudden rush of politeness. "If you would be kind enough to give her our regards?"

"I will, of course," said Poppy, adding conscientiously, "But, as I'm sure you recall, I've recently moved in with my Aunt Esther. Both my aunts thought it advisable," said Poppy, determined not to get side-tracked again from her assignment, "and I agreed."

Sherman Pearse produced a condescending smile. "Well, if you'll extend our regards to your Aunt Esther as well, we would appreciate it."

"Certainly Mister Pearse," said Poppy, wanting to upbraid him for his manner, but sticking to her mission.

Mister Pearse sat down next to his wife and took her hand; he spoke quietly yet firmly to Poppy. "I'm told you know Inspector Loring, Miss Thornton, and I must believe that you know he is working on our case, very sub rosa for now. Commissioner Smiley is in agreement that we need to keep as much of this investigation out of the public eye as is possible. Commissioner Smiley is a prudent fellow, for all that he was born in Scotland. We spent yesterday resolving particulars in that regard. Not only are we eager to protect our privacy, but we're hoping to avoid the kind of hysteria that arose around the Leopold-Loeb case, which is assuming that there has been a kidnapping, which I am not prepared to concede." He patted Missus Pearse on the shoulder as she shuddered.

"I can see why you want to do all you can to prevent that kind of publicity; it's hard enough to have your son missing—to have to dodge the press to get to the mailbox is an unnecessary burden; if I can do anything to lessen your encumbrance, I will, to the limit of my position," Poppy said, making a few cursory notes to demonstrate her earnestness. "I'll do what I can to see you're not exposed."

"I'm pleased that you do appreciate our situation; this way, you'll understand the conditions I'm going to impose upon you for this interview." His tight smile had the look of an expression he had developed since youth as a way to gain the cooperation of those he regarded as underlings. "I'm sure you understand."

"Yes, I do; I'll make note of them," said Poppy, readying her pencil.

"First, I want you to assure me that you will not speculate on any aspect of the case beyond what I tell you today."

"I agree, so long as you will permit me to use information Inspector Loring may vouchsafe me in terms of what he is undertaking; I hope that by including the police in my report, it will be clear that the investigation is being properly pursued," Poppy said, using as direct a tone as she dared. "It could be seen as bias if I don't include what the police are doing."

Mister Pearse weighed this and said, somewhat reluctantly, "So long as you distinguish between his comments and mine, I will not protest."

"What's second?" Poppy asked.

"That you refrain from mixing any of Merrinelle Butterworth's utterances with your coverage of my remarks. There has been far too much excitement about her outbursts than is seemly in this situation; I will not allow anyone to trade on our misfortune. Say what she will, neither Missus Pearse nor I was ever apprized by GAD that he had made an offer for Miss Butterworth, and if he had done so, we would have repudiated it and him." He wagged a finger in

Poppy's direction to emphasize his point.

Missus Pearse dabbed her eyes with the edge of a lace handkerchief; she turned away from her husband and bit her lower lip.

Poppy wrote no Merrinelle in her notebook; much as she would have liked to pursue this assertion, she realized that the quiet vehemence of Mister Pearse's words made it obvious that this would be a mistake, as would commenting on Missus Pearse's distress would be. "Is there anything else you require?"

"Yes. You must promise to messenger a copy of any article you may write to us before it is to appear in the *Clarion*, and to abide by any excisions I make in it." Now he sounded more implacable than ever.

Poppy chose her words carefully. "Within the limits of my authority at the *Clarion*, I will endeavor to do so; my editor is the man who has the final decision on that," she said, knowing her authority was negligible at best; she promised herself to tell Lowenthal about this proviso, as a good faith gesture. "We'd like to have a photograph of GAD, to run with my piece."

"A photograph?" Mister Pearse said as if he had never heard the word before.

"It makes the information more accessible for most readers. If they have some sense of GAD as a person, they'll pay more attention to what's reported," Poppy said patiently.

"I'll arrange for one to be delivered to you," Missus Pearse promised Poppy after a quick scan of her husband's demeanor.

"If it will help, certainly you shall have it." Mister Pearse lost a little of his stringent behavior. "Excellent. Then I think we may proceed. Ask away."

"Can you tell me when you last heard from GAD?" It was a simple question and one that was easily answered.

"It was four pages long, on postage bond, written on both sides of the sheet. It was posted from Vienna," said Missus Pearse before her husband could answer. "On the 19th of July. It arrived here on the 8th of August. He paid for rapid post, as he has done throughout his travels, not wanting to cause us undue worry."

Mister Pearse cleared his throat. "He was staying at the Londoner Hotel in Vienna. It caters to those who speak English. We've been in contact with the management there, and they have informed us that GAD checked out on the 21st, in the morning."

Poppy wrote down the dates. "What did he tell you in his last letter, if you don't mind talking about it?"

Missus Pearse had recourse to her handkerchief once more. "He told us more about the Living Spectres, how much they had endured, how dedicated they were to peace, and—"

"My dear," Mister Pearse cautioned, nodding in the direction of the door. "We can discuss this shortly."

With this warning, Missus Pearse went silent as a stout man with curly, bright-red hair and a florid complexion, dressed in a cook's tunic and tan trousers, came into the conservatory and went to the service closet.

"Ah, Huntsman. I would like you to make a pot of tea and a pot of coffee. As you see, we have company." Mister Pearse gave Poppy a warning look that indicated she was not supposed to ask questions in front of the staff.

"I prefer the heartier teas, Miss Thornton," said Missus Pearse in her most courteous voice, "What about you?"

"Coffee, please, with one sugar and a little cream," Poppy said and resigned herself to a spate of small-talk while the cook went about preparing the requested items at the service closet. "Thank you."

After a brief, cumbersome silence, Missus Pearse asked, "Do you enjoy your work for the paper Miss Thornton?"

"Generally speaking, yes, I do," said Poppy, wondering when people would stop asking her that.

"Reporting on crime seems like a...an unusual choice for a woman, especially an unmarried woman of good station in life," Missus Pearse said.

"Not every woman I've met would like it, but it suits me down to the ground," said Poppy, making no apology for her direct response.

"It must be your father in you," Missus Pearse murmured.

Poppy was fairly certain that she should ignore that last, but decided to respond. "No doubt he influenced my understanding of journalism early in my life, and I have had the advantage of a very good education, but my father was a travel writer, and had more in common with his sister Esther than with the work I do. Both of them have been providing much interesting information on foreign places—my father in his books, my aunt from our discussions. But my interests are turned in other directions. I find it useful and challenging to report on crime, and I am grateful for having had the opportunity to do work for which I seem best-suited."

"Does your brother approve of your vocation?" Mister Pearse asked, sounding disgruntled. "I wouldn't have thought so."

"No, he doesn't, and neither does my Aunt Josephine, which shouldn't surprise you, Mister Pearse," said Poppy as genially as she could. "Tobias prides himself on being a traditionalist, and often expresses his disapproval of our mother, who, as you know, was a Suffragette. He—Toby—has relegated me to the category of oddity." She admitted to herself that this was more than small-talk, but did not abandon it. "What about Auralia? I understand she's persuaded her husband to run for Congress."

"Yes. William was not convinced he could win, but Auralia has encouraged him to try; she has told him that he will never know if he can serve if he does not put his name forward. She's offered to organize a staff for him; he will run in the mid-term election in 26," said Mister Pearse, not quite proudly. "He's not from Pennsylvania, you know, but she has talked me into making a contribution for William to begin in planning his campaign. Auralia has assured us that he will do very well in the election. She has already spoken to the local Republican committee about it." He turned to frown at Huntsman. "How much longer will you be?"

"Less than ten minutes," the cook promised him. "The water is just coming on to boil, and I have the coffee-grounds ready to put in the strainer. The second hot-plate burner has been turned on and will be fully heated in another three minutes."

"You may return to the kitchen as soon as you serve us," said Mister Pearse with the confidence of a man who did not often have his orders questioned. "And say nothing of this meeting to the staff."

"Very good Mister Pearse," said Huntsman, and went on assembling cups, saucers and spoons.

Missus Pearse asked, "Is there any news of Eustace? After Esther's party, I have wondered what the situation is. Eustace has been gone a long time."

"I'm sorry," said Poppy, and knew more was expected of her. "If anyone has had word of him, I haven't been told of it."

Hearing this, Missus Pearse sighed. "It's the not knowing that makes it so unbearable, isn't it?" She raised her lace handkerchief again. "I have already lost one son, so I know I can stand that if I must. But this—"

"Yes, the uncertainty is difficult to weather," said Poppy, consoling herself with the thought that she was telling the truth, as far as she could.

"I sometimes think if I knew what had happened, no matter how dreadful, I could deal with it far better than this...this vacuum that is the case now." Missus Pearse was about to continue, but caught another warning stare from her husband, and so said only, "I am glad you're doing this interview, since you know from experience how demanding this waiting can be. I rely upon you to keep the line."

Mister Pearse was frowning. "Are you feeling tired, my dear? Would you like to retire for an hour or so?"

Missus Pearse did not bother responding to this blatant suggestion and said, "Thank you, Sherman; I'm fine. But I do find it trying to discuss this."

Since Poppy was aware that Isadora Pearse had been expostulating on her fears for her missing son at every opportunity for almost a month, she tried to frame an appropriate remark. "That's not usual for anyone having to deal with circumstances like these."

Missus Pearse nodded. "Thank you for understanding," she said in the tone of automatic good conduct.

Wanting to take control of the conversation once more, Mister Pearse said, "We're relying on you to bear that in mind when you write about GAD."

"I'll do my best, Mister Pearse," Poppy said, wondering how many times she would have to relieve his anxiety in this regard.

"You're a sensible young woman, thank the Good Lord," said Mister Pearse, his manner so deprecatory that Poppy wanted to scream; she contained the impulse, but knew that she would have to say a number of uncouth things in her auto when she was through here. "Breeding always shows, doesn't it?"

"Such a comfort," Missus Pearse whispered, making Poppy's exasperation worse.

"Then let me finish what I'd like to ask you, and be on my way back to the *Clarion*." She readied her pencil yet again.

Huntsman put an end to this ponderous attempt at making light conversation. "The tea is almost ready, and the coffee will be in a minute or so." He had selected a large pot for the coffee, a tall Wedgewood one with a pattern of ivy-wreaths around it. For the tea, he had a bulbous china pot with a celadon glaze; he had a strainer of tea waiting in its open top into which he poured boiling water, saying softly, "Always tea to the water, never water to the tea." He put the lid back on the pot, resting it above the strainer, and stepped back to set up the grounds-basket in the neck of the coffee pot. As soon as he was satisfied with the level of grounds, he reached for the kettle to pour water through the grounds.

Poppy watched Huntsman as if fascinated with what he was doing, but actually taking a little time to rephrase her next question. "What a wonderful aroma," she said, to account for her interest in Huntsman's activities.

In response to this observation, Missus Pearse said, "Yes. If only coffee tasted as good as it smells, I would drink a great deal more of it."

Poppy attempted to say something in defense of coffee, but was relieved of the problem as Huntsman set trivets on the tray for the two pots, and put them in their place, before carrying the tray ten feet from the service closet to the round teak table in the center of the sitting area.

"Bear in mind that the tea and the coffee are very hot," Huntsman said before he withdrew.

Once Mister Pearse was sure that Huntsman was out of earshot, he said, "Now, where were we Miss Thornton?"

Poppy consulted her notebook in order to appear attentive. "You were going to tell me something about the contents of his last letter."

For the last several minutes, the conservatory had been darkening as the clouds thickened overhead; now the first spatters of serious rain tapped on the glass arch above them, sounding like pebbles cascading on a sheet of tin.

"Oh, dear," Missus Pearse said, glancing up as if expecting the whole roof to fall in.

Mister Pearse would not allow himself to be distracted by his wife's anxiety. He gave an experimental orator's cough. "He wrote from Vienna, as you've already heard, informing us that he was planning to take some provisions to the Armenian refugee camp outside of the city. He was troubled on their behalf, and wanted to alleviate their suffering as much as he could. A Quixotic gesture, but that is to be expected from GAD: not an ounce of common sense. What would have been far more helpful would have been to address the Austrian government directly, to alert them to the situation with the Living Spectres, but GAD has always been one to want to have his hands on the problems he sees. When he was still at the Alexandrian Academy, he worked with the orphans of parents who had died of the Flu. Your brother informed us of GAD's project then, and I went at once to speak with him directly. He would not listen to me when I animadverted against such reckless disregard for his own health. This preoccupation with the followers of Ahram Avaikian is more of the same. Folly. Complete folly."

"Sherman, please," Missus Pearse protested.

Mister Pearse rounded on his wife, speaking acerbically. "I am aware you do not disapprove of what GAD has done as much as I do, yet you will allow that I have been inordinately patient with him. And, had he not ventured to undertake his so-called rescue mission, he would very likely be back here, in his own country, and beginning his university career, instead of wandering about Austria on a fool's errand."

"I will concur with most of your last statement, but I cannot and will not deprecate his inclination to help those less fortunate than himself. You may see it as a failing in him, but I do not." Missus Pearse got to her feet. "I find I am getting tired, after all, and so I will excuse myself. Please apologize to Huntsman for me: I cannot bring myself to drink the tea. I'm sorry, Miss Thornton, but my nerves are very—" She turned away and escaped through the door into the main corridor beyond, her sobs muffled by her handkerchief.

Mister Pearse had risen and taken a step or two after her. "Isadora..." he said placatingly; when it was apparent that she would not return, he heaved an exasperated sigh and looked directly at Poppy. "I trust no mention of this incident will appear in your account of this meeting." He returned to his seat. "She's easily overset and the last weeks have frayed her nerves. You'll keep this to yourself."

"I'll keep it out of my story," Poppy said, making a note to herself to ask Loring what he thought of Missus Pearse's state of mind.

Returning to his place on the couch, Mister Pearse said, "Perhaps you'll let me pour you a cup of coffee before we continue? It would be lamentable to have it and the tea go to waste. Or would you rather have the tea?" He saw Poppy shake her head as he reached for a cup-and- saucer. "Coffee it is then. You said cream and sugar, I think."

"One sugar and a dab of cream," Poppy told him, hoping that she could still coax some information out of him.

"Right you are," he agreed, and prepared her coffee with more cream than she liked. Handing her the cup-and-saucer along with a napkin and a spoon, he went on, "When last I spoke with Inspector Loring, he told me that he had contacted an investigator in London, one who is willing to search for GAD. I am preparing a dossier for this Mister Blessing, which I will send him shortly, so that he has our most current apprehension of GAD's circumstances. Mister Blessing should receive it in six days or fewer, and he will then proceed to Vienna, at which time he will wire me to inform me how he plans to proceed. Miss Butterworth and my wife may fear that GAD has been abducted, but I believe the most prudent thing is to contact the Armenian groups he said he was going to aid, to determine if he is with them, and not embrace any rash theories until that bridge has been crossed. If GAD is not among the Living Spectres—a ridiculous and untempered appellation, in my opinion—then I will authorize Mister Blessing to undertake more drastic measures."

Poppy was struggling to keep up with what Mister Pearse was saying, but had the presence of mind to ask him, "How much of this am I at liberty to include in my article? I want to make sure your wishes are regarded in my work."

Mister Pearse paused in the preparation of his own cup of coffee. "Let me reiterate: you are not to mention anything about a possible kidnapping. You may say that a foreign investigator has been engaged to pursue inquiries on the Continent on behalf of GAD's family, but I would rather you do not use Mister Blessing's name in your report. I would prefer that you not mention the Living Spectres specifically."

"My editor may require that I do," Poppy said, knowing full well that Lowenthal would insist upon it, but she also was pleased that Mister Pearse's instruction was not as rigorous a limitation as she had feared he might impose. "To the extent that I might influence him, I'll do what I can to comply." Saying this, Poppy suspected that Lowenthal would not run Aunt Esther's piece on the Armenian group if Poppy failed to mention the Living Spectres, or at least the

Armenian refugees, in her story. "It may be out of my hands."

"Just so." Mister Pearse clicked his tongue in disapprobation. "If the choice is between mentioning the Living Spectres in the article or have no article at all, I won't oppose it, though I ask that you not sensationalize them."

"I wouldn't do that, in any case." Poppy picked up her cup of coffee and took a sip that almost burned her tongue. "Hot." She set it down.

"Give it a little while to cool," Mister Pearse recommended.

"I will," said Poppy, and for the first time, noticed a spangling light drifting among the elephant ears and philodendrons. "How long had Holte been with them?" she asked herself. "Mister Pearse," she said, returning to their discussion, "Have you made any plans to go to Europe yourself, or will you leave the case to your investigator?"

"That will depend on what Mister Blessing discovers. I will not entirely rule out going there myself, but if Mister Blessing deems it unnecessary, then I will remain here and deputize Mister Blessing to act to return GAD to his family. I would rather not draw attention to his activities by my presence." He paused, looking up at the increasing rain. "No matter what my wife may think, I am not unaware of the danger my son may be in, and I am cognizant of the various outcomes that might result from this latest undertaking. I hope that GAD will have learned his lesson by the time he returns. He cannot save the world, and it is well past time that he should give up grand romantic notions."

"Is that what you think he's done?—taken on an ill-considered knight-errantry? Truly?" Poppy asked, watching Mister Pearse closely for any nuance of expression he might reveal.

"Naturally that is how I see it. Anything else would be unthinkable. I'll grant that GAD is an enterprising young man, but his efforts in the name of hopeless causes shows that he has little grasp on the realities of the world. He has not yet realized that life is not an adventure, nor is it a crusade. It is a great pity that he was ever encouraged to do so. Your Uncle Maximilian has much to answer for." On that final note, he picked up his cup of heavily creamed coffee and drank, making it a sign that the interview was over.

TWENTY-FIVE

HOLTE WAITED UNTIL POPPY WAS HALF-WAY BACK TO THE CLARION TO MAKE himself known. "Not the easiest of consultations, was it?" he asked as Poppy pulled up at a stop sign.

"No, it wasn't." She pulled her arm in and rolled up the window, glowering at the rain that spattered the windshield, undaunted by the wiper-blades, saying as she did, "I'd forgotten what an insufferable man Sherman Pearse can be."

"Perhaps he wasn't so difficult to you when you were younger." It was an obvious suggestion to Holte, but it raised Poppy's hackles; he decided to clarify his point. "You were a student when last you saw him, weren't you? A young woman not yet embarked on your career. You were still in your aunt's care, and dependent upon her. Not nearly so dangerous as you are now, a self-sufficient professional. He probably felt uneasy."

"Ha," said Poppy, "and ha."

"Men who are that authoritative usually are so because they are frightened," Holte persisted. "It took me a long time to realize that, but I grasp it now."

Poppy honked her horn at a messenger on a bicycle, saying as she did, "Do we have to talk about this now?"

"You seem to want to," Holte replied. "It's better you say it to me than blow up at Gafney, or take it out on Lowenthal."

"Because they're afraid of me?" Poppy asked incredulously.

"Not as much as Mister Pearse was. He's so frightened that the prospect of admitting it is making him—"

"Don't you go defending him," she told Holte, all her aggravation of the past hour welling up inside her. "He's infuriating. I had to bite my tongue every time he spoke to me. I almost expected him to pat my head—or Missus

Pearse's. And the way he talked about Uncle Max, I wanted to wring his neck."

"Yes," said Holte. "And who is this Uncle Max? You haven't mentioned him."

"Uncle Max was my paternal grandparents' second child. Regis was the oldest. Then Max, Esther, and Josephine, and finally my father. Sherman Pearse was right about one thing: Max liked GAD. He liked me too, and my father." She tapped her horn as a man in a military overcoat started into the street. "He should watch where he's going."

"And you should watch out for the pot-hole," Holte said, nodding in the direction of a broad puddle in the middle of her lane.

"Thanks," she said through clenched teeth; she drove another block, then said, "Pardon my brusqueness. I don't mean to bark at you, but—"

"But you want to release some of your pent-up exacerbation. I'd want to do the same thing, in your shoes. If I weren't noncorporeal, I might have taken a punch at him, on your behalf." He became slightly more visible. "I meant what I told you: Pearse is the sort of man who is terrified when he can't be in charge. Having his son missing, and being unable to face what might have happened to his heir, is making him worse."

She laughed sardonically. "If you were in my shoes, he wouldn't have treated you the way he did me. You're male in a man's job, and that would be acceptable to Sherman Pearse, as much as anything ever is."

"He would not have seen me as a colleague; only like one of the hired help, and would have expected deference on my part; I knew officers in the Army when I was still spying, cut from much the same cloth," Holte said at his most conciliating. "And although Mister Pearse thinks of spies as men and only men, I have known six women who served as spies, much the same as I did. One was a waitress in a restaurant in Arnhem; I was her contact for a while. She had more courage than almost any other person, man or woman, in our network, and more pure nerve."

Poppy's chuckle was sad. "You're right—Mister Pearse would never believe that: a woman and only a waitress."

"I don't doubt that," Holte said. "The trouble is, he believes that the world accepts his standards and therefore he has no reason to examine what he thinks, which saves him from having to realize that he's afraid. If he were not in such a high position, that would be awkward or foolish. But between his wealth and social placement, he probably isn't even aware that how he conducts himself can offend others, and if he did have some inkling of it, it would not be likely that it would matter to him."

"Don't give him the benefit of the doubt. I'm in no mood for it, although you're probably right." She braked suddenly as a small, bedraggled mongrel ran into the road, yapping at a horse- drawn wagon laden with crates of poultry. "Ye gods!" she cried out, accompanied by a counterpoint of horns from other autos and trucks.

"Hold steady," Holte said quietly. "Let the rest of them panic. If you notice, the pace has been slowing down. There's some other obstruction up ahead."

"Is that what you did as a spy? Held steady?" Poppy asked even as she took his advice. "And yes, I see that there's some kind of tangle a little farther along."

"I held steady whenever possible. If you'll spare me a moment, I'll see what the cause is." He slid out through the passenger door and swooped around the confusion, and returned to the Hudson. "This will break up shortly. There is a road-crew up ahead trying to get the water standing on the road to drain away. An old Ford is stuck in the puddle that's not draining." He gave the appearance of settling back down on the passenger side of the seat. "You may want to turn off on the next street and make your way back to the *Clarion* by an alternate route. Clearing what's ahead could still take some time."

"Thanks," she said curtly, and rolled down her window to signal for a right-hand turn. At the first break in the traffic, she veered away from the increasing snarl, jockeying into position next to the curb and rounding the corner. "What does this seem like to you? You're noncorporeal, as you keep reminding me, so all these physical intrusions must strike you as inconvenient at the least. Or do you miss them? Perhaps some of both?" She went slowly down to the next intersection and signaled to turn left.

"Occasionally, I do miss corporeality; for the most part, I've become accustomed to being a ghost," he said. "But corporeality is the reality of the world of the living, and I ought to be willing to accommodate it." He fell silent, then asked, "Have you decided how you're going to tell Loring about Overstreet? Or are you going to avoid the whole thing?"

Poppy found herself chuckling. "I think I might suggest that he contact

Hank, and ask him if there is any way that the *Belle Helene* could have made it through the hurricane. He and Hank were talking at the party last Friday, and Hank loves to hold forth about sailing. And I think Loring might want to talk to Quentin Hadley about the yacht. Or I might."

"That should help deal with the situation," said Holte. "But there is a very strong chance that Quentin Hadley went down with the ship."

"Have you encountered his ghost, or is that a guess?"

"No, I haven't found him in the dimension of ghosts, but I didn't know to look for him until I spoke to Overstreet. I still don't know it for certain, but it does seem likely; worth following up, in any case."

"You could be right," Poppy said.

"I could find out, if you'd like?" He watched her for a moment. "Would you be willing to call Hadley and Grimes to find out if Quentin Hadley is in the office? If he is, that should make it clear that he hasn't drowned at sea, and that would answer a few questions without fuss."

Poppy laughed uneasily. "Why didn't I think of that? On what excuse?"

"Some kind of follow-up. Why not say it's about the federal investigation on the counterfeit antiquities? Customs is still trying to get information out of Hadley and Grimes, aren't they? And you're covering that story. The courts in Pennsylvania are not working to clear the way, and that means there's something going on under the surface. If you approach them as someone sympathetic to their situation, they might be more forthcoming than not. Encourage them to set the record straight." He mused on the possibilities while Poppy jockeyed around a furniture van double-parked in front of a warehouse.

"I suppose that would work." She honked the horn as a man with a hand-truck stepped into the street without bothering to look for traffic. "Are they all half-asleep this morning?" she asked the leaking sky, then spoke to Holte. "Sorry. I'm still riled up at Mister Pearse. I shouldn't take it out on hapless drivers. And is it still morning?"

"A few minutes past noon," he told her, since he was trying to be scrupulous about time; his loss of time in the world of the living bothered him, and he was attempting to pay attention to it.

"So some of them are hungry for lunch, and are in a hurry to eat." She glanced in the rear- view mirror. "There's an impatient fellow in a Cord back there, trying to weave in and out of lanes to get down the street faster." She moved into the left-hand lane and rolled down her window again to signal for her turn; the Cord came abreast of her Hudson, and the man at the wheel began to gesture in Poppy's direction, as if to shoo her out of the way. "I'm turning left," she yelled back at him, and moved her arm to signal more forcefully.

The man in the Cord grew more irate and swung into the intersection to move around her and cut her off. Poppy honked her horn again and jammed on her brakes; the Cord hurried off, sending a plume of water back on Poppy's Hudson and soaking her left arm. "Ye gods!" she burst out.

"Gods had nothing to do with it," said Holte.

Poppy slowed down as she rolled her window up, and took a second to inspect the damage to her coat-sleeve. "I hope something can be done to fix this; I've only had it four months."

Holte said something under his nonexistent breath that was probably a curse, and he raised himself up through the roof of the car so that he could watch the progress of the Cord. When he saw the Cord turn right two blocks down, he sank back onto the passenger's side of the bench. "He's going toward Independence Hall."

"I hope the police stop him before he does something really stupid." She gripped the steering wheel, her knuckles white with exertion.

"Would you like me to follow him and get the number on his plate?" Holte offered.

Poppy considered this for half a block, but finally said, "No, don't bother. It's not worth the trouble it would cause." She clutched down to first gear as she prepared to make another left turn. "I want to get back to the paper and write my story. Then, I hope, Aunt Esther and I can indulge in a late lunch."

"Why not have that now?" Holte suggested.

Poppy shook her head. "I'm too edgy. I'll enjoy it more if I turn in the story first, and then Aunt Esther and I can talk about her appointment with Lowenthal. With luck, I'll have my story in Lowenthal's hands by then, and that will help me feel less harried." She shifted into second gear as she rounded the turn, and drove past the old Presbyterian Hospital, a relic of the Civil War, now scheduled for demolition. Three more blocks to the *Clarion*, she told herself. Don't get rattled.

"There's a policeman directing traffic up ahead," Holte observed. "Best to slow down until you've passed him."

"Well, that's reassuring," Poppy remarked, and rolled down the window to signal for another left turn. When Poppy drove into what she had come to think of as her parking alley, she located a place next to the Inkwell, the tavern where reporters and pressmen went for coffee and sandwiches; it had an openly secret rear bar where beer and whiskey were available to those in the know. As soon as she had banked her wheels, she said to Holte, who was now only a kind of pale smudge next to her, "Why so quiet?"

He became a bit more defined. "I have been thinking about Overstreet. He's confused about being dead, and how he got that way, but I want to find out as much as I can about his time with Nelson and Quentin Hadley. Overstreet might not know how he was killed, but he had some time on the *Belle Helene*, and he might be able to remember what they talked about after they left Montreal."

"Does that mean you're going back to the dimension of ghosts to talk to him? Or will you be looking for one of the Hadleys?" Poppy asked, feeling a bit slighted by this very sensible plan; she gave herself a scolding for her hurt feelings. "When do you plan to leave?" That sounded more civilized, she decided.

"Not at once," said Holte. "I want to find out what you learn from Hadley and Grimes first, so I have a place to start."

Poppy peered out at the steady rain, sighed, and opened the door. "I should have brought my umbrella," she said to Holte. "It's under my desk. I didn't think I'd need it."

"Well, get your things and keep under the eaves if you can," Holte recommended, flowing out through the front windshield. "At least there's a sidewalk. Not all alleys have them. Not that that helped you earlier."

Poppy had set off at a brisk walk, her brief-case swinging from her left hand, her purse clutched in her right. "I know that," she assured him, wincing as she stepped into a two-inch- deep pool next to a down-spout.

"Only a little more than forty feet to go," he said. "Don't move too quickly, you'll just splash more water."

"I hope I'm not completely drenched," she said, picking up the pace a bit more, and paying as little attention as she possibly could to the water sloshing in her right shoe. She was almost trotting by the time she got to the front of the Addison Newspaper Corporation building; she forced herself to slow down as she went up the rain-slicked marble stairs to the massive revolving front door. She stepped into the moving wedge as soon as she could, and sighed as she made the half-circle into the lobby. She touched her hair and found it wet, as she knew it would be. "It's all of a piece," she whispered.

"Rain isn't personal," Holte reminded her from a few inches ahead of her. "It isn't there to make you uncomfortable."

"No, it's not," she murmured as she made for the stairs.

"And it is breaking up. You should only have clouds in another hour or so." He rose up the stairs a couple of steps ahead of her.

"Are you certain of that?" she muttered.

"As certain as a ghost can be," he said, and changed the subject. "Are you going to call Loring before you get to work on your piece about the Pearses?" Holte drifted along beside her.

"I'll give it a try, if you'll stop being so reasonable," she said under her breath, taking care not to let her wet shoes slip on the steps; if she should trip, she knew her male colleagues would not let her hear the end of it. "But I'll check with Hadley and Grimes first; that way, I'll have information on two stories for Lowenthal."

"A very good idea," said Holte, sounding encouraging. "That should help you with Loring as well."

Poppy did not bother to answer Holte; she was already thinking about how to present what he had told her to both her editor and Inspector Loring. It would require a great deal of diplomacy with each of them, and Poppy had to acknowledge that just now, she was not in a very diplomatic frame of mind.

"I'll be back shortly," said Holte, starting to rise above her.

"Where are you going?" she asked in a whisper.

"I'll tell you when I get back," he promised, and vanished through the ceiling.

By the time she reached her desk, Poppy was already half-way out of her wet coat. She hung it over the back of her chair, put her brief-case on her desk next to the Remington, and her purse into the locking drawer on her left. She removed her notebook from her brief-case, then returned it to its place next to her chair. After opening her notebook and setting it next to her phone, she lifted the receiver from its cradle and, once again changing her mind, gave Inspector Loring's number to the switchboard operator who said, "One moment please," before connecting her to Loring's phone.

The voice of the man who answered was not familiar, and when Poppy asked for Loring, the man at the other end said, "He's out."

"When is he expected back?" Poppy asked, trying to keep her exasperation in check.

"Don't know. Two, three hours maybe. Is this urgent? I could connect you with another of our inspectors."

"Would you be good enough to leave him a note asking him to call Miss Thornton at his earliest convenience?" She used her most professional tone. "I'll be available after three."

"Is this urgent?" The answerer sounded skeptical as he repeated his earlier question.

"I have information that might be useful to him, about an on-going investigation."

There was a short pause and then the man said, "What's your number, Miss?"

"He has it," she snapped, hoping that the man would do as she asked. "Thank you," she added, and heard him hang up. To calm herself again, she put together her bond, carbon paper, and onion-skin sandwich and rolled it into her typewriter. She centered the carriage and typed in:

PARENTS QUESTION FATE OF MISSING HEIR and then sat still, trying to decide how best to begin her report on the interview with the Pearses, keeping Sherman Pearse's requirements in mind. She recited the requisite needs for the opening paragraph of a story: who, what, when, where, why, and if needed, how. With these rules in mind, she began to type.

Mister and Missus Sherman Pearse have authorized an English investigator, working from London, to undertake a search for their oldest son, Gameal A. D. Pearse, 18, who has been missing in Europe since late July. This decision comes after several weeks have passed since their last communication from him, which was sent from Vienna, Austria. The Pearses as yet do not believe that this silence is the result of foul play, but wish to locate their heir, if only to put their family and friends at ease in regard to the safety and location of their son. There is some indication that Gameal Pearse might have been providing some sort of assistance to a group of Armenian refugees, although this has not yet been confirmed. Gameal Pearse was scheduled to begin his university studies over a week ago, which has added to his parents' concern. They are hoping that the work of Mister Blessing, the English investigator, can set their minds at ease and dispel some of the rumors about Gameal Pearse's present circumstances, and request that anyone having contact of any kind with young Mister Pearse while in Europe inform Inspector J.B. Loring of the Philadelphia Police Department of the nature of that contact, where and when it occurred, and any other relevant information in that regard. Mister Sherman Pearse is anxious to resolve this mystery as soon as is possible, and to that end, the Pearses request that their privacy be respected during this difficult time.

When there is reliable news, the Pearses have pledged to this reporter to release it to the public. Until such time as more is known, the Pearses decline to be interviewed by anyone except those in official positions working directly on the case, on the advice of their attorneys and those officers of the law actively involved. They, and the United States Department of State, thank you for your cooperation.

Poppy read this through, then nodded once to herself. There was no specific mention of Merrinelle Butterworth, which ought to satisfy Mister Pearse's stricture. The tone of the piece was not sensationalistic, but direct enough to keep Lowenthal happy. She pulled the papers out of the typewriter platen and put them down beside her notebook. Time to call Hadley and Grimes, she decided, and once again signaled the operator to make the call.

"Hadley and Grimes, Certified Public Accountants," said the carefully cultured voice of the receptionist. "To whom may I connect you?"

"Mister Quentin Hadley," said Poppy.

There was a minuscule pause, and then the receptionist said, "Mister Quentin Hadley is not available today."

Bingo! Poppy told herself. "Then I'll speak with Mister Tinsdale, Mister Hadley's assistant. I'm with the *Philadelphia Clarion*, and I have some questions I would like to ask him, regarding his employer's present whereabouts." She had met Tinsdale when she had gone to interview Quentin Hadley shortly after

Madison Moncrief's murder; she remembered a fastidious man with a single-minded alliance with his employer. "I realize that he may be out at lunch, but I hope to have a word with him in regard to the state of the federal inquiries regarding Mister Hadley's positi—"

"I'll connect you," said the receptionist.

Two rings later, the phone was answered. "Mister Quentin Hadley's office, his assistant, Clifford Tinsdale, speaking." His voice was crisp and cool, as if Tinsdale were addressing an unwelcome caller. "If you are calling about a canceled appointment, please ask the operator to direct your inquiry to Mister Bloom."

"Good afternoon, Mister Tinsdale. This is P. M. Thornton of the *Clarion*. We met last spring, a few days after Mister Moncrief's untimely death? I was wondering if I might have a word with Mister Hadley?"

Tinsdale's tone got frostier. "I'm afraid that Mister Quentin Hadley is not in the office today, Miss Thornton. He isn't expected in."

"When would I be able to reach him?" Poppy said, hoping to goad Tinsdale into revealing what, if anything, he knew about Quentin Hadley's current whereabouts.

"Mister Hadley is away from the office for...another week, we believe."

Poppy could tell that Tinsdale was on the brink of hanging up on her. "Can you tell me where I might reach him? You see, we're doing a series of articles on the state of the federal investigation of counterfeit antiques and Customs fraud. I was hoping that Mister Hadley could help us to clarify the issues involved. The Justice Department has not been very forthcoming on details, and we would like to present an unbiased picture of how matters stand."

To Poppy's surprise, Tinsdale took the bait. "Mister Hadley is on vacation; he is expected to be in Jamaica tomorrow or the next day, and has pledged to wire us of his safe arrival, and to inform us of when he and his cousin will be going on to Cuba. It was part of his arrangement with us that he would keep in regular contact with us. He and his cousin have been sailing together for the last ten days, and they wire every time they make port."

"Then you have some notion of where he might be now," Poppy said, to keep Tinsdale talking.

After a slight hesitation, Tinsdale said, "They began their trip leaving out of

Mystic, Mister Hadley's cousin Nelson having sailed up from Cuba with a companion who left when Mister Quentin Hadley came aboard. They went up into the Maritime Provinces to pick up another person, then went down the coast, bound for the family's vacation home in Cuba. They included a stop-over in Jamaica—just a day or two, and then back north and the vacation house near Santiago de Cuba—as part of their itinerary, which is where they should have been yesterday, but hadn't counted on encountering a hurricane. They have probably sought a safe harbor to wait out the storm." He paused, then plunged on, "It may take a day or two longer for him to get through to us this time, because of the hurricane. But we're expecting to receive news of him in the next two or three days, at most."

"Oh, yes, the hurricane; it is dangerous to sail when such a storm is raging," said Poppy, as if that had only now occurred to her. "Would you be good enough to call me back when you hear from him? I'd like to set up an appointment with him when he returns."

"I'll let him know when I respond to his wire. And I'll keep you informed." Tinsdale paused. "Well, good-bye, Miss Thornton."

"And to you, Mister Tinsdale," Poppy replied, a grin dawning; perhaps, she thought, this day would not turn out too badly, after all. She picked up her phone again and asked the operator to connect her to Rudy Beech in Florida, offering the number Neva Plowright had reluctantly supplied, and waiting while she heard the rings on the far end of the line. After nine loud clangs, Poppy was about to hang up when someone answered.

"Hello?"

Poppy was so startled that she nearly dropped the receiver. "Hello? Is this Rudy Beech?"

"Who are you and what do you want? Make it snappy. I'm busy doing clean-up. We've had a hurricane."

This was not a promising beginning, but Poppy took a deep breath and began to speak. "I'm P. M. Thornton with the *Clarion* in Philadelphia calling to speak with Rudy Beech in regards to his missing half-sister, Loui—"

"Louise Moncrief," he cut in. "Don't you people understand what I don't know means? I haven't seen her, I haven't heard from her in over a year. If you have any questions, talk to Titus van Boew, he's her lawyer. Don't say I sent you." And with that, he hung up.

Poppy sat still for several seconds, then hung up, thinking, if this is Neva Plowright's idea of family closeness, they must have had a difficult time as children. Then another thought struck her: who else had phoned Rudy? His reference to another caller or callers troubled her as she went through her notes again. "Well, I don't think he'll tell me if I phoned again, at least not this week," she murmured, putting her attention on her story. She closed her notebook and decided it was time to get a cup of coffee.

TWENTY-SIX

AUNT ESTHER EMERGED FROM LOWENTHAL'S OFFICE HALF AN HOUR AFTER SHE entered it, her countenance composed and her step firm as ever. She was dressed much the same way as she would if she had been going to speak to the National Geographic Society: her suit was conservatively fashionable—a jacket of tan wool over a simple, pale-mauve, pin-tucked silk blouse, with a pleated skirt the color of milk-chocolate that was hemmed the standard four inches above her ankle; she had a narrow-brimmed hat of tan felt perched on her neatly rolled hair—in addition, she had her small portfolio in her hand, her raincoat over her arm, and her purse slung over her shoulder. Threading her way through the maze of desks, she approached Poppy's, where Poppy was just finishing typing up her notes for Lowenthal's perusal, with only a short sentence on her contact with Rudy Beech. "I'm not interrupting, am I?" she asked as Poppy looked up from her work.

"Not at all, Aunt Esther; I'm glad to see you," said Poppy, smiling without hesitation. "How did it go?"

"I hope you'll tell me that over lunch. I haven't decided. He's not easy to read, your Mister Lowenthal." Esther shrugged philosophically. "I hope my presentation was enough to convince him that my information is worthwhile." She covered her mouth with her hand, concealing a yawn. "I must admit that after our...interview, I guess I'd call it, I'm famished; I feel as if I've hiked five miles."

"Not unexpected," said Poppy, slipping her two single-spaced pages of notes into a manila file folder. "Lowenthal's got a schedule to keep, and that means all of us must keep working full steam."

"What are you working on?" Esther inquired, her eyes brightening. "Anything exciting?"

"Not really, not for you and me. I had an interview this morning with the Pearses. Most of what I've done is boil it down to basic information presented as emotionlessly as possible. Mister Pearse demanded it."

"I'll wager Isadora didn't," said Esther. "Not given the way she's been behaving."

"She went along with him, reluctantly, I thought," said Poppy, taking her purse from the drawer and removing her brief-case from its place under her desk. "He's pretty imposing."

"He's an arrogant martinet," said Esther tranquilly. "I never understood why she married him. Her family is almost as rich as his, so money wasn't the reason."

"His position is pretty impressive, and his brother is in the state legislature, which must count for something," said Poppy, putting away her notes and retrieving her purse. "I made a couple of phone calls while you were with Lowenthal, and I need to be back here by three, in case there's more I have to do on the story I filed shortly before you arrived. It's pretty brief, and Mister Pearse insisted on seeing it before it goes to press. Lowenthal has sent my copy over to the Pearses by messenger, just in case. They'll provide a photograph for the paper."

"I don't imagine that the Pearse's demand sits well with Lowenthal," said Esther. "Most reporters don't do peer-group reviews, do they?"

"Not the way you do for the National Geographic, or for academic publications, but we do have to be sure of our sources, and check the accuracy of any quotes we have, and our basic sources need to be vetted by another source," said Poppy, reaching for her coat on the back of her chair. "I don't know what it is that Mister Pearse is expecting; I wouldn't be surprised if he asked for changes just to make sure we all know that he's calling the shots. I kept the story brief and to the point, as he wanted me to, but that doesn't mean that he and I will see eye-to-eye."

"I wouldn't hold my breath," her aunt advised.

"No; I don't plan to. I'm tending to think that he won't give blanket approval. Sherman Pearse, as you say, needs to be in charge, or he has for as long as I've known him." She paused, thinking of what Holte had told her in the Hudson, then shook it off. "I've been told that he used to harry his staff relentlessly. HOB was turning out just like his father, and GAD his opposite, but I guess you know that."

Esther looked around the room, and finally saw the clock. "One-forty. We ought to get underway."

"Do you have any place you'd like to go for lunch?" Poppy asked, securing the cover on her typewriter as a last duty before departing.

"I haven't been to Cooper's Grill in the last three years. I know it's ten miles from here, but I'd like to see how it's faring, with Prohibition and all. It must be the very devil for all those hoteliers and tavern-keepers who depend on regular patrons who do business over drinks." She started to make her way through the city-room desks, knowing that Poppy was behind her. "This is quite a busy place for early afternoon," she remarked over the clatter of typewriters.

"First deadline is at one-thirty, the second at three-thirty, when everything has to be in."

"When does the paper go to press?" Esther asked as she reached the door.

"Regional edition goes to press at two-twenty, the trucks leave at three; Metropolitan goes to press at three-thirty, so that papers can be on the street no later than five. Most of the time, we get it out promptly." Poppy recited this as if she no longer paid much attention to the schedule; it had become automatic. "There's a bit more slack in the sports pages, but that's because afternoon games and such don't always finish on time."

"Doesn't the *Clarion* bring out extra editions?" Esther asked as they started down the stairs. "I know I've seen them on the streets from time to time."

"Yes, it does, but not very often, and not necessarily for sports. I think the last time there was a sports extra was in 1921, after the Dempsey versus Charpentier fight. I'd started at the *Clarion* only two months before, and I couldn't believe how much excitement there was for a boxing match. Everyone was talking about the contest. It wasn't just the championship that excited the public as much as it was the one-point-seven million they took in at the gate at the fight itself that attracted attention."

"That's an impressive haul, if you ask me," said Esther, moving out of the way of a young man in a dark-blue suit who was in a hurry. "Do they all smoke, or is it my imagination?"

"It often seems like it," said Poppy.

Esther nodded. "One-point-seven million. What a lot of money to watch two men hit one another in the face."

"It garnered a lot of press. We brought the extra edition out at six-thirty p.m., but then, the fight didn't begin until three in the afternoon, and we had reporters standing by to monitor the wire. We had to chase the paper that day," said Poppy, speeding up to avoid another reporter in a hurry. "As to the smoke, most reporters do, and never more than when coming up on deadline. Some days the city room is foggy with it."

"I trust you won't take up the habit," said Aunt Esther, then added, "I used to smoke occasionally, but I believe I have lost the taste for it. I have certainly gotten weary of the odor of cigarettes. Pipes aren't quite so bad, but they too can end up smelling like charred rags. Cigars are the worst." Once they were out of the Addison Newspaper Corporation building, Esther suggested that they hail a cab. "It will save you having to find a parking place when you return," she said at her most practical, "and I will get home without adding to your delay. I know you can afford the cab fare. This isn't just for our mutual convenience—I wouldn't want to give Lowenthal any reason to have doubts about me, or you. He knows we'll talk, since we live under the same roof, but I don't want him to think either of us will take advantage of our relationship."

Poppy nodded, and stepped to the curb, her hand lifted, her hair blowing in the wind; she was pleased that her new crop was not as disorderly as her former style had been, and that it had dried while she worked at her desk. "I'll be happy to pay for the cab Aunt Esther."

"There's no reason for you to do that. If you want to, fine, but I'll pay for my cab, going home." She came up to the curb, clutching her portfolio against the gusting wind.

"If you'd like it that way," said Poppy, buttoning the collar on her coat. "Hang on to your hat Aunt Esther."

She pressed it down more firmly. "I will. At least it's only wind," she remarked and sighed. "There's more rain on the way."

"That seems likely," Poppy said, remembering what Holte had said, and went toward one of the new Checkers cabs that pulled up in response to her summons. She opened the back door and held it for Esther, then climbed in beside her. "Cooper's Grill, on We—"

"I know where it is," the driver said in a thick Irish brogue, his arm out to warn approaching traffic that he was moving back into the stream. "Nine-and-a-half miles from here."

"That's right," said Esther, settling onto the upholstered rear seat. "Be careful of mud- puddles, please."

The driver began to whistle under his breath; it sounded a little like "The Minstrel Boy," but it was not loud enough to be certain.

During their taxi-ride, neither Poppy nor Esther spoke about anything but their coming engagements for the rest of the week; both of them were aware that a great many jarveys were not above selling overheard gossip to the *Tattler* and the *Bugle*. Poppy had the uneasy sensation that Aunt Esther was keeping something from her, but supposed that it had to do with her interview with Lowenthal, and so was able to keep from pestering her about it, knowing she would hear about it soon enough. When they were about five blocks from Cooper's Grill, Esther said, "Miss Roth is taking a week off in mid-October. Her nephew is getting married, and she's going to help her sister get ready for the occasion. She may leave a little early if her family needs her for more than they agreed upon. I've authorized her two weeks' leave, if she needs them."

This was the first Poppy had heard of it, but she took the news in as unruffled a manner as she could. "I hope she will enjoy the wedding."

"So do I." Esther paused a moment before informing Poppy, "Since I may be in South America by then, think about whether you'd like to take on a temporary housekeeper for the time Miss Roth is gone."

Poppy felt startled. "Would that be necessary for only a week or two? I'd think we could rattle along well enough for so short a time, wouldn't you?" Yet even as she asked it, she thought it might be wise for any number of reasons. There could be developments in the Pearse case, and the search for Stacy, Derrington, and Louise might heat up again, and then who would take care of the house, and Maestro—not Missus Sassoro, or Galliard.

"I'd recommend that you have someone, preferably someone you know, take over the post for that period. Miss Roth might have someone she can vouch for, but you'll want to interview whomever you consider for the post. It's always wise to have an available substitute for just such circumstances as these. You'll know best what will suit you." She turned to stare at a large touring auto up ahead, escorted by four motorcycles ridden by men in heavy-weather gear. "What a grand vehicle that is. Three rows of seats."

"I believe the governor rides in one of those," said Poppy, not as engrossed in the fine auto as Aunt Esther was. "His has a siren."

"That one is very imposing without the siren; I wonder whose it is," said Esther, and sat back once more; Poppy still had the feeling that there was more to Aunt Esther's disquiet than Miss Roth's coming absence.

Not quite ten minutes later, the cab drew up in front of Cooper's Grill, and the driver asked for a dollar, two bits.

Poppy handed this over, with a fifteen-cent tip. "Thank you," she said perfunctorily as she opened the door to get out; a sudden gust struck her afresh, and she felt her damp hair toss. She took a firm grip on her purse and stepped up onto the curb. "Be careful Aunt Esther; it's getting blustery."

"I'm right behind you," Esther said, taking her portfolio and squirming to the edge of the seat. As she emerged from the taxi, the wind made a snatch at her hat; she once again held her hand on the crown as Poppy closed the taxi door for her.

Cooper's Grill had been built twenty years ago, intended to be a gathering place for local big-wigs to congregate in relative seclusion. It had ended up catering to the nouveau riche, and because of that, had gained a carefully cultivated reputation for lavish dining and discreet waiters. There were three dining rooms—one done in light-blue wallpaper with a pattern of intertwined spring flowers, one with murals of windjammers leaning through rough seas, and one of polished oak paneling set off by portraits of race horses—and a now-neglected bar turned into a smoking room in the Art Nouveau building; in addition there was a private reception room at the top of a flight of stairs, reserved for the use of politicians, merchant princes, formal receptions, and distinguished foreigners, which this afternoon was not in use. The maître d' who greeted Poppy and Esther was on the shady side of middle-age, a man with a genial smile, a carefully groomed moustache, and a formidably genial manner; his tuxedo was slightly out of date but showing no signs of wear, and went well with the building. Bearing leather-bound menus as if carrying holy relics, he escorted the two Thornton women to one of the enclosed booths at the rear of the largest dining room, the one with the polished paneling.

"It wouldn't do for such ladies as you are to be seen dining without a male companion, if you'll pardoning my mentioning it," he informed them, as if this were new to the place.

"Whatever you think best," said Esther before Poppy could object, adding to Poppy in a whisper, "The booths are warmer, and we won't be disturbed."

The maître d' opened the burgundy-velvet curtain that fronted one of the booths, and a small bell jingled with the motion; he indicated the bell. "This will summon the waiter and will announce his arrival; if you have any requirements for him, he will answer your ring; it sounds in the kitchen as well as here," he explained, then set down the menus. "Jeremy will be your waiter. He'll be with you shortly. Enjoy your luncheon." He stood aside so that Poppy and Esther could choose their places among the four chairs, then let the curtain drop, the soft ringing of the bell accompanying his departure.

Esther chuckled softly. "This is pretty much the way I remember it," she said, hanging her coat on the brass coat-rack next to the curtain. "They've put in more light fixtures, but kept with the stained glass."

"Are they real Tiffany, do you think?" Poppy asked as she dropped her coat over the back of her chair.

"If they aren't, they're very good copies," said Esther, sitting down opposite her niece. "Now, tell me what you think of my chances of getting an opportunity to tell the story of the Living Spectres?"

"I can't be certain," Poppy said cautiously. "But if the Pearses agree to keep the reference to the Armenian refugees in my story, I think you stand a good chance of doing at least a side-bar—more if it looks like there is someone else besides Merrinelle Butterworth who's heard from GAD since the end of July and knows something about his interest in the Armenians, which will add credibility to what you have to report." She realized that Esther was not wholly convinced. "No one else at the paper can tell as much about them as you can, and that means you have an advantage, and Lowenthal knows it."

"I hope you're right," said Esther, glancing at her small brooch watch. "How long do you think it will take Lowenthal to make up his mind?"

"Nothing more than a day, unless there's new information," said Poppy, unfolding her napkin and spreading it on her lap. "If that turns up, you'll get another twenty-four hours beyond that."

"Good Lord Harry!" Esther shook her head. "How do you keep up with such a pace?"

"You get used to it, and I have to admit that most of the time I like it," said Poppy. "I remember when I was in college, working on the weekly paper—four sheets, one of them advertising—and how rushed it all seemed. My first job, at the *Pennsylvania Women's Companion*—you remember how frustrating I found it after the first month—wasn't much more demanding, but it got me a file of stories to use with Lowenthal."

"Weren't you on the society pages when you first went to work for him?" Esther asked. "You didn't like it much."

"Unfortunately, yes, I was. Garden parties and book clubs, occasionally a wedding or a funeral. Aunt Jo was pleased that I was working on the *respectable* part of the paper. I'd probably still be there, but for the Moncrief murder."

"Yes," said Esther slowly, and ventured out onto conversational thin ice. "Speaking of my sister, she phoned me about ten this morning, all excitement. It appears she may have heard from Stacy."

So that was it, Poppy thought. No wonder Aunt Esther was in no hurry to bring it up. "What do you mean, *appears?*" she asked.

"She told me that she had a post card with what she thinks is a Brazilian stamp on it with the message: *Hurricane nowhere near me. Don't fret. E.*"

"Nothing more than that?" Poppy asked when Esther did not volunteer anything else. "*No 'Having a Wonderful Time. Wish you were here'?*"

"That's what she told me."

The reporter in Poppy took over. "Has she informed the police?"

Esther attempted a laugh. "Jo, talk to the police? About Stacy? Are you serious? She said that she would never deal with the police so long as they believed her Eustace was a suspect in any wrong-doing."

"That sounds like Aunt Jo," said Poppy.

Again Esther hesitated. "I was thinking that if we could learn a little more about where the card came from, I might be able to take a side-trip on my way up the Amazon, just make a few inquiries, to see what comes up. You never know what you'll find if you don't look," she said, raising her chin.

"I wouldn't recommend it, not with Stacy. He's dangerous. I should know."

Poppy caught her lower lip in her teeth, recalling the hours she had spent in the warehouse basement. "I'd say avoid him if you happen to come across him."

"Perhaps we can come up with some sort of plan," Esther said as if this notion were new to her, but Poppy could see was not.

"What sort of a plan?" Poppy asked, her suspicions rising. "It can't be just a sketchy thing, not if you have Stacy in your sights."

"Perhaps we could get some suggestions on what might be the best strategy to use in locating him," Aunt Esther ventured in a manner that confirmed Poppy's sense that her aunt had worked all this out already, one she was planning to put in motion once she arrived in Brazil. "You know more about this than I do. Is there someone who can advise me how I might go about locating him? Someone you can trust."

"Whom did you have in mind?" Poppy said, deliberately taking her cue from Esther.

"Someone reliable, who is connected to the case," said Esther, her eyes lighting up. "Whom would you recommend?"

"Someone connected to the case you say?"

"Well, that would probably save some time," said Esther with her best cherubic smile.

Poppy frowned, trying to determine how to proceed. "This puts me in a bit of a quandary. Not simply because I'm close to the investigation, but I have... obligations."

"Inspector Loring—I know. He wouldn't be able to intervene in this case, not in South America, no matter how much he might want to. Yet he could have a few ideas I could employ if I decided to search for Stacy." Esther shook her head, as if weighing the options for her journey. "In a pinch, you could talk to Lowenthal about it, couldn't you? I'm sure he has contacts in South America through the press, and could put me in touch with som—"

"And how could I corroborate what you've told me when I ask his advice? Aunt Jo wouldn't confirm the post card even existed if the police ask her about it; what makes you think that she would discuss it with—" She broke off to order her thoughts, then resumed, "And if Aunt Jo isn't talking to the police, she surely won't say anything to anyone with the press, including me. Especially me, since she thinks it's my fault that Stacy's a suspect."

"You could mention it to Loring, or to Lowenthal, as a supposition. Either one of them ought to be able to make suggestions, hypothetically," Esther persisted. "Bring it up theoretically, or use some other, similar device that would not let them in on what has actually happened."

"I suppose I could," Poppy said. "I ought to tell Loring, whatever else I do; I know that. But there isn't much to hang on it for Lowenthal."

"It's worth a try. He seems to have a good opinion of you and your work," said Esther.

Poppy chuckled. "News to me. He was probably trying to get on your good side."

"I don't think so. He called you plucky, and seemed to be proud of what you did on the Moncrief murder investigation."

"Which is still open," Poppy reminded her as she opened the menu, then asked the question she knew her aunt was hoping for. "What do you recommend? Not about the food, about the card."

"I just thought you'd want to know about the card." Her mask of innocence slipped a bit. "There's been no progress in finding Stacy, and this might be a lead. You know the case has bogged down, and I presume you would like to see it active again. So now you know about the post card. What you do about it, if anything, is up to you." Esther picked up her menu and squinted at the page. "I really must get new reading glasses; I'll call Doctor Sawyer later today," she murmured as she strove to make out the elegant script. "The Buttered Cod Baked in Parchment sounds good."

"What about the Veal Cutlets?" Poppy asked. "In Italian Herbed Cream Sauce?"

"Sounds pretty rich for lunch—you might not be hungry by dinnertime," Esther said. "But if you're hungry now, don't let me stop you."

"I won't," said Poppy. "A pity there's no wine on the list."

"Um," Esther agreed. "I wonder if the Lamb Chops with Leeks and Mushrooms is good? I don't recall what their version tastes like."

"Try it and find out," Poppy suggested, and heard the bell tinkle as the curtain was drawn back.

"Would you prefer coffee or tea to start with? We serve water with the meal, but if you'd like some now, I'll bring it, if you like?" the waiter asked with slightly overdone courtesy.

Poppy and Esther exchanged glances and said at the same time "Coffee with one sugar and a little cream," and "Black tea with a teaspoon of milk—Assam, if you have it."

"We have English Breakfast," the waiter told her, "And some Russian Caravan, which costs ten cents more per pot."

"It'll do," said Esther. "The Russian Caravan."

The waiter nodded smoothly, and repeated their order. "Would you prefer crescent rolls or bread?"

This time aunt and niece agreed on crescent rolls.

"I'll bring them directly, and will take your luncheon order then, if you're ready." He whisked himself away.

"Well?" Poppy asked. "What do you think of the place?"

"It's not the same as it was," Esther said, and went on briskly, "But so little is, and in any case, memory can play tricks about the old days."

"That's so," Poppy said, wishing she knew what Aunt Esther was actually referring to, and doubted it was the change in selections on Cooper's Grill's menu.

"I must say, they've kept the place up well," Esther said as a kind of compensation for her possible lapse in memory.

"Did you come here often, when it was new?" Poppy asked.

"Three or four times a year, as I recall," said Esther. "I think I will have the lamb."

Poppy gave the menu a last, thorough perusal. "And I'll have the Beef Rib in Pan Gravy with Shredded Cabbage and Pine Nuts," Poppy decided.

Esther reached out to ring the bell. "Let's tell Jeremy."

Poppy nodded agreement, knowing that it she would get nowhere pursuing the matter of the post card now. "Yes. Let's. I'm hungry."

TWENTY-SEVEN

POPPY HAD BEEN BACK AT HER DESK FOR TWENTY MINUTES WHEN LORING returned her call. After the most terse of greetings, Poppy asked, "Have you talked to Hank yet, or would you like me to phone him first?"

"Is that what you wanted to talk to me about? Whether or not I want you to smooth the way with your cousin for me?" Loring inquired. In spite of his pleasure at the sound of her voice, he was tired and a bit peevish; he offered his version of an apology. "It's been a rough day, and I'm out of sorts."

"Asking about Hank was an earlier question. I have more to tell you now." She took a breath and waited for him to interject whatever he liked, then, when he remained silent, she said, "Aunt Esther told me over lunch that Aunt Jo had a post card from Stacy, most likely in the early post."

"Oho," said Loring, his tone guardedly interested. "Do you know where it came from? Can you tell me more?"

"No, not very much; I can only tell you what Aunt Esther told me over lunch. Judging from what she said, the card would have had to have come this morning, in the early post, probably because Aunt Jo did not receive it yesterday, morning nor evening. From what Aunt Jo told Esther, the stamp on the card is Brazilian; the message on it let Aunt Jo know that the hurricane was not near where he is." She waited again, then went on, "It's nothing more than a couple sentences, but I thought you'd want to know."

"Did he give any indication where that might be, beyond the stamp?" There was genuine curiosity as well as a little skepticism in his voice.

"Not that I know of," Poppy replied carefully; she studied her desk-lamp to see if it flickered—a sure sign of Holte's presence—but its shine remained steady.

"Have you seen the card itself?" Loring pursued.

"No, I haven't. Neither has Aunt Esther, but she reported that Aunt Jo called her this morning to tell her about the card. If there was anything more to their conversation, Aunt Esther didn't mention it." Poppy went quiet while she pondered what else to tell him. "I could ask her if Aunt Jo told her anything else."

"Would it do any good?" Loring made no effort to hide his doubts.

"Do you mean with Aunt Esther or Aunt Jo?"

"Ultimately, Aunt Jo," said Loring.

Poppy had a prompt response. "She's not likely to talk to me about it if I called her; she still blames me for Stacy's troubles."

"Do you think she'll let you see the post card if you asked her?" Loring asked.

"No, I don't think so," Poppy admitted.

"Me, too," he conceded, and abandoned the topic of the post card. "What was the other thing you wanted to tell me?"

"I called Hadley and Grimes. Quentin Hadley isn't in the office today and isn't expected back soon. He's sailing with his cousin, bound for Cuba via Jamaica, according to his secretary, a fastidious fellow named Clifford Tinsdale, who was surprisingly talkative for a man in his position, and I don't quite know what to make of what he said—he told me more than I expected without coaxing. I think it might mean that he's worried, with the hurricane and not yet hearing that Nelson and Quentin have arrived in Jamaica, or anywhere else, for that matter."

"Not a good time for sailing. Hurricane Sylvia savaged that part of the Atlantic, and could still damage the Carolinas, though the Weather Service says it's dying." He paused, and when he spoke again, he had lowered his voice. "Am I to assume that Hadley and Grimes have not heard from Quentin?"

"Not yet," she said. "But with all the damage the storm did, he might not be able to telegraph the office yet. Transmitting cables might be down, or telegraph offices wrecked."

"I'll call the Coast Guard and find out what they know; they'll have the most current information," said Loring with growing exuberance. "There might be something worthwhile in all this. About time."

"I hope so." Feeling oddly guilty for not telling him that the *Belle Helene* might have sunk, Poppy went on, "If I find out anything more about Stacy, you'll be the first to hear about it." She wondered what Holte might be able to turn up in the dimension of ghosts, where she guessed he had gone.

"Thanks. If I learn anything, I'll pass it on," Loring assured her.

This was a good time to hang up, she thought, but instead she asked, "Have you any news on the Pearse case?"

"Not yet," he said, echoing her earlier response. "I gather that Blessing has agreed to go to Vienna and see what he can find."

"That's good, isn't it?" She started doodling on her desk-blotter with her pencil. "It gets things moving, doesn't it?"

"It's better than nothing," he said. "Blessing seems like the kind of man who can be trusted; I'm not sure I can say the same about the Austrians."

"Why?"

"They have trouble enough without bothering about the Armenian refugees or one missing American college student. Think of what's going on in Germany—the inflation there can't be good for Austria." He cleared his throat.

"Have you said anything to the Pearses about this? Not the inflation, the difficulty of dealing with the Austrians."

"No; they're apt to make a formal complaint about it if I say anything," he said, still quietly. "All we need is diplomatic red tape fouling the works."

"You mean that they'd interfere on that level?" Poppy increased her doodling.

"That's exactly what I mean, and it's the one thing we can't afford. It's hard enough to get the Austrian police to do anything about GAD now; add pressure and it will be doubly so." He swallowed audibly. "That's off the record, of course."

"I thought so," she said, a bit distractedly; she found it disconcerting to have Holte missing when there had been potential news about Stacy as well as developments on the Pearse case. Her doodles grew still more extensive.

As if he had read her thoughts, he asked, "Anything useful from your invisible friend?"

Poppy dropped her pencil. "You know there isn't, since there is no such person," she said, more brusquely than she had intended. "Sorry. I'm still a little flummoxed about Stacy."

"I can see why," said Loring, and faltered. "If you don't want to get dragged into this part of the investigation, just tell me and I'll make sure you aren't kept informed."

Poppy reacted at once. "Oh, no. I want to know everything, even though I might not like it. I don't want to have it left to my imagination." She winced at the recollection of the nightmares that had followed her ordeal for more than a month after it had happened.

Loring's voice brightened. "Atta girl. I'll let you know what I find out from the Coast Guard, okay? And you can let me know if you learn anything more about your cousin." He was quiet for a second or two, then said, "Sorry. Have to go. I'll talk to you tomorrow or Friday." He took an audible breath. "If anything else turns up—"

"I will keep you informed," she said, and to her own perplexity, added, "Good luck." She located her dropped pencil with her toe and began to roll it out from under her desk to where she could bend down and reach it.

"Thanks. You, too," he said, and hung up.

After retrieving the pencil, Poppy sat still for more than a minute, staring at the far wall with her eyes focused some distance beyond it, her mind very nearly blank. When Gafney, three desks away, began coughing, Poppy recalled where she was and called herself to order, then got out bond, carbon paper, and onion-skin, aligned them and rolled them into the platen of her typewriter, although she had no idea what she was going to write. As she began to make a summary of her appointments and interviews of the last ten days, she could not shake off the nagging question, "Where is Chesterton Holte?"

It would have startled Poppy to discover that Holte was not in the dimension of ghosts, but riding in a first-class train carriage on its way through the tempestuous night en route from Brussels to Vienna; he had caught up with N.Cubed Blessing as the detective had left his taxi at the train station in Brussels, bound for the ticket booth and platforms beyond; that was at sunset. Now he was going over the information that Blessing had received from the Pearses' London solicitor that morning, reading over his old co-ordinator's shoulder.

"How much credence do you give this?" Blessing asked, holding up the sheaf of papers.

"I'd say that it's largely factually correct, but that means that a great deal has been left out," said Holte. "Sherman Pearse is a punctilious man, but he does not usually take well to displays of emotion, which is why this dossier reads like a summary of school progress. That, and the solicitor isn't apt to include emotional content."

"Mister Pearse is paying for airborne delivery of his records to Vienna, but that might only mean that he is impatient," Blessing remarked as he rewound his muffler around his neck, for the railway car was growing chilly, first class or not.

"It's more than that: his wife thinks GAD has been kidnapped, and the longer there is no word from him, the more Mister Pearse may have to accept that as a possibility, and the outcry that goes with it. I believe that Pearse is hoping for a swift resolution to the case, so that the publicity around it is minimal." Holte adjusted himself along the luggage rack, although this was more for Blessing's benefit than his own.

"Then he isn't indifferent to his son," said Blessing, looking reassured. "I was beginning to think that Mister Pearse was relieved to have his son among the missing."

"Well, GAD is the heir; Pearse and his wife lost their oldest son about four or five years ago. On the other hand, GAD is not the apple of his father's eye, although he is worried about the lad's being missing." Holte was now lying horizontally in the luggage rack above Blessing's seat rather than hanging in the air in front of it.

"Do they have any other children?" Blessing asked.

"I haven't seen them, but Poppy says there are four girls and one boy—the boy is quite young—beyond GAD."

Blessing nodded emphatically. "So the missing heir is important to him."

"And especially to his mother; she's almost frantic." Holte floated down to the open place beside Blessing and did his best to sit on it without sinking into the seat.

"Is that a problem?" Blessing glanced toward the window as a cluster of lights appeared in the distance ahead.

"Mister Pearse has a strong dislike of the spotlight, as most of his class do, and Missus Pearse has been telling everyone she knows of her fears for her son; it is only a matter of time until there is a public outcry. Mister Pearse has forbidden the Philadelphia police to open an official file on this case, for fear it will end up in the *Inquirer* or the *New York Times*. In addition, a young lady who is not an acceptable daughter-in-law to the Pearses has spoken to a...disreputable newspaper about GAD's disappearance, so there already is a degree of public awareness that GAD has vanished, however questionable the publication may be. The young lady herself comes from New Money and has a flamboyant nature, living in high alt, as my mother used to say. The other thing that Mister Pearse dreads almost as much as public attention, is the Federal Bureau of Investigation; he believes that they are too eager for attention, and that that could complicate the return of—"

"I understand," said Blessing. "And I agree with Pearse to a point. Too much of a hue and cry can interfere with a proper investigation, as you have reason to know."

Holte lowered his head. "Lamentably." He did not like to be reminded of his near- exposure as a spy while on his first mission in Holland, when a passing remark to a schoolboy ended up in the evening news. "I can sympathize with Pearse without having to like him. And good thing, too." He would have liked to have made a greater show of his disapproval of Sherman Pearse, but was frustrated by his lack of corporeality.

Blessing neatened the papers he held. "I'm going to take a little while to think this over, so that I can be prepared when I arrive in Vienna."

"You won't get there until late Thursday, assuming there are no delays, and you make your connection in Strasbourg," Holte reminded him.

"I'll need a fair amount of time to sort out the variables in this case, and riding in a train is a fine place to ruminate," Blessing said at his most reserved. "Tell your latest...hauntee that you have spoken with me, if that will be useful to your mission."

Holte paused, then went ahead and asked, "In all that information, what, if any of it, is about the Living Spectres?"

"Not very much: according to the Viennese sources, the group is led by the Armenian Orthodox Priest, Ahram Avaikian, numbers roughly two hundred adults and fifty or so children. They are sworn pacifists, are seeking a place to settle permanently, and most of them are as near to destitute as it is possible to be. Nothing new there."

"No, it doesn't sound like it," said Holte. He shook off the sudden gloom that had settled upon him. "Well, I guess I'll be off, then. I'll try to seek you out again in a day or so."

"Bring me news of any developments you can; you're much faster than the post." Blessing took out his pipe and tobacco pouch.

"I will, and thank you." Holte prepared to rise out of the train and proceed at ghost-speed to Philadelphia.

"Just one thing," Blessing said, halting Holte's departure.

"What is it?"

"If you find GAD Pearse in the dimension of ghosts, try to discover where he's buried and what happened to him, would you? So I can inform his family. It's the least I can do." Blessing reached into his inner jacket pocket and drew out a lighter. "I'd offer you some, but I know you would not enjoy it."

"I'll let you know if I learn anything about GAD." Holte did not respond to the jibe about the pipe.

"Tally-ho," said Blessing, as Holte faded from sight and left the train; it was the same thing N.Cubed used to say to his spies as he sent them out on assignment, Holte recalled, as he hastened westward.

He arrived at Esther's house shortly before six, and found Poppy and Esther in the sitting room with drinks in their hand and a platter of finger-food on the table between them; Holte took care to avoid the overhead two-bulb fixture, but was not so lucky with one of the sconce-bulbs which flickered as he moved along the wall. He saw Poppy turn toward the fixture, an expression of near-welcome on her tired features.

"Not another bulb going," Esther complained. She set down her balloon-glass of twenty- year-old brandy and got up from the settee to go tap the offending bulb; it stayed strong. "Must be the wind, though if it is, you'd think more than one light would blink, wouldn't you?" She glared at the sconce.

"It could be a fuse," Poppy suggested.

Esther shrugged. "We'll find out soon enough, if the lights all go out," she said, and came back to her place on the settee. "They say we'll have more rain tomorrow, if you believe the Weather Service."

"So I've heard," Poppy said, and had another sip of cognac. "I'm going to buy a proper raincoat this coming Saturday. I can't continue to ruin my cashmere coats. The one I wore today is a dead loss, and I only have two others. I don't even know if it's worth donating my wet one to St. Clement's charity-box."

"Someone could make a child's coat from it, I'd think," said Esther.

Holte found a comfortable place near the ceiling in the southwest corner of the room and settled down to watch and listen.

"Why not go out tomorrow? I'd wager that Lowenthal would give you an extra half-hour for lunch if you told him what you wanted to do. He can't want you to go about dripping while you work, can he." Esther picked up a bacon-wrapped broiled scallop and used the toothpick transfixing it to dunk it into the fig-and-olive tapenade. "I don't know how Missus Sassoro comes up with these treats, but I have to say I'm always delighted when she does." She bit the scallop with its portion of bacon neatly in half.

"It's her heritage coming out," Poppy said, not quite seriously.

"Possibly, but whatever accounts for it, I'm very pleased with the results," said Esther chewing, and took the rest of the scallop with the same precision.

Poppy tasted her cognac again, and stared at the ceiling, looking for the faint but familiar smudge that identified Holte; she did not spot him at first, and when she did, she gave a little smile. "I don't know what was so exhausting about today, but it has knocked the stuffing out of me." She wanted to rub her eyes, but feared that it would smear her mascara.

"A good meal and a hot toddy this evening should set you to rights, come morning," Esther said with her usual energetic encouragement. "The rain makes life a little enervating, but a good raincoat will help that. The sooner you get one, the sooner you won't feel the damp so much. There's nothing to be gained from delay, not with winter coming. You might look for a pair of galoshes, as well. You don't want to go around in wet shoes all the time, do you? I've noticed that you've had wet shoes."

This pragmatic advice took Poppy's attention away from her search for Holte, and she said, "I suppose you're right, but I do hate shopping in the rain. It's so dreary."

"Dreary or not, the sooner done, the soonest mended...or fixed," Esther said, more bracingly than before.

"I'll see what I can arrange," Poppy said, succumbing to her aunt's energetic support. "It'll depend on how the news goes whether Lowenthal will spare me the time."

Satisfied that she had set Poppy on the right track, Esther abandoned her affectionate ballyragging. "Have a scallop or two before I eat them all; I won't have any appetite for dinner, and that would annoy Missus Sassoro," she recommended.

Obediently, Poppy selected one of the scallops nearest to her on the platter, and poked it into the tapenade. She took a bite and was pleased to agree with her aunt: it was delicious. "I'll have another shortly."

"See that you do," said Esther, taking a more generous swig of her brandy. "This is just the thing on a dank night like this one."

"Yes," said Poppy, and helped herself to a second scallop. "You mentioned winter: do you think we'll have an early one?" As she spoke, she wondered if Holte could offer any advice on the weather, or if, by being noncorporeal, he had no need to pay attention to it.

"Galliard says it will be a hard one, though not very early—something to do with the pyracantha berries." She selected another scallop. "How's the winter coat growing in on that dratted cat of yours?"

"He has a lot of fur at the best of times, so it's hard to tell," Poppy said around the scallop she was consuming.

"Miss Roth tells me that he sheds a lot," Esther said. "Not a complaint, mind you, but an observation."

"She told me that she'd like to take the carpet-sweeper to him, so she wouldn't have to do the floors every other day. I said she could, if she could catch him." Poppy picked up a tea-napkin and wiped the grease from her fingers.

"I have to confess that I didn't expect to like him, but he's appealing, in an aloof sort of way." Esther finished her brandy and added a bit more to her glass. "I'm going to be in this evening, the last time this week, so I want to make the most of the peace and quiet."

"It's your house Aunt Esther," said Poppy. "You may do as you like in it."

"That's not Jo's opinion," Esther said with a sharp laugh.

"Well, no, it wouldn't be. She is wedded to her notion of correctness, and at this point, there's no changing her. I surmise that you and she have had words recently? Beyond her morning call. How did you come to speak to her twice in one day," Poppy said, putting her hand over the top of her glass in response to Esther's proffer of the bottle of cognac.

Esther nodded. "I made the mistake of calling her this afternoon when I got back from lunching with you. I intended to learn more about the post card, but she accused me of snooping—which I was—and decided to rake me over the coals in regard to everything she could think of. Hearing about it all from her, you'd believe that I deliberately snubbed everyone in our social set, and that I had cast a shadow over all the family because of it. Since Isme Greenloch declined to attend our party, the rumors have been buzzing among the upper crust, most of whom are cautious about including me among their guests unless I have an acceptable escort with me, in any case."

"But you're busy the rest of the week, in spite of that," said Poppy.

"Two evenings are reciprocal invitations for our party, Isme Greenloch's being the most significant, because she decided not to come to ours. She's attempting to make amends for the slight. And Moira Sauers has asked me to speak to the Women's Political Society about the coming election. There's a small honorarium, which I shall donate right back to the group. We may have the vote now, but there is much more to be done."

"What will you be speaking about?" Poppy inquired.

"Oh, the usual: women's place is not wholly in the home, that there is no error in getting an education to do more than teach grammar school, run the local library, or nurse the sick and injured. Marriage isn't the only honorable career for females. Eugenia Perkins will probably take me to task for advocating a turn away from womanliness, meaning marriage and motherhood. She usually does. I know better than to fight with her, there's no point to it. At least she supports the vote for women, which is more than many others do. Yet I hope some of the younger women attending will at least think about what I say, and get enough backbone to stand up to the family pressures." She sighed. "It's not easy, as you know as well as I, but in the long run, it's worth the struggle."

Holte moved a little closer to the two women, his curiosity piqued.

"If they have an ounce of sense, they will listen to you," said Poppy. "I did."

"And see what it's got you: you're excluded from a number of high society occasions because you're a journalist." Esther did her best to laugh.

"You see how crushed I am," Poppy said, clasping her free hand to her brow in her best tragic manner. Then she abandoned her joking. "Speaking of exclusions, who is the other reciprocal hostess?" she asked, wishing she could find out where Holte had been; she would have to hold her tongue until later, when they were alone.

"Professor Timms," said Esther with a moue of aversion.

Poppy could not stop a wry smile. "Does that mean you will have to endure the lovely Missus Timms?"

"Beatrice will be the hostess, no doubt. I'm guessing that the event is Langton's idea—he was pretty distressed at the way she behaved here, and he's the sort who tries to make up for awkwardness. I've asked Judge Stephanson to come with me; Benedict knows how to handle difficult people."

"Beatrice and Benedict," Poppy mused with the hint of a grin. "Mightn't that be too tempting for her?"

"You're not going to blame Shakespeare for Beatrice's bad manners, are you? It isn't his fault that the two names have a resonance beyond the immediate social scene. Besides, she doesn't need such an excuse to flirt." Esther drank most of her brandy and poured a little more. "I can't endure the thought of going alone, and it would only create more gossip if you come with me: two women who work for a living at such a gathering. Shocking."

"That's a bit...daunting," said Poppy. "You'd think having a job is the same as having leprosy."

"To many of them, it is," said Esther, and continued less animatedly, "Don't take umbrage. Our set isn't the only ones to think that a woman's first obligation is to marry and have children, and that those who do not are, at the least, odd, if not pitiable. The middle class can be just as stuffy, and can take more pride in being so."

Holte slid closer to the two women, listening with heightened interest to what they were discussing; he hoped for another insight into their opinions.

"I'm aware of that. Aunt Jo used to remind me that with my trust fund—which I agree is generous—I shouldn't have to work, and technically, that's true. She occasionally said that I owed it to my father to marry and have children, since my trust would support a family comfortably—ten thousand dollars a year is a lot of money, but—" Poppy was surprised at the intensity of her emotion; she decided to explain. "But it isn't the money Aunt Esther, it isn't. I want to do something useful with my life."

"Isn't having children useful?" Aunt Esther asked quietly.

"Perhaps, for those who have a natural talent for it. My friend, Mildred Fairchild, does have such a gift, and I'm happy for her." Poppy shook her head. "I don't, and I know it. I need to be taking on the world, the way my mother used to do, before she became ill. Her work with the Suffragettes was inspiring."

"Your father thought so, too, and was glad to see you following in her footsteps. He told me how proud he was of the way you were growing up. He'd be delighted to know you're a working newspaperwoman." She drank the last of the brandy in her glass. "That's enough of that. I'll be light-headed if I continue to indulge."

Poppy had another small sip of her cognac and considered setting the glass aside, half- empty. "There'll be wine at dinner, I suppose?"

"Missus Sassoro has a good bottle of claret set aside for tonight, to go with the duck in raspberry sauce, and the mashed turnips with cream cheese. It's the last time we'll have fresh raspberries this year."

"Sounds delicious," said Poppy, and helped herself to another scallop. "The other six are yours Aunt Esther."

"Don't be ridiculous," said Esther. "I can't possibly eat them all. Have one more, please."

"One, but no more," said Poppy, capitulating. She finished the one she was eating and took another. "This is my last."

"Your cat is going to be lucky tonight—at least two scallops with bacon, maybe three." She suddenly stretched, flexing her right foot. "Don't worry. I just had a stitch in my thigh."

"Are you all right?" Poppy asked, a rush of concern coming over her.

"I'm getting old, that's all, and my body reminds me of it from time to time." Esther selected another scallop. "This will do it for me." She sat back against the cushions on her settee.

Poppy grinned. "Maestro will be pleased."

TWENTY-EIGHT

"I THOUGHT YOU'D LIKE TO KNOW THAT BLESSING IS ON HIS WAY," HOLTE SAID apologetically, hovering near the end of her bed while Poppy sat at her vanity table, brushing her hair; she was wearing her bathrobe over her new, silk pyjamas, and had already used cold cream to clean her face—a small wad of tissue paper was at her elbow in testament. It was only ten-thirty, but Esther had gone off to make notes for her address to the Women's Political Society, and Poppy was glad to have a chance to relax. She had got into her bedclothes and begun her nightly routine: removing make-up—what little she wore—and brushing her hair the recommended one hundred times.

"On his way to where?" Poppy asked.

"Vienna; it's his first step on his hunt for GAD," Holte answered. "I thought you'd like to know."

"I'm glad you've told me," said Poppy, almost losing count of the strokes; it was something around fifty-nine, so she thought fifty-eight, just in case, and continued on steadily. "I suppose that Blessing wired Mister Pearse before he left?"

"Yes, he did. And he wired Inspector Loring, as well, so he would be able to assess the progress of the investigation. I believe it was a wise precaution to make sure Loring does not have to depend on Mister Pearse for his news from the Continent." He moved so that he was a little more visible in the half-lit room. "Blessing told me when I visited with him on the train."

"I assumed you'd gone to the dimension of ghosts," said Poppy, as much to keep him talking as for any information.

"Not yet. I want to be better prepared before I start asking more questions," Holte said. "You know how important research is, don't you."

"I do," she agreed. Sixty-six, sixty-seven, sixty-eight...

"It occurred to me that I needed know more of what's going on here, in the world of the living, before I returned to the dimension of ghosts. I need to be able to sort out what is true, what is remembered, and what is imagined, before I go much further on this Pearse matter."

"You don't have to do it, though I'm grateful that you do." Poppy stopped brushing momentarily, and looked directly at the pale sketch of a man almost reclining on her bed. "If you were alive, this would be scandalous."

"A good thing then that I'm not," he countered with unflagging good humor.

"I should think so," she said, and smiled in spite of herself.

Holte could sense that she was avoiding something, so he said, "There's something else on your mind."

Poppy assumed a hauteur that was more like Aunt Jo than herself. "It's very unbecoming for a gentleman to force an issue with a lady."

"I thought you didn't like being considered that kind of lady," Holte shot back. "You certainly gave me that impression earlier." He paid no attention to Maestro, who had hissed at him and then hurried under the bed.

"I don't, but I don't like being pushed, either. Cajolery might work better, if it isn't too demeaning." She resumed her brushing.

"You really don't want to talk about it if you're willing to get on your high horse. What is it?"

"That's not cajolery," she pointed out.

"Then tell me what's bothering you, and I'll stop." He had grown more perceptible, his voice more a sound in the room than an echo in her mind.

She sighed heavily. "There are so many dead people around Stacy: Madison Moncrief, James Poindexter, Percy Knott, now indirectly, Quentin and Nelson Hadley, and Miles Overstreet. I can't help remembering that strange warning I was given when I went to interview Quentin Hadley last spring. That I was in danger. After the episode in the locked cellar, I thought it was over. Now I'm not so sure. What if there are more dead?"

"You don't include Julian Eastley?" Holte inquired levelly.

"No. Should I?"

"Tangentially, yes." He saw the appalled look in her eyes; he went on, "He wouldn't have been driving out on that road if Louise Moncrief had not left town, which she wouldn't have if her husband hadn't been murdered, and possibly she wouldn't have fled with Stacy and Warren Derrington, but that's not such a sure thing."

"I think you're stretching a point," Poppy said.

"Do the police see any connection?" Holte was sitting up now, fully concentrating on Poppy.

"Inspector Loring does," she said.

"That hardly counts," he said.

"You're being persnickety," she told him, and once more picked up her brush. Eighty-two, eighty-three, eighty-four...

"You have to be, if you're a spy—persnickety, and a bit...paranoid, as the alienists call it." He floated closer to her. "You know you're not responsible for any of those deaths."

Poppy could not bring herself to look at him. "I tell myself that, but I don't believe it, not entirely. If I hadn't pursued Madison Moncrief's death, perhaps some of the others would not have died."

"Even if you hadn't been assigned to the story, one of your colleagues would have been, and Denton North would be gathering evidence of antiques counterfeiting and Customs fraud, to say nothing of the problems that were developing among those who were likely part of the counterfeiting-and-smuggling ring; any one of those things would have made the murders possible." He said this with cool deliberation, and went on less austerely. "You aren't responsible for what they decided to do, and you may be in a unique position to contribute to the apprehension for those in the conspiracy. That should reassure you."

"But, ye gods! Stacy and Derrington would not have come under scrutiny so quickly, and—assuming that one or the other of them did the killing—they might have gone away before needing to kill any more..."

"Including Stacy's attempt on you," Holte interjected. "No wonder you're feeling tired, carrying all that around with you," he said, now half a step behind her, his manner more sympathetic. "Has it occurred to you that if you hadn't investigated Moncrief's death, and put some pressure on Stacy, that your cousin might have got away with at least one murder, and very likely more?"

"Don't make fun of me," she ordered him.

"I'm not," he rejoined. "I'm pointing out something that would be obvious to you if it were happening to anyone else."

She set her brush aside and slumped in her chair. "I keep thinking about Derrington and Louise. If they're with Stacy, are they in danger from him? Or he from them?"

"That isn't your responsibility, Poppy. You haven't told any of them to kill anyone; those murders are their choices, not yours, and they, not you, bear the burden of them." Holte saw her stiffen, and fell silent.

"Do you feel that way about the agents who worked for you?" She looked forlorn as she asked him.

"No," he said bluntly. "Because I was the one who sent them into danger, and they were aware of the risk. Your father was one of those who died because of me, which was entirely different. My men, and women, knew what they were getting into; your father did not. I might have been able to save him, but that would have led to the death of a great many more men, so I chose the...the lesser of two evils, and I'm in the process of recompensing those who suffered because of what I did, knowingly and with full awareness of the peril I was imposing on those who were ignorant of the danger I—"

Poppy bit her lower lip. "Doesn't it bother you?"

"It certainly does. That's why I'm haunting you—remember?" He was losing patience with her, as much because he did not like having to think back on all he had done in the name of King and Country, as because he was worried on Poppy's behalf. "It took me a while to work out what damage I had done while I was doing good, but I've got a handle on it now."

Taking up one of the used tissues, Poppy wiped her eyes. "I'm sorry for being such a ninny. It's just that sometimes it all catches up with me—you know how that is—and I begin to feel sorry for myself. It's most unseemly in me; I apologize for being so self-indulgent."

"It's not unseemly at all," said Holte. "And for what it's worth, you're one of the least self-indulgent persons I have ever encountered."

"It's kind of you to say that, but I would be horribly chagrined if I had an outburst like this in the city room of the *Clarion*." She gathered up her tissues and let them fall into the waste- paper basket at the edge of her vanity table. "And no doubt, I would rue the day I let myself give way."

"I can't picture you doing that," said Holte. "It's not your style at all."

"Well, I can picture it, and it makes me want to hide under the bed with Maestro; I know what a lapse like that would mean for me—back to the society page," said Poppy, trying to keep her voice from shaking. She mustered her tattering reserves and exclaimed, "Ye gods! What a goose I'm being."

"Hardly a goose," said Holte at his most avuncular.

Poppy was unconvinced. "If you want to go away and give me time to collect myself, I wouldn't blame you at all. I'd do it if I could."

"I would blame me. I won't be offended by your tears or your dismay, or anything else," he said. "You hide your strain well, but I can tell that it's been growing in you for some time. So I'll listen if you want to talk, or I'll talk if you'd rather listen."

Maestro emerged from under the bed, did a double flip with his tail, and went to curl up in the corner, his back to the room.

Poppy leaned forward, her elbows on the vanity table, her chin propped in her joined hands. "If only there could be a break in the Pearse case, something positive that I can report on instead of having to cover all the fears and anxieties of the family, I think I'd feel better. Or if I could get something more than ephemeral traces of Stacy, so that he could be pursued, I'd have some hope for retribution. If that makes me unworthy, so be it."

"Well, it doesn't, not in my eyes; your cousin has a lot to answer for, and should," said Holte, holding still to the extent that he could. "I'll do what I can to glean more information from the ghosts who are tied to the case, to find out if there is anything they can tell me about Stacy, but that's about all I can do, other than follow Blessing to Europe and see what he discovers, if anything, about GAD. I've been planning to do that for a little while, and now I think it's necessary."

"That *if anything* is what has me worried. What if there is no sign of GAD, and that he simply vanished, and no one ever finds out how that happened?"

"No one *simply vanished*, not if he's traveling with a passport. It may take time to find him, and I can't tell you what shape he'll be in, but someone, somewhere will know what has happened to him." He slid over toward the end of her bed. "I haven't found him among the ghosts, so I take it he is still alive."

"But what if he's not?" Poppy stared at Holte, her eyes like hot coals. "Or what if he's a prisoner, and his captors have no intention of letting him go?"

"Once we know where he is, something can be done," said Holte. "Your Aunt Esther's old friend from the diplomatic corps could still pull some strings, couldn't he?"

"You mean Arnold Schultz?" Poppy considered the possibility.

"That's the man. He looks like he still has some grit in him."

"He probably does, from what Aunt Esther says," Poppy allowed, more speculatively than before.

"He might be able to lend a hand to N.Cubed, in an unobvious way," Holte continued. "It wouldn't have to be official. Many of those kinds of activities aren't."

"But it could take months to find out what the Pearses need to know," Poppy protested.

"Don't borrow trouble," Holte said, hovering over the folded blanket on the end of the bed. "I'll do as much as I can to keep up with Blessing and to ask more questions in the dimension of ghosts, and I'll report back to you before Friday, probably earlier. Will that suit you, or would you prefer me to stay here."

"To buck me up, you mean? No, it's better that you do the kinds of things only you can, and get back to me as quickly as you're able. I appreciate your dilemma, but I'd like to think I can handle myself by myself for a day or two." As a demonstration, she made herself sit up, her spine straight, and her head raised. "If I'm going to be a crime reporter, I'm going to have to get used to disappointments and dead ends, with or without your support."

"If that's what you want," said Holte cautiously. "I'll do what I can. If I'm lucky, I'll be back by Thursday night, Friday morning at the latest. Keep in touch with Loring; he'll have news from Blessing in a little while."

"You're sure of that?" Poppy asked.

"Ninety percent sure," he told her, moving off toward the ceiling. "And your aunt is right—you need a raincoat."

"Thanks so much," she said, rallying herself in order to be a bit sarcastic; she watched him disappear through the ceiling, then stared bleakly at herself in the mirror. After five minutes of this melancholy pursuit, she left the vanity table, turned off the central light fixture, and got into bed; her reading light was on and there was a copy of Sheridan LeFanu's grand Victorian gothic tale *Uncle Silas* on her night-stand, which she picked up and opened to the bookmark she had put in place the night before. She read the previous page to remind herself of what was going on, and moved ahead in the tale. Good, old-fashioned horror, she thought. Nothing like the modern world of world-wide war and actual murder victims. She settled back on her pillow and let herself get lost in the story.

A little while later, Maestro sauntered out of the corner and took his place at the foot of the bed, purring loudly.

Slipping through the ceiling, Holte decided to start with the dimension of ghosts first. There were sufficient questions to put to the various ghosts he had been in contact with that he wanted to begin his interrogations now. Besides, Blessing was still on the train, and would be for a day or two longer, and with the flexibility of time in the dimension of ghosts, Holte was sure he could make more progress there than in a first class railway compartment. He floated through the invisible chaos of ghostly streams and eddies, looking sightlessly for Moncrief or Knott or Overstreet as a place to begin. To his amazement, he found Knott first, drifting with a jumble of hurricane victims and paying no heed to their plaintive, silent howls.

"*Knott?*" Holte addressed him from a distance. "*I'm Chesterton Holte.*"

"*Holte. I remember you, don't I?*" Knott came to as much of a halt as he could in the convoluted mass. "*You're the one looking for Stacy Dritchner, Warren Derrington, and Louise Moncrief, aren't you? Are you looking for me to learn about them?*"

"*I am. I was hoping that you might answer a couple of questions for me.*" Holte moved a little farther outside of the cycling current of ghosts. "*Not only about Stacy and Derrington and Louise, but connected to them.*"

"*You've talked to Overstreet, or so he told me a while ago.*" There was a guarded quality to his observation.

"*I have, as much as I could.*" Holte sailed a little nearer to Knott. "*Overstreet was still fairly confused. He hadn't yet realized that he had been murdered when I spoke to him.*"

Knott did something that was like acquiescence. "*He's beginning to figure that out, and he's getting angry about it. I hope he doesn't try anything reckless.*"

"*What might that be?*" Holte asked, trying to imagine how a ghost could be reckless in the world of the living.

"*I'm not sure, and neither is he. I think he wants to cause some kind of physical scene, or at least make the attempt; he can't rattle chains and he can't shove the living down stairs or under a train, not that he wouldn't like to,"* said Knott. *"And not that it would do much good Quentin and Nelson are here, both drowned during that hurricane that battered along the outside of the Caribbean a day or two ago. Or more. I'm not really sure of the time. You know how that goes."*

"None better." This was the kind of information that Holte was seeking. *"Have you seen them?"*

"As much as anyone sees anything in this place. It felt like them, but they were so dazed, I could be wrong." He drifted a short, non-distance away from Holte.

"Were they bound anywhere in particular?" Holte asked, keeping up with Knott. *"Did they mention their destination?"*

"In this place? There's no such thing, and you know it. I would have thought that they had a port in mind in the world of the living." Knott gave another of his non-laughs. *"I couldn't tell you where they are now, but I haven't seen them since that one time, shortly after they arrived. Not that I've made any attempt to search them out. I'll wait until they remember more of what has happened to them before I speak to them again. I don't think Quentin wants to talk to me, as much as I want to talk to him."*

"Why is that?" Holte wanted to keep Knott telling what he knew.

"I'm not sure—it may be that he hasn't fully realized where he is yet—but it may have something to do with that antiquities fiddle that he and Dritchner and Derrington worked out with me. Quentin was the one who kept the books, and he did a fine job of it. The government's after all of us—not that that means anything now. The Attorney General can't reach us here." His ghostly non-chuckle troubled Holte.

"So there was something illegal going on," Holte said.

"Depends on what you mean by illegal. We were providing high quality copies of legitimate pieces—nothing shoddy—to people who were inexperienced enough to buy them. I had some of the real thing, but for museum-level prices, and those were the ones we had copied, then arranged for the originals to be sold privately. Getting the copies into the country was a different juggle, but one that worked as well as our methods of importing the originals. Quentin handled the paperwork for Customs; top notch documentation. I was surprised when someone twigged on what we were doing."

"Why is that?"

"Because of all the care Hadley and Grimes took with our records and such. What Vincent and Paxton worked out was good enough to pass muster with their own firm—which is saying

a great deal. James Poindexter didn't winkle it out for more than a year of snooping, and Moncrief only scratched the surface of what we had been able to accomplish. Most of their people didn't cotton on to our game at all." At the mention of the senior partners of Hadley and Grimes, Knott seemed to contract within himself. *"Damned clever, those two pictures of rectitude. I sometimes wonder what their grandfathers would say if they knew what Vincent and Paxton are up to."*

"I'm afraid that neither of their grandfathers are still here to be asked," Holte reminded Knott.

"No; more's the pity," Knott conceded. *"Do you know when they moved on?"*

"Only that it was before I got here," said Holte.

"When was that?" Knott asked.

"Spring of 1916," said Holte, hiding his reluctance to talk about his execution. *"I got here unexpectedly, so I was extremely confused, not unlike Overstreet. It took me a while to get sorted out. By the time I was ready to begin haunting, it was 1921, and this dimension had been filling up with Flu victims for three years, and I was ready to get on with it."*

"Oh, yes. That was a bad time. Worse than the Great War," Knott said, unconcerned. *"I'm just as glad it's over with. Good times are coming back, though we aren't there to share them."*

"You haven't been gone from the world of the living all that long," Holte reminded him.

"Not in comparison to some, that's true. But I haven't lollygagged about, either. As soon as I realized where I was, I put my mind to finding out how I came to be here, so I can do something about it before I move on." Knott seemed genuinely optimistic, which surprised Holte.

"Do you think you'll be ready to do that so soon?"

"Yes; why not. Once I settle the matter of my death, there will be no reason to linger here, will there? I might as well get on with the next step as quickly as possible. I intend to resolve all unanswered questions I may have without giving in to the lethargy so many of those here have shown. Eastley, for example, drags around in a state of torpor, feeling sorry for himself. I used to have a high opinion of him, but no more. I cannot look on such passivity with sympathy." Knott swirled around Holte, disrupting the nearest cluster of ghosts.

"You must have some books of your own to balance before you move on," said Holte.

"I suppose I do. I'll cross that bridge when and if I come to it," Knott responded.

Holte thought Knott's remarks were a bit cold-blooded, but he kept his opinion to himself. *"So in your dealings with Stacy and Derrington, did either of them ever give you a hint of where they might be going when the left the US?"*

"I've already looked in most of those places, but not very successfully," said Knott, making a movement that was very like a shrug. *"I couldn't find any of them, and not for lack of trying. If I think of anything more, I'll tell you next time I see you...if I remember. I've been warned by Moncrief that I may forget."* He was drifting away again.

"You've looked all through Brazil? All through the Caribbean? Where else?" Holte was astonished at the idea of such a thorough search being possible in the short time that Knott had been dead.

"Most of both. If there is another place I might find them, I haven't found out where it was. In South America and the Caribbean, I couldn't pick up scent or sound of them. I had a tingle that might have been Derrington at one point a little while ago, but it was vague and when I tried to follow it, I couldn't manage to close in on it."

"It was probably a place he had been in his recent travels," Holte said, by way of consolation.

"Or intended to go. Overstreet said something about meeting Derrington in Cuba, and I think that was the place where I got the itch. Not that it was an actual itch—you understand, I'm sure. It didn't last long enough for me to pursue it, so I didn't linger, and went on toward Brazil. No point in wasting time, was there? I think Overstreet told you about that."

"That he did." Holte could feel a kind of noncorporeal heat building up in Knott.

"If you catch up with him, will you let me know where he is? I do want to find out whether he or Stacy actually killed me. If they're both still alive. When I locate them I'll do something about what they did to me." There was an undercurrent of fury in Knott's words, and he began to spin in the greater whirlpool of ghosts that lapped near the two of them.

"If I find out anything reliable, I'll let you know," Holte promised, and moved away from Knott before he became entangled in Knott's simmering rage. He flowed through the dimension of ghosts, but caught no trace of either Miles Overstreet or Madison Moncrief, and eventually *slipped* back into the world of the living just as Poppy was getting ready to leave for work.

TWENTY-NINE

DICK GAFNEY WAS ON HIS FOURTH CIGARETTE, AND IT WAS NOT YET NINE O'CLOCK. The city room was filling up with reporters, but for once Gafney paid little heed to them. He sat hunched over his typewriter, busily pounding the keys, swearing softly when he made a typo. At one point he almost pulled his master, carbon, and copy out of the platen in order to start again, but instead, caught sight of Poppy heading for her desk, and made a slighting comment about her coming in late. "If you're catching up on your beauty-sleep, Thornton, it isn't working."

Poppy did not give him the satisfaction of answering back; she took the cover off her Remington and sat down. She had already spent an hour with a Lieutenant Walter Ely of the Coast Guard in the Harbor Master's office, trying to find out as much as she could about ships unaccounted for after the havoc wrecked by Hurricane Sylvia; Lowenthal had given her the go- ahead to do this as soon as she arrived at seven-forty, and she was not about to waste time wrangling with Gafney, whom she realized had come in late. She took out her notebook and thumbed through four pages of scrawl, trying to decide how best to approach the various reports that Lieutenant Ely had provided, along with his estimate of how long it would be until a more accurate list could be compiled. It was not very much, but it did address the state of the search for missing vessels, storm damage, and made way for other accounts as the week went on; there was enough general interest in that to make Lowenthal accept what she wrote, even if it was not tied to either of her on-going stories. She began preparing to type up her notes as a way to help work through all the material she had, when her phone rang. More grateful than annoyed for this interruption, she picked up the receiver. "Thornton," she said.

"Poppy, it's Loring. I just came from interviewing Genevieve and Tatiana Pearse. Would you have time enough for lunch today? I've got some questions I'd like answered, and not by either of those girls." He sounded a bit out of breath but also stirred up by whatever GAD's two sisters had told him.

"If you like," Poppy answered, relaxing a little from the tension that she had developed while listening to Lieutenant Ely explain the loss of life and ships that had been recorded in the last three days. "Where would you like to meet, and when?" She was cheered by the thought of a delay in writing her story for Lowenthal; she would tell him that lunch with Loring could provide some more recent information on the Pearse investigation.

"What about Coulson's Chop House? It's about half-way between us and it's open at ten- thirty. How about eleven-thirty? I'll meet you there. They have some good cherry cider this time of year, if you want something other than tea."

"Coulson's it is. Eleven-thirty." She took a pencil out and wrote the time and place down on the corner of her desk blotter, next to her most involved scribbles. That done, she prepared to resume work on her notes, and made up her mind that when she handed them in, she would tell Lowenthal about her lunch appointment with Loring. With that thought to buffer her against the appalling statistics Lieutenant Ely had provided her, she continued to transfer them to her story, separating the commercial ships by ports of registry and country of origin, yachts and pleasure craft by whatever information she was given. After that she went on to the vessels that were missing but had not been confirmed sunk. Forty minutes later, she went and knocked on Lowenthal's door, her article and her notes in a manila envelope, the notes paper clipped together.

"Come," Lowenthal bellowed, revealing that he was not in a very good mood. As Poppy came in, he swung around in his chair and glared at her. "What have you got?"

"Coast Guard reports on ships sunk and missing in the wake of Hurricane Sylvia; the Hadley yawl is on the list," she said as crisply as she could. She took the seat opposite his, the desk between them, and handed over the envelope. "I can get an update tomorrow or the next day, if you like, or later today if it's urgent."

Lowenthal opened the envelope and pulled out the sheets of paper it contained. He held his arm out to read them, squinting from time to time as he read the pages. "Lots of property damage, it looks like," he remarked as he reached the end of the story. "Too bad for the Florida Keys, by the tone of it. Over two hundred people missing in the Keys. Not a good sign for Florida in general."

"To say nothing of the Caribbean islands," Poppy added.

Leaning back in his chair, Lowenthal gazed up at the ceiling. "The Caribbean islands are not that significant to most US shipping companies; no reason to do more than a cursory report on them. What has happened to them is their look-out, even though there may be some businesses here that are connected to various Caribbean corporations; there aren't enough of them to merit more attention."

"That's true enough," said Poppy, "but that doesn't change the impact of the hurricane."

"No, it doesn't." Lowenthal put the papers down. "It also doesn't change the fact that you handled this well, Thornton, and that's to your credit. We'll run it on page one, because it is timely, but below the fold. There's enough Philadelphia business tied up in east coast shipping that this will make us look on top of things—we can't leave all the money stories to the *Constitution*." His reference to the *Clarion*'s sister paper was, as always, slightly sarcastic.

"No, sir. And a hurricane is much more exciting reading than stock market fluctuations." She offered a facetious smile to show her agreement.

"Not that most of our readers give a damn about the market, so long as it keeps going up." He did not bother to apologize for his strong language.

Poppy waited a second or two, then ventured, "I'd like to have lunch with Inspector Loring today, if that's convenient. He has some more information about the Pearse investigation."

"Such as it is," said Lowenthal at his most sardonic.

"Truly," said Poppy. "Such as it is. But don't you think that another bit of news will keep the public interested in what's happening? The Pearses are an important family in this part of the country, and this story has some unusual elements. It means we can avoid the questions about the ransom demands, at least for now, and the Pearses will appreciate that. They want that kept quiet for as long as possible."

"Yeah, there's nothing like leaving out news to sell papers." said Lowenthal. "Or putting emphasis on things many of our readers aren't interested in. Such as, it isn't happening here in the US. Not exactly what I had in mind. We're supposed to cover Pennsylvania news, or national when it's appropriate, but Caribbean? Or European?" He mumbled something under his breath, and then said. "Oh, well. Why not? Just make sure you turn in your notes from your lunch to me. I'm not paying you to flirt."

Poppy bit back a sharp retort and stood up. "Thanks, boss. I'll make sure you have my notes before I leave at five."

"See that you do." He waved his hand toward the door. "Nice work, Thornton. Now get back to it."

This second compliment so startled Poppy that she almost walked into the doorframe as she started back to her desk.

"Oh, another thing," Lowenthal called after her.

Poppy stopped. "What?"

"Do you think that aunt of yours could do a couple hundred words for Friday's edition?" He asked it so nonchalantly that Poppy knew he had been planning to broach the matter with her since she had knocked on his door.

"You'd better ask her," said Poppy. "I can give you her phone number."

"I have it already. I'll give her a call before lunch." Satisfied that he had accomplished his purpose, he clapped his hands. "Chop-chop, Thornton."

"So the boss let himself be finagled," Gafney said to Poppy as she resumed her place at her desk. "You certainly know how to reel him in."

"Not that I did," said Poppy, doing her best to stay focused on her work rather than Gafney's carping. "I've never had the knack for such persuasion."

"Don't try the innocent act with me, lady. You're up to every rig in town, and I know it." He punched his typewriter keys as if they were piles. "He may not understand what you're doing, but I do. And don't you forget it."

Poppy stared at her Remington, trying to remember what she had intended to write. Nothing came to mind. She prepared a bond, carbon paper, onionskin sandwich and rolled it into the platen. There had to be something she could write about between now and when she had to meet Loring at Coulson's Chop House, though nothing occurred to her. She started to doodle on her desk-top blotter, but even that did not help her focus on what she wanted to do. "Blast and ruination," she said to the empty page in front of her.

Tony, the chief copy-boy, stopped across from Poppy and handed her a note, offered her a cynical smile that did something creepy to his fifteen-year-old face, and said, "Hope it's worth it," and with that, ambled away.

Poppy took the note and opened it.

Miss Thornton,

I am saddened to tell you that we have just received word that a portion of Nelson Hadley's yacht, the Belle Helene, has washed up on Cabo Cruz in Cuba, severely damaged and with no one, living or dead, aboard. I fear we must consider them lost at sea. This office will provide appropriate information to be included in my employer's obituary before close of business today.

Sincerely,

Clifford Tinsdale

Poppy read through the note twice, and then picked up her phone, asking the operator to connect her to Lieutenant Ely at the Harbor Master's Station. She would get her confirmation on the sinking and then begin work on the tragic loss. She thought over the *tragic loss* description and made up her mind to use it in the story she wrote.

The operator came back on the line. "That number is busy, Ma'am."

"Please try again in ten minutes." Poppy glanced at the city room clock. "And at ten minute intervals for an hour, if necessary," she added before she hung up, and began to doodle. After five minutes of waiting for the connection to go through, she decided to check with Vital Statistics, to repay Rob Gentry for his giving her the information on Julian Eastley's fatal accident. She signaled for the in-house operator and gave her Rob Gentry's number, then waited for him to answer. "Gentry? Poppy Thornton here," she said when he answered his phone.

"Well, hello, Miss Poppy. What can I do for you today?"

"It's something I can do for you. I've just had a note from Hadley and Grimes, from Quentin Hadley's secretary, telling me that Quentin and his cousin Nelson appear to have been lost at sea during Hurricane Sylvia; part of Nelson's yacht washed up on Cabo Cruz in Cuba. You might want to check it out. We should be getting obituary material from Hadley and Grimes later today. For now, I'm planning on calling the Coast Guard as soon as we're off the phone, for confirmation." That much was true, but in the name of candor, she said, "As soon as I get confirmation from the Coast Guard, I'll let you know. In the meantime, you may want to check with Mister Tinsdale at Hadley and Grimes."

"Thanks. Will do," said Gentry.

"One more thing," Poppy said. "There's no mention of bodies being recovered, just parts of the boat."

Gentry gave a low whistle. "Call me back after you talk to the Coast Guard, if you would."

"Happy to," said Poppy, and hung up. She checked the clock again, and resumed scrawling on the corner of her desk blotter, trying not to count the seconds. By the time the call went through, twenty minutes later, Poppy had added more than four square inches of tiny drawings of unlikely plants and animals.

"Miss Thornton?" said Lieutenant Ely.

"Yes, Lieutenant. I was wondering if you could check on some information that just came in at the *Clarion*—about one of the missing pleasure boats?"

"Do you have a name for this craft?"

"It's a two-masted yacht, a yawl, out of Mystic harbor, the *Belle Helene*. It may also be registered in Santiago de Cuba. The owner is Nelson Hadley." She paused, wondering if he would say something; he did not. "I had a note from Hadley and Grimes that the boat was found washed up on Cabo Cruz. Can you confirm that for me, please?"

There was a silence at the Coast Guard end, and then Lieutenant Ely said, "It appears that may be correct. We have no specific report yet, but there is a preliminary notification that was wired in half an hour ago that describes a badly wrecked yacht that sounds like the vessel you mean. Only half the name has been found, but *Belle He* is very likely to be *Belle Helene*, and from what they tell me, it is a yawl, which is the kind of craft you're looking for. If I find out anything to the contrary, I'll phone you as soon as I learn of it."

"Much appreciated, Lieutenant," said Poppy, and as soon as she had hung up, she called Vital Statistics to relay the unofficial identification to Rob Gentry.

"Something hot, Thornton?" Gafney asked, his question filled with doubt.

"Nothing that would interest you," Poppy shot back. "Shipping news."

Gafney laughed and lit another cigarette.

Poppy spent the next half hour putting together a short piece on the missing yacht and then went to hand it in to Lowenthal.

"Doesn't look like either Hadley made it," Lowenthal said after he had skimmed the report. "You'll have to do an expanded piece when you get the final word from the Coast Guard. This is enough for now."

"That's encouraging," said Poppy, thinking that it was strange to be satisfied with writing up a few hundred words on the loss of a ship at sea. "I'll be back by one."

"You leaving early?" Lowenthal asked, his brows rising in surprise.

"Loring requested it. I think he wants to get ahead of the regular lunch crowd, so we can have some private conversation; he may have new information that's a bit...touchy. He's interviewed two of the Pearse girls and he may have something more about the latest situation with the family." Listening to herself, she thought this sounded pretty lame, but she saw Lowenthal nod, and felt relief at that sign.

"So long as there isn't anything that will set off Mister Pearse's temper, it's good enough for me." He regarded her thoughtfully. "If you need until one-thirty, I won't mind. Just make sure that you take the time to get the whole story."

"You know I will," said Poppy, and went out to put on her coat and pick up her purse and brief-case.

"Another outside job?" Gafney asked at his most snide.

"Yes, not that it's any business of yours," Poppy countered, and made her way out of the city room and down the stairs.

Arriving at Coulson's Chop House, Poppy found a parking slot in the lot behind the restaurant. She set the hand-brake and got out of the auto, her purse and brief-case in her right hand. After locking the Hudson's door, she went into the Chop House, and looked around the somewhat darkened interior of the dining room; only three of the tables and one of the booths were occupied. She saw Loring seated in the booth on the far side of the room, to the side of the kitchen doors; she waved and started toward him.

"Ma'am?" said a young waitress hurrying up to her.

"I'm meeting with the inspector. You needn't seat me," Poppy said in the way she imagined Aunt Esther would say it; she kept walking in Loring's direction, leaving the waitress to go back to the reception stand to gather up menus for them. Sliding into the seat opposite him, she set her brief- case and purse on the bench next to her, after she removed her pencil and notebook, and asked, "So what did you think of the Pearse girls?"

"Hello to you, too." Loring took his tone from Poppy. "Stay seated, won't you?" He did not wait for her to do it, but launched into the reason he had asked her to join him. "Regarding the Pearse girls: I liked Genevieve; she's a very self-composed girl for sixteen, and she's forthcoming without being effusive. By the way, she told me that GAD had a terrible crush on you when he was thirteen and fourteen. Did you know?"

"Not really; I've only heard about it recently," Poppy answered, wondering what—if anything—this had to do with what Loring wanted to know about the Pearses. "I used to listen when he talked about his creatures and his fascination with nature. He seemed bright and a little out of step with his family, something I could understand. But there's six years difference in our ages. I never thought of him as anything more than a kid until last year, when I came across a letter to the editor in the *Constitution*. The idea that he had had a crush on me never entered my mind. Is that important?" She glanced up as the waitress came up to them to hand them menus.

"Who knows?" Loring replied, then kept silent.

The waitress took this as her cue. "The special today is meatloaf with a baked potato and celery root. It's one sixty-five with coffee or cider." She was practicing sounding enthusiastic at the high price. "There's Vermont cheddar cheese in the meatloaf."

"Thank you," said Loring. "We'll have some cider now and order a little later."

"Yes, sir. I'll be back with your cider in ten minutes," said the waitress before turning away and going back to her post near the reception desk in anticipation of the noon-time crowd.

"What else did Genevieve tell you?" Poppy asked him, the menu lying unopened in front of her, her pencil poised over her notebook.

"She said that GAD did have some kind of understanding with Merrinelle Butterworth, but had not mentioned it to his parents, for fear of their interference with him. He was worried that if he and Merrinelle became engaged now, there would be an uproar that would mean that they would have to wait to marry until he had graduated from his university at the least. He was worried that Merrinelle might not like that long a delay, but he could not think that it would be a good move to elope. Too much of a scandal."

"Not surprising," said Poppy while she made a couple of notes.

"When I asked her about what she thinks is going on with GAD, she didn't sound troubled. She told me that she believes that he is doing just what he said he would do, which is a change from what Merrinelle said to the *Tattler*." Loring lowered his voice. "Genevieve also mentioned that in the last two days, her father has received five demands for ransom for GAD's safe return, and he's furious. He blames Merrinelle for the new demands."

"Five ransom demands?" Poppy repeated. "From the same person or group?"

"No. According to Genevieve, all are from different postmarks, all make different claims about GAD's condition, and the amounts they're demanding vary from twenty thousand dollars to half a million."

Poppy wrote this down, saying as she did, "No wonder Mister Pearse wanted to avoid publicity."

"No wonder," Loring echoed. "The thing that bothers Genevieve is that one of those demands might be real, but there's no way to be sure."

"Missus Pearse must be beside herself," Poppy said. "She's been imagining horrors ever since GAD dropped out of sight, and five ransom demands won't lessen her anxiety." She took a moment to think. "Did any of the demands originate from outside the country?"

"Genevieve didn't think so; she didn't see any foreign stamps on the envelopes, but that doesn't mean that a letter from Austria wasn't sent here and remailed; that would take time, and unless the ransom demand was sent over a week ago..." Loring shook his head. "I'd like to have a look at those letters, but Genevieve told me that Mister Pearse has been fit to be tied about the ransom demands, and wants to tear them all up. Missus Pearse won't let him, or so Genevieve told me. Tatiana had another view of the situation."

"No doubt." Poppy thought about the state of the Pearse family, and frowned. "I can phone them, to ask about the ransom demands, or find an excuse, but I don't think that would be a good idea. Knowing Sherman Pearse, he would think that I was taking advantage of my association with the family."

"That's likely," Loring admitted, signaling Poppy to be quiet as the waitress brought their ciders, saying to her as she set down the tall, beer-glasses. "Give us another ten minutes, if you would."

"The lunch crowd will be starting to arrive by then," the waitress warned.

Poppy opened her menu and looked over the possibilities. "Let's tend to this now. I'll have the corned beef sandwich, with the pickle and potato salad," she said.

Loring handed his menu to the waitress. "And I'll have the special, and a cup of your beef-and-barley soup."

The waitress had taken out a notepad and began to write with a broad-tipped pencil. "Anything else?"

"Not for me," said Poppy, surrendering her menu.

"Same here; don't put a rush on them," Loring told the waitress, and watched as she opened the nearer of the two kitchen doors. Once that swung closed, he leaned forward. "Can we get back to Tatiana?"

"I wasn't aware we had begun," said Poppy, smiling to take the sting out of her remark. "What did you make of her?"

"I don't really know. She's a peculiar mix of sly and mercurial; I'm still guessing about half of what she said to me. One of her comments bothered me: she said she was certain that GAD was faking his kidnapping to get money for those Living Spectres of his."

"That sounds like something Tatiana would do, not GAD," Poppy said,

One of the parties at a table in the middle of the room—a group of three middle-aged men—got up and went to the reception desk to pay; the tallest of the three left two bits on the table for a tip.

"Why do you say that?" Loring inquired. "Not that I doubt you, but you have to admit that it is a possibility."

"Because Tatiana has always been surreptitious, and she's become capricious. She's not above being deliberately misleading, and taking pride in being so. GAD's the opposite. If he wanted money for his Living Spectres , he would ask for it directly, not create an elaborate scenario that could backfire. That's not his nature, but it certainly is TRA's." Poppy took her glass of cherry cider and tasted it. "Not bad. In fact, pretty good."

"I'm pleased you like it." He looked around the dining room; the patrons at the other occupied table did not appear to be ready to leave. "Then you don't put much stock in her suspicions."

"No, I don't. As you say, they might be true, but it's more likely just TRA's—Tatiana—stirring the pot." She looked down at her half-page of notes. "I have some news for you, by the way."

"Okay," he said warily. "What now?"

THIRTY

"I HAD A NOTE FROM QUENTIN HADLEY'S ASSISTANT THIS MORNING, INFORMING me that Quentin and his cousin, whose yacht they were sailing, are missing and considered drowned in the hurricane." Poppy saw that Loring was startled. "The wreckage of Nelson's yawl, the *Belle Helene*, washed up near Santiago de Cuba. The Coast Guard has given provisional confirmation of the loss."

"Quentin Hadley is dead?" Loring asked, as if he had not heard what she said.

"It certainly looks like it. The yacht he was on broke up and sank."

"What about his cousin? And Miles Overstreet?" Loring asked, gathering his thoughts.

"It seems likely that they're gone, too. So far as anyone knows, they were all on board." Poppy felt abashed for her fib; she took a sheet of paper from her brief-case and held it out to him. "This is a copy of the note I had." She had typed it out shortly before leaving the *Clarion*, anticipating this moment.

Loring looked over the text, shaking his head slowly. "I'll have to check this out. Thanks for the warning."

For some reason she could not identify, Poppy felt warmth rising in her face. "We did agree to share information. I'm just doing my part," she said, determined to hide her confusion.

"For which I am grateful," said Loring. "This is going to throw the District Attorney's and the federal government's investigation into a cocked hat with those men dead, and no actual witnesses to confirm it. Maybe they'll turn the case back over to the police and leave the heavy- weights out of it."

"Why do you say that?"

Loring shook his head. "Because it means that they'll have to shift some of their focus to other members of the firm, and none of them want to do that, not when they were getting their ducks in a row. That shift alone will slow down the speed of the District Attorney's and the Attorney General's inquiries, and that will give Hadley and Grimes more time to cover their tracks, which could mean that there will be even more heat on Stacy and Derrington. Not that there's anything we can do directly." He took another sip of his cherry cider. "I'd like to find one or the other of them, and soon. We need a lid on this."

"But why? Wouldn't you rather have the lid blown off?" Poppy stared at him, trying to discern his reasons for such an unrealistic desire.

Loring stared down into his glass of cider as if attempting to read signs in it. "There are too many rich and powerful people who have their hands in this, one way or another, and such men are well connected, which could open even more locked doors to public scrutiny, and that means that whatever is there to be found won't be there long. I don't want to end up spinning my wheels."

"In other words, politics," said Poppy with a cynicism that was almost equal to that of Dick Gafney's. "That could be a problem."

"We're feeling pressure already, and that's a strong indication that it can only get worse. So far, the District Attorney is prepared to continue his search for Stacy and Derrington, but he's cooling on Louise. If Hadley and Grimes can sweep their activities under the rug, then I'm not certain that there will be much effort spent in tracking down your cousin and his friend." His expression turned apologetic. "I don't know how much more they'll let me do, Poppy, if Hadley and Grimes manage to slide out from under this."

A spurt of anger went through Poppy as she considered what the implications of this could be. "There have been three murders for sure in this case, and two questionable deaths. Doesn't that mean anything?"

"It won't if there are no culprits to drag into court, and the way things are going, that's not impossible. They're already starting to run for cover." Loring's eyes had taken on the exhausted look they had had when he and she first met. "I wish I could say something less disheartening, but if we can't find a lead..." He turned one of his hands palm up, then blinked. "Three murders? What three murders? Do you mean Poindexter, or have I miscounted?"

Poppy realized that she would have to summon up some kind of explanation other than Holte to account for her slip of the tongue. "I was thinking of

Overstreet," she said. "He went down with the ship, didn't he? Through no fault of his own."

"If you think the rescue in Montreal was a trap instead, which I gather you do. But why bother to save him in the first place? They didn't have to pull him out of the river. They could have let him drown without any discredit to themselves." Loring was doing his best to sound sensible, but there was an uneasy note in his voice.

"The Mounties might have been able to save him, and that would have put him right back where he was," Poppy remarked. "He didn't want to be extradited, did he?"

"Exactly. Why take the risk of testifying? But that could have been prevented in other ways. What was the point of rescuing Overstreet?"

"On a whim, do you think? Or an out-burst of sympathy for him? That doesn't sound like the reason the Hadleys would do anything. No, they had a purpose in saving him, and in arranging their elaborate efforts for doing it. Overstreet didn't jump off that bridge impulsively. He must have known that the yacht was coming for him. I don't think Overstreet would have gone into the river otherwise. He doesn't seem the type to take such a chance, not without knowing he wouldn't drown." Poppy turned a page in her notebook and waited for what Loring would tell her now.

"No, he doesn't," Loring admitted.

"That's not assuming that the Hadleys rescued him for no specific reason—a kind of altruism, in fact, which, you're right, doesn't seem in character." She took a little time to ruminate. "What if Overstreet knew something the Hadleys needed to know, or thought that Overstreet had such knowledge? What if they wanted to get him where the law couldn't reach him, and use that isolation to compel him to reveal something of importance to them?"

"What kind of thing would be that important? What would it mean to them, to take such a chance?" Loring asked, intrigued at this idea.

"Oh, I don't know. Perhaps Knott's records of his transactions with Hadley and Grimes. Or a register of those who provided Knott with his counterfeit antiques, or those who helped to smuggle some of Knott's wares into the country." She knew she would have to ask Holte to find out more from Overstreet, so she could provide Loring with more possibilities. "I've been thinking about this, you see? The rescue has bothered me, and I've been trying to work out why it happened. It had to have been planned; it was much too fortuitous to have been happenstance. This was what I came up with. The one thing that doesn't fit is the hurricane, but that wasn't a factor when they made their plans, was it?"

"No, it wasn't," Loring agreed, beginning to concentrate again. "I take your point, and I think there may be something to it. I don't know if my superiors will agree, but I'll see what I can do with it. Keep searching; however you came up with this, follow the clues." He rubbed his chin, a sure sign of cogitation, and was about to speak when Poppy interrupted him.

"If you dare say anything about an invisible friend, I may leave." It was an empty threat, and both of them knew it, but Loring backed off.

"I won't. But you will admit that you come up with some uncanny guesses; I'm supposed to be skeptical of unverifiable information—it's part of the job." His attention was claimed by a group of six men at the reception desk, and he averted his face. "That's Captain Bannerman in the brown suit. It wouldn't be good for him to see me with you."

"Do you think he'll bother to look?" Poppy asked, dropping her voice to match his.

"He might. He started on patrol, and that means he takes stock of his surroundings even now. Very canny fellow is Bannerman." He shifted his position on the bench and kept his head turned away from the middle of the dining room. "At least this booth is fairly dark, and being near the kitchen doors should help. Most people don't like to sit here."

"Did you know he would be coming here?" Poppy could see that Loring was rattled.

"No, I didn't. He doesn't tell me his plans. He and his cronies usually lunch at The Irish Harp. That's out of the picture now." That gathering place had fallen on hard times since Prohibition had begun, but there was a group of men in key positions in city government who had kept The Irish Harp afloat; a recent foray by Brigadier General Smedley Butler's men had ended the tavern.

"Wasn't it raided?" Poppy recalled a forty-point headline about the effort; there had been a fair amount of excitement about it.

"Two weeks ago, yes. A dozen barrels of beer were seized, and ten cases of whiskey. General Smedley Butler was crowing about it. The *Inquirer* gave it a lot of coverage."

"That's the *Inquirer* for you," said Poppy, watching as the waitress led the group of men through the dining room and into the room reserved for private parties. "You'd think that none of their reporters ever touched a drop, the way they carry on."

"Well, Markham must be the exception to the rule, then," said Loring wryly; Damian Markham covered the municipal courts for the *Inquirer* and had been arrested for driving and drinking at the same time more than once.

"Of course," said Poppy at her most demure. "And none of this group has a flask with them." She nodded in the direction of the new arrivals.

"Oh, sure," Loring agreed, with a roll of his eyes. "If the whole gang is going to be here, there'll be a dozen more along shortly," he went on more seriously. "I should have realized that they would be scouting out a new location for their bi-monthly gatherings. I'd like to be invisible about now."

"That's one way to deal with it, but then, there was no reason to think they would come here. There are a number of other places that would be glad of their patronage, and no doubt this is one of those trial runs." She set her purse on the table and put her notebook and pencil away. "In case anyone bothers to notice, I don't want any of them curious about why I should be taking notes." She drank a little more cider. "How does that sound to you?"

"Reasonable," said Loring.

"Then let's wait for our lunches and talk about the weather, or something ordinary," Poppy suggested. "Then neither of us will have to worry about who may be listening."

He gave a slow smile. "I guess I can live with that."

"So can I," Poppy said, and settled back against the straight booth wall behind her. "Are you planning anything for the weekend?"

"Nothing much. I thought I might actually read a book, something light and amusing, to counter all that's been going on." He drank a bit of his cider, and did not bother to look in the direction of the next group of five men arriving.

The waitress escorted these new-comers to the private room—the one with the sailing prints on the wall—handing out more menus as she held the door open for them, then returned to the reception desk.

"Did you see anyone you know?" Loring asked.

"Commissioner Smiley. He didn't even notice me, but then, why should he? He was talking to a tall man in an expensive suit who uses a cane and walks with a limp," Poppy said. "I don't think I know him, but I couldn't be sure." She frowned at this admission. "He has that sleek look—he might be in politics."

"White hair and a long face?" Loring guessed.

"Yes," Poppy answered. "Who is he?"

"He's a lawyer, doing mostly business law, and slippery as they come. Lincoln McCullough, the top man at Templeton Ramsey Harrison and McCullough. He does a lot of work for the Republicans. Not that the Democrats don't have their own sharks as well." Loring sighed. "It's amazing how much politics figure into everything, isn't it?"

"Yes, it is; I used to think that there was a hard line between politics and business, but not anymore," said Poppy, and changed the subject to Aunt Esther's forthcoming article for the *Clarion*, and what Lowenthal was expecting from her, a discussion that filled the time until their meals arrived and they could settle down to eating.

While Poppy and Loring were huddled over their food, Chesterton Holte was once again trying to locate Miles Overstreet in the dimension of ghosts. He drifted along through eddies and whirlpools of the dead, searching for the wavelength that would identify Miles Overstreet from the thousands and thousands and thousands of other noncorporeal presences. After what seemed to be a long time, he came upon Overstreet moving along with a number of hurricane victims, as if seeking the company of others who had died at sea.

"Overstreet," Holte called voicelessly.

Overstreet did not respond for a while, but then turned away from the conglomeration of ghosts and came back toward Holte. *"Do I know you? I think I know you."*

"Chesterton Holte. We did meet, shortly after you arrived here." He said this as genially as he could, for it was obvious that Overstreet was not yet accustomed to his current state.

"Oh, yes," Overstreet said vaguely. *"You were asking about someone..."*

"A couple of someones, as matter of fact," Holte confirmed. *"Quentin Hadley and Warren Derrington. I need to find them."*

"I was supposed to meet Derrington in Cuba; I was with Quentin on Nelson's yacht." Overstreet said with more certainty. *"I think he's here somewhere. I mean Quentin. So's Nelson. Are you going to look for them?"*

"Not just at present," said Holte. *"I was hoping you've remembered what you talked about while you were sailing with them."*

Overstreet moved in a way that would have been a shaking of his head, if he had had a body. *"Nothing much. Just smatterings."*

"Can you tell me about those?" Holte persisted.

"Something about a bank in British Honduras, I believe. And something about the Gray Goose. It's a steamer, and fairly small one, owned by a friend of the Hadleys, and of Percy. The captain of the Gray Goose is a friend of the Hadleys." This repetition seemed to comfort Overstreet.

"You mean Percy Knott?" Holte asked, to be sure.

"He's about the only Percy I know. Knew." Overstreet said, a touch sadly.

"What was it about the Grey Goose? What was the connection?" Holte kept his questions unhurried, so as not to alarm Overstreet.

"Sorry," Overstreet said. *"Can't remember. I think the friend who owns it has gray in his name somewhere. Or it might be goose."*

Holte could sense that Overstreet was starting to fade on him, so he made one last attempt to get an answer from Overstreet. *"Did you ever talk about smuggling?"*

"Smuggling," Overstreet said as if trying to decide if he knew what that word meant. *"I don't think so. But so much of that seems...fuzzy."* He was about to float away, but then brightened. *"Come to think of it, though, I believe Quentin did say something about the amount of smuggling that went on in that part of the ocean...more than booze was coming into the US along the East Coast. He thought that was funny...So did Nelson. I don't know why."* He paused, then did the equivalent of a shrug. *"That's about it."*

"Thanks," Holte told him, wanting Overstreet to remember him as well-intentioned, in case he should need to consult him again.

"It's...nothing..." Overstreet responded as he drifted back among the ghosts of the hurricane-dead, swirling away with them into the mist that was the dimension of ghosts.

Holte hovered as the tide of ghosts swept on, and tried to locate Quentin or

Nelson Hadley in the mass, but he could not discern them. After a while, he gave up and went in search of Madison Moncrief.

"You back again?" Moncrief asked as he became aware of Holte. *"Have you found out what's happened to my wife yet?"*

"Not yet," Holte said. *"Poppy's been trying to locate her step-brother, but—"*

"Why does she want to talk to Rudy? He's an invert. Louise didn't get along with him after she found that out. She was ashamed of him. Who wouldn't be?" Moncrief was agitated by this. *"He doesn't know anything you could use, I'd wager."*

"We don't know that—not for sure," said Holte. *"Maybe Louise has used him as a way to keep in touch with some of her friends without being obvious about it, or revealing where she is."*

"You might be giving her more credit than she deserves," Moncrief said. *"She's not a stupid girl, but she is impulsive, and what you're describing would take more planning than she usually..."* His words became distant. *"Pay no attention to me. I'm beginning to see that I never really knew Louise, only my idea of her. For all I know, she could be the most calculating woman on the face of the earth."*

Holte could not help but feel sorry for Moncrief. *"That's unfortunate, Moncrief,"* he said, recalling how little Sybil had responded to him when they encountered each other in the dimension of ghosts, and how much a stranger his wife had become to him. *"I'm sorry it had to come to that—feeling that you and she were not as close as you thought."*

"Well, you know how it is. I'm starting to remember many things, and from this perspective, those things look much different than they did when I was alive. I can tell that Louise often put on a performance for me; she knew what I wanted to see, she provided it, and I was delighted." He wilted. *"Not that other wives don't do that—and some husbands, too, but not so many— but I no longer believe that she was simply accommodating me as wives are expected to do."*

"I'm sorry," Holte said.

"Don't be. It's part of what we do here, isn't it? When we understand, then we can move on. Nowhere is it written that we have to like what we understand." He became a bit smaller and a great deal tighter. *"I'm starting to wonder if our marriage wasn't a kind of scheme cooked up by Louise and Stacy. I asked Eastley about it, but it's too soon to suggest that to him. He was vehement in his insistence that Louise was the ensoulment of virtue and rectitude, and wouldn't consider anything else. He's gone off; won't speak to me. He thinks I should be penitent for even entertaining the possibility that Louise would do such a thing as*

dissemble about our marriage. He regards my doubts as heresy."

"That's unfortunate." Holte was about to slip away, back to the world of the living, but halted when he heard Moncrief add, *"I don't know if it's crazy, but I can't help thinking that Louise was after me because I worked at Hadley and Grimes. It could have been because of the money I inherited, but Hadley and Grimes played a part in it, I'm almost convinced."*

"What makes you think that?" Holte asked sharply.

"Shortly after we met, she said that it must be exciting to work in a business where there were so many secrets about money. She laughed when she said it, and I thought it was a charming and playful remark, but now I'm not so sure. I think, perhaps, she was being more forthright than I gave her credit for." He began a slow spiral, closing in on himself.

"Did you tell her much about your work?" Holte moved a bit nearer to Moncrief. *"What did she ask about?"*

"Oh, nothing very specific, and I told her mostly dribs and drabs, as you do. At the time, I didn't think she was interested. Now, I have to wonder."

"Have you remembered anything else?" It was a risky question, but Holte wanted to learn as much as he could from Moncrief.

"One thing. Shortly after he introduced us, I asked Stacy why—since he was obviously taken with her—that he didn't pursue Louise. He told me that he wasn't rich enough to be able to afford her. Not that he was poor at the time, but he wasn't nearly as rich as I was. I took this as a go-ahead, and went after her, with, as I supposed, Stacy's blessings. Stacy never acted jealous or forlorn, but that might have been because he had no reason to be either of those things."

For the second time Holte said, *"I'm sorry,"* and *slipped* back into the city room of the *Clarion* in time to hear the bell sound for turning in the stories for the evening's editions to the composition department.

THIRTY-ONE

"THAT WAS WHAT HE TOLD ME," HOLTE REPORTED TO POPPY AS SHE SAT AT HER typewriter in the study at Aunt Esther's house; it was a few minutes past eight, and Poppy had just finished writing a piece on what had been confirmed in regard to GAD's foreign travels; she would hand it in first thing in the morning. "Overstreet only remembers a few things about the time on the *Belle Helene,* and most of it is trivial. He did have some recollection about a discussion about smuggling, but I don't know...I've done as much as I can to call it forth, but I haven't figured out how to discover more."

"Has what he told you been useful?" Poppy asked.

"I'd like to think so. He's been helpful in some information about Hadley and Grimes. I'd like to learn more, but that's going to take time." Holte drifted around the end of the desk and moved into a sitting position six inches above the surface of the hutch. "I don't know to what degree Moncrief figured out about Stacy's and Derrington's chicanery; he hasn't dealt with that yet; he's still trying to reassess his marriage, and Louise. "

"Do you think that Moncrief was in on it? On the smuggling and such?" Poppy asked, determined not to listen to the branch banging on the side of the house as the wind rose.

The lights in the room flickered. "Nothing to do with me," Holte assured her.

Poppy got up and lit the candles in the Indian brass candelabra that stood on the Oriental chest on the far side of the room. "Just in case," she explained as she came back to her chair. "About Moncrief, then: has he been dealing with his own role in discovering the smuggling and fraud, or is he concentrating on Louise?"

"Not really; Louise is more important to him, and he's not prepared to think that she might have something to do with his murder." He moved a little so that she could see him a bit more clearly. "I do think that Stacy and Derrington faked their argument as a way to engage Moncrief's sympathy in some way, to disarm him, on the night he was killed. From all I can tell, Stacy and Derrington never actually had a falling out; it was just pretense, a way to draw out how much Moncrief suspected."

"That sounds like Stacy more than Derrington to me," Poppy said darkly.

"You're not giving Derrington enough credit. If Moncrief had happened on something that was clearly illegal, I think he'd be more likely to approach Derrington than Stacy." Holte paused to summon up what he believed. "If Moncrief sought out one or the other of them, I'm assuming that whomever it was pleaded innocence in regard to the fraud and such, and then asked to see what Moncrief had discovered in private, which gained him access to Moncrief."

"With Louise's help, do you think?" Poppy asked.

"It's not impossible, but that's less certain; I'm of two minds about her role in Moncrief's murder; I need more information before I make up my mind about that," Holte allowed. "I know it was thought that she was greatly upset by the premature delivery—the loss of a baby distressed Moncrief as much as it did Louise, or perhaps more—and most of their friends believed that she was seeking some kind of diversion from that by planning a party, but I am not at all certain that she was as distraught as Moncrief supposed she was. I wouldn't be surprised if that idea has crossed his mind by now." He looked around the study, noticing for the first time that Poppy had brought in a small electric heater to warm the study. "It is getting chilly, isn't it?"

"You don't feel it, do you," said Poppy.

"No. But I can see that you do," he told her. "I gather Esther isn't in this evening; there's no fire in the sitting room, and the rest of the house is dark. Miss Roth is back in her apartment, I suppose."

"Yes. She is. And Aunt Esther will be out tomorrow evening as well." Poppy stifled a yawn, then took the papers out of the platen and reached for a manila envelope. "I should buy these by the gross," she remarked.

"Or the fifties, at least," Holte quipped. "How does it feel, just you and Miss

Roth in the house?"

"You're forgetting Maestro," Poppy reminded him.

"Not likely," Holte said. "Missus Sassoro and Galliard don't live in, do they?"

"You know they don't," Poppy said, trying to figure out what was on Holte's mind. "In a while Miss Roth will be away for a week or two. We'll see how I manage then. Why are you asking?"

"Do you feel safe?" It was posed innocuously, but there was concern in his tone.

"So far," Poppy said. "Is there some reason I shouldn't?"

"Not that I'm aware of." Holte moved nearer to the ceiling, as if preparing to depart.

Poppy was not ready to give up on his latest discussions in the dimension of ghosts. "So what else did you learn from Madison Moncrief? And Miles Overstreet, for that matter?"

Holte floated down a foot or so. "Moncrief is remembering more than he was a couple of weeks ago; you know that. It's been long enough since his death that he's beginning to recall more specific things surrounding the event itself. He did say that he was having second thoughts about Louise and Stacy, about their friendship, in case it might be something more."

"In what way?" Poppy asked, leaning forward.

Holte hesitated. "He used to think that their friendship was platonic, but now he's changing his mind."

Poppy almost laughed. "I might have thought the same thing as Madison did, because I didn't think that Stacy would do anything so...underhanded. But I no longer think that. I wouldn't be amazed to find out that they were... involved." She wrote Lowenthal's name on the manila envelope and put the two bond sheets into it. "There. I'm done."

"It's a bit early for bed for you, isn't it?" Holte remarked, looking at the carriage-clock in the top shelf of the bookcase. "It isn't even eight-thirty."

"I think I'll make some chocolate milk and add a little brandy, then sit down to read a good book." She went to turn off the heater and to pick up the candelabra. "Come with me, and tell me more of what you found out from Moncrief." She shoved the door all the way open and started down the hall to the kitchen. As she walked, Maestro came running in order to amble in front of her, occasionally meowing until he noticed Holte, and hissed.

"One day I'm going to fall over on you," Poppy warned the cat, struggling to hold the candelabra upright.

Holte rose to the ceiling, but remained almost overhead. "He can be a nuisance."

"He probably thinks the same of you," Poppy said, and pushed the hall door open, then turned on the overhead light in the kitchen. "Missus Sassoro always leaves this room so clean."

"Didn't Missus Bourdon do the same?" Holte asked. "I'd have thought your Aunt Jo would expect rigorous cleanliness from her cook."

"Oh, yes. But Aunt Jo's kitchen is more old-fashioned than Aunt Esther's. This place can be spick and span in a way that Aunt Jo's can't." She put the candelabra on the cook's table in the center of the room before she went to the refrigerator to take out the open bottle of milk, removing the small paper cap as she did so. "I don't suppose you want any," she said to Holte.

"Even if I did, I wouldn't be able to drink it," Holte said, watching Maestro mince around the cook's table. "You better give my share to him."

"That's what he's expecting," Poppy agreed, and went to get the smaller sauce pan, and then a shallow bowl as well as a wedge of thick, dark chocolate. She put these down on the cook's table, then poured milk into the bowl and set it on the floor for Maestro. "Drink that and stay out from under my feet," she told him, and then poured more milk into the sauce pan and carried it to the stove, where she took the box of matches, struck one, lit the smallest burner, and set the sauce pan on top of it.

"When did you learn to make hot chocolate?" Holte asked.

"When my mother was ill, so we wouldn't have to wake the housekeeper. She—my—mother didn't like people to fuss over her."

"How old were you?" Holte was now slightly a foot off the floor and a step behind her.

"About fourteen, I think; maybe a little younger: thirteen." She picked up the wedge of chocolate and lowered it into the warming milk. "Sometimes I'd put a little vanilla extract into it for her, when she was having trouble sleeping."

"Did it help?"

Poppy shrugged and took a spoon from a jar of cooking utensils on the counter next to the stove. "She liked it. I guess it did." She began to stir the milk slowly, watching the chocolate wedge move around in the pan. "What else about Moncrief? Anything?"

"Not very much. Overstreet is beginning to sort things out, but I don't think he understands about being murdered, let alone why. That's going to take more time."

"Does he have any idea about where Stacy and Derrington, and Louise, for that matter, are?"

Holte moved and the overhead light flickered. "My fault," he said, then resumed his observations. "Overstreet has said that he was supposed to meet Derrington in Cuba, I think at the Hadley's vacation house, but I'm not sure about that; that's where the Hadleys were bound. Santiago de Cuba is the nearest city of any size, but I would have thought that Havana was a likelier choice, if they were trying to do business. Wherever it was, Overstreet has been pretty consistent about the appointment, so I'm convinced that it was his intention to go there."

"I understand about the Hadleys, but why would Derrington be at the Hadleys' vacation house? I'd think that you're right: if Derrington wanted to see Overstreet, he would plan to meet somewhere else, some place more convivial to schemes—wouldn't you, in his situation?" Poppy inquired as she reached into the cupboard for a mug.

"That's a bit more of a puzzle," said Holte. "Overstreet hasn't told me that. And I'm guessing that they were planning to meet at the Hadleys' house, being that Overstreet was on the *Belle Helene*. Derrington is part of the Hadleys' social set, isn't he?"

"Yes, he is, but Overstreet isn't," Poppy said, resuming her stirring.

Holte mused on this. "You're right. They'd meet elsewhere."

"Maybe that's something to look into," Poppy suggested. "The next time you leave the world of the living behind."

"It's a good suggestion," Holte said. "If I can do that, along with keeping track of N.Cubed. Just now, that's a priority."

"You mean in his hunt for GAD?" There was a perceptible hesitation in her question.

"Yes. That's my plan. I think the more you know, the more easily you will be able to deal with the Pearses. It's pretty difficult to speak with them at all, now that they've had ransom demands." He paused. "Blessing has told them that he will wire them on his progress at least twice a week; if you're familiar with what Blessing has discovered, you can frame your approach to them with that in mind."

"So long as I don't know enough to make either Sherman or Isadora decide that I'm in on it in some way." Poppy gave a half-yawn, half-sigh and dipped the end of one finger into the sauce pan. "Almost ready."

"Are you going to tell the good inspector about any of this?" Holte asked. "Or would it be too difficult to explain how you came by the information?"

"I don't know. You're right—I'll have to figure out a way to present it to him that won't make it sound as if the source I got it from wasn't you, and that might be dodgy," she replied; the chocolate wedge was almost melted, and she stirred it in a figure-8 motion. "He's curious enough as it is. I don't want any more remarks about my invisible friend, thank you."

"Is there someone who might have mentioned something to you, someone whom you could designate as a source?"

"I can't think of anyone off-hand. Do you think Moncrief or Overstreet might be able to advise you on that?" Poppy turned the flame down under the sauce pan.

"Moncrief might be able to think of someone. I don't think Overstreet knows anything about that kind of connection." Holte thought a little longer. "I'll see what Overstreet has to say the next time I see him. And Moncrief, as well."

"What about Julian Eastley? Could you get him to talk to you?" Poppy asked.

"He might, if I can find him. He's been absent from his usual places, and that makes it difficult to locate him. He's upset with me. He's also irritated with Moncrief." He moved away from the stove. "He seems to be holding onto the idea that Louise is blameless and needs him to protect her reputation."

"That's a bit over the top, isn't it? Or doesn't he talk to Moncrief any more, if he's angry? Are they on the outs with each other?"

"I don't know. I might give Eastley a try, just to find out his opinion, assuming he'll talk to me at all. I hope he will, but there's no guarantee." Holte slid around the kitchen, taking care not to get too close to the ceiling light. "Can you think of anyone in your group of friends who might receive mail from Louise, or Stacy?"

Poppy did not answer at once, and when she did, she said, "I could try Neva Plowright again; things may have changed since our last conversation. I don't think Rudy Beech will talk to me; he did hang up on me when I reached him. By the sound of it, I'm not the only reporter who's tried to get through to him." For a second she remembered his acerbic reaction to her phone call, and the vitriolic tone in his voice; she had not given this more than a passing thought at the time, but he had sounded as if others—not necessarily reporters—had been in touch with him. She decided that she would make another attempt to find out about that, and returned to what she had been telling Holte. "It's pretty obvious that Stacy isn't likely to contact the men here in the US he was in business with, not with the Attorney General after him."

"And I doubt that those who were would volunteer much on their own, with the federal government snooping around," Holte said. "Their living associates may have decided that it is prudent to remain silent."

"Why do you say that?" Poppy bent over the stove, sniffing critically.

"Because at least three of them have been murdered; if there were others in on the frauds and smuggling, I don't think they'd want it known that they had any association with Stacy beyond the social one."

Poppy was astonished. "You think Stacy would sneak back into the country to kill some of the others? That's assuming there are others."

"No, but I suspect he could hire it done," Holte said.

"Oh." She let herself mull this over for a short while. "Do you think he knows I'm still alive?"

"I have no idea," Holte said with a hint of regret. "If he's in contact with someone in your group, then he probably does. If he's not, then I wouldn't think so. He made a very good attempt to make sure you were not discovered until it was too late."

"That's a very appalling thought; he might want to finish what he started, mightn't he," she said, making it a bit of a reprimand. "Still, you're probably right—there's no way to be sure. I do hate all this uncertainty—half-answered questions, partial truths, inconclusive information." She used a potholder that hung on a length of twine to take the sauce pan off the stove and pour its contents into the waiting mug. That done, she took it to the sink and filled it with water from the hot tap. "Should I be worried, do you think?"

"Not just at present, no; Stacy has other fish to fry, some of them more inconvenient to him than you are. You've already talked to the police and the Attorney General of the state and some of the men associated with the federal investigation, so it would be useless to silence you now that your damage has been done. If anything should happen to you now, there's every chance that it would be seen as something ordered by Stacy."

"Because I made a report?"

"Yes, Poppy. That gives you a certain kind of protection. At this point, if anything, no matter how accidental should happen to you, it would create more suspicions than it would end, and Stacy doesn't seem to be the sort of man who would accept that kind of hazard for no good reason."

"He might do it in a fit of pique." Just saying the words made Poppy uncomfortable.

"Coming back to the US would be a major risk for pique," Holte said. "If you like, I could be on the look-out for him."

"Yes, please," she said quietly. "If you don't mind."

"That's why I'm here; to help," he pointed out, rising another half-foot up in the air. "I hope you won't mind if I expand my duties for the time being."

"So long as they don't raise too many eyebrows, I'd be foolish not to say yes." She shook her head once. "I'm sorry, but I can't help resenting the need for your help."

"I gathered that a while ago," said Holte.

"Your understanding doesn't make it easier." Saying this, she tested the side of the mug, then picked it up and carried it into the breakfast nook, turning on the lights as she did. "Make yourself comfortable." She sat down just as Maestro came into the breakfast nook to join them.

"Oh, I will." He wafted in and made as if to sit in the chair opposite hers.

Maestro yowled at him, arching his back for emphasis, and made a run at Holte, but did not try to take hold of him, preferring to stay near Poppy.

"Calm down, you noisy cat," Poppy admonished him as he rubbed against her shins. "If you can't behave, then go into the pantry and catch some mice."

"Has he actually done that—catch mice?" Holte rose a short way above the chair, out of the cat's easy reach. "It doesn't seem his style, does it? I wouldn't think his pride would allow him such...humble tasks."

"Yes, he has caught mice. Missus Sassoro has found the leftover bits—paws and tails and such—in front of the pantry door. So far, he's accounted for six of them that we know of; there may be more in other parts of the house. Aunt Esther says she'd rather have a cat attend to the mice inside than have to set out poison."

"That's a sensible precaution in a pantry, with all that food stored there," Holte said approvingly. "But what about mouse traps?"

"Missus Sassoro doesn't approve. She says that the dead bodies and the bait attract ants." Poppy stared at the larger window. "The wind's rising."

"Probably the last of the hurricane blowing itself out," said Holte.

They sat in companionable silence for a few minutes, then Poppy tested the side of the mug, nodded, and drank her chocolate while Maestro prowled around her feet, muttering to himself, and Holte gradually rose toward the ceiling, becoming invisible as he went.

THIRTY-TWO

Saturday, Poppy's half-day, went from weekend-quiet to wild excitement shortly after nine in the morning with the breaking news that the Napier robbery gang had been arrested before dawn and were now in police custody; so far six men were in jail, but there were supposed to be two more who were still on the run, and speculation was running high among the reporters as to where the men could be, and what might become of them. Poppy watched the eruption of exhilaration and took a degree of satisfaction that the capture of the jewel thieves would knock her story on the hunt for GAD off the front page; the Pearses would approve.

"Tough luck," Gafney said to her, chuckling around the cigarette dangling from the corner of his mouth.

"I'll weather it somehow," said Poppy, thinking that Gafney had been hoping for some such event to get her by-line off the front page of the paper.

"You keep on telling yourself that, dearie," he recommended as he resumed typing on his story that would surely be the lead for the day.

Poppy took a deep breath and looked at what she had managed so far:

> *Missing Pearse heir has not yet been located in Austria. The investigator working on the case in Eastern Europe has informed the family that he is moving on to Bratislava, in Czechoslovakia, based on new information he has obtained.*

Reading this over, Poppy knew it was useless to say that if there was no trace of the Living Spectres in Bratislava, or that Blessing would go north, toward Brno, looking for any sign of them; for most of their readers, Bratislava might as well be the far side of the moon. She decided not to mention this, in case Blessing should change his plans as he went along, or that Sherman Pearse would be displeased at Poppy revealing so much about the investigation. Doing her best to shut out the noise around her, Poppy attempted to come up with some way to imbue this rather colorless announcement with a bit of excitement nothing came to mind, so she put that story aside and began to compose an article about Hurricane Sylvia and how it had plowed through the Caribbean and along the southern coast of the US. This was going a bit better when she heard Lowenthal shout for her from his office. "Coming boss," she yelled back, trusting he would hear her as she picked up her purse and left her desk.

"Come in," Lowenthal bellowed as Poppy reached his door. "Sit down."

"I will," said Poppy, and did.

Lowenthal leaned forward as if to impart something private to her, but his voice was still loud enough to command naval maneuvers. "I had a note from— never mind. He's associated with the Department of State."

"Ye gods! Is this about GAD Pearse?" Poppy asked, surprised. "What's happening? Has he been locat—"

"No. This is your other case. This guy's one of those on the South American desks at State," he declared. "Your cousin may have been spotted in Venezuela, but that's not certain. They have a photograph. I thought you might want to get on it before the rest of the city room is through writing up the Napier robbery arrest story; you don't want the others chiming in on your territory. You'll be ahead of most of this paper, and most of the rest of the press in Philadelphia, for that matter. They're all caught up in the Napier story."

"Do you think other papers will be chasing this story about Stacy? Isn't the Napier story more important now?" she asked, thinking that it was like Lowenthal to shift her from her second- chair position on the Napier case just when it was finally heating up; she swallowed her indignation and listened to what he had to say. "Do you think one photograph will fire up the investigation again?"

"If the Venezuelan photograph turns out to be a solid lead, you bet I do," Lowenthal said. "And more than anyone on this rag, you're the one who's earned the chance to get there first."

Poppy thought this through, and asked, "Am I supposed to talk to this person you know in the Department of State?"

"No, not yet. He won't be taking an active role in the investigation—yet. If this ends up looking worth a follow-up, then I'll make the call for you to vouch for you. For now, there's a person you can call there—never mind the cost, I'll authorize it—and he should be able to tell you the basics. I've let him know someone from the *Clarion* would call that number in the next half hour. If it does turn out that this is a lead worth following, this'll get the ball rolling."

It took Poppy a short while to work out how to respond. "Do you want me to do this because it's my cousin, and I want to see him caught, or because I can identify him?"

"A little of both," Lowenthal admitted. "I'll bet you a lunch at the Blind Pig Grill that this could be the break in the case you've been looking for."

"If it's that kind of break, I'll buy *you* lunch at the Blind Pig Grill, boss," Poppy promised him.

"No, no. Wouldn't do for one of my reporters to host me there. Nope, I'll take you if it all turns out, and no nonsense about it." He began to twirl his forelock around his fingers, as he did when he was thinking. "Come up with as much as you can from the Department of State, and let me see your notes, and then you can get to work on up to four inches for Monday's paper. How does that sound to you?" It was clear to Poppy that Lowenthal wanted her on this, no matter how slim a lead it might be; he confirmed this by adding, "You have a real advantage on this, Poppy. You can make a difference."

"Challenging," Poppy replied at once. "I'll get right on it."

"Good." He handed a file-card to her across his desk. "That's the number and the extension for the fellow you should talk to. Tell him you're with the *Philadelphia Clarion*, and then tell him what this is all about. He should have your name on his calendar by now, and you should be able to get everything current on the sighting."

"If it is a sighting," Poppy added, being careful.

"Yeah. If it is." Lowenthal coughed. "Well, get on with it. Chop-chop."

Poppy rose, saying, "I'm going, boss," then paused. "How did my aunt's sidebar go for you?"

"Very good. Nothing too high-brow in tone, and explained in language that most of our readers can understand. I was afraid we'd have to tone it down some, but she came through with a sensible piece. I'd use her again, if the need arose." He stopped, then continued. "You can tell her I said so, if you like."

"It would be better coming from you," said Poppy, and hoped she had not gone too far with Lowenthal. "But I'll mention it if you prefer."

"I'll send her a note later today," said Lowenthal, an amazing concession, coming from him.

Poppy looked at the number on the card Lowenthal had given her. *Potomac 7-435, ext. 39.* She would have to have the outside operator connect her, it being a long distance call. At her desk, she hesitated, as much because of the continuing noise around her as any doubts she might have about how to approach the fellow on the other end: Lowenthal had scrawled *Chambers Mobray* under the phone number. "Where does the Department of State find the men with such names?" she wondered; "do they have a special committee for searching them out?" Satisfied to leave her question unanswered, she picked up the receiver and signaled for an outside operator. Once she had given the number and the city of its destination, she got out her notebook and pencil and prepared to write.

"Chambers Mobray," said a slightly nasal voice with a distinct New England accent to it; there was a moment of static on the line, and then he added, "Good morning."

"Mister Mobray," Poppy said at once. "This is P. M. Thornton, of the *Philadelphia Clarion,* and I have been assigned to the Dritchner and Derrington investigation. My editor, Cornelius Lowenthal, has instructed me to contact you about a possible sighting in Maracaibo, Venezuela of Eus—"

"I know who you are, Miss Thornton, and that you have a family connection to Eustace Dritchner," Mobray said crisply. "I am more than willing to assist you in any way I can, but I hope that you will, in return, assist me."

There was a shout from three of the reporters as the AP wire began to chatter.

Mobray's remark brought Poppy up with a start. "I assist you? How?" She took a deep breath and went on in her most professional voice, "Of course I'd be happy to, in any way I can."

"Very good," said Mobray. "I have in hand a report from our embassy in Caracas; I received it two days ago, and I am now beginning the next step of our investigation. I will arrange for a messenger to deliver it to you the day after tomorrow. It is from...one of our field operators in Maracaibo," he told her, studiously avoiding mentioning the man's name, "and it purports to be a photograph of Eustace Dritchner at a restaurant there. It was taken last week, and was not considered important until a man in the embassy made a tentative identification of Dritchner, at which time we ordered our man in Maracaibo to keep watch on the man in the photograph, to get his name, if possible, and to wire us who he is, or claims to be." The static returned, and then faded. "What we need now is the confirmation of this identification, which I hope you will be able to provide. We spoke briefly to his mother earlier this morning, and she refused to have anything to do with us." He cleared his throat. "She made it very clear that she will not cooperate with us in any way if it could be damaging to her son—if the man in the photograph is her son."

"Oh, dear," said Poppy, not at all surprised by Aunt Jo's intransigence. "I'd apologize on her behalf but—"

"We understand he is her son, Miss Thornton. Such ties rarely break." There was a speculative note in this observation.

"Don't worry Mister Mobray. I have no reason to shield my cousin from the consequences of his activities."

"So I've been informed; Arnold Schultz told me that you are one of those who will be testifying at his trial for the prosecution, when and if he is apprehended. With Mister Schultz vouching for you, I am willing to include you in our work, reporter though you may be, since you have an interest in the outcome that marches with our own; I hope I have not misjudged you Miss Thornton," said Mobray at his most unctuous.

"I want to see my cousin punished probably more than you do, Mister Mobray."

"That is my understanding and it is why we are having this conversation: you have nothing to gain in refusing to assist us. If I thought that you might also want to protect Dritchner...Well, I would not have agreed to discuss this with you."

"I appreciate that," said Poppy.

"My one reservation is that I caution you against gossip," Mobray warned.

"Hey!" Gafney shouted, holding up his finished report. "Above the fold Lowenthal! You promised. It damned well better be there!"

Poppy felt her ears grow warm, and knew she was blushing in anger at

Mobray—gossip, indeed; she would have liked to upbraid Mobray for his high-handedness, but she knew that would not serve her purpose in any way. She held her tongue just long enough to be certain she would not shout at him. "I'll do what I can for you, Mister Mobray, and I won't talk publicly outside of my editor's office. I will not publish anything without checking with you first." As she said that, she knew she was not being honest—she would be sharing whatever she found out with Inspector Loring, and probably Aunt Esther as well.

Mobray coughed quietly. "So I suppose I don't have to ask you to keep what I tell you to yourself?"

Poppy cupped her hand to her ear to keep out the noise of the city room. "Excuse the ruckus, Mister Mobray; we have a breaking story here." She did not wait for his reaction. "For now, yes, I understand. But I can't pledge to do it forever, since I must answer to my editor and it is our job to report the news," Poppy came back quickly. "Please keep in mind that I work for the *Clarion*, and I am assigned to report on this case, and have been for several months. My editor will expect something from me about this potential discovery, and it's my job to see that he has it. It's the nature of our business."

"I'm aware of that," said Mobray. "Shall we say that you will not publish anything until you have an opportunity to examine the information I will be sending you? We can discuss your next step after you've seen what we have on the man we suspect is your cousin, Eustace Dritchner. Will that satisfy you?"

"I think that I can live with it," said Poppy. "Can you at least tell me what I'm about to receive?"

"Certainly," said Mobray, a hint of relief in his manner. "The package you receive will contain the field agent's report on the sighting, the evaluation and recommendation of our office here, as much information as the person in the photograph provides us, and a copy of the photograph that was taken. The sooner you can provide your opinion on the man in the photograph, the sooner we can act on his presence, if such action is called for, and the sooner I can release you to write about what you've seen." Mobray gave a careful cough. "If you have doubts, do not hesitate to voice them. We would far rather have an uncertain response than one that is emphatic, but in error." He changed his tone. "What more may I tell you about the sighting, Miss Thornton?"

Poppy was ready for his offer. "You said something about a field agent? The one who took the photograph? Can you tell me anything about what a field agent of his sort does, and why he took his photo of the man who might be my cousin?"

Mobray took a few seconds to answer. "This is not for public dissemination, but I will tell you that we have men associated with the Department of State whose duty it is to observe and report on the activities of Americans abroad, particularly those who may be involved in...questionable enterprises, as we suspect is the case with Eustace Dritchner. You must understand that it is essential that we do not make the identities of such men public."

"Probably with excellent cause," said Poppy. "In regard to Stacy—he has been into some very shady dealings, it turns out."

"It is unfortunate," Mobray said by way of agreement with her. "The work these agents do is of a clandestine nature, and I cannot reveal anything more than what I have told you."

"I accept that." Poppy looked at the notes she had taken, and decided to tear them up as soon as she was off the phone, as a gesture of compliance. "As to what I know, it is probably less than you do: Stacy seems to have been part of a smuggling operation, and a participant in the forging of antiquities, as well as Customs documents. I don't know what else he may have done." That, too, was less than the truth, but Poppy knew better than to mention what she had learned through Holte.

"You know the facts as we have them. There are some other possibilities, but they are still matters of speculation, not certainty." Mobray clicked his tongue.

"My business is filled with uncertainties," Poppy told Mobray, and was rewarded with a burst of static. "But we in the newspaper business don't have to do more than confirm what we say from two sources, nothing as demanding as what is required in court." Listening to herself, Poppy thought she sounded like an obsequious boob, but hoped that would reassure Mobray.

"In this case, you will have to be very diligent." Mobray cleared his throat for emphasis. "Even when you are permitted to write about our conversation, the function of the agents may not be included in your story. Is that clear?"

"It is clear," said Poppy. She watched Gafney take a cigar from his desk drawer and prepare to light it. As if the cigarette smoke isn't enough to deal with, she thought, and missed what Mobray said. "Pardon me, Mister Mobray, but would you repeat that? I don't think I heard you clearly. The city room is—"

"I said: if you mention anything about the agents, you could be open to federal charges. We cannot afford to compromise any of our men in the field."

"Oh." Poppy put a line of exclamation points in her notebook. "I'll keep that in mind while I work."

"Good." Mobray spoke over the static on the line. "I'll expect to hear from you no later than two p. m. on Tuesday. Is that acceptable to you?"

"So long as I don't have to be out of the office on another story I'm following, yes, it is. If I am not here, I will return your call as soon as I return."

"Very good. Thank you, Miss Thornton," Mobray said, and hung up before Poppy could say anything.

Poppy sat still, caught up in everything she had heard from Mobray. What if it turned out that the man in the photograph actually was Stacy? What then? Should she tell Aunt Jo, or would it be better to say nothing? And what if he was not Stacy? Which did she want it to be? If it was Stacy, what was he doing in Venezuela, in Maracaibo? The card with Brazilian stamps confused her: Aunt Esther had said that Aunt Jo had told her that Stacy's post card had Brazilian stamps on it, and that was a long way from the north coast of Venezuela. Was the card meant to throw Stacy's pursuers off the track, or had he some other use for having it posted in Brazil? She picked up her notebook and tore out the two pages of notes she had made and then ripped them into small strips before dropping them into the wastebasket that she shared with Gordon Steenbroek, who covered public works for the paper, and who was presently attending a meeting on the need for new, wider roads in the city. Steenbroek, unlike Gafney, would not go through the wastebasket to look for tidbits, as he called them. Pleased with her destruction, she put the card with Mobray's name and number on it in her purse and prepared a single sheet of bond on which to make her notes; she would tell Lowenthal to destroy it when she gave it to him before leaving for Aunt Esther's house and a quiet afternoon.

THIRTY-THREE

As Poppy got into her Hudson at ten minutes to one, she heard Chesterton Holte speak from the passenger side of the front seat. "When would you like me to have a look around Maracaibo?"

Pulling her door closed, Poppy said, "So it *was* you on the line," she said as she settled herself behind the steering wheel.

"I thought you must have realized that," Holte said, becoming more like a shadow than a flaw in the windshield. "Would you like me to make a short jaunt to South America?"

"Not yet." She studied the traffic in the alley.

"But you were aware that I was listening in," he persisted.

"I wasn't at first. There was so much other noise..." She started the engine, adjusted the choke, and waited the recommended two minutes for warm up before rolling down the window to signal that she was pulling out of her parking space.

"The Napier news. That's going to be around for a couple of days, at least, which gives you a bit more time to look into the sighting, if it is a sighting." He was silent for a short while. "Do you think they'll catch the missing member of the gang?" He looked around. "You can pull out now."

"Thanks," said Poppy, a bit more brusquely than she intended. "Sorry. I'm preoccupied." She released the brake, put the car in gear, and eased into the alley.

"Small wonder." Holte watched her. "You could do with a nap."

"I'm not so paltry as that," Poppy informed him. "I can hear troubling news without having a fit of the vapors."

"I know that," Holte said patiently, and stopped talking until she had made the turn at the corner and was headed toward her aunt's house. "I'll be off shortly. I want to find Knott and bring him up to date on events."

"If you mean about Stacy, you might want to wait until I'm sure that the photograph is of him; I'm trying to withhold judgment until I see what the Department of State has," Poppy said, edging around a large van pulled by two huge Belgian Draft horses. The onside horse turned toward Poppy's Hudson and tossed his head, snorting. "I guess he doesn't approve of autos," said Poppy.

"Or he might be bored," Holte said. "Many of the horses pulling caissons in the Great War grew restive if they had to stand for a long time, or were kept working past their usual hours."

"Most horses are like that," Poppy said, and sped up again, moving into the flow of traffic. "Have you seen N. N. N. Blessing recently?"

"Not for a few days. I'd just as soon give him a little time to get the feel of the investigation before I go to speak with him. He's just getting settled into the case, and he will need a day or two to decide how to proceed; he should be in Vienna by now, but he's hardly had time to unpack his duffle. He will have to get whatever information the police have before he makes up his mind about what to do, and how to do it." He noticed a paper boy on the curb ahead, brandishing copies of the *Tribune*. "Keep an eye on that lad. He looks excitable."

"So do most paper boys," Poppy said, but double-clutched down to second gear, just in case. "What does the headline say?"

Holte eased half-way out the passenger door, and read aloud, "*TWO SHIPS MISSING IN POLAR EXPLORATION FEARED LOST.* There's a two-column story beneath, but I can't make out what it says."

"No need. We've been covering the search, Daffydd's on it." She pronounced the clever Welshman's name *Daveth*, and wondered in passing why he clung to the traditional spelling of it, since almost everyone got it wrong. "The Coast Guard finally confirmed their conclusion. Too bad," Poppy said, and drove the next mile in silence. After she had passed the Friends Day School, she said, "I wonder how many people go missing in a year? Not only in disasters, but simply vanishing."

"Quite a number of them," Holte said. "But no one actually vanishes: everyone is somewhere."

"Yes, but not everyone else knows it," said Poppy, slowing down.

"That's true," Holte said, recalling the bombed and burned villages he had seen before he died, and the wandering refugees who trudged in the wake of the armies toward what they hoped was safety.

"But do you have any notion how many?" Poppy asked. "Thousands, do you think, or just hundreds?"

"Thousands sounds more accurate; there are a lot of missing people left over from the Great War, and another group of those who are unaccounted for from the Flu. Big emergencies always leave a trail of those whose fates are unknown."

"And how many of those are dead?" Poppy tapped her horn in warning to a young woman walking a frisky dog along the sidewalk.

"Many are, but not all. Certainly a third of them are still alive," Holte said. "More living spectres, in a way."

"Ye gods!" Poppy was so struck by this remark that she almost ran through the next intersection without stopping. "I hadn't thought of that, but you're right. There are all manner of living spectres, aren't there? The Armenians aren't the only ones with a claim on that title; there are countless living spectres, aren't there? People who have lost connection with their own pasts, and have no means to regain them. In a way, GAD fits the description as well, and so do Stacy, and Derrington, and Louise."

"True enough," said Holte, and fell into a reverie that lasted until Poppy pulled up in front of Esther's house; as Poppy got out of the auto, he shook himself out of his preoccupation, and said, "I'm going to do a little exploring. I'll be back tonight."

"Should I expect you at any given time?" Poppy asked as she locked the Hudson's driver- side door.

"I don't know. If I'm not back by nine tonight, don't wait up." He drifted out through the roof. "Wish me success," he said as he faded into a smudge of mist.

Poppy watched him go until there was nothing to see; puzzled but unworried, she went up the steps and onto the porch, where she stopped to get out her key, only to have Miss Roth open the door for her.

"Thank goodness you're back. Come in, come in," she urged, all but dragging Poppy inside.

"Ye gods!" Poppy exclaimed. "What's happened?"

Miss Roth flung up her hands. "Judge Stephanson proposed," she wailed. "Miss Thornton is upset."

Poppy blinked. "I take it that Aunt Esther refused him?"

"She always does," Miss Roth said fatalistically.

"Always?" Poppy repeated. "Does this happen often?"

"Once a year for as long as I've been here—probably longer," Miss Roth said as she closed the door and urged Poppy in the direction of the parlor. "It always upsets her. Always. But she never tells him it does."

Poppy almost tripped in astonishment. "He proposes? Every year?" She was astonished that Aunt Esther had never mentioned it.

"Usually nearer to Thanksgiving, but with Miss Thornton leaving in four weeks or so, he spoke up earlier. Miss Thornton is...a bit—" Without finishing her thought, she knocked on the closed sitting room door. "Miss Thornton? Miss Poppy is here."

"Have her come in," Aunt Esther called. "You can leave the door open. You don't have to shut me up in here."

Miss Roth pushed the pocket-doors wide and stepped out of Poppy's way. "Have you had your lunch yet?" she asked Poppy.

"Not yet," Poppy said, and looked into the sitting room warily, not knowing what she would see. "Aunt Esther?"

Miss Roth leaned near to Poppy. "I'll have Missus Sassoro get to work on something for you. I'll bring it in, when it's ready, and something for Miss Thornton, as well; something hot and nourishing. She'll need it." Having said that, she hurried off in the direction of the kitchen.

Poppy lingered in the door. "Aunt Esther?" she repeated, noticing that a half-empty bottle of rum was on the coffee table, and that Esther had a glass in her hand. "What's wrong Aunt Esther?"

"Come in Poppy." Esther was sitting on the arm of the settee, her hair slightly disordered, the color in her face high. "Don't worry; I'm not distracted, only a little drunk. Come in and sit down. Have a bit of the rum, or some cognac. I dislike drinking alone." She achieved a slightly lopsided smile.

Poppy went to the chair nearest to the settee and put her brief-case down beside it. "Miss Roth told me something about Judge Stephanson..."

"He proposed." Esther sighed. "Occasionally I think I should accept, just to see what would happen. He'd probably faint."

"Aunt Esther!" Poppy burst out.

"Well, he probably would, but he would expect me to follow through, which I wouldn't," she said, sounding a trifle morose. She regarded her niece through slightly unfocused eyes. "For heaven's sake, pour yourself a drink Poppy. You'd think you'd never been around anyone a bit into the wind, and I know that's not true."

"No, it's not," Poppy said as she went to the tray on the cabinet behind the settee; she took out the bottle of cognac and poured herself three fingers in a tulip-glass, reminding herself as she did that she had not eaten since breakfast, and that it would be wise to go slowly; she was about to replace the bottle when Esther interrupted her.

"Bring it over here. I don't want you jumping up and down every ten minutes," Esther said, waving Poppy back toward her. "Have a seat and get comfortable."

"But what's wrong?" Poppy asked again, and took a small sip of her cognac. "You like Judge Stephanson, don't you?"

"Yes, I like him. I'm very fond of him," Esther conceded. "If I were ever going to marry anyone, it would be Benedict Stephanson. But I am not going to marry, not at my advanced age: why should I? I am not in my dotage, and neither is he, but it's not as if I'm going to need a name for my children. I'm well enough off not to need his money, and I am high enough in society to be above the usual suspicions. I don't need his position or his social standing to ensure my place in the world." She took a swig of rum and went on, "It's not that he isn't a worthwhile catch. He's a good man, no doubt about it."

"Then why are you so...disquieted?" Poppy was beginning to feel worried about Aunt Esther's condition; this was a side of her aunt that Poppy had never seen, and it unnerved her. "Haven't you got used to his proposing?"

"No, I haven't; I get jumpy when he makes his annual proposal," said Esther, her words a little too precise for complete sobriety. "You see, I like things the way they are. I enjoy his company; he's an excellent companion. He has always been kind to me, in his way. I trust him in most matters. He does not condescend when he talks about my work, he does not try to tell me how to conduct myself, and he purports to admire my independence."

Poppy felt baffled. "Then what do you find distasteful in his proposal?"

Esther wagged a finger in Poppy's direction. "That he wants *marriage*. I have no desire to be any man's legal chattel, and he knows it, but he can't help himself. He grasps why I say no, but he feels compelled to offer anyway. He wants to *protect* me, he says, and I suppose he means it, but he doesn't know what he is asking me to give up for his sake, and money is the least of it." She finished the rum in her glass and poured some more. "It's not as if I haven't explained it to him, time and time again. He has said that he is aware of the disadvantages that marriage imposes on females, and then he tells me that he doesn't see marriage that way—and of course he wouldn't. He tells me that he would let me run my own affairs. *Let!* As if I needed his permission to do so—which I would, if I married him, come to think of it."

"He's a judge; he must see the results of marriage in his courtroom from time to time; doesn't he comprehend that you have made up your mind?" Poppy watched as Aunt Esther started to pace around the sitting room. "Isn't there some kind of contract you could make, if you accepted him? Something that would grant you more independence than is permitted in most marriages?"

"That's not what bothers me," said Esther, taking another sip of her rum.

"Then what is it?" Poppy asked, bewildered.

"I want to maintain my financial autonomy, and in this state, that would not be possible," she said bluntly.

"Do you mean you wouldn't retain the proceeds of your work and title to all you own before marriage?" Poppy was shocked at the depth of her feeling, and wondered if she could attribute it to her first sip of cognac.

"Technically—" She stumbled over the word and took another run at it. "Technically, there is a way that includes appointing an executor, which is bad enough during my lifetime, but it could be challenged by his heirs when I die, and in most such cases, the heirs prevail."

"Does he have heirs?" Poppy asked, dumbfounded; Aunt Esther had never mentioned them before.

"Oh, yes. I thought you knew. He has three children, all grown now and two with families of their own: Victoria, the youngest, lives in Cambridge with her professor husband and four children; Ralph lives in Cleveland—he's never married; he plays the French horn and teaches music there—and Walter, the oldest, lives in Arizona, for his health; he was gassed in the Great War—he was an officer then; he led his men into mustard gas—his wife and he decided to follow his doctors' advice and move to a warm, dry climate. They have one child, a son who is presently an officer in the Navy. Benedict's first wife died twenty-six years ago of a severe case of measles, of all things, which she got from one of the children. Amanda was a very sweet woman—I liked her then, though I doubt I would now: too compliant—who could deal with all the day-to-day aspects of life, which left Ben free to work on his legal career."

"Then you knew her?" Poppy was nonplused at learning this.

"Yes. I met Ben through Amanda. She was a member of the same discussion group that I was; we talked about world events. They were very popular before the Great War, discussion groups—almost as popular as mummy unwrappings were, shortly after you were born, and for more than a decade after. Discussion groups were more lady-like than sewing bees had become; we were supposed to do more than gossip."

Poppy took another, larger sip of cognac. "You're joking, aren't you? About the mummies?"

"Not at all," Esther said. "Jo was fascinated by them; she must have tended a dozen unwrappings in the years before war broke out." She poured a splash more rum into her glass. "You were at the Smithson School for Young Ladies then, I believe, and your mother did not approve of mummy unwrappings as entertainment."

Mentally unraveling this tangle of information, Poppy asked, "Why would you think that Judge Stephanson's heirs would not honor their father's wishes in regard to his estate?"

Esther heaved a prodigious sigh. "Because I've seen it before, and I have no wish to spend my waning years tied up in legal wrangles, thank you." Her *th*s were becoming more *z*s.

"You're assuming you'd outlive him," Poppy pointed out.

"It's likely I would. I'm younger than he, and I live more actively than he. Gardening is not the same as exploring, you know."

"And you're sure it would come to that?" Poppy asked before Esther could wander down another conversational path. "That the heirs would lay claim to your portion?"

Once again Esther sighed. "If they didn't, I'd be astounded. I have a fair amount of my own money—not a vast fortune, but I'm more than comfortable, and it would become Ben's money if we ever married. Unless he made a separate and specific provision in his Will that my funds should be returned to me upon his death, they would be lumped in with his money, and his heirs would have first claim on it." She took a good swig of her rum, and explained. "I've seen it happen many times," she repeated with intensity, "before a father dies, the children all pledge to accept the terms of the Will, and then, when the parent is no longer about, disputes break out, especially if there is another wife in the picture, a woman not their mother. They wouldn't have minded if Amanda got all Ben's money—not that I'd want all of it—but they'd be outraged if I did try to recover my own."

"But would it have to come to that?" Poppy asked, and was denied an answer when Miss Roth appeared in the door with a tray in her hands.

"Italian soup and toasted cheese sandwiches. Missus Sassoro says she'll push dinner back an hour—you can come into the parlor at seven instead of six, and dinner will be served at eight—so you will have an appetite for the meal. It will be lamb chops and sautéed rhubarb with a side-dish of steamed cauliflower with butter and cheese." She came into the sitting room and put the tray down on the coffee table, next to the bottle of rum. "The coffee is hot, there's cream and sugar." She pointed them out.

"Thank you Miss Roth," said Aunt Esther with owlish formality. "I'll bear that in mind."

"You might want to have a lie-down after you finish up here," Miss Roth hinted broadly. "Should I go in and close the draperies in your bedroom so you can rest this afternoon? I'll tell anyone who phones that you're not available."

Esther rolled her eyes. "If you think I'm that far gone, you might as well." She came back to the settee and plunked herself down on it. "There. Are you satisfied?"

"For now," said Miss Roth, and left aunt and niece alone.

"Where were we?" Esther asked Poppy, who was pouring herself a cup of coffee.

"You were telling me about inheritance battles," Poppy said as she used the tongs to pick up one cube of sugar from the bowl on the tray.

"Yes, I was, wasn't I?" Esther eyed the sandwiches with misgiving. "The soup smells very good, but I'm not so sure about these cheese sandwiches."

"Ye gods, why not?"

"Because it smells as if she's toasted them in margarine, not butter," Esther said bluntly. "I can't bear the taste of margarine. Dreadful stuff. Might as well use lard instead."

Poppy could tell that Aunt Esther was about to go off down another conversational rabbit hole, and decided to stop her. "Which of Judge Stephanson's heirs would you expect to attempt to break their father's will?"

"I don't know," said Esther. "But once we married—*if* we married—control of my money and property would pass into Ben's hands, and would end up part of what they fought over; I have my own heirs to think about."

After adding the usual dollop of cream to her coffee, Poppy remarked, "And who might they be? Since you haven't any children."

"I have you, for one, and Hank. And Linus, Bethany, Jacob, Estelle, Francis, and Bertram, not that I feel any obligation to Regis' children—they're all well established, and like Regis, they disapprove of the way I live my life." She steadied herself as she reached to pour more rum into her glass. "I don't feel any sense of family obligation to them, nor they to me. You and Hank are another matter."

At the mention of her oldest uncle's children—all of whom were more than a decade older than she—Poppy blanched, and said the first thing that came to mind. "Just Hank and me, not Stacy?"

"Good Lord, no! Not Stacy. Never." Esther drank more rum. "No. Not Stacy," she repeated for good measure, and drank down the last of the rum in her glass before pouring out another three-fingers'-worth into it.

Poppy took this all in. "If you're telling Judge Stephanson no because of Hank and me, I wish you wouldn't. I can manage very well on what my father left me, and I plan to work as long as some paper will hire me. I'm doing well financially; I've been investing most of my annual allotment of inheritance, and depositing a quarter of it in a small but very reliable local bank; I try to live within my salary in most things. What you charge me to live here is a pittance, so if providing me and Hank an inheritance is all that's holding you back, Aunt Esther, don't—"

"Of course it's not all," said Esther abruptly. "I enjoy my way of life, and, fond as I am of him, Ben would want me to curtail my exploring. He's been telling me for the last three years that a woman of my age shouldn't go about on her own, visiting remote places populated by what he calls *unscrupulous natives*. As if the civilized world is any better when it comes to a lack of scruples. Look at the level of corruption in this city. What native in New Guinea can aspire to that?" She set down her glass and reached for the soup spoon on her side of the tray. "I suppose I'd better get into this; Miss Roth will hector me if I don't. She doesn't approve of my being drunk."

"I think she's trying to keep you from making it worse with indulgence."

"True enough. That's because she thinks I'm getting drunk by accident," Esther scoffed. "I'm getting drunk on purpose, so I don't end up raging about the house. I'd rather muddle my thoughts for a while than end up ranting." She set her glass next to the tray. "I try not to rant when I'm afraid."

"Are you afraid?" Poppy asked, alarmed to hear it.

"Of course I am. Any woman on her own is afraid unless she's insane or foolish. I saw this when I was quite young, and I told myself then that I would face my fears before they took hold of me, and decide how to deal with them while I still had my wits about me, so that I would not be driven to panic when the fears proved genuine. Most fears aren't real, you know—they're small worries blown out of proportion and given power through panic." She wagged a finger in Poppy's direction. "Don't let yourself be fooled by fears. Look them in the eye. You'll end up being a puppet, dancing to your wildest imaginings if you don't."

Poppy mirrored Esther's motions. "Don't tell me you're afraid of Alexandra Roth. I won't believe you."

"Not afraid in the usual way, but I do enjoy peace in my household," Esther said quietly. "And she's right to a point—I ought to sober up before evening."

Poppy found herself at a standstill, having no more ideas on how she might pursue her aunt's determination to hold the man who loved her at arm's length, so she tasted the soup and found it quite satisfying; she resigned herself to a quiet afternoon following this unconventional lunch; she had to admit that she was worn out. "Are you staying in tonight?" she asked Esther when she was half-way through her bowl.

"Yes; it's going to be an early night for me; I'm going to bed shortly after we have dinner. I'm actually tired for a change." Esther picked up half her sandwich and bit into it cautiously. "Oh, good," she said around her mouthful of toast and cheese. "Missus Sassoro went to the Italian grocery and got provolone." She pronounced all four syllables. "I do like that one."

"Don't you like cheddar?" Poppy asked as she reached for her sandwich.

"On many things, but I prefer provolone or asiago in my toasted cheese sandwiches. It reminds me of the time I've spent in Italy." Esther smiled as she chewed.

"Then make sure you tell Missus Sassoro grazie per questo," said Poppy, dredging up the phrase from her Italian lessons of a decade ago; then she bit into the sandwich and decided she agreed with Aunt Esther, at least about the cheese.

THIRTY-FOUR

Chesterton Holte slipped into the dimension of ghosts, to make a few inquiries before he went on to see how Blessing was progressing. Although there was no day or night in the dimension, there were places that were marginally brighter than others, and he started in one of them, hoping to seek out Moncrief or Overstreet, their emanations being the most familiar to him now. After a while, he followed their trail to an energetic swirl, not far from a mob of Ceylonese rice farmers killed in a tidal wave who came surging by; here he found Madison Moncrief with Julian Eastley, moving as little as was possible for ghosts.

"So it's you again," said Moncrief as he noticed Holte.

"Yes, it is," Holte told them. *"I was hoping you might help me out."*

"Which one of us?" Moncrief asked.

"Eastley, if he's willing," said Holte, and saw that Eastley was starting to slide away. *"It's nothing to Louise's discredit."*

Eastley hung in the emptiness. *"Your word as a gentleman?"*

"If you insist, yes," said Holte, and went on before Eastley could change his mind. *"Do you recall Louise saying anything about Maracaibo? It's a city in—"*

"Venezuela. Yes, I know. She was always talking about South America—how exotic and romantic it was. She often told me how much she wanted to go there."

"Did she?" Moncrief asked in amazement. *"She never said anything to me, beyond wanting to go to Rio for Carnival."*

"She told me that you weren't fond of traveling," Eastley said.

"Not fond of traveling? I'd proposed a trip to Europe, but she turned it down; said she didn't want to go there until they had cleaned up from the Great War." Moncrief shifted away from the rice farmers. *"She and Stacy used to joke about running off to Rio if*

things went bad. I never took them seriously."

"What is it you want to know?" Eastley asked, prickling. *"So far I am not hearing much to her benefit, from either of you."*

"Was Rio the only place she wanted to go?" Holte asked, wanting to keep on track.

"Most of the time, yes. She did say something about hoping to go up the Amazon, to see what it's like. I vetoed that," Moncrief said. *"I told her it was too dangerous. The river is a wilderness for the most part, and there are insects and animals that are far from friendly, not to mention potential natives. When the river floods, half of the forest is under water, and the maps of the river's course become useless, and it is said that one may easily become lost there."*

"Which one might," Eastley chimed in. *"A lady like Louise should never expose herself to the kind of risks such a journey would require."*

"When I told her how long it might take, she changed her mind, or at least she never mentioned it again. I didn't think any more about it." Moncrief swung toward Holte. *"What's this all about?"*

"Stacy may have been spotted in Maracaibo," he said without preamble.

"According to whom?" Moncrief's dubiety was obvious.

"The US Department of State," Holte responded. *"They are going to send a photograph to Miss Thornton that they believe may be of Stacy."*

"Good gracious," said Eastley.

"Just Stacy? Not Louise?" Moncrief asked.

"They're not certain that it is Stacy; that's why they've contacted Poppy. They tried Josephine Dritchner, to no avail; she refused to talk to them, or so I understand," Holte said. *"Apparently it's only Stacy they're asking about; there was no mention of anyone with him."*

The rice farmers began to swirl away from the Holte and the two ghosts he was consulting; their moaning soughed like wind through trees.

Moncrief was growing more alert. *"When did this happen?"*

"A short while ago," said Holte. *"I'll know more in a few days, when their packet of information arrives."*

"I still think it's horrid of Dritchner to smirch Louise's reputation the way he has. He might be escaping the law, but to let it be thought that Louise fled with him...Unpardonable." Eastley would have stamped his foot if he still had a body. *"A short note to her family could stop all the whispers. Dritchner is a man of breeding, and this is the least he could do, isn't it?"*

Moncrief made an impatient sound. *"When will you stop idealizing Louise?"* he demanded of Eastley. *"She was my wife, and if anyone should be upset—"*

"Then you should defend her good name," Eastley said, his manner truculent.

"When I'm convinced she deserves it, I will," Moncrief promised. *"Until then, I'll say what I think."*

"If you continue in this vein, Moncrief, I shall have to seek out other company." Julian Eastley began to fade off toward the rice farmers.

Holte decided that he should leave these two to quarrel among themselves. *"Thank you both,"* he said, floating away from them and casting about for Overstreet or Knott. He searched for a whiff of either ghost, and finally caught a trace of Knott. Increasing his speed, Holte hastened toward a cluster of African orphans dead of water parasites, and passed through them, closing in on Knott.

Knott had not lost any of his determination to find Derrington and wring information out of him, but for now he was turning in figure-eight loops, much as if he were pacing a floor, had there been floor to pace in the dimension of ghosts. As he became aware of Holte's approach, he decreased his speed and hung in speculative quiet as Holte came up to him. *"What are you doing here this time?"* he inquired testily.

"Looking for you, among other things," Holte replied.

"Really? Do you have any news for me?"

"In a manner of speaking. There have been developments in the search for Dritchner, and I thought you might want to know about them." He summed up what he had learned during Poppy's conversation with Mobray, and ended with, *"So you see, if the man in the photograph turns out to be Stacy, we may be able to narrow the search."*

Knott did not respond for a long moment, then said, *"I looked through Maracaibo. If he had been there, I would have found him."*

Although Holte doubted that, he said, *"It's likely that he's traveling, and wouldn't have been there when you looked. The card he sent his mother was sent from Brazil."*

"Where in Brazil? It's a big country." Knott sounded aggravated; if he had had a face, he would have been scowling.

"I don't know. I haven't seen it, nor has Poppy, not yet."

"Then it's little more than a rumor," Knott said dismissively.

"It narrows the search," Holte repeated.

Knott slid away a short distance, then came back toward Holte. *"You're being damned frustrating, Holte."*

"That's not my intention," Holte reminded him.

"I realize that," Knott said, not quite as brusquely as he had been, doing his ghostly equivalent of speaking; he dropped down below Holte, motioning him to follow. *"By the way, I'm more certain than ever that Derrington killed me, with Dritchner's help. I wouldn't have thought that he had it in him, but I've been remembering, and I believe that it was Derrington who came to my home the night I was killed. I know that he phoned me. He wanted to talk about the counterfeit antiques and something about Dritchner's other activities. That part I haven't recalled yet. Something happened a little later, that isn't at all clear to me. I believe he brought a mace-and-chain with him, saying he wanted me to authenticate it, because he didn't trust Dritchner with such evaluations any more, at least I think that's what happened. I know there was a mace-and-chain involved. That's what was used to kill me, I'm pretty sure. Vicious things, those mace- and-chains."*

"That they are," Holte agreed.

"I wish I could remember all of it, but it still escapes me. I don't like that."

"Few of us do," said Holte as a gesture of consolation. *"Those of us who die... unexpectedly...often take a long—"*

"—time to remember," Knott finished for him. *"I understand that, but I still don't like it. I'm almost certain about the mace-and-chain. The rest is still...unfocused."*

"That's not surprising," said Holte. *"There's no going on until the memories are straightened out and you take the time to wholly acknowledge them. I don't want to go off on wild goose chases."*

"Yes; yes, I know all that. But it wears on me, these delays and lacks of completion."

"It's easier once you stop being angry," Holte told him.

"So I've heard; I'm not persuaded that losing the anger is necessary. It's the thing driving me to find out what happened. Without it, I'm afraid I'd drift around in the kind of confusion I see in so many others in this dimension," Knott was abashed to admit this, and he showed that by curving away from Holte. *"I think I may have another go at Maracaibo."*

"Would you know Stacy if you saw him?" Holte asked.

"I believe so. Remember, I bought my business from his father. The first time I met Stacy, he was about fourteen, as I recall, and the last time was when he graduated from...one of the Ivy Leagues; I can't recall which one. He was about twenty-one then. He can't have changed so much in the intervening years that I would not know him on sight. I may have seen him

again, more recently, but I can't bring the encounter to mind." Knott was farther off now, preparing to slip away to the world of the living. *"If it comes back to me, I'll tell you about it the next time I see you."*

"Will you let me know if you find Derrington?" Holte called voicelessly after him.

"If you're around, I will." For Knott, this was a binding commitment; he shimmered and was gone.

Holte was far from satisfied, but he was aware that he had done all that he could for now from Moncrief, Eastley, and Knott, so he began a methodical exploration for Overstreet, flitting from one part of the dimension of ghosts to another at rapid speeds, his noncorporeal senses set to hone in on Overstreet. Finally Holte came upon him near a vortex of earthquake victims from New Zealand. *"How is it going for you?"* Holte said as he approached Overstreet.

"I know you, don't I?" Overstreet asked.

"Chesterton Holte," he said. *"We've met a couple of times."*

"You're the one who asked about my time on the Belle Helene, *aren't you?"*

Encouraged by this accurate recollection, Holte said, *"Yes, I am. I was hoping that you might have more complete memories of that."*

"Sorry," said Overstreet. *"Not that I'm aware of."*

"Has anything else come back to you?"

"Not really. Bits and pieces. You know how that is." Overstreet studied the New Zealanders rotating near him. *"How long will it take them to remember how they died, do you think?"*

Holte had no immediate answer for that. *"As long as they need, would be my guess,"* he said as he saw Overstreet's attention begin to flag. *"As for you, can you tell me about the bits and pieces?"*

"If you like," said Overstreet, and went silent.

"Your bits and pieces?" Holte urged.

Overstreet came back into focus. *"Oh, yes. I was just thinking."* And again, he fell silent.

"Overstreet," Holte prompted. *"It's important. Tell me what you do remember."*

"If you like. I haven't made sense of it yet." Overstreet moved a little closer to Holte. *"I think there must have been some kind of argument on the boat...It had to do with travel plans...but I may be wrong about that...I believe I was supposed to meet Derrington in Cuba...but Nelson said we'd get around to that after we went to Jamaica...he said it was*

important...*There was something he was planning to pick up in Jamaica...if he told me what it was, I've forgotten...and he claimed it was more important than my appointment with Derrington. I...must have said that Cuba was nearer than Jamaica...well, it is.*"

"*Yes,*" Holte agreed. "*It is.*"

Overstreet made a motion of justification. "*Thank you. I reminded them—both Nelson and Quentin—but Nelson wouldn't budge...I would have paid him to let me off...he got mad at that...They both did...one of them...said that I hadn't told them enough to be let off...I think it was Nelson, but it might have been Quentin....Nelson was the one steering the boat...I know that's right.*"

"*When did this happen? How far were you from Canada?*" Holte was troubled by Overstreet's distracted state.

"*I don't know...you've seen the ocean...it's hard to judge distance when...all you can see, day after day, is water. Like being here.*"

Holte did his noncorporeal version of a sigh; Overstreet was a long way from being able to give a full account of what he had experienced in the days before his death, and there was no point in pushing him. "*I've got to leave you for now,*" he told Overstreet. "*I may be back, but later.*"

"*That's good to know,*" said Overstreet remotely, and wafted away in a directionless sort of zig-zag.

Holte took a little time to wander among the ghosts in the hope of finding someone who might be able to tell him more, but it was a futile exercise, and he gave it up fairly quickly, slipping back into the world of the living in time to find Poppy still in her study at Aunt Esther's house, a stack of notes next to her typewriter; the clock said forty-two minutes past eight, and the two lamps were lit, revealing Maestro curled up on the visitor's chair. Holte swung around the end of Poppy's desk and made a kind of bow. "Still busy?" he asked in order to alert her to his presence.

Poppy looked up just as Maestro raised his head and hissed. "Oh. You're back," she said, looking a bit harried.

"I am." He noticed that there were no completed sheets of paper lying on the desk. "Having trouble with work?"

"In a way. We had a late dinner. I've only been at this for about ten minutes."

"Ten minutes? That is a late dinner." He approached her, increasing his visibility as he came.

"I did get some work done this afternoon, but then I had a call from Sherman Pearse. He gave me a tongue-lashing because he now has nine ransom demands for GAD's safe return, and he's decided that it's my fault." She shook her head. "I know I'm not supposed to be thin-skinned about this, but I'm afraid he got my dander up. I said some things he found offensive."

"Such as?" Holte inquired.

"I called him a martinet and a blowhard," she admitted. "Not very professional, I'm afraid."

"Are you saying he isn't a martinet and a blowhard?" Holte was incredulous. "From what I've seen of the man, you had him pegged. Do you think you were wrong?"

"Ye gods, no!" Poppy slapped her hand on the top of the desk. "He's both those things, and more. But I shouldn't have lost my temper."

"Why not? Pearse lost his, didn't he?"

"That he did," Poppy said. "And I was fool enough to follow his example. Pearse hung up on me after he said he'd get me fired for—"

"He can't do that," Holte interrupted her. "You don't work for him, and I don't think Lowenthal likes it when Old Money tries to tell him what he can and can't do. He's not fond of politicians, either, come to think of it."

Poppy was not so sure about the Old Money. "He went along with Pearse's demand that he approve what I've written, and I'd been civil to Pearse before now."

"Lowenthal wants the story, but not if it means trouble for you."

"It bothers me, knowing that Pearse is being so...so pugnacious. If I were a man, he'd probably expect me to fight with him—fisticuffs."

Holte did his best to sit on the edge of the desk, and so only sunk an inch into its surface. "What does your aunt think about this?"

Poppy looked away from him. "I haven't told her."

"Why on earth not?" Holte asked her.

"I don't want her rallying to my cause," Poppy said in a small voice. "She's apt to drive over to the Pearses' house and give them a piece of her mind, and then the fat would really be in the fire."

"I can see how that would be unpleasant, but how could it—" He saw the distressed look in her eyes and stopped. "All right. Tell me why that would be a bad thing. You've made no secret of your disapproval of Mister Pearse's behavior, so why would your aunt's support not help you?"

Poppy flung up one hand. "It's hard enough doing my job as it is; having my relatives and old friends taking sides would make it even harder. I don't mind being an oddity, but I have no wish to become an example—good or bad, depending on which side of the issue people chose. It's bad enough that nearly everyone I know disapproves of what I do. If it meant difficulties for the paper, Lowenthal would be displeased at the least: he says his reporters are supposed to cover the news, not be it."

"Are you sure of that?" Holte asked calmly.

"Sure enough that I don't want to take a chance on it," said Poppy, and retrieved a handkerchief from her pocket to wipe her eyes. "Ye gods, what a ninny I am."

"Hardly that," Holte reassured her. "You're a little on overload, and no wonder."

Poppy bit back the retort that rose to her lips, and said only, "You may be right."

There was a knock on the door, and Miss Roth said, "Miss Thornton, you have a visitor. I've put him in the parlor, and I've offered him coffee and a drink."

"Who is it?" Poppy asked, trying to adjust her mascara.

"Inspector Loring, Miss," said Miss Roth.

Poppy gave a little shriek. "I'll be out in a couple of minutes. Please ask him to wait, if you would." She turned to Holte. "I should go find out what he wants."

"Your company would be my guess," said Holte, obligingly rising toward the ceiling and circling above Maestro. "I'll come back a little later."

THIRTY-FIVE

INSPECTOR LORING STOOD UP AS POPPY CAME INTO THE ROOM. "SORRY TO DROP in on you unannounced like this; I hope you don't mind." There were circles around his eyes and his shirt, under his tweed jacket, was rumpled, and his tie loosened a bit.

"Looks like you've had a long day," Poppy said, motioning to him to sit down. "Make yourself comfortable, Loring—no need to stand on ceremony with me." As she said this, she felt a bit embarrassed; she covered this by telling him, "Miss Roth will bring you whatever you asked for, and probably something more, for hospitality's sake."

"I gather I caught you working," he said, a bit apologetically.

"You did, but I'm glad you're giving me an excuse to stop; I wasn't doing very well. You're likely to help me shake the cobwebs out of my thoughts." She took the far end of the couch from where he sat in the wing-back chair. "What's been going on? More about the Napier capture?"

Loring shook his head. "The Robbery boys have got a bead on the last man. It's not my look-out. No, that's not what's bothering me."

"Then what is?" she asked. "Because you do have something on your mind."

"I do, and I know you can help me figure out how to handle this awkward situation. You know the people better than I do." Loring sat forward, put his elbows on his knees and his chin in his hands. "I had a telegram earlier today, and I've been trying to confirm what it said. No luck so far, and I've been working on it for most of the afternoon and into the evening. I'm at a bit of an impasse."

"Oh?" She felt her curiosity awaken. "What about the telegram?"

"It was from Blessing. He's just leaving Bratislava for Brno, on the night train. He has learned from what he believes is a reliable source that GAD is in jail there." He heard Poppy gasp. "That's what I've been trying to confirm. Blessing said he'd hold off notifying the Pearses until he can discover if it's true and, if it is, what can be done about it."

"Ye gods!" Poppy exclaimed. "In jail? Why? What did GAD do?"

"That's what I'm trying to find out, as a first step; I've sent a telegram to our Embassy in Prague, asking if they can verify this claim, but no answer so far. But it's late there, and I'll probably have to wait until Monday morning before I hear from them; I had Sergeant Barech, who knows Czech, draft a telegram to the Brno police for me and sent it off around four." Loring said, and noticed Miss Roth approaching with a tray. "Let's attend to this after we're private again."

Miss Roth brought the tray to the coffee table. "I've taken the liberty of providing cognac and rum as well as coffee and some toast with shrimp-paste or potted ham for you; the potted ham is on the rye bread, the shrimp-paste on the white toast. Have what you want."

The three of them did not notice a faint flicker in the floor-lamp behind the couch.

"Thank you, Miss Roth," Poppy said, and added, "Will you tell my aunt that Inspector Loring is here?"

"Certainly," said Miss Roth, adding, "I'll be going to my quarters after I have a word with Miss Thornton. So if you'll put the tray in the kitchen when you're done?" and with that, left them alone.

"So, Inspector, what may I give you?" Poppy said, recalling all her lessons in etiquette; she handed him one of two napkins on the tray.

"It was very nice of Miss Roth to provide rum and cognac," Loring said with a faint smile. "I'll have a bit of rum, and after that, I'll decide about the rest."

"Coming up." Poppy obliged him, pouring two fingers of rum into the taller of the two glasses on the tray. "Enough?"

"Fine."

As she gave this to him, she said, "You'll let me know when you make up your mind about the sandwiches."

"I will," he said as he took the glass from her. "Are you going to join me?"

Poppy reached for the cognac bottle. "I am. Anything to shake up my head.

Or, if it puts me to sleep, I'll know I've been pushing too hard." This was a maladroit confession for her, but she was gratified when she saw Loring actually smile. With that for encouragement, she took her glass and poured in a little over a finger. "There." She lifted her glass to him. "To good times ahead."

"Good times," he echoed. After his first sip, Loring began to relax, more from conviviality than the impact of alcohol. "I stopped sending telegrams around five, and I've tried to get hold of someone in our Department of State to find out how to go on from here. There aren't many about the place on a Saturday afternoon."

"Have you said anything to the Pearses yet?" Poppy asked, setting her glass down next to the tray.

"No; I don't want to alarm them if I don't have to; I should have something from Blessing in the morning, after he gets to Brno and finds out what he can about GAD." He had another sip. "I hope Blessing knows how to handle situations like this, because I don't."

"And you said that Blessing hasn't sent a telegram to the Pearses; is that right?"

"No, he hasn't; he's waiting for my recommendation and some actual confirmation, which strikes me as sensible, especially dealing with Mister Pearse." He faltered, coughing a little. "It isn't easy to break the news—if it is news. I don't want to pass on information if it turns out to be wrong. Pearse said he didn't want gossip and rumors, he wanted hard facts, which is why I wired Prague; I hope they can give me something concrete without masses of red tape." He had a little more rum.

"Don't you know how to do that? Get the information you want? Surely you had to deal with local governments during the Great War?" Poppy asked.

"I did, and I wasn't much good at it. Finding and identifying bodies was hard enough in itself, but when there were no certain ways to know who was who, and what army they'd fought for, there are headaches that are beyond anything you can think of."

She picked up her glass again. "I can imagine. I know what it took to get my father's remains back from Belgium. Months and months of forms and telegrams, made more difficult because my father was an American civilian, not a soldier in uniform. But the US wasn't in the Great War yet when he was killed, so we had to arrange most of it ourselves. My Uncle Regis handled the bulk of it; he had the highest access of any of us."

"Not very pleasant, all those hurdles to jump over," Loring said in sympathy.

Poppy shook her head, and shifted the subject. "But it seems GAD is alive, in all likelihood—the Europeans are generally prompt in their death notifications—which ought to be good news for the Pearses. Doesn't that make a difference?"

"I hope so," said Loring devoutly. "*Seems* isn't good enough, though, not for Pearse." He had a little more rum. "I have to phone Pearse this evening, to provide his daily report, and I'm at a loss to know how to do it. If I withhold information, Pearse'll be furious when he finds out, but if I tell him what I know, he'll—"

"—be furious. You're right about that." She reached for the coffee pot and poured some into her cup. "Would you like some?"

"Okay. I guess I'd better," Loring said. "I don't want a muddled head."

"Then have a sandwich or two. That should sop up the rum," she said. "I'm not very hungry; as I mentioned, dinner was late."

"Thanks," he said, setting his glass aside and taking one of the shrimp-paste sandwiches. "I don't feel hungry, but I probably am; I haven't eaten since two this afternoon."

Poppy looked startled. "You must be famished," she said. "Would you like something more substantial? I could go into the kitchen and make you up a small plate." She saw his surprised expression. "I know my way around a kitchen. I'm not a great cook, but I do more than boil water."

"I didn't mean..." He cleared his throat. "Sorry. Yes, I did. Most women of your..."

Poppy bridled at this. "You mean upper class women don't always have domestic skills? You're right about that; many of us don't. But I was fortunate to have a Suffragette mother who insisted that her daughter be able to fend for herself in such matters; I can do basic cooking, I can handle cleaning and repairing, and I can manage money. It's all stood me in good stead, and I'm grateful to her in more ways than one."

Loring was a study in consternation. "Poppy, I didn't—I apologize."

Seeing his discomfort, Poppy softened. "You're right, Loring. Yes, I can cook enough to keep from starving, but Missus Sassoro outdoes me at every turn, and I like it that way. I wish she were here now, but in her place, I can make you up a plate, if you decide you want one." She put sugar and cream in her coffee and then reclaimed her glass of cognac, which she lifted in his direction. "Eat your sandwich and then we'll talk about how to approach Sherman Pearse."

"Cautiously," he said, before taking his first bite of his sandwich. "I realize the man is demanding."

"That he is," Poppy agreed. "I didn't think so when I was younger and we were visiting the family, but in retrospect, I can see that he had to be in charge of everything, and still does. He must be impossible if there is real disorder in the home. No wonder Isadora is given to emotional outbursts; I'd scream too, if I were married to him. He's a tyrant at heart. I'm surprised that she is willing to put up with him."

"Then have you anything to advise me in dealing with him?" He took a second bite of his sandwich, smiling a little.

"You're right about caution." Poppy took a little more cognac, and did her best to summon up her opinions. "If I were you, I wouldn't tell him much; I might say that you are awaiting word from Prague, and you hope to have news for the family on Monday, if not sooner. That should reassure him without giving the impression that you are dragging your feet. Additionally, it might be prudent to say as little as possible about what you've heard, and you might, in your telegram to Blessing, mention the same approach for him. Once you inform him of the possibilities, they will become certainties in Mister Pearse's mind."

Loring swallowed his third bite of sandwich and said, "If you think that will work. He could insist on knowing the whole."

"It should be better to tell him that you're following a few promising leads than telling him too much of what is not verified," Poppy said, and saw a blur on the far wall; she realized that Holte was observing.

"Okay," he said again, and had another sip of rum before taking a third bite. "Anything else?"

"You might tell him that Blessing is also working to follow his current leads, and will report to Pearse as soon as he has contacted the appropriate Czech authorities, which may take a little time. It reminds Pearse that you and Blessing are working together, not in competition." She set her cognac aside and picked up her coffee cup. "It would be like Pearse to try to play you off against one another."

"I thought it might be something like that," said Loring. "I'll try to warn Blessing when I send my next telegram."

"Bear in mind that Mister Pearse likes people he considers beneath him to be deferential, so present what you wish to tell him with respect and modesty, accede to him as much as you can, be acquiescent. The more humble, the better." She was a bit surprised to hear herself say so, but she decided not to modify her remarks.

"A lot of the upper crust are like that," said Loring, and nearly choked as he heard laughter from the door; he set his sandwich down and got to his feet. "Good evening, Miss Thornton."

"Excuse me Inspector," said Aunt Esther. "I didn't mean to interrupt, but as Miss Roth mentioned you were here, I thought I'd better come welcome you to the house. Do sit down and eat. You look like you could use some food."

Loring muttered a kind of thanks, and resumed his place in the chair. "Your niece as I were just discussing the latest developments in the GAD Pearse investigation."

"So I gathered," said Esther, coming into the parlor. "Don't worry; I won't stay long."

"You're busy?" Poppy asked.

"I'm starting to make lists for the Amazon trip. I have a lot to do before I can depart, which I want to do in fewer than twenty days, if possible." She came in and pulled up the ottoman for a seat. "I have to budget my journey for the National Geographic Society and submit it by next Wednesday. They don't like writing blank checks."

"Hardly unusual," said Poppy, indicating the two bottles on the tray. "May I pour you some of your excellent drink, Aunt Esther?"

"No thank you, not just at present. I indulged earlier, and now I'd rather devote myself to doing calculations and such, which requires that I try to keep my head clear, more's the pity. I may have something later, as a nightcap. But that needn't stop either of you from having a nip or two. You both go ahead and enjoy yourselves." She moved to study Loring. "You look weary, Inspector."

"I am weary Miss Thornton."

"Then let me advise you to have another sandwich when you finish the one you're working on. And have more coffee than rum, if you intend to work tonight." That said, she shifted her attention to Poppy. "I had a call from Denton North today, about a rumor that Stacy has been seen in Venezuela. Is there any truth in that?"

Poppy told herself that she should have anticipated that the Department of State would be in touch with Philadelphia's District Attorney. "I don't know, yet. I may be able to be specific by Tuesday."

"So there has been some progress," Esther said. "About time."

"There *may* be some progress, but that depends on a proper identification," Poppy corrected her. "I don't know what Denton has heard, but so far all there is, that I'm aware of, is supposition, and that's the problem the Department of State would like to solve."

Esther regarded Poppy narrowly. "Is this something new, or did you know about it this afternoon?"

Poppy took on the question directly. "Yes, I did know about it, but I didn't want to bring it up. You were concerned with other matters."

"So I was. Pardon me for being...preoccupied," Esther said somberly.

"When I find out one way or another whether or not Stacy has been seen, I'll let you know," Poppy vowed. "I may even inform Aunt Jo."

Aunt Esther shook her head. "Best let me do it; she won't want to hear it from you." She turned toward Loring. "How does this appear to you, Inspector? Do you think that Denton North is on to something at last?"

"If Stacy is identified, then it might prove helpful, although from what I little I've heard of this, I'm not getting my hopes up; South America is a very big place, and there are a vast number of bolt-holes to hide in," Loring said before taking a last bite of his sandwich. "If Stacy is moving about, then it will be hard to get on his trail."

"It would be like Stacy to lead you on a merry dance all over South America, I'm afraid." Esther said, and added, "He would enjoy that."

Poppy offered the plate with the potted ham sandwiches. "Have another. I don't think I have room for any of them."

"Yes, please do," Esther seconded. "I hate seeing food go to waste, and I don't think the cat likes sandwiches."

He held up one hand. "I'll stick with the shrimp-paste, if you don't mind. The potted ham reminds me too much of Army food. We ate potted ham for dinner six days out of seven when I was in the Army."

"As you like," said Poppy, replacing the plate she held and exchanging it for the one with shrimp-paste, extending it in Loring's direction.

Loring took the next-to-last one, nodding his thanks; he addressed Esther. "How long do you plan to be gone Miss Thornton?"

"Five to six months, weather permitting—it could be a bit longer," she said. "I'm relieved that Poppy will be here in my absence."

"No more than I am," said Poppy.

"If I could persuade the National Geographic Society to lease me an aeroplane—I did so in Siberia—I could accomplish more than I can by taking boats up the river, but they're worried I'll crash and be stranded." Esther snorted contemptuously. "They're fools, all of them. As if I could not be stranded in a boat!"

Loring was about to say something, but changed his mind and had another sip of rum; then he said, "The Amazon is a long river: how far are you going?"

"I'd like to go to all the way to Iquitos, but that may not be possible, the way things stand now." She stood up. "And I need to get back to working out the finances and supplies. It's good to see you, Inspector. I trust your current inquiries will be successful. If you'll excuse me?" Without waiting for a response, she turned and left the room.

"An astonishing woman, your Aunt Esther," Loring said. "It must be the very devil to keep up with her."

"I wouldn't even try. I only hope I can be half so hale and hearty when I'm her age," said Poppy, a hint of wistfulness about her.

"You'll be marvelous at her age," Loring told her, his ears turning red, and bit into his sandwich.

"Why, thank you Loring," Poppy said playfully, as if she thought he had been teasing her, which she did not, but she could not bring herself to acknowledge the compliment in any other way.

The floor lamp flickered again, and this time both Poppy and Loring noticed it. For several seconds neither of them spoke.

At last Poppy said, "Spooks," before she picked up her coffee cup, satisfied that she had, for once, been honest about Holte's presence.

Loring stopped chewing. "If you say so."

THIRTY-SIX

BLESSING WAS ON THE NIGHT-TRAIN FROM BUDA-PEST TO BRNO, LEAVING
Bratislava at one-forty a. m. with stops at Malacky and Kuty before Brno; he
had reserved an upper berth and was trying to stay asleep as the train made
its way north; the man in the bunk beneath him was snoring vigorously, as if
in hope of orchestral accompaniment. To make matters worse, portions of the
track were in need of repair, and the train took those stretches slowly, swaying
erratically; it would therefore arrive later than the posted 5:10 a.m. time, for
which Blessing was grateful; he would be able to get breakfast without a long
wait. The greatest difficulty was proving to be falling asleep in the swaying
bunk. He wadded his pillow into a new shape and tried to get his mind to
quiet—images of GAD in a cell worried at him like a dog at a bone, along with
the problems that might well lie ahead—but so far had little success. Just as he
began to doze, there was a gathering of what might be smoke at the foot of his
bunk, and an ill-defined form took shape.

"Sorry to wake you," said Chesterton Holte.

"What are you doing here?" Blessing grumped at him.

"I want to ride along with you, to find out if, and why, GAD Pearse is in jail,"
said Holte.

"Sweet Jesus, spare me," Blessing muttered.

"I understand that you and Inspector Loring have exchanged telegrams,"
Holte said, paying no notice to Blessing's annoyance.

"Yes," Blessing said quietly. "I telegraphed the parents immediately
afterward, informing them that I was going to Brno on a lead, and that if it
proved accurate, I would telegraph them again by evening. Loring was right
to suggest that I give them no additional information. I haven't met Sherman

Pearce, but I can tell that he is an absolutist, as many wealthy men are. He reminds me of Colonel Haycroft." Ghost and investigator shared a shudder at the mention of Haycroft's name. "Pearse is bad-tempered to boot," Holte said when he had put the obnoxious colonel out of his thoughts. "Don't mind my tagging along. I want to be able to keep Miss Thornton apprised of my progress, and following you will make it much easier for me to do that. I may even be of some use to you, incorporeal though I may be. For example, locked doors are no barrier to me, which might provide opportunities you can't manage on your own." He hung near the ceiling of the bunk compartment, hardly more visible than the pale shine emitted by the small night-light above Blessing's head. "Miss Thornton is somewhat acquainted with GAD, and it may be that her name will be useful if you make direct contact with the lad; it would lessen the stigma of working for his father."

This last awakened Blessing completely. "How does she know him?" he asked, struggling to keep his voice low; from the bunk below came a stentorian crescendo of snores, and Blessing motioned Holte to be silent.

"Only you can hear me," Holte reminded him when the noise started to lessen. "If it helps, I won't raise my voice."

"But *I* can't hear *you* over that." Blessing waited until the honks and buzzes quieted, then repeated his question and waited for Holte's answer. "That's better. Now, what was it you wanted to tell me that couldn't wait until morning?"

This abrupt question did not bother Holte. "Miss Thornton's family socialized with GAD's when they were children. Poppy is roughly six years older than GAD, and I understand he had a crush on her when he was a boy—may still do, for all I know. You should mention that she's a reporter with the *Philadelphia Clarion* now, when you speak to GAD, and is in a position to plead his case publicly, if that's what GAD wants. He might find a reference to her more reassuring than the knowledge that his parents are looking for him, which I would guess he knows." He gave Blessing a little time to take this in, and then continued. "You might also want to mention GAD's sister, Genevieve. She's more like him than most of his family, and seems more sympathetic to his actions than some of the others."

"I'll bear that in mind," said Blessing, and yawned. "Is there anything else that you feel can't wait, or may I—"

Holte rushed ahead with the last of his news. "The Pearses are going to be talking to Arnold Schultz; he recently retired from the American Department of State—and incidentally, is a friend of Poppy's Aunt Esther. I've heard that he's fluent in German; I don't know about Czech, but apparently, he has had experience in this part of Europe, and will be set to twisting some arms come Monday morning. If he is as capable as most think he is, there may be ripples as far as Brno."

"That could be inconvenient, if there is more going on than I've learned thus far; local police don't like being interfered with," said Blessing. "I'll bear that in mind, too." He moved his pillow so that he could raise his head. "Is there anything else?"

"I have a few questions for you, if it's all right," Holte told him, his manner pragmatic. "Your answers may make it possible for me to go ahead and...um... shorten the length of time you will need to gain access to GAD."

"And how do you plan to do that? You're noncorporeal, or have you forgot that?" Blessing yawned suddenly. "Pardon."

"No, I haven't," Holte said amiably. "I plan to use it to my advantage. If I can discover where GAD is being held, I can provide you that information, so that if officials try to give you the run-around, you can cut them short; they may try to claim that they don't know where he has been detained, and therefore require you to wait a day or two before speaking to him. You can tell them a colleague found out where GAD is, which, technically, is true."

"That would be useful, I'll admit," said Blessing, yawning once again. "What do you need to know?"

"First, do you know if GAD is still with the Living Spectres, the group around Ahram Avaikian, the Armenian Orthodox priest? In his last letter home, he said that he was." It was moments like this when Holte missed the ability to take notes; he concentrated on Blessing's answer in the hope of remembering it accurately.

"That's difficult to say. I understand that some of the group has remained near Vienna—a few of them have work, and would rather stay where they can make a living than give up the little security they have. The rest, according to those left behind, are hoping to find work in the forests around Brno, logging and clearing brush, that sort of thing. Avaikian has said that he is certain they will be welcome there." Blessing yawned again. "My translator wasn't so sure about it. He thinks that Armenians will have difficulties in most places."

"How do you rate your translator's understanding of the Armenians' situation?" Holte moved a little nearer the head of the bunk.

"He did his job well, and has had a fair amount of dealings with the Living Spectres; I gather he knows whereof he speaks; his German was quite good, his English a little less so. Assuming GAD is in Brno, that would suggest he's connected to the group or has accompanied them this far, which provides a place to start. We must aspire to being worthy of the help of those in local government."

Holte knew from his living experience that when Blessing's speech got flowery, it meant that he was becoming nettled, so he asked only one more thing. "Is there any reason to suppose that GAD has left them?"

"Not that I know of," said Blessing, and pummeled his pillow back under his head. "If you don't mind? I'll have to be awake in a few hours, and at my age, I need to rest before I undertake to address local officials."

"Sleep well. I'll see you at the station when you arrive," said Holte, and slid out of the train to leave it behind him as he sped north, arriving in Brno a short while later; he circled the old part of the small city, trying to get the layout of the main buildings.

The Town Hall was fairly obvious, facing the largest church across a broad market-square, with formidable stone buildings flanking it. Four wide streets converged there; there was also a lattice-work of narrow alleys surrounding the old buildings. Surely, Holte thought, the jail must be somewhere in the vicinity, and he set himself to searching. By the time the clock in the steeple struck four, Holte had narrowed the possibility down to two buildings, one behind the Town Hall, isolated in a diamond-shaped tower of five storeys with narrow windows and a studded steel door, the other in what was probably the police barracks, between the church and what appeared to be the law courts. The second building being nearer, Holte went around the barracks and gained entrance through a heavily barred window; he found himself in a vaulted cellar lined with iron doors, three centuries more recent than the building itself; the air was still and dank. Four ceiling light fixtures spaced about fifteen feet apart provided scant illumination to the place; at the far end of the avenue of doors there was another door made of iron bars, beyond which a man in some kind of uniform dozed, a large ring of keys in his hand. Pleased at his discovery, Holte began a systematic search, flitting along the ceiling from cell to cell, taking stock of the occupants, and moving on. As he went, the light fixtures in the corridor ceiling flickered. Holte paid little attention, trying to make the most of his time so that he could finish his inspection of the cells and still be able to meet Blessing when his train got in.

The third time the lights failed, then brightened, the guard work up, crossed himself, and shouted something in Czech that Holte assumed was "Who goes there?" or some similar challenge as he grabbed the pistol in the holster on his belt; Holte did not bother to answer, but he dropped down almost to the floor in order to keep the lights burning steadily; he continued his search, seeping into cells through the doors. He took care to observe without disturbing, wanting only to be able to explain to Blessing what he had observed.

Of the eighteen cell doors in this room, Holte soon discovered that two cells on the east side of the corridor were empty, the others on that side occupied by three or four men each, all of them in working-man's clothing, one of them with blood spatters on his hands and face; on the west side of the corridor only one cell lacked an occupant. The cell next to the vacant one held a single man, dressed for hiking in Jodhpur trousers and a canvas safari jacket over a hand-knit fisherman's sweater; far from the dress of the Living Spectres. He lay on a thin, hard mattress in the lower bunk. Holte came to inspect this figure more closely: the man was young, with a short, fair beard, and curly hair that was below collar-length; there were a few fading bruises on his face and, on his left hand, scraped knuckles. Holte had seen the photograph of GAD Pearse that his parents had provided to the *Clarion*, and so recognized him at once. GAD was thinner now than he was in the photograph, Holte thought, and in need of a bath and some grooming, his skin tanned from a summer out of doors; as GAD turned on his bed, Holte could see that there were calluses on the palm of GAD's left hand, Holte could not make out GAD's right. He passed through the door, noting its number—16—and headed for the train station a few minutes after the clock in the steeple struck four-forty-five.

The train arrived half an hour late; the station-master announced its coming to a waiting room with only nine living occupants, most of whom were sleepy, but summoned the energy to gather their belongings and move out onto the platform beyond, into the tinted glare of sodium lamps that lined it, where they made an irregular line near its edge; most of them turned to the south, anticipating the train.

Holte drifted onto the platform behind them, watching the sky for signs of dawn. He found a place near the pass-through for arriving passengers, and settled in as the train came into sight, its headlight brighter than the moon.

Blessing was the fourth man into the pass-through, his overcoat unbuttoned over his rumpled traveling suit and navy-blue roll-neck pull-over, his hat set forward on his head, putting his face in shadow. He carried his duffle in his left hand as he trudged forward.

Holte fell in beside him. "How was the journey? Did you get any sleep?"

"No, I didn't sleep, and not for want of trying. The track immediately south of here is a menace." Blessing did not seem surprised to have Holte with him again. "Are there any taxis available at this hour, or do I have to walk to find a hotel?"

"I'm sorry; I didn't notice," Holte said as they emerged from the pass-through to the front of the station.

"Did you have a look around the town?" Blessing asked Holte while he cast about for a taxi.

"I did. There's a nice hotel about four long blocks from here and not quite two blocks from where they're holding GAD Pearse," said Holte. "The hotel is the Vaclav IV, after one of the medieval kings. You can be there in ten minutes."

"How far is it from here?" Blessing asked, almost whispering.

"Less than a quarter mile. I can guide you, if you like."

"I guess you'd better. I don't imagine I'll be able to find a taxi until sunrise." He set his jaw. "Lead on, Holte. Not too quickly; I have no reason to rush, and I'm tired."

"As you wish," said Holte, dropping down to street level and setting off into the warren of ancient streets.

"And what's all this about you finding GAD Pearse?" Blessing demanded, a bit more loudly. "How did you manage that?"

"He's in jail, as you've heard; the report was accurate, and Brno has only one jail. That jail is under what I think is the police barracks; GAD is in cell sixteen.

He appears to be in fairly good shape, given the circumstances. It looks as if he has been in a fight, or mistreated I don't know by whom. That's all I've learned so far. I can't tell you what he's charged with, but at least we have located him, and that should make your work here easier." Holte faded as he passed through an old wagon at the side of the street. "I don't know if he's wholly by himself, or if some of the other prisoners are part of Avaikian's Living Spectres; there are other men in other cells, but who they are, I can't tell you. I don't know if the Living Spectres wear special garments, or ordinary laborers' clothing."

"How did he look to you?" Blessing asked. "I mean GAD. You said *fairly good shape*, but what does that mean?"

"Worn. He's lost weight from what I saw in his photograph," Holte said, taking up his place three steps ahead of Blessing. "I saw a few signs of mistreatment, but he was fully clothed and under a blanket—"

"Any other signs of misuse? Bruises or cuts?" Blessing was beginning to pant. "Will you slow down a little?"

"Glad to," said Holte, doing so. "A few bruises, but no serious cuts, or other indications of manhandling that I could see, but he was fully dressed, and short of sliding through the blanket and his clothes, there was nothing else that I noticed."

"I'll have to ask him when I talk with him." Blessing's breathing steadied at the slower pace. "Where is this hotel you mentioned?"

"Fewer than three more blocks. Not far at all," said Holte. "How do you plan to get to see him? Do you intend to start with the jail, or with the courts?"

"As a foreigner here, I should start with the courts," said Blessing. "Stop. My shoelace is undone." Without waiting to see where Holte was, Blessing knelt down and retied his shoelace, then stood up. "Much better. These old cobbled streets demand a lot of shoes, don't they? And old joints, for that matter."

"I suppose so," said Holte, reminding himself that Blessing was aging and was very much corporeal. "Veer right at the next intersection."

"I will," said Blessing, picking up his satchel and moving on.

The Vaclav IV was about two hundred years old, a handsome structure of the early eighteenth century with a mansard roof atop four storeys, a porticoed entrance and a large double door that, at this hour, was locked.

"There's a bell," Holte pointed out to Blessing.

"Good thing, too," said Blessing, tugging on the pull; there was a faint clanging from deep within the hotel.

A few minutes later, the night watchman came to open the door. "What do you want?" he asked first in Czech and then in German.

"I'd like a room," said Blessing in the local language. "I just arrived here."

The night watchman gave him a thorough once-over, then nodded. "Come in," he said in German. "I can accommodate you."

"Thank you," said Blessing. "And may I arrange to be called at eight-thirty? I have a commitment at ten. "

"Certainly," said the night watchman as he stepped behind the reception counter. "How long do you intend to stay?"

The light over the register that the night watchman had opened now blinked twice; the night watchman swore.

"I don't know—possibly a day or two, but perhaps as long as a week," said Blessing, and reached into his coat for his small, buckled portfolio, where he had his passport and other papers. "Here. N. N. N. Blessing, of London, England," he said, handing it over along with his card.

"Very good, Herr Blessing," said the night watchman, as he examined the passport carefully, and put the business card into his breast pocket. "What is your business in Brno? I need you to be specific."

"I am here on legal matters; I am to locate a family member for my clients," Blessing said, watching while the night watchman wrote this into the register. "I don't know how long that's going to take, so I don't know how long I'll be here."

"If you will sign and fill in your address?" the night watchman asked, indicating the lines in the register that Blessing was to use.

Blessing wrote in the spaces the night watchman had indicated. "I will need a bath in the morning. May I arrange for that with you?"

"I'll put it in the book. At what hour would you require it?"

"Eight forty-five."

"Very good," said the night watchman. "I've put you on the floor above. The bath room is at the far end of the hall; the toilet room is next to it, on the right."

"Thank you," said Blessing, taking up his satchel and reclaiming his portfolio and passport. "Do you expect a deposit?"

"For the bath, yes. You may pay in marks, if you like."

"How much?"

"Two hundred; the inflation in Germany has had a great influence on us, I'm afraid." The night watchman lifted one hand to show there was nothing he could do about it. "I hope that it is no inconvenience. I can hold off taking the full amount if you have a partial payment and will visit the bank in the morning."

"That won't be necessary," said Blessing. "I anticipated the need for cash, and took out a goodly share of it before I left London." He included a half-crown as he handed over the amount requested in English money.

The night watchman almost smiled. "Thank you, Herr Blessing."

"It would be surprising if the inflations didn't impact the Czech economy; it certainly had an impact on England, in trade," said Blessing without complaint. He found his billfold and took out the money. "Will you have a receipt for me for the amount?"

"When you wake up, Herr Blessing." The night watchman made notes on a pad of paper next to the register. "Will you want breakfast in your room or would you prefer it in the dining room?"

"In my room. I have work to prepare and I need to do it in private." Blessing paused. "Eggs and sausages, with black coffee, if you can manage that?"

"Indeed we can. What time would you like those brought up?" He blotted the fresh ink in the registry and put the fountain pen aside.

"At eight-thirty; when I want to be wakened," said Blessing.

The night watchman turned to the pigeon-holes behind him. "Room 103; at the top of the stairs"—he pointed them out—"the first room on your left." He handed over the key. "Please return it to the desk clerk when you go out, Herr Blessing. I would wish you a good night's sleep, but you haven't enough time for that. I trust you'll be able to rest a little," he said with a chuckle at his own wit.

"Unfortunately, that might not be possible, but thank you," Blessing said as he shouldered his duffel and made for the stairs.

The room was of a good size—Blessing estimated fifteen by twelve feet containing a high sleigh bed made up with a satin comforter and six pillows, a chest of drawers with a mirror and a ewer of water atop it, an armoire, a small table with two chairs, and three lamps, one of which—the one at the bedside—was on. There was a thick carpet on the floor, covered with woven designs of wild flowers, and the walls were painted a light shade of blue-green. Three windows faced east and looked out on the side-street. Blessing put his satchel on the end of the bed, opened it, and took out a thick file, then a pair of pyjamas, a bathrobe, and a shirt and waistcoat; he hung up the robe, shirt, and waistcoat, then slowly got undressed, hung up his suit, dropped his roll-top pull-over into the duffle, and got into his bed clothes.

"Do you think you can get to sleep now?" Holte asked from a place near the top of the armoire.

"If I draw the draperies, I'm certain I can." Having said this, he went to the window and pulled the dark-green velveteen draperies across the windows. "There."

"I'll return a little after eight, shall I?" Holte asked

"Where are you going?" Blessing asked, and reached to pull the metal string to turn out the light.

"I'm going back to GAD's cell. I want to see how he's doing." Holte began to sink through the floor.

"I'll see you in a couple hours." As if to emphasize this, the nearest church steeple's clock struck five forty-five, and Holte was away into the night, moving with ghostly swiftness through the dark streets. He hastened to the police barracks and slid into basement cell 16; GAD was still lying on the bunk, sleeping fitfully, the single blanket he had been provided pulled up to his head. Holte took his place in the upper bunk, and waited. An hour later, a clang announced the beginning of the prisoner's day; Holte dropped down to the floor as the ceiling light in GAD's cell went on, and GAD mumbled and yawned, stretched tentatively, then slowly sat up; Holte watched him, and concluded that, young though he was, GAD's muscles were stiff from the night on the thin, hard mattress. He observed GAD get to his feet, run his fingers through his hair and over his beard, then stretching once again, yawning a third time, and coughing once. Reluctantly GAD began to fold his blanket, and then swung it onto the foot of the bunk.

There was a rattle of keys, a door at the other end of the corridor slammed open, and a voice shouted an order; aware that it would be a while before his door was opened, GAD sat back down on the lower bunk, and stared at the chamber pot in the corner, but did nothing but listen to the opening and closing of doors along the corridor.

A quarter of an hour later, GAD's cell door was flung open, and a square-built man with an equally square jaw shiny from shaving, wearing a uniform that Holte did not recognize, ordered GAD out; he obeyed, and Holte followed the two of them along to the latrine, where GAD stepped into a doorless stall before going to the sink to wash his hands and face. There were signs that other men had been there a few minutes ago, but now there was only GAD and the man in the uniform, who took GAD back to his cell and locked him in. Holte watched GAD a short while, then returned to Blessing after he had made a rapid tour of the Town Hall and the courts building. He would recommend that Blessing go to the Town Hall before visiting the courts building.

Pinkish, watery sunlight was shining, the sun a bright glare in thin clouds east of the city when Holte once again passed through the window and draperies into Blessing's room; the clock on the table said eight forty-one. There were sounds of activity from the kitchen and four of the rooms, a sign that the day had begun and the staff was preparing to deal with the hotels' guests. Holte drifted up to the ceiling and let his thoughts wander until there was a sharp knock on the door and Blessing came rapidly awake.

"Herr Blessing?" a voice asked from the hallway. "I have your breakfast. If you will open the door?" His German was stilted but understandable.

"Bitte," said Blessing as he went to the armoire and took out his bathrobe, pulling it on over his pyjamas before going to answer the door, where a young waiter stood with a tray in his hands.

"Your breakfast," the waiter informed him unnecessarily.

"Ja. Put it on the table, if you will."

The waiter obeyed. "Your bath will be ready in fifteen minutes," he informed Blessing, pocketed the tip Blessing handed him, and left the room.

Holte floated down to the end of the table, looking like an attenuated bit of filmy cloth. "GAD is awake. It appears that they're isolating him: he's by himself in his cell, and he did not wash with the other men. There was a guard on him the whole time."

Blessing had taken a look at the heap of scrambled eggs and the four patties of sausage. "Sit down Holte. You make me nervous." He inspected the crockery coffee pot, lifted the lid, and frowned. "Looks like silt."

"Did you get any rest?" Holte asked as he settled himself into the chair opposite Blessing, not quite on the seat.

"A bit. I'll have to retire early tonight. I don't think there's going to be time for a nap today, and I'll need to be tip-top to handle this case." He picked up a fork and tasted the eggs. "Fresh. That's something. Any idea why they're keeping GAD away from the others?"

"No. It could be nothing more than he doesn't speak Czech, but that's just a guess. If I were you, I'd suspend judgment until you can ask him yourself." Holte leaned forward, penetrating the table at sternum height. "What will you tell him when you see him?"

"I haven't made up my mind; I'm going to wait until I know what he volunteers to tell me." Blessing cut into the largest sausage patty with the edge of his fork. "Thick," he said.

"But cooked through?" Holte said.

"Almost too much." Blessing nodded. "No danger of trichinosis here."

"That's reassuring," Holte agreed, and shifted the topic of conversation. "May I make a suggestion for a way to approach GAD?"

"Is this more about mentioning his sister—Genevieve, wasn't it?" Blessing had a little more of the eggs.

"Yes, and Poppy Thornton. I know I've said this before, but these two names will inspire more confidence with GAD than a mention of either of his parents—his father in particular."

"We've agreed about that, last night in the train," said Blessing.

"I'm pleased you remembered; you were quite sleepy," said Holte.

"I recall that you did tell me Mister Pearse is difficult, and I read his letter that came with his shipment of documents; he has some very stringent demands that he calls instructions, most of which have no application here in Brno; I hope he decides to stay in America. Having him here would be a disadvantage," said Blessing, striving for neutrality in his expression. "I'll decide about which of his orders to obey after I see the young man."

"Do you want me to come with you?" Holte asked.

"No; check back with me this evening, and I'll let you know how things went. You can advise me on what to tell Mister Pearse in my telegram. I need to be careful when I prepare it, since I suspect that no matter what I find out, Mister

Pearse will not be pleased." This last was muffled by another wedge of sausage.

"Probably not," Holte agreed.

Blessing swallowed and had a sip of coffee before he spoke again. "Just as well that we got here on Sunday night; I'll have the opportunity to catch the officials—whichever ones I may have to deal with—before they're soured by the demands of the week."

"That's if there aren't matters left over from the past week," Holte said.

Blessing shook his head. "I'm going to remain optimistic."

"Then if you don't mind, I'll absent myself for most of the day; you don't need me to help you fill out forms. There are things I can do while you deal with the officials, things that might help you speed matters along." Holte started to rise at an angle, bound for the ceiling and the outside. "I hope that all goes well for you today."

"So do I. I'm planning to buy the local paper, to find out what I can about the incident that put GAD in jail." Blessing drank more coffee.

"That's right. You know Czech. I forgot that for a moment. Apologies," Holte said, feeling chagrined that something so important had escaped him.

"No need to apologize. I'll use German for the most part while I'm here. I'll see you later," said Blessing as he poured himself a second cup of thick, dark coffee.

"Good luck," Holte said as he glided up and out of the room and into the glare of the morning.

THIRTY-SEVEN

Tuesday morning got off to an early start: Poppy had hardly emerged from the tub and pulled her bathrobe on when Miss Roth called her downstairs to the phone; she picked her damp towel off the bathroom floor, and called out to Miss Roth, "I'll be down in two shakes of a lamb's tail." She had caught her Aunt Esther's expression. "Ask whoever it is to wait, if you would." It was not quite seven a.m.

"It's Inspector Loring," Miss Roth informed her, adding knowingly, "He'll wait."

Spurred on by knowing who was calling, Poppy abandoned her usual morning routine and made her way downstairs to the phone. She took the receiver from Miss Roth with a nod of thanks and said, "Good morning, Inspector. What is ?"

There was a minuscule hesitation, then Loring began his rapid report. "I had a telegram a little after three this morning—a long one—from Blessing; the delivery boy got me out of bed."

"What's the time difference with Czechoslovakia and here?" Poppy asked, not willing to try to work it out in her head; she could hear edginess in Loring's voice, so let him talk.

"Four or five hours; probably five," said Loring, who was not quite sure himself. "I apologize for calling so early, but I wanted you to know what Blessing told me," he explained, going on almost at once, "He's located GAD and had a couple of conversations with him. GAD really is in jail—according to GAD, for disturbing the peace—though the formal complaint is for inciting a riot. Blessing said he thinks the disturbing the peace charge is just as excuse for keeping GAD in jail until they can come up with more serious charges; he is waiting to find out what those might be before recommending any specific action to the Pearses. The alleged disturbing the peace resulted when GAD supposedly interrupted a meeting at the Town Hall last Wednesday, speaking on behalf of Father Avaikian's Living Spectres, who were staging a protest—by all accounts a peaceful one—about the harassment they had experienced at the hands of some young men from the city, last Thursday night. GAD's German must be fairly good, since he doesn't know Czech, and he said enough to rile the magistrates about the Living Spectres, or so the paper says." Loring took a deep breath. "Part of GAD's plea was in the paper. Blessing was impressed, and said that GAD was quite articulate, if the account of the meeting is to be trusted."

"GAD took four years of it, as I recall, and four of French, at the Alexandrian Academy," said Poppy, coming fully awake speedily. "He's got an ear for languages."

"The Alexandrian Academy? Where your brother is headmaster?" Loring asked.

"The very same. It's a good school academically, in spite of Toby. What's the rest of your news?" She tried to prepare herself for whatever Loring might have to say.

"Okay," said Loring, and obligingly resumed his narrative. "Anyway, GAD caused quite a stir and he was arrested and flung in jail, where he remains. There is pressure from some of the leading citizens of the city to have the Living Spectres go elsewhere, according to the report. There is some mention of a ruction outside the hearing in which a few of the demonstrators were accused of throwing rocks and such, but there is no actual proof of it. Blessing spent all of the morning and half the afternoon with GAD yesterday, trying to learn the whole story of GAD's incarceration. Along with many other things, he told Blessing that he was ashamed to contact his family, knowing how much his parents disapproved of his European trip in the first place. He was hoping to handle the problem on his own."

"Ye gods! How was he planning to do that from a jail cell?"

"I don't know. Blessing didn't say," Loring admitted.

"You must have had a very long telegram," Poppy remarked.

"That's what I told you; it cost Blessing a small fortune to send; it's a good thing Mister Pearse is paying all Blessing's expenses." Loring cleared his throat. "Blessing will be working with the law courts for the next few days to try to get GAD out of jail, which looks likely, providing GAD agrees to leave Czechoslovakia and return to the US. If GAD digs in his heels and refuses to go, then more serious charges are likely to be forthcoming, some of which could keep him in jail for several years."

"And the Living Spectres?" Poppy asked. "What about them?"

"I don't know. Blessing didn't mention them except to say that they are in the area. Blessing hasn't been able to contact them." Loring hesitated, then rushed ahead. "I wanted you to know this in case you hear from Mister Pearse. I don't want you to be unprepared; he's apt to be...excitable when he gets Blessing's telegram."

"You mean that Blessing wired you first?" Poppy said, perplexed.

"Yes. He's been sending his information to me in advance of his report to Pearse. He says that he doesn't trust Pearse not to do something foolish, and so wants me to be forewarned of that possibility, and do my best to dissuade him."

An idea struck Poppy. "What if GAD insists on staying? What kind of serious charges are we talking about?"

"There's already the inciting to riot, and likely worse to come, but is it likely that GAD would not agree to leave the country?" Loring asked, surprised.

"I think it's possible," she admitted.

"Sweet Je—" he began, then stopped himself. "Sorry. He wouldn't be that... quixotic, would he?"

"He might," said Poppy.

"If GAD does that, I hope Blessing will send another telegram to me at once. That never crossed my mind, not realistically, and now it's going to haunt me until I have word from Blessing, or Mister Pearse." Loring swore under his breath. "What a mess."

"That it is," said Poppy. "But it's only conjecture."

"For now. I should phone Pearse in a little while, before he calls me. I want to ease him through the news if I can; he tends to go off half-cocked and he doesn't brook correction. I have to tell you, I pity the people who work for him. It's hard enough to be doing my part of the job. If I had to answer to him, and only to him..."

"No wonder you phoned me in advance of speaking with Pearse. Thanks," said Poppy, wondering why she had heard nothing more from Holte; "had he played a role in any of this?" she asked herself, but could provide no answer. Surely, she thought, Holte would know what GAD had decided to do.

"If he should phone you, will you let me know? I mean Pearse," Loring said.

"You're more likely to hear from him before I do; you have the public ear, according to Mister Pearse, which he does not approve of. He believes—or he used to believe—the police should not talk about their cases with the press until the whole matter is tried in the courts, and even then, he would like to keep the police and the press apart; he's not fond of the press," Poppy said, beginning to feel chilly as the dampness from her body soaked into her bathrobe, or that was what she told herself it was. "Unless he's changed on that point, he'll want to instruct you, much the way he appears to be dealing with Blessing, and me."

"I'm not sure that Mister Pearse is giving Blessing hard orders, but I hope it's not the case. Blessing works best when allowed leeway in his dealings," said Loring. "Blessing knows what's going on far better than the Pearses—or I—do, and it's wise to give him free rein on this."

"If you can, find out if the Czechs follow through with more serious charges, and what those charges might be." Poppy continued to feel cold growing within her. What on earth had GAD got himself into?

"Of course. And good luck when you talk to Mister Pearse. He's going to be in a bad mood." Loring sighed.

"Tell you what: I'll phone you if I hear from him if you'll phone me if you do," she said, and noticed that Miss Roth was gesturing in her direction. "Hang on a minute, Loring, would you?"

"Okay," he said.

"Missus Sassoro would like to know when you want your breakfast," Miss Roth whispered.

"In twenty minutes or so. Is Aunt Esther up yet?" Belatedly she put her hand over the receiver.

"No, not yet." Miss Roth glanced at the clock.

"Then make it half an hour. I don't need to be at the paper until eight-thirty this morning." That settled, she spoke again to Loring. "Sorry. There are a few household things...You know what it's like."

"That I do," said Loring. "If you hear anything else about GAD today, from anyone, will you let me know? Please? I won't even ask what your source is, if it's the reliable one you won't reveal to me," he hinted broadly.

"If you like; the same applies to you," Poppy said, trying not to sound too accommodating. "If I don't get an assignment that takes me away from the office, I will be waiting for your call at my desk. Otherwise, I'll call you this evening, or you may phone me, say after dinner, when we've both had time to unwind?"

"I will. Thanks. Talk to you later," Loring said, and before Poppy could make her farewells, he hung up.

While Poppy went back up the stairs, she pondered what Loring had told her. How unlike GAD it had seemed, to hear that he had caused a ruckus at an official meeting; that was so different to the boy she remembered, who was content to pass hours by himself, spent his holidays alone in the forest, and could not bear the sight of an injured animal. She could not decide if Sherman Pearse would be pleased or disappointed to hear of it. But what had Blessing told Pearse in his telegram? Had it been as extensive as the one Blessing sent to Loring? She went into her room and closed the door, preparing to dress, but found it hard to concentrate on choosing clothes. After dithering for ten minutes—and mentally upbraiding herself for her lack of concentration—she selected an iris-colored long jacket and a slightly paler bell-shaped skirt with a trumpet hem. For a blouse, she took out one that was yellow-ochre with a double-shawl collar. She reminded herself to take her new raincoat, just in case, for there were scattered clouds in the sky. Her selections made, she began what now felt was the tedium of dressing, then putting on her very modest make-up-mascara, a little face powder, and a little lip rouge. If I were only five years younger, she thought, I might be a flapper; considering the possibilities, she realized that it was unlikely that she would break so much with tradition, or would enjoy the frenetic energy being a flapper seemed to require. Having settled that to her satisfaction, she turned her attention to the final stages of her dressing; the last thing she selected was a pair of shoes, and after careful consideration, she took out the pair of tan pumps with the princess heels; they were low enough for work, but stylish.

From his place on the bed, Maestro regarded her with a jaundiced eye, then set to vigorous grooming of his fur.

Going downstairs, Poppy discovered Missus Sassoro busy in the kitchen, although Miss Roth was nowhere in sight. "Oh, good morning, Miss Poppy," she said as she caught sight of her in the doorway. "Miss Roth has gone out to the morning market for me. I'm out of spinach for dinner, and I was hoping for a few new potatoes for the soup. It's important to get to the market early. All the best vegetables are gone in the first hour." Behind her, the stove had three different vessels on it, each belching its own kind of steam.

Poppy nodded to her. "Good morning Missus Sassoro. What am I going to have this morning?"

"Your usual coddled eggs, with a pat of butter, and Miss Roth is planning to bring back some fresh-baked muffins from Fletcher's Bakery. I expect her to return in the next ten minutes, if that's no problem for you." She stopped and sighed, then turned to Poppy, a look of chagrin on her countenance. "Pardon me. I'm worried for my husband. He has a growth on his back that is going to be removed on Friday, and his doctors have told me that it may mean he will not be able to continue in his work. Your aunt pays me well, but not enough to make up for the loss of his salary, if it comes to that."

"I'm very sorry to hear that Missus Sassoro," said Poppy with complete sincerity. "I hope that won't be necessary."

"We all are Miss Poppy. I feel ashamed that I should worry about money when his life may be at stake, but I can't help it. I have my children to think of, as well as my husband, who is a proud man, and would not like having his wife support him. Two of my sons have offered to leave school and get jobs, so their father need not continue to worry, but for now, I will not permit that. They need their education, even my two girls do, though their need is not so urgent, no matter what your aunt says. It will be some time before any of them are wholly on their own." There were tears in her eyes; she dashed them away with the back of her hand. "My apologies. I shouldn't have mentioned it."

"Ye gods, of course you should," said Poppy at once. "I'm astonished that you aren't hanging from the light fixtures, gibbering. I know I'd probably be." This was less than the truth, but it did describe how she had felt for the eighteen months it took her mother to die.

"You're most kind to say that," Missus Sassoro said as she used the edge of the dishtowel as a handkerchief.

"Have you told my aunt about any of this?" Poppy asked.

"Not really; it's not her concern," said Missus Sassoro. "Not with her leaving again so soon. I shouldn't have told you, but it's so much on my mind." Then she changed the subject. "I'm about to put the coddler into the boiling water, Miss Poppy." She nodded toward the saucepan on the right-front burner. "If you'll go in and sit down, I'll have your coffee and coddled eggs out in less than five minutes. You'll want tomato juice, as well, won't you? Or would you prefer something else? I have apple juice."

"Yes, please; tomato," said Poppy, stepping through the open pocket doors into the breakfast nook; she sat down and turned her attention to what Missus Sassoro had told her, and tried to decide how much to pass on to Aunt Esther about GAD; not that she was worried that Esther might gossip, but with so much misinformation about GAD already being passed around, Poppy did not want to add to it. She found herself wishing that Holte were with her, to advise her, and to add his take on what she had heard. She sat down at what had become her usual place at the table, one of two laid for breakfast.

As if he had read her thoughts, Holte came in through the south-facing window, and wafted up to her. "This is going to be a hurried visit; I want to get back to Brno to hear what the magistrates decide." He leaned forward. "I have a message for you Poppy."

Poppy blinked at him. "Where have you been?" she asked, keeping her voice low so as not to draw Missus Sassoro's attention.

"Following the court's hearing of GAD's case; it's been quite a carnival, in its Slavic way," Holte said, coming down to stand more or less at floor level.

"In Brno?" Poppy wanted to be certain she understood him. "The court there is taking on GAD's case in Brno? No change of venue?"

"Certainly, in Brno. The magistrates are listening to the Living Spectres just now, and will be doing so for a couple of hours more, so I thought I'd come and tell you what GAD has agreed to do, since he refuses to write to his family about any of this, or ask for their help directly."

Poppy's misgiving increased. "What would that be?"

"Blessing tells me GAD's going to send you an open letter, with permission for you to print it in your paper, so everyone will know what he has done, and why; he wants to explain the reasons he has taken on the cause of the Living Spectres when so many have forgotten their suffering. He trusts to your discretion, or so he told Blessing. It took Blessing most of the morning to convince GAD that the charges that were being assembled against him would keep him in a cell for a decade at least."

"What sort of charges are we talking about?" Poppy asked, trying to resist the dread that was increasing within her.

Holte would have taken a deep breath if he had had lungs. "GAD's said he's not going to leave the Living Spectres until they are properly settled somewhere they can be safe, but he is promising not to cause any more public disruption in Brno. That's contingent upon the more serious charges against him being dismissed. He is willing to agree to stay out of the city with the Living Spectres, and to leave Czechoslovakia as soon as they are settled elsewhere. He will be allowed to undertake to help the Living Spectres get fair treatment when they have found a place where they can live—to assist them in their negotiations with whatever authorities are involved—assuming that those negotiations can be done in German, but not in Brno. He's exiled from the city, and that's not negotiable, little as GAD likes it. That's the substance of what Blessing will be telling Mister Pearse; he'll send you a telegram tonight or tomorrow."

"How is GAD, do you know that?" Poppy asked, feeling a bit breathless.

"Somber. When he was informed that the magistrates were prepared to level a charge of attempted murder against him, GAD was deeply shocked," Holte said.

"Attempted murder?" Poppy shrieked softly. "How did they manage to come up with that?"

Holte shook his head. "When the Living Spectres were marching on the magistrates' building a few rocks were thrown, and GAD is the one accused of throwing them; the Living Spectres are known to have taken vows against committing violence, and since Americans are reputed to be rowdy, the suspicions about rocks devolve to GAD; they do not accept the account that the same group of young men who raided the Living Spectres' camp had anything to do with the stones being thrown, although GAD insists that it was they who did. The magistrates are not persuaded; they say that it was a reckless thing to do, and might well have injured or killed people in the street."

"That's ridiculous," said Poppy.

"Maybe," said Holte, "but that's what's being held over his head. And the Czechs mean it: they'll lock GAD up for as long as they can, as an example to obstreperous foreigners." Holte moved a little closer to Poppy, his faint countenance taking on a little more definition. "Those courts aren't like American courts; they'll do it and think no more about it."

"Sherman Pearse will be enraged," said Poppy, just in time to startle Missus Sassoro bringing in her coddled eggs and a small pot of coffee.

"Miss Poppy?" Missus Sassoro said uncertainly.

"I'm sorry—thinking aloud." She smiled as best she could and moved her woven place- mat to provide easier access for the coddler.

"My Teobaldo does that. Says it helps him decide how to do things." She poured coffee into Poppy's mug.

"Your husband?" Poppy guessed.

Missus Sassoro laughed. "No. My oldest. He'll be fourteen in February, and doing well in school, God be thanked. I am determined that he will go to high school, and to a teachers college."

"What does Teobaldo think of that?" Poppy asked, her curiosity stirring.

"He is willing," said Missus Sassoro in a steely way. She indicated the creamer and the sugar bowl on the table. "Filled this morning as soon as I got here."

"And they're most welcome," said Poppy. "Is Aunt Esther up yet?"

"I believe so. And Miss Roth is parking now; your muffins will be ready shortly." She almost curtsied and went back into the kitchen.

Holte, who had been watching this exchange from the foot of the table, looked directly at Poppy. "Would it be better if we talked in the Hudson? So you wouldn't have to explain why you're talking to...um...yourself?"

"Yes," she murmured. "I'll be leaving here in fifteen minutes, right after I give Maestro his breakfast. He's being allowed to have all his meals in the kitchen now, starting yesterday."

"I'll keep that in mind, and avoid him; can't have him hissing at empty air when the staff is about," Holte said, and sped out through the window.

Poppy went back to her coddled eggs and was about to add a spoonful of sugar and a bit of cream to her coffee when Aunt Esther appeared in the arched door of the breakfast nook, where she paused as if surprised to see her niece at the table ahead of her.

"Good morning," Poppy said as her aunt pulled out her chair and sat down, a frown darkening her features. "Is anything wrong?"

Esther was in her most formidable suit—the one she saved for public lectures and formal meetings—a charcoal worsted frock-coat with a straight skirt with a deep kick-pleat in the rear; her blouse was mauve silk with matching froths of lace at collar and cuffs. "I hope not," she said at her most foreboding. "I have to appear before the Grants Board today. The Society will decide how much of my travels they are willing to finance, and let me know what they expect me to do for them." She drummed her fingers on the table. "I loathe having to do this every time. They don't do it to the men after the first two or three expeditions; the explorers submit their plans and their budget, the Board reviews them, and decides how much to pay for, no fuss, no questions. I have to appear before them every time. This is the eleventh time in fifteen years. I could just spit!"

"If you do, please use your napkin," said Poppy with a propriety she did not feel.

At that, Esther laughed. "Thank you," she said, and looked over at Miss Roth, who had come to the breakfast nook door. "Nothing to worry about. My niece just made a very clever remark," she informed her housekeeper.

Miss Roth kept her opinion to herself. "Shall I tell Missus Sassoro to start your breakfast now Miss Thornton?"

"Yes, if you would, please. I'll begin with two of those delicious-smelling muffins. With butter and blueberry preserves." She turned back to Poppy. "That was very kind of you. I had got myself into a lather again, and that would not have helped me."

"You're welcome," said Poppy, still a bit baffled.

Esther leaned back in her chair and raised her voice. "Missus Sassoro, may I have coffee now, before my muffins? And after that, I'd like some diced ham with shredded potatoes, if you would? I'm not in a great hurry today."

"Very good Miss Thornton," Missus Sassoro called back.

Esther dropped her napkin into her lap and smoothed the place-mat. "I don't know what comes over me; I always tell myself to keep my resentment in check, but it comes back anyway. You'd think I'd have more self-discipline after all these years."

"Why?" Poppy sipped her coffee. "I haven't got the knack of it yet; frustration is frustration, no matter what."

"Hiram Schippers is the worst—always implying that I'm too old and too female to go *gadding* about in foreign places." Esther snorted. "No matter what my family may believe, I've never gadded in my life. That's not what I'm doing, and never will be. Schippers thinks it is unbecoming of me to want to travel to remote parts of the world, and that it is his duty to stop what he calls my *excesses*. Pompous old fool."

"You certainly haven't gone *gadding*," Poppy said, and went back to her eggs. "You've *traveled*, you've *explored*—no gadding in that."

Missus Sassoro brought in a mug of coffee for Esther and a glass of tomato juice for Poppy, set them down, and went back into the kitchen.

"I hope they'll cover the cost of an aeroplane rental. I'll use my own funds if I have to, but it looks so much better if the money comes from the National Geographic Society than out of my accounts." Esther sighed. "They may balk at the cost of the stateroom on the *Evening Star*, as well. They would like it if I traveled second-class instead of first."

"Don't borrow trouble Aunt Esther," Poppy recommended.

"You're right—I'm tilting at imaginary windmills, or I hope I am. So tell me," Esther said in a brisker tone, "what's on your schedule for today? I need to get my mind off my defense to the Grants Board."

Poppy could not help but smile. "I'm supposed to get a packet from the Department of State today, that's about—"

"—whether the man in Maracaibo is Stacy?" Esther interrupted, and nodded along with Poppy. "I'd almost forgotten that. That should be interesting. Anything else?"

"I'll be talking with Loring later today about developments in GAD's case." She could tell that Aunt Esther wanted more information, so she added, "He gets regular telegrams from Blessing—the investigator?—who apparently has found GAD in a Czechoslovakian jail." She did not want to appear too certain of this because that might lead to questions she would find difficult to answer without complicated explanations.

"GAD? In jail? Whatever for?" Aunt Esther exclaimed.

"That's what I'm hoping to find out; Loring thinks that they may be trumped up charges," said Poppy, not wanting to get into how much she did and did not know about GAD's situation, for fear of adding in some of what Holte had told her. "I'll be talking to Lowenthal about the little I've learned regarding GAD's predicament."

"Jail," Esther mused again. "Sherman will be livid. Isadora will be hysterical." She stared into her coffee as if to find confirmation in its depths. "I hope you don't have to deal with either of them."

"Thank you Aunt Esther. I hope I don't, too," said Poppy.

"And as long as we're discussing unpleasant things, are there any new developments on the Hadley and Grimes investigation? And what happens next if the photograph is of Stacy? Or are there any plans around that?"

"Not that I've heard. If it's slow today, I might give Tinsdale a call, but I don't think he'll have any news he'd be willing to pass on, and I doubt anyone else at Hadley and Grimes will talk to me, so I must contain myself with patience. No use letting my speculations run wild." As she heard herself speak, Poppy became frustrated once more.

"But you may have to prepare yourself for a number of eventualities," said Aunt Esther sagaciously. "Including having to stand up to a barrage of accusations from Sherman Pearse."

Poppy shuddered. "Talk about borrowing trouble. I might as well give it a try and phone them, just to keep my hand in, bearding the lion in his lair before he starts roaring." Then something occurred to her. "I might try to call Rudy Beech again. I'd like to know who's been talking to him. Before he hung up on me, he said something that's been eating at me: I think he's had other inquiries about Louise, and I'd like to know who was asking."

"He's Louise's half-brother, isn't he? The one the family doesn't talk about." Esther tasted her coffee and put the mug down. "Too hot."

"That's the one," said Poppy. "I've been watching the papers to see if there are reports in any of them that originated with Beech." She had another bite of egg.

"What are you hoping to learn from him?" Esther asked.

"I want to know if he has heard anything from Louise, and if so, what it was; it's worth a try." As she said it, she thought it sounded simple enough, but she had an inkling that it would not be so. "Neva told me Rudy and Louise were close as children, and although they became less so, it might still be enough to give her reason to contact him instead of any of her friends here in Philadelphia."

"Is she with Stacy?" Esther mused aloud.

"I don't know. I'd like to find out, along with a number of other things," said Poppy, a bit of grimness in her tone.

"You aren't the only one," said Aunt Esther. "What a tiresome man Stacy has turned out to be. I can almost feel sorry for Jo."

"Why is that?" Poppy asked, and took the last bite of her eggs.

"Well, to have two of her four sons die before she did is painful enough, but to lose both Cosmo and Reginald, and to be left with Stacy..." She shook her head to finish her sentiments. "Hank is a good man, but Stacy is not. If Cosmo had not been killed in the Great War, he might have amounted to something afterward; he had taken an interest in electronics, if I remember correctly. Reginald was a promising anthropologist before the Flu got him, and Jo was proud of him in a vague sort of way, not unlike her feelings toward Hank and his work on yachts and aeroplanes. She'd like it better if he weren't making money at it—that would take the blot of profit off the family escutcheon, but it is getting governmental approval and that appeals to her she can talk about it without sounding immodest." She made another try at her coffee and found it drinkable this time. "Not that she would ever turn against Stacy, but having the law after him is putting her capacity to deny the obvious to a severe test."

"I'm afraid you're right about that," said Poppy.

Missus Sassoro brought in two plates with warmed muffins on them, and the butter-dish. "I'll have your ham and potatoes done in less than ten minutes Miss Thornton."

"Take all the time you need, Missus Sassoro," said Esther, reaching for the butter-knife. "These will keep me busy for a while." As soon as the cook had returned to the kitchen, Esther went on, "I'm sorry for blathering on, but it helps me to compose myself."

"I understand the impulse," said Poppy.

Esther broke one of her muffins in half and buttered both of the halves. "I'm sure you do." She bit into the muffin and smiled around it. "Heaven."

THIRTY-EIGHT

CHESTERTON HOLTE WAS SEARCHING THE DIMENSION OF GHOSTS FOR PERCY Knott when he came upon a new ghost wandering aimlessly through the whorls and currents of noncorporeal presences. *"Derrington?"* he asked, to be sure of his startled recognition.

The ghost stopped. *"You know me?"*

"You're Warren Derrington, aren't you?" Holte did his best to conceal his astonishment. *"How do you come to be here?"*

"Where is here?" Derrington drifted a short nondistance away. *"I thought I was in the hospital, then Stacy came to see me...or maybe I dreamed he did...and now I'm here."* He began to spin, but was able to stop. *"What happened?"*

As much as Holte wanted to ask Derrington if his death had been helped along by Stacy, he knew that Derrington would not yet be able to answer that question. *"Why were you in the hospital?"* Holte asked, choosing an indirect approach.

"There was a hurricane...and the Hadley house lost most of its roof and the east wall as well...the noise was dreadful...I think a beam fell on me, or perhaps it was the wall...I can't remember which...A pair of the servants found me and got me to the hospital. I had some broken bones—my right arm and leg were in casts...I'm fairly certain of that...They said I had a fever, but I don't remember whether I did or not. I can't feel the bones any more." He stopped abruptly.

Holte took a little while to respond. *"That sounds like a rough go."*

"I don't know much Spanish, but I think I was told the priest was coming...and then Stacy showed up—if I wasn't delirious, which I might have been...I know I was part of the time."

"You'll figure it out, in time," Holte assured him. *"What were you doing at the Hadley's vacation house?"*

"Waiting for Overstreet...He was going to join me...I'm afraid I've disappointed him; I should have left a note when...the servants took me to the hospital; I was not thinking clearly then...Santiago de Cuba is closer, you see...Closer than Havana...We were supposed to meet in Santiago de Cuba...once the Hadleys got him out of Canada...That yawl of Nelson's can make very good time when its engine is assisting the sails, especially on a reach."

"You've sailed with Hadley, then?" Holte said, not wanting to inform Derrington that Overstreet was here in the dimension of ghosts, not waiting to contact him in Cuba.

Derrington was more sure of himself about events not associated with his death. *"A few times, mostly when Stacy and I were vacationing...It seems an eternity ago...We once spent almost a week in Cuba while Quentin worked out some arrangements regarding our antique reproductions, so they would pass muster with Customs. Stacy's clever at those sorts of things, and Quentin knew how to make the arrangements almost invisible to inspection. That's coming to an end."* He faltered on this last, then went on, *"We would work in the morning and sail in the afternoon. Nelson was there most of the time, but he wasn't part of our plans. He often slept late, in any case; he spent a lot of nights at the casino. Nelson likes to gamble."*

"Have you come upon either Nelson or Quentin here yet?"

"No; are they here? I didn't know."

"They may have been drowned in the hurricane. Their boat broke up, so it's likely they didn't survive," Holte said, trying to ease the blow.

"That's...unfortunate. It means I needn't have waited so long for Overstreet. Sad." Derrington stopped himself from drifting in a circle.

"Do you remember how long you've been waiting?" Holte asked, hoping to keep Derrington doing the ghostly version of talking.

"Not really. The days run together when you're in a place like the Hadleys' vacation house; one day much like another, and no clocks to keep you at your tasks. In the hospital they had me on morphine, so everything is a bit hazy. Sorry." Derrington became more aware of his surroundings. *"They still are a bit hazy. I don't recognize anyone. I don't know you... or do I?"*

"We haven't met, but we have...acquaintances in common: Madison Moncrief, for example, and Percy Knott."

Derrington winced. *"Pity about Moncrief. I should have handled it better."*

Holte was fascinated by that little addition. *"You should have handled what better?"*

He paused, then urged Derrington on. *"What it are you talking about?"*

"You know," Derrington said miserably. *"The killing."*

"You killed Madison Moncrief?" Holte would have shouted if he had had a voice.

Derrington began to spiral, but did not stop explaining. *"Yes, I did. I didn't like killing him, not even with Louise helping by putting sleeping pills in his brandy. But Stacy was right Moncrief was getting too close; he knew too much, and was putting materials together that would have ruined us if they had been released to the Attorney General. I agreed to make it look like a suicide; I thought the chandelier was a good idea, that it was more plausible that he would hang himself than would take too many sleeping pills. I wanted to make sure they didn't suspect Louise, and the hanging should have thrown them off her scent, but in the end, the police worked out that it wasn't a suicide, but didn't come to think that Louise had anything to do with it. Stacy said I made it too complicated—just shove a hatpin in behind his ear, he said, turn it around a couple of times, and that's all it would take to do the job. The wound might not be noticed at the autopsy, and suicide or a stroke would be the finding."*

Holte was familiar with the need of new ghosts to talk about what they were able to remember as part of the process of understanding what had happened to them; he gave Derrington a little time to contemplate what he had said, then prompted him, *"Moncrief is here, you know, if you would like to apologize?"*

"Apologize? You mean for killing him?" He lapsed into contemplative silence, then said, *"I suppose I should."*

"It might help," Holte was being deliberately vague, not wanting to force comprehension on Derrington, for such imposition often brought about more confusion, rather than providing clarity to the recently ghosted. He had one other question to put to Derrington. *"Did you kill Knott, as well? Because if you did, you should know he's very angry with you for doing it."*

"Oh, no; I had nothing to do with that." Derrington was distressed now, and so he spoke quickly, breathlessly, as if he had breath. *"Stacy did that one, saying I had made such a hash of Moncrief he couldn't trust me to take on Knott. It sounded like Stacy didn't manage much better than I did: there was blood everywhere. You should have seen his overcoat. Stacy had used the mace-and-chain he had brought with him, and somehow got hold of one of Knott's sabers after Knott had wrested the mace-and-chain out of Stacy's grasp; Stacy's first swing had caught Knott in the shoulder, not the head. That's when Knott fought back, and almost got the saber away from Stacy, but by then, Stacy had cut him pretty badly,*

to say nothing of the damage he had done with the mace-and-chain, and Knott was losing strength in a hurry. He told me—Stacy, not Knott—that he had been bruised on his chest, where Knott landed a lucky blow, but that made it possible for Stacy to slice open Knott's thigh, and that was pretty much the end of it. Stacy had to throw away his suit and overcoat; they had so many stains on them. He cut the garments into rags and tossed them into the Delaware, ten miles downstream from Wilmington. I went with him, to make sure no one saw us." He was beginning to pull back from Holte. *"I don't know who you are, and—"*

"I'm Chesterton Holte. I hope you'll talk to me again?"

"—and I want you to leave me alone now. I have to think." Without another word, he slid away into the nearest helix of ghosts, leaving Holte to consider what he had just heard. Stacy had killed Knott, assuming Derrington had told him the truth, and had not diverted his account from his own experience. For a moment he considered searching out Moncrief, or even Knott, but then changed his mind. He had more pressing business in the world of the living; Blessing would be readying his report shortly, and Holte wanted to know how the magistrates had decided GAD's case. With that in mind, he *slipped* back into the world of the living, finding himself not far from the Vaclav IV Hotel, with the last stains of sunset shining in the west like molten lava, and its light burnishing the old stones of the city so that they shone like bronze. Paying little heed to the people still on the street, he hurried toward the Vaclav IV, only to be briefly halted by a torrent of angry barks from a smallish dog on a leash. Rising into the air, Holte put the ferocious animal below him and continued on at about third-storey level. Sliding into Blessing's room through the ceiling, he found the investigator seated at the small table, a pad of paper open before him, and his fountain pen in his hand. "Have you had your supper yet?" Holte asked as he became more visible.

"There you are," Blessing said, sounding more tired than Holte expected him to be. "It's been quite a day, I can tell you that. If you ever need me to take on another case like this one, I may do away with myself."

"Why so difficult? Do the magistrates want to put GAD in jail after all?" Holte did his best to occupy the other chair at the table.

"The magistrates want him, and the Living Spectres, out of Brno. You know about that, and GAD isn't willing to do it unless the Living Spectres are provided a place where they can set up their own village. No, it's GAD's father who is determined to undermine all my efforts. The magistrates are requiring that Mister Pearse guarantee the price of GAD's passage back to the US." He scrubbed his hand through his thinning hair. "Mister Pearse is not inclined to do that. He says it's GAD's fault he's in this situation, and he can get himself out. Mind you, Mister Pearse is also trying to offer bribes to the magistrates if they will release GAD from jail—he says Missus Pearse insists on it."

"Can GAD afford a steamship stateroom?" Holte asked, dreading the answer.

"He hasn't enough for a bunk in steerage; he's spent his funds on the Living Spectres. Without help from his family, he's pretty much stranded," said Blessing, making a gesture of resignation. "I've been trying to find a way to pad my accounts enough to provide GAD a second- class ticket, but I can't help but wonder if Mister Pearse is likely to compare my charges with what I quoted him originally, and I wouldn't want to have to defend my actions to him; he might refuse to pay me for all my services. He seems the sort to do that, doesn't he?"

"I'd have to agree," Holte said. "Is there some way his mother might be able to—" He stopped. "No, I guess not."

"I could get him as far as Southampton Waters, and add that to my outlay, but there's no way I can cover his ticket without taking it in the pocket-book, and that is not a good way to run a business." Blessing rubbed his eyes. "Damned annoying."

"Is funding all that's keeping GAD from going home? I thought he was threatening to remain here with the Living Spectres." Holte looked down at the pad of paper.

"He is," Blessing said with a harsh sigh. "The magistrates are being firm about him leaving. They have agreed to make sure that the Armenians have a place to live, and a chance to work, as GAD was trying to secure; we don't have that in writing yet, but I hope we will soon. The magistrates agree for now that working in the forest would be a good solution for the Living Spectres, and Avaikian is satisfied with that resolution. GAD is more skeptical, and wants to see if they're going to follow through, once GAD is gone. I've recommended that GAD sleep on his options; I'll have another go at him in the morning."

"If the Living Spectres are satisfied with the arrangements for them, why is

GAD being so stiff-rumped about staying?"

"Some of it is his concern for the Living Spectres, but that's only part of it. He's worried about what his father has planned for him; Mister Pearse is insisting that GAD return and begin his university career, keeping—as his father puts it—his nose to the grindstone to make up for all the trouble GAD's put the family through." Blessing shook his head. "And I can't say that I blame him for wanting to stay with the Living Spectres."

"Nor I," said Holte. "What about this letter you mentioned? Is that a done thing?" He saw Blessing raise his eyebrows. "Does GAD really want to send an open letter to Poppy so it can appear in the *Clarion?*"

"Yes; he's been adamant about that. He wants to remain in Europe for another year, and to makes sure the Living Spectres are successfully established, wherever that might be. He plans to write a book about his experiences with them. I'm going to tell Loring about it in my next report. The magistrates in Brno aren't too pleased with GAD's literary ambitions, and I fear that if I mention it to Mister Pearse that he might disown the lad." Blessing stared down at his notes. "I can't decide how to present the court's decision to Mister Pearse. I doubt he's going to like anything I can tell him about the proceeding; he already thinks that I've bungled my mission. Do you have any suggestions in that regard?"

"Not just at present," said Holte, and made up his mind that this was another thing to take up with Poppy when he got back to Philadelphia.

"So tell me," said Blessing with a feigned indifference, "is your current hauntee willing to print such a letter in her paper?"

"It isn't up to her, it's up to her editor, and it will depend on the letter itself, I reckon." Holte cogitated for a few seconds. "If it's full of recriminations and justifications, I'd guess Lowenthal would turn it down—or the paper's attorneys would. If it's informational and not obviously self-serving, then I think there's a chance that Lowenthal would accept it."

"Would you mind if I pass those suggestions along to GAD, presenting them as my own? I don't want to try to describe you to GAD—I'd have no credibility left with him by the time I'd finished." Blessing shrugged, and turned his thoughtful gaze in Holte's direction. "I think GAD should know how to present his experiences."

"Go ahead; tell him it's your idea. Stress the importance of tone in editorials," said Holte. "Something along *more in sorrow than in anger* lines."

"Yes." Blessing made a note to himself.

"Will the magistrates ultimately allow GAD to remain for a year, do you think?" Holte asked after a brief silence.

"I have no idea. I doubt they'll agree to allowing him to stay anywhere in the vicinity of Brno. I don't really understand the Czech soul very well," Blessing told him.

"Are you going to advocate for GAD's plan?" Holte pursued.

"I'm leaning that way, but it might be out of my hands. Mister Pearse is considering sending one of his attorneys here to—as he puts it—talk sense to GAD and the court." He let his breath out slowly and stared up at the ceiling. "I hope he changes his mind."

"I take it you don't think that would help," said Holte.

"Not at all. GAD would get his back up even more than it is, and he would take a more pugnacious stance against whatever his father does; he's the right age to do that, and in my opinion, Mister Pearse is asking for it, as the Yanks say. If GAD gets too pugnacious, the magistrates might reconsider their decision and put him back in jail with all charges in place, and then we would be in a stew." Blessing noticed that he had ink on the tip of his right index finger. "Blasted pen's been leaking."

"Are all the parts properly screwed together?" Holte asked.

"I ought to check," Blessing said.

Holte rose from the table. "Well, I'll leave you to it. I don't envy you your position. I trust you'll find a solution all the parties can live with."

"Thanks ever so," said Blessing sarcastically. "Are you planning on coming back this way any time soon?"

"In a day or so, I will, unless something comes up. In the meantime, I'll find out as much as I can in Philadelphia, so I'll have useful information to provide, in appreciation for all you've done." He waved his insubstantial hand, and was out through the roof, moving at ghostly speed, following the sunset westward, and emerged in front of Poppy's desk at the *Clarion* about three in the afternoon, to find Poppy reading through a stack of papers, with a photograph propped on her typewriter's keyboard. "That's the photograph the Department of State thinks is Stacy?" he asked softly, and heard her give a little yelp. "Apologies for my abrupt arrival," he added.

"Something spicy in all those pages," Gafney caroled out, waving his cigarette suggestively. "Why not share it with the rest of us, honey?"

"Something confusing; not nearly as salacious as you'd like," Poppy said, and lowered her voice to a whisper. "Where have you been?"

"In the dimension of ghosts and in Brno, and I have news from both places," he told her. "Do you want to postpone hearing what I have to tell you until you're in your auto?"

"Um-hum," she said.

"Shall I leave you to your work?"

"Um-hum," she repeated, surreptitiously eyeing Gafney to see what he might be up to.

"Is the Hudson in its usual place?"

Poppy stared at Holte and nodded.

"I'll see you there a little after five, why don't I?"

"Um-hum," she said again.

Holte was already headed for the window, looking like a large smattering of dust motes as he went. Only when he was outside the building did he realize that he had not found out if she thought the photograph was Stacy or not. Something else to discuss on the way home, he told himself, and drifted on toward the Mayes Brothers store, three blocks away; it would be a good place to pass the time.

THIRTY-NINE

IT WAS NEARLY FIVE-THIRTY WHEN POPPY LEFT THE CLARION. SHE HAD PUT ON her raincoat against the rising wind, and her hair had become a tousled mess by the time she got into the driver's seat. She set down her purse and briefcase before starting the engine, reviewing all the things she had written so far for the Department of State messenger, who would return in the morning to collect the file along with her comments on the various documents that had accompanied the photograph.

"Good evening," said Holte from the general area behind her.

This time she was not startled; she turned around and could just make out a partial outline of Holte reclining two inches above the actual seat. "Good evening to you," she said pleasantly as she adjusted the choke. "It seems that you've been busy today."

"In my way, yes, I have." He came through from the back, taking his place in the passenger seat, about two inches below the upholstery. "What would you like to know first?"

"Is there any progress in GAD's situation?"

Holte chose his words carefully. "That's uncertain as yet, but there are negotiations going on that should help get the case settled, providing no one does anything foolish. That's the reason that Blessing is eager to keep Mister Pearse, or any of his underlings, out of Czechoslovakia their presence is more likely to exacerbate the situation than resolve it; GAD is not yet completely out from under the attempted murder charge. The locals have closed ranks around a young group of hooligans, and will not balk at keeping GAD in jail for years to justify their loyalty. But as things stand now, there is reason for cautious optimism." He saw Poppy nod. "So far, it looks like it can work out to everyone's satisfaction."

"Is GAD still planning to send a letter to me for the *Clarion* to publish, or is that up in the air?" She rolled down her window and signaled with her arm that she was going to pull out into the alley even as she pressed in the clutch and put the Hudson in gear.

"That's one of the things that's being negotiated; the magistrates want to send GAD home, but he wants to stay in Europe," Holte noticed that Poppy had not yet turned on her headlights, and so pointed that out to her. "There is another wrinkle in all this: I gather from Blessing that Mister Pearse is not willing to pay GAD's passage home, and there could be a problem there. I don't know if that is contingent upon any conditions laid down by Mister Pearse, but it wouldn't surprise me."

"How like Sherman Pearse," said Poppy, turning on her headlights. "Better."

"Mister Pearse is also threatening to send an attorney to Brno to take on the magistrates, but with what goal in mind, I can't imagine. Blessing doesn't think that's a good idea." Holte moved forward through the front seat so that Poppy wouldn't be tempted to look into the back seat while she was driving.

"What's involved in getting GAD released? What you've said up til now sounds worrisome. Is it more than a question of bringing him back across the Atlantic, or persuading the Czechs to release him?" asked Poppy, frowning. She had slowed to get around a double-parked Oakland. "I wish drivers wouldn't do that. It ruins the flow of traffic."

"There aren't any open spaces on this side of the block," Holte remarked. "I don't think the driver cares about the flow of traffic."

"Anything more about GAD?" Poppy asked, uninterested in excuses for the Oakland's driver. "Is he still in jail?"

"He hadn't been released when I left Brno," Holte answered cautiously.

"But arrangements are on-going?" She dropped down to second gear and eased into position to pass the Oakland; it was going to be a tight squeeze.

"Nothing is fixed, though they are close. Blessing has been appealing to the magistrates to agree to let GAD remain—which GAD wants to do—but with the Living Spectres, outside of the city. I think I told you he plans to write a book about them?"

"He just might do it; of all his family, he's the one most capable of it," said

Poppy, half enthusiastically, half uneasily. "Anything else?"

Holte took a half-dozen seconds to decide how to broach the matter; he took the direct approach. "While I was in the dimension of ghosts, I saw Warren Derrington."

"Warren Derrington? Are you sure?" Poppy tapped her horn as she inched around the Oakland.

"We may be noncorporeal, but we do have ways of recognizing one another," Holte said, a touch of stiffness creeping into his manner.

Poppy held up one hand. "I didn't mean anything against your noncorporeality. I merely meant that you only saw him once or twice, and both times were brief."

"True enough. When I asked him if he were Derrington, he said yes, and some of what he told me was persuasive. It's Warren Derrington, all right. And he's a bit disoriented. Nothing odd about that."

She hesitated, then made herself ask, "I take it this means that he's dead?"

"In Cuba, fairly recently," Holte confirmed. "He died while in the hospital, recovering from injuries he received due to the hurricane. He's not much good on time."

"I understand that time is problematic for ghosts," said Poppy. "What happened?"

Holte summarized what he had learned from Derrington, ending with, "It's possible that Stacy killed him. He told me he either saw or dreamed he saw Stacy and very shortly thereafter left his body."

"Stacy killed Knott and Derrington?" Poppy sounded perplexed.

"If Derrington is remembering correctly, which isn't necessarily the case, but it seems likely. His account fits with the facts as you know them. That may not be conclusive, but at least it explains a number of things." He saw that she was attempting to think this through. "I'll find out more as Derrington becomes accustomed to his new existence, but for now, I'm willing to believe him, and say for certain that Stacy killed Knott. I'm going to reserve judgment about Stacy killing Derrington."

"I hate to say it, but that sounds like Stacy, doesn't it?" Poppy said.

"Unfortunately, it does."

Holte's agreement gave Poppy an instant of baffled resentment, followed at once by a deep sense of vindication. She shifted into third gear and picked up speed. "If only there were some way I could tell Loring about this."

Holte had anticipated this, and was ready with a response. "I'd hold off a while, if I were you, at least until I can nail down some provable factors that he could investigate. If you mention what you know now, it would only lead to more unanswerable questions, and there are quite enough of them already."

Poppy took a different tack. "Does Derrington know where Stacy is? Or Louise, for that matter?" She signaled for a left turn.

"If he does, he didn't mention it," Holte told her. "And even if he does, that information could become out of date quickly. I have a feeling that Stacy isn't in a hurry to put down roots. He might be en route to Valparaiso, or Lima, or Tahiti, for that matter."

"I know," Poppy said. She slowed for the stop sign at the end of the block. "I wish we had better information on where he was going, or with whom."

Taking his cue from her, Holte said, "I don't know if he and Louise are together, or ever were, once they left this country."

"Overstreet doesn't know about that, does he?" Poppy slammed on her brakes as a man on a bicycle appeared in the cross-street ahead; she honked her horn. "Those contraptions should have headlights."

"No argument there," said Holte.

"Is there any reason to hope that we can locate either Louise or Stacy without Overstreet's help?" She sounded upset, and Holte could see why.

"I haven't come across Quentin Hadley in the dimension of ghosts yet, and I've never met his cousin, Nelson, so I'm at a loss as to where to go next, unless Overstreet can remember enough to set me on the right track." Holte saw the tension in her shoulders, and added, "I'll keep looking. Word of a Canadian."

"I hope you're serious, because I'm unable to think of anything more to do." Poppy looked glum. "What a coil we're in."

In an effort to console her, Holte said, "You have the photograph, don't you. What's your opinion? Is it Stacy?"

Poppy shuddered inwardly. "I want Aunt Esther to have a look at it, just in case. If it is Stacy, he's gained weight, and changed the cut of his hair, and grown a moustache, but I'm almost positive it's he. There. I've said it."

Holte mused a bit, then said, "A post card from Brazil and now a photo in

Venezuela, as well as a possible appearance in Cuba."

"What do you make of it?" Poppy asked. "I think he's up to something, but I can't think what it would be."

"It's likely he is," said Holte as Poppy turned onto Aunt Esther's street. "But what?"

"Whatever it is, I'm sure I won't like it," Poppy muttered. "It could mean that he had something to do with Derrington's death. If he visited Derrington in the hospital, he might have done something to make sure that he kept his mouth shut." As soon as she said this, she became convinced that was more than a guess, and she felt a spurt of both anger and guilt rise within her.

Holte was about to second her words, but thought better of it, and remained silent for the next five minutes in the auto. Finally he said, "I may return to Brno tonight or tomorrow. I want to see how things are progressing."

"If they are progressing," said Poppy.

"Yes." Holte paused. "I wonder if I might ask a favor of you—on GAD's behalf?"

Poppy did not answer at once. "What is it?"

"I know you've experienced some...inconveniences in dealing with the Pearses, but if you could talk to Missus Pearse about the problem of GAD's transportation home, work out something that the magistrates of Brno would accept—an open ticket on a reputable ship, perhaps?—that would make it possible for GAD to come home when he has his book completed, then I think it might be possible to get his charges reduced, and have him out of jail."

"What does Blessing think about this?" Poppy asked, rolling down the window to signal for a right-hand turn.

"I haven't mentioned it to him yet. I only thought of it just now. I would like to have your opinion before I speak with Blessing." Holte hesitated, sorting out the possibilities that this solution might create. "Do you reckon that Missus Pearse would be amenable to talking with you about this?"

Poppy shrugged. "No idea. I can phone her this evening, and see if she'll talk to me at all. If she does, I can try to get an idea from her; she doesn't want her son in jail, accused of murder, and that may give her some reason to stand up to her husband without any hysterics or recriminations."

"Do you believe that's possible?" Holte asked as Poppy picked up speed across the intersection.

"I'm going to find out," said Poppy. "Just as soon as I get home."

"Mind if I listen in?" Holte asked.

"Mind? I'm expecting you to," said Poppy as she turned into the long cul-de-sac that led up to Aunt Esther's house. Poppy remained silent while she looked for a parking place, hoping that the one directly in front of the house had not yet been taken. She settled for the place across the street, set the brake, turned off both the lights and ignition, collected her purse and briefcase, got out of the Hudson, locked her door, and hurried across the street just as the porch light came on. As she reached the small porch, she heard a meow of greeting as Maestro ran up to strop himself on her legs.

Before Poppy could bend down to scratch the cat, the door opened and Miss Roth said, "I saw you drive up, Miss Poppy. Come in." She stepped back to allow Poppy access to the entry- hall; Maestro scooted ahead of her, and toddled off toward the kitchen.

"Thanks," said Poppy. "Is my aunt home yet?"

"Not yet. I don't expect her for another forty minutes," said Miss Roth.

"Then, if you don't mind, I'll get into the proverbial *something more comfortable*," said Poppy, and went up the stairs with her purse and brief-case in hand, planning what she would put on that would be both appropriate and less constricting than what she had on.

After hanging up her coat, she got out of her suit, taking the time to examine the hem on the skirt before consigning it to the laundry bag. The jacket quickly followed the skirt, but she decided to keep the blouse. She took her black trousers off the hanger, considered them, and nodded approval. She then removed her silk stockings and garter-belt, then donned the merino-wool trousers. As she buttoned them up, she decided that her rope of pearls would be enough to make her ensemble dressy enough for dinner at home, and went to her jewelry box; she doubled the rope once and dropped it around her neck, taking the time to check her appearance in her pier mirror, and was about to go back downstairs to call Isadora Pearse when she decided to change out of her shoes in favor of a pair of black, low-heeled dancing pumps. Satisfied with the results of her activities, she descended the stairs, calling out as she reached the foot, "Miss Roth, I need to make a phone call. I shouldn't be long." Without waiting for an answer, she went into the phone alcove and gave the operator the Pearses' home number.

"Good evening," said a voice that Poppy had not been expecting to hear.

"Genevieve?" Poppy asked, surprised that neither the butler nor the housekeeper had picked up the receiver. "This is Poppy Thornton."

Genevieve Pearse made a squeak of recognition. "Poppy. How are you? I've been following your stories in the *Clarion*. Gosh."

"Is that a good gosh, or a bad gosh?" Poppy asked, rapidly revising her plans for dealing with the Pearses; she came close to smiling as she heard a crackle of static on the line.

Genevieve laughed. "A good gosh, of course. Are you calling about GAD?"

Poppy was relieved at Genevieve's understanding. "Actually, yes, I am. I'm very glad you answered the phone." This next part she knew would be tricky. "I've had some news from...a colleague of mine, about GAD. This colleague has connections in Eastern Europe, and he sent me a...clipping from the paper in Brno, and I was hoping to get your parents' opinion of it." She gave a self-deprecating chuckle. "Fortunately he provided a translation."

Genevieve took a sharp breath. "My mother and father are out tonight—they're dining with Senator Cummings. Mother wanted to cancel, but father—well, you know what he's like. He told her that she must come with him. Do you want me to tell them that you called?"

Poppy's thoughts ran ahead of her tongue so rapidly that she almost stuttered when she answered. "I d-don't th-think I can wait," she replied. Then, as if the idea were new to her, Poppy said, "I don't suppose you'd be willing to listen to me and pass on what I tell you to Sherman and Isadora? That way, one or the other of them can give me a call in the morning."

"That would be hunky-dory," said Genevieve in a conspiratorial whisper.

"Thanks," said Poppy, and readied her comments and questions for GAD's favorite sister. "I gather you know that GAD is in jail in Brno?"

"I do. We all do," said Genevieve.

"And have you heard that GAD is at risk for being charged with attempted murder?" Poppy asked, more carefully.

"I thought it was inciting a riot," said Genevieve, clearly shocked.

"Both charges are being discussed," said Poppy. "The thing is, there's a problem with the magistrates in Brno: they want GAD out of their city, and country. The charges may be dropped if GAD leaves Czechoslovakia, and in fairly short order. They—the magistrates—want assurances that GAD will return to the US as soon as possible." She paused to let this sink in. "The trouble is that GAD can't afford passage, and your father—"

"—won't provide it," Genevieve finished Poppy's sentence for her. "I know all about that. Mother is very upset about that, which only makes father more obdurate. Everyone but Tatiana is walking on eggs because of it."

"I'm sorry to hear that." Poppy said quite sincerely. "Do you know that GAD wants to remain in Eastern Europe with the Living Spectres for a year, so he can write a book about them?"

"No," Genevieve exclaimed. "Good gracious, why?"

"I think it's because he believes that no one in this country is concerned about what happened to the Armenians of the Ottoman Empire in 1915 and 1916. There were very few who escaped the massacre of their people, and those who did have been displaced refugees who are not welcome in most of Europe." Poppy paused, to give Genevieve a chance to comment; when Genevieve remained silent, Poppy went on, "Hasn't he said something about this in his letters home?"

"Yes, but father said that GAD is exaggerating, trying to make a case for his irresponsible behavior," said Genevieve.

"Well, excuse my bad manners, but that's absurd. GAD is sincere and is willing to put his freedom, and possibly his life, on the line for Father Avaikian's group. That's a very courageous thing to do, whether you agree with GAD or not," said Poppy, with feeling.

There was another brief burst of static on the line.

"Do you know this for sure?" Genevieve asked.

"Close enough to for sure," said Poppy. "I'd be willing to bet on it."

There was a second of silence from Genevieve, then she whispered, "Then why does father keep saying that GAD's making too much over these Armenians?"

Poppy answered honestly. "I wish I knew, Gigi. GAD's doing everything your father claims to admire: standing up for the down-trodden, speaking out against injustice, and all the other civic virtues. You know him much better than I do."

"I thought I did," said Genevieve softly.

Poppy decided that she had said enough; Genevieve was upset and Poppy had no wish to make her distress worse. "Anyway, I'd like to know what has brought your father to his intractable position, because he is putting GAD at greater risk than is necessary. If you'd be kind enough to tell your parents what I've told you, and ask them to call me to provide a comment, I'd be most grateful."

Genevieve said something almost inaudible, then dared to raise her voice. "This source who provided this information—your colleague? Is he reliable?"

Poppy listened to the static for a second, and answered, "For the time I've known him, he's never steered me wrong."

"All right," said Genevieve. "I'll talk to mother and father when they return tonight. How early may they call you in the morning?"

"Here, after seven am; at work, after eight-thirty. I'll be leaving the house a little after eight." She paused. "Thanks, Gigi. I hope this works out."

"So do I," said Genevieve, and without waiting for any leave-taking, hung up.

Poppy replaced the receiver in its cradle and sat in the alcove for a minute or two, reviewing everything that had been said. She half-expected Holte to semi-appear to talk over what she and Genevieve had said. When that did not happen, she rose from the small telephone table and went into the parlor to wait for the arrival of her aunt, and any news from the National Geographic Society about the funding of her journey up the Amazon.

FORTY

AUNT ESTHER STUDIED THE PHOTOGRAPH THROUGH NARROWED EYES. "I WISH the focus had been a little bit better, but I have to agree with you, Poppy: it's either Stacy or his doppelganger, and I don't believe in doppelgangers." She had read through the various reports and other documents, and now thumbed through them one last time. "What was the name he gave the photographer again?"

The clock in the entry hall struck six-thirty; neither Poppy nor Esther paid it any attention.

"Esteban Driscoll, claimed to be from Arizona. He said most of his friends call him Steve. He had a passport that confirmed what he was saying." Poppy found this new development in the search for Stacy a bit off-putting; the idea of shedding one identity for another struck her as distasteful. "But Esteban Driscoll seems so...artificial."

"It's quite a western affectation, I agree, but it has its uses. E. D. It would match any monograms he might have on his clothing and luggage, and Esteban sounds a lot like Stacy without being obvious. I never thought he wasn't intelligent, but the uses he turns his brains to—" Esther looked around the parlor "Goodness, it's getting late. I would have thought we'd have finger-food by now. I wonder if I should venture into the kitchen to find out what's going on?"

"You could pour us both a drink—I'm feeling ready for one, after going through all this paperwork." Poppy began to gather up the papers and photograph and return them to their manila envelope.

"We should have something to eat," Esther said, and smiled a little as Maestro dashed through the kitchen door, into the dining room, and finally slowing down in the parlor; there were sounds of dropping metallic things in the kitchen, and exclamations of distress. "You know, I didn't much like the idea of a cat in the house when he first arrived, but he's grown on me. And Missus Sassoro says he's caught over eight mice since he's been allowed run of the house, so he's earning his keep. He actually deigned to allow me to scratch his chin yesterday. I've been honored, I guess." She got up from her chair and went to the high-boy to retrieve two bottles and two glasses. "I'm assuming you want cognac?"

"Yes, please," said Poppy, watching Maestro curl up on the ottoman.

Aunt Esther had just finished pouring their drinks when Miss Roth burst into the sitting room, a tray in her hands with two covered dishes. "I'm sorry, I'm sorry Miss Thornton." She was slightly out of breath. "We had a problem in the kitchen; that's why we chased the cat out. It's taken care of now, but it'll put dinner back half an hour. I'm so sorry."

"What on earth happened?" Esther asked, picking up the two glasses to make room for Miss Roth to put the tray on the coffee table.

"One of the pot-holders caught fire, and it spread a bit before Missus Sassoro and I got it out. For a little while, I wished we'd had a garden hose in the kitchen, but it would have made a soggy mess, so it's just as well there wasn't one. There's some smoke-tracks on the wall, and the paint on one of the counters blistered, but there's nothing more drastic than that." Having taken a step back after setting down the tray, Miss Roth looked ready to bolt from the room.

"Where was the pot-holder, that it could catch fire?" Esther asked with no show of distress.

"It was on the counter next to the stove," said Miss Roth. "As near as we can figure, the hanging loop was near enough to the burner that it smoldered and then charred and..." Her words trailed off.

"Ye gods, didn't you smell it?" Poppy wanted to know.

"With salmon baking, and French onion soup about to go into bowls with cheese, a little charring wasn't easily detected. I am sorry, Miss Thornton. So is Missus Sassoro."

"What else are we having, beyond the salmon and the soup?" Poppy asked, wanting to help calm Miss Roth.

"A cabbage boiled in milk with pine-nuts, and rum-baba for dessert," said Miss Roth, glad not to have to talk about their attempts to restore order to the kitchen. "There was going to be a side-dish of deep-fried potato croquettes, but I'm afraid they're a total loss."

"I suppose there was a grease-spatter around the burners that would account for the pot holder bursting into flame?" Esther asked. "I gather the pot-holder is a dead loss too, and perhaps the deep-fryer as well?"

"Yes, Miss Thornton. The hanging-loop was next to the deep-fryer, which was starting to spit. It must have had enough oil on it to be vulnerable to the burner. It and the deep-fryer will have to be replaced." Miss Roth summoned up her courage and said, "If you need to take the cost of the loss of food and equipment and any repainting that needs to be done out of my salary, go right ahead. I should have been more alert. Missus Sassoro had her hands full. I should have noticed—"

"Miss Roth, I'm not going to do anything so paltry." Aunt Esther sounded a bit bored. "Work out what needs to be done and give me a list tomorrow evening, if you would. Right now, once the basic damage is cleaned up, there's not much more any of us can do until Galliard has a look at it, and that won't be until Sunday night. The house didn't burn down around us, you and Missus Sassoro took matters into your own hands successfully, and all I need to think about now is dinner being a little late on an evening when I have nothing more planned than finishing work on my revised journey's budget." She studied Miss Roth's face, looking for indications that she was regaining her composure. "Would you like me to inspect the kitchen?"

"Thank you Miss Thornton, not yet; by the time you finish your dinner, the kitchen will be more presentable," said Miss Roth, sounding almost like her usual self. "I'll go tell Missus Sassoro that you're willing to have dinner postponed." She almost ran from the parlor, leaving Esther and Poppy to remove the covers on the dishes.

Esther took a generous swig of brandy. "God, I hate fires."

Poppy was a bit surprised at this announcement. "You didn't sound like it." Poppy removed the lid from the nearer plate and uncovered a half-dozen pastry shells filled with chopped baby clams in cream sauce with minced scallions and pepper.

"You don't imagine that I'd have strong hysterics in front of the staff, do you?" Esther took umbrage at the very thought.

"No, but I would sympathize if you did," Poppy said, setting the lid aside. "What's under the other lid?"

"Celery sticks stuffed with cashew-butter, by the look of it. Not quite up to Missus Sassoro's standards, but since she stopped the house burning down, I won't complain." Esther took more brandy and reached for the bottle to refill her glass. "I'm a bit shaken. You start on the finger- food. I'll need to get a little more brandy into me before I'll trust my stomach with food."

Poppy was feeling a bit jittery herself, and had a taste of her cognac. "It's a frightening thought, being in a burning building."

Esther made a determined effort to get beyond her quaking nerves. "The world is filled with things that are frightening; they're all around us. We might be killed at any moment by any number of accidents or calamities: lightning could strike, an auto might hit you as you walk down the street, you could choke on a fish-bone, an aeroplane might fall out of the sky, a cut finger could lead to deadly infection, you could slip on a muddy patch and crack open your skull, you could be bitten by a venomous serpent, and so forth. Any sensible person is aware of the risks, but learns not to dwell on them. That doesn't mean we ought to succumb to those fears, as you well know. We should get on with living and do our best to disregard the hazards of mortality." She had another go at her brandy. "I'll be better shortly."

Poppy took one of the pastry shells and had a tentative bite of it, agreeing as she did that it was not up to Missus Sassoro's standards. "Still, it's pretty tasty."

Esther took another, smaller sip and put her glass down. "Let me have one of those shells. I don't think I can stand the crunch of celery yet."

"The cream sauce is a little bland, even with the pepper," Poppy said as she held the plate out in Esther's direction.

"Consider me warned," said Esther, taking one. "I'll inspect the kitchen after we have dinner, in case there's something still too hot in there."

"Would you like me to come with you?" Poppy offered as she put the plate back down.

"No reason to; I'm not a poltroon, you know." She bit into the pastry shell, and said around its flaking edges. "I see what you mean. Bland."

"The texture is nice," said Poppy, trying to mitigate her criticism.

Esther nodded, then swallowed. "It has been a trying few days for her, and the rest of us."

Poppy did not respond for a short while, and when she did, she asked, "Do you think we're ever going to find Stacy? The photograph doesn't help us find him, does it?"

"I think that depends on Stacy; if he's arrogant enough not to change his appearance again, then perhaps our Department of State can circulate his likeness throughout South America and find a way to bring him back," said Esther, wiping her fingers. "Why do you ask? Do you want him found, or not?"

"I don't know," said Poppy, and watched the lamp on the high-boy flicker. "If I could be certain that he would be held to account for what he has done, then yes, I would. But I don't want him back if he's going to find some way to squirm away from any charges brought against him. I'd rather be frustrated than abashed."

"That may require you to testify against him in open court," Esther warned. "Jo would be infuriated if you did that."

"I know, and I wouldn't like either her wrath or the exposure of the court. But without my testimony, his conviction would not be a sure thing—and it might not be assured with it—but given that the others he may have succeeded in killing can't appear in court, I would have to undertake to represent them all." She remembered what Holte had told her about Stacy, about how many deaths he had caused, and she shuddered.

"It isn't only the murders that could earn him prison time. If the federal government gets its hands on him, he won't be able to wriggle out of the charges against him; you can rest assured of that. There's too much evidence of wrong-doing for him to claim he didn't understand what was going on. Fraud, along with forged documents, and cheating on Customs with those counterfeit antiques; that's not acceptable." Aunt Esther shook her head vigorously. "You're right: they might not be able to get him for his attempt to kill you, but I don't think he'll get off scott-free. That's assuming he's caught at all. He could end up on the run for a long time."

"That bothers me, too. If he plans to spend his life avoiding capture, who knows if we can find a way to..." Her words faded, and she sighed.

"Yes. It's a daunting prospect." Esther had another sip of brandy, and said, "You've hardly touched your cognac. At least try to swallow a little of it."

"If you like," said Poppy, and dutifully had some. "Have you heard from Aunt Jo about any of this?"

"Not a word since the post card incident. Josephine Dritchner, who in her way is as much his victim as anyone, is still locked on the conviction that Stacy has done nothing wrong, and she despises me for my doubts on that issue. There are times a sister is a more obdurate opponent than any man I can think of." Esther took another of the pastry shells. "For an improvisation, these aren't too bad, once you get used to them."

"What about the celery sticks?" Poppy asked.

"Not yet. I'm still too queasy from Miss Roth's account of fire in the kitchen. Would you like some?"

"No thanks, I don't like celery very much." To make up for this lack, Poppy had another sip of cognac.

Esther shrugged. "Then let's hope Miss Roth will enjoy them." She had another pastry shell, and bit into it. "I'm liking these better; they may be a bit insipid, but that's soothing, in its way." She realized there was only one left on the plate, and gave Poppy an embarrassed smile. "I'm sorry. I seem to have eaten more than my share."

"It's fine with me. I'm not very hungry." As she said it, she realized it was true. "I'd better wait for dinner, or I won't eat more than a few bites."

"You're still unnerved about Stacy?" Esther licked her fingers before wiping them once more on the napkin Miss Roth had provided.

"That, and I'm hoping that Lowenthal will take on the open letter that GAD sends. I'm worried that he might not, and then I'm afraid that GAD will be in for more trouble than he knows. Not the sort of thing he would comprehend, since he's been acting with good intentions." Poppy saw the light flicker again; Maestro lifted his head enough to glare in that direction. She wondered what Holte was making of their conversation.

"If Lowenthal decides against running the letter, it's not your fault. It may be unfortunate for GAD if that happens, but he's the one who put himself in this position, and he's the one who will have to answer for it. Mind you, I'm benignant in the matter of his troubles, and I admire his impulse to try to help the Armenians, who have suffered more than most of us realize, but I know there is little I can do for GAD, or for the Armenians, for that matter, and I will not allow myself to fret about something that is out of my hands," said Esther. "Lowenthal will want to make the decision about the letter in terms of what he thinks will sell newspapers, not what will help GAD, and that's his job. You don't have to do more than present the letter if you think it's appropriate, and your responsibility ends there."

Poppy thought this over as she had a bit more cognac. "That may be hard to do. I feel that I owe him my help, since he's sought it."

"That's your mother talking. She felt responsible for the fate of all womankind."

"What's wrong with that?" Poppy demanded.

Esther looked directly at Poppy. "You were given a great deal of responsibility when you were still quite young, when your mother became ill. I'm not saying your mother didn't need someone's help, but when it fell to you as the primary attendant, I told your father that it was unfair, that you hadn't learned to separate yourself from the needs of others; I tried to convince him to hire a day nurse, but Oliver said you wanted to do it."

"And I did. I hated feeling that there was nothing I could do for her, when she had done so much for others, herself," said Poppy, feeling uncomfortable.

"That's understandable," Esther said. "But it was unrealistic to make you her major support. Had you been seventeen or eighteen, that would have been another matter, but you were too young for such burdens. You had your schoolwork and your French classes, and your comportment lessons, and caring for a dying woman was asking too much of you. It gave you an exaggerated sense of responsibility. In your profession, that could exhaust you." She studied Poppy's demeanor. "I'm not rebuking you, I'm giving you the benefit of my opinion, although you didn't ask for it. Take it or not, as you like, but at least agree to think about what I've said. If it will make matters easier for you, do as much as you can to cover GAD's story, but remember that it is *his*, and don't entangle yourself. That's my opinion, and that's all it is." She took the last pastry shell.

"You sound like Lowenthal," said Poppy, feeling she had to say something. "He's always telling us that we are the voice of neutrality. A couple days ago, he got after Gafney for bluntly taking sides in a story he's covering, such things being for the editorial page, not in with the reporting." In spite of herself, Poppy relished the recollection of Gafney's chagrin. "I try to keep that in mind when I work."

"Lowenthal's a sensible man," Esther approved as the light blinked twice. "Damn and blast. Another bulb going."

"It could be trouble on the line because of the fire," Poppy said, glancing at Holte who was floating up toward the ceiling.

"I hope that's all it is," said Esther with feeling, adding, "I don't want to offend you, Poppy; I want to see you get through life with as few bumps and bruises as you can. I appreciate your concern for GAD's circumstances, just as I think it generous of you to be sympathetic to Missus Sassoro's worries about her husband—you're good-hearted, which is to your credit, so long as you don't let it consume you."

"You know about Missus Sassoro's husband's health?" Poppy asked, trying to disguise her amazement with an attempt at a knowing demeanor.

"Certainly. I'd be a poor employer if I weren't aware that there is something seriously wrong with Cesare, but I'd be a worse employer if I intruded where I might not be welcome. Family crises, as you know, are often best kept private, particularly when there has been no request for outside aid." She caught her lower lip in her teeth. "If Celeste Sassoro wants my help, she knows she can ask for it. I'll let her know the same is true for you before I leave for South America. But until she does ask—if she does—don't volunteer; it would make her feel vulnerable and beholden at a time when either or both would be frightening. Let her keep her pride for now. She's under enough strain as it is." She drank most of what was left in her glass; she refilled it.

"All right; I'll do my best not to," Poppy vowed, but with a twinge of conscience. "I wouldn't want her to think that I don't care that she is enduring a difficult time."

Aunt Esther held up her hand. "You've misunderstood me. There are times that the illusion of normality is more reassuring than forcing the issue of an emergency; it helps keep the crisis from compounding."

"Aren't you ignoring your own advice by artificially maintaining that illusion?" She was puzzled when Aunt Esther laughed. "What's funny?"

"I've told you my opinion. You're free to ignore it. I felt it would be remiss of me not to point out some the hazards of your work, and why you might not see them yourself. GAD has his problems, so does Missus Sassoro, and almost everyone you'll ever meet—I'll wager that your Inspector Loring has his troubles, as well; in his line of work, it would be strange if he didn't; his being protective of you is commendable, though it has its limits, which is good for you both. You have only to think about Jo, and her constant efforts to dismiss Stacy's misdeeds because she is inwardly afraid that she is responsible for how he behaves, which she is not; Stacy's made his own bed and he should lie in it. I would hate to see you end up doing the same thing in your own style. That's all." She put the lid back over the celery sticks, stood up and smoothed her skirt. "Dinner should be about ready. Shall we go into the dining room and sit down?"

Poppy drank the last of her cognac and followed her aunt; she could sense that Holte was still with them, and made up her mind to ask his opinion later that evening, and hoped she would not have to wait until Esther had gone off to bed to inquire.

Her opportunity came when she had gone to the study to complete her notes to hand over to Lowenthal on the following morning. She had done a half-page of summaries about the Department of State's materials when Holte came through the closed door and approached her. "I was wondering when you'd show up," Poppy said with more nonchalance than she thought she possessed.

"I see you're busy," Holte said, becoming more visible.

"Nothing that can't be interrupted," Poppy told him, swiveling her chair away from her typewriter. "Anything more to report?"

"Not just at present," Holte answered. "I was thinking I might take another stab at finding Quentin Hadley among the ghosts, and see what he remembers of his last few days among the living. If he does, it will be another piece of the puzzle."

"Do you think you can? Find him?" Poppy heard Maestro yowl outside the study door, but made no effort to let him in.

"If I take the time to do it properly, I should do. It strikes me that he may be able to tell me where to look for Stacy, and perhaps to tell me what Stacy may be planning." Holte sank into the desk up to his waist. "If you have something to go on, it may help you to be less anxious about him."

"I want to get him back here to face up to what he's done. I want to see him revealed for what he is. If he really killed Knott and Derrington, he has more than his attempt on me to answer for," she cried out, adding parenthetically, "That was a very poor sentence; Lowenthal would make me rewrite it."

"That sounds more like you," Holte approved. "When grammar and syntax are the worst thing you can think about, that's improvement."

"Well, I do my best to speak as well as write with concision," Poppy said, raising her chin to make her point.

"And you do it well," said Holte. "For the rest of what I might say, take note that I am biting my metaphorical tongue.'"

Poppy chuckled. "Duly noted."

"I want you to know that I think your aunt gave you some very good advice. You would be wise not to become too deeply immersed in the stories you cover; you need to marshal your energy, not wear yourself to flinders." He came toward her. "You can do a better reporting job if you don't allow yourself to get dragged into the actual cases you cover."

"Stacy made that impossible when he tied me up and locked me in the warehouse basement. Up to that point, I could have remained uninvolved, but once he did...what he did, I was in it up to my neck."

"I'm relieved to hear that you're aware of that," said Holte, and went on, "You have a portion of your life invested in Stacy's activities, whether you like it or not."

"I don't see how I could avoid it." Poppy gazed toward the night-darkened window, seeing her face reflected in the glass, almost as insubstantial as Holte's figure that appeared embedded in the surface of her desk. "Cousins we may be, but his actions involved me in his activities beyond all remedy. GAD, I'll admit, is hardly on the same level, though my friendship with him is hard to put aside, since I like him. I'm pleased that Mister Blessing is making me tangential to GAD's particular problems. I'll do what I can to persuade Lowenthal to publish the letter he's going to write, but short of embarking for Europe myself, that limits my participation in his life." She tossed her head to show her independence from the Pearse family. "Lowenthal says he wants a piece from me when GAD's letter comes in, to accompany it and remind the readers of what has happened, but other than that, unless something drastic happens, that should be the end of it, though if he writes his book, I may do a profile on him when it's published. I expect I'll have another assignment in a day or two; he's going to keep me on crime for the time being. He reminded me this afternoon that impartiality is paramount in reporting, and I have no dispute with that."

"It is good to know that you understand the principle," said Holte.

"I pay attention to what my editor tells me; I'm not a complete novice at these things."

"I knew there was a reason I like Lowenthal; he's an admirable fellow, and a credit to his profession," said Holte. "He's protective of his reporters, in his way. That's a virtue for a man in his position."

"That he is," said Poppy. "In his way."

"I'll be off, then, shall I?" There was a bit of reluctance in his tone.

"If you like," said Poppy, turning back toward her typewriter.

"I'll see you in a day or two—sooner if I find out anything useful." He was moving slowly upward, his feet about eight inches off the oaken top of the desk.

"That would be fine," said Poppy, deciding that she would call Loring before she went to bed, to let him know about GAD's letter and to confirm that the photograph was of Stacy, who was now known as Esteban Driscoll, according to the Department of State. It would be a good way to end the day, she told herself as she resumed working on her notes.

EPILOGUE

G AD'S LETTER ARRIVED AT THE C LARION ON THE LAST DAY OF S EPTEMBER, AND was delivered to Poppy's desk by Neal Galloway, the newest copy-boy on the floor, a fourteen-year-old from one of the most run-down parts of the city. "Those are a lot of stamps," he observed as he handed the envelope to Poppy. "Where do they come from?"

"Czechoslovakia," said Poppy, and saw the blankness in Neal's eyes. "It's in eastern Europe, below Poland and next to Austria. Go into the morgue and look at the world map on the wall." It was the pride of the *Clarion* morgue, twelve feet wide by nine feet high, a floor-to-ceiling four-color print occupying a wall all its own. "Start at Vienna and go east-by-south to Bratislava, or north and a bit west to Prague."

"Right you are Miss Thornton," Neal said with an enthusiasm so patently false that even Gafney laughed.

"For your own good, Neal," Poppy admonished him. "If you're going to be in the newspaper business, you're going to have to be familiar with the world. You might not need to know these things often, but when you do, you'll need them urgently."

"Right you are," Neal repeated, retreating in disarray.

"You sure told him, honey," said Gafney loudly, and grinned as his comrades laughed again, coughed, and lit another cigarette.

Poppy rallied. "I could say much the same thing to you," she told Gafney. "But you don't want to listen to a woman."

"Why should I?" Gafney shot back.

Before Poppy could say anything, Harris spoke up, sounding bored. "Put a sock in it, Gafney. It's all old hat, in any case. She does her job as well as the rest of us."

Gafney swore comprehensively and glowered in Poppy's direction, but remained silent.

"Anyone here collect stamps?" Poppy called out. "If you want these, let me know."

Miss Stotter called out from her desk next to Lowenthal's office, "My nephew does. I'll take them."

"I'll hand them to you when I go into the boss' office," Poppy promised her, and carefully opened the envelope to remove the four, closely typed pages. With a degree of trepidation, she began to read, skimming over the half-page of thank yous and expressions of appreciation that served as GAD's cover letter before beginning the actual text of the letter to his family. The salutation was brief and respectful, but then GAD took on the meat of his concerns:

> *I regret that my decision to assist these unfortunate people, the Living Spectres, who are among the very few to escape the massacre of the Armenians undertaken by the now deservedly defunct Ottoman Empire, has so deeply disappointed you, but I believe that I have a responsibility to do what I can—and it is little enough—to alleviate the suffering of these remaining few. I did not arrive at this determination lightly, or with the intent to cause you any dismay. I have attempted to live up to the principles you have applauded in others and have instilled in me throughout my life...*

Poppy read on through each paragraph, looking for signs of self-indulgence or grandiosity, and found none. By the time she finished, she felt on the verge of tears, so she took her handkerchief from her purse and carefully blotted the edges of her eyes, taking care not to smudge her mascara, then stood up, picked up the letter and the envelope, walked to Miss Stotter's desk where she handed that harried individual the envelope, then went off toward Lowenthal's office, hoping that there was no one there ahead of her, for she did not want to wait a minute longer than necessary to put the letter in her editor's hands. She rapped once on the door, when she realized that Lowenthal was on the phone; Poppy clicked her tongue in annoyance, and tapped her toe until she heard him hang up, then knocked twice on the pebbled glass that displayed *Cornelius Lowenthal, Day City Editor* in large, black, Roman letters.

"Come," said Lowenthal.

Poppy opened the door and went in, and noticed that Lowenthal's thinning hair was more than usually disheveled. "I have something for you, boss," she said before taking the chair across the desk from him.

"You finished with the interview with Denton North already?" Lowenthal asked abruptly.

"No, not yet," she said. "But I have the open letter from GAD Pearse to his family. It came in half an hour ago."

"Then you've read it," said Lowenthal.

"I have. I think it's useable." She held it out to him. "Have a look at it and tell me what you think."

"Stay where you are," he ordered her as he began to read, nodding occasionally, and pursing his lips twice, a sign that he thought something was wrong. When he was done, he looked over at Poppy. "Not bad. Not bad at all. It needs a little trimming, and there are a couple of clauses that need fixing, but for an eighteen-year-old kid, it's pretty damn good."

Poppy knew that this was high praise coming from Lowenthal. "Then you're going to run it. I'm glad to hear it."

"I am. You can do a brief summary of events, and it'll go on tomorrow's edition. I want you to call the Pearses and tell them that we have the letter, so we won't have Mister Pearse storming in here to complain. He can write a letter to the editor, and we'll run it as a response, if he insists." Lowenthal said this with relish, anticipating the clash with ill-disguised glee.

"I'll talk to Missus Pearse and explain it to her. Isadora Pearse will know how to handle her husband better than I do," said Poppy, not entirely convinced of this herself.

"Deal with it however you like, just make sure they're informed," said Lowenthal. "Did Denton North tell you why the District Attorney is going to arrest only three of the senior men at Hadley and Grimes, and not the whole lot of them?"

"Not exactly, no," Poppy admitted. "The whole of the office is being cagey about it."

Lowenthal hooted derisively. "Playing politics. I knew it!" He grinned with relish. "This is going to get hot in the next week or so. I want you to stay on top of it, Thornton. You know more about the case than anyone else in the city room. Just be careful to get confirmation about every single fact you mention, even if it's only that the day was sunny."

"I will," said Poppy.

"And keep your emotions in check. We need hard-nosed reporting on this." Lowenthal laid both of his thick hands palm-down on his blotter pad. "You have good reason to be caught up personally in the investigation, but don't give in to the urge. This whole long case has been a kind of trial-by-ordeal for you, and so far you're doing great, but I want you to leave your missing cousin out of it unless North brings him up. You got me on that?"

"I got you boss," said Poppy.

"Good. Now go back and finish writing up the North interview. I want to have it in hand in thirty minutes. I'm going to work on this letter for a while." He motioned for her to leave.

"I'm on it boss," Poppy assured him, and went toward the door.

"Chop-chop," Lowenthal called after her.

Poppy completed the interview story and handed it in with five minutes to spare.

"That's great," Lowenthal said when he had read it through. "He's an arrogant son-of-a—" He stopped himself.

"That he is," Poppy said.

Lowenthal chuckled. "Tell you what: you take the rest of the day off, no loss of pay. You've been burning the candles at both ends over the whole Hadley and Grimes investigation, and you could use a little rest. You and your aunt go out to dinner, or something nice like that. She'll be on her way in three weeks, won't she? Something like that, anyway—so you and she should spend a little time together before she goes."

Startled by this unexpected gesture, Poppy blurted out, "Thank you boss. I'll see you tomorrow."

"Just make sure you call the Pearses tonight."

"I'll do it from home," Poppy told him. "This is very nice of you, boss."

"Yeah. Keep that in mind." He pointed at his door. "I'm busy. I have a paper to put out."

"I'm going," she said, and did.

Traffic had not yet built up, so the trip to Aunt Esther's house took less time than it usual; Holte did not accompany her, and Poppy decided it was because she had left early. She let herself in the front door and called out, "Miss Roth, I'll be in the study," while she hung up her coat. In the study, she sat down to add to the growing file of notes she had compiled during her conversations with Holte, information that she hoped to be able to confirm when and if Stacy were ever brought to justice. She was rolling bond, carbon paper, and onion-skin into the platen, when she heard her name.

"You're home early," Holte remarked, taking on the appearance of a faint charcoal sketch.

"Lowenthal gave me two hours off," she said. "Where have you been recently?" It had been three days since he last called on her.

"I've been following up on what Quentin Hadley remembered."

Poppy gave this a little thought. "You mean about Stacy wanting to start a new antiques company in British Honduras?"

"That's the one."

"Did you have any luck?" Poppy watched as he grew a bit brighter.

"I'm beginning to make progress. At last." Holte gave a sound that was vaguely like a sigh. "I think I'm on to something."

"I hope so," said Poppy. "For both our sakes."

"Both? What does it have to do with me, beyond my asking questions of the recently dead?" Holte asked, drifting by her horizontally.

"Aren't you trying to balance the books? Doesn't your help get you closer to the time when you can move on, as you call it?"

"That is a consideration, but there are a lot more people out there that I haven't haunted yet, who deserve my attention." He sounded quite serious, but his tone, and his manifestation both lightened. "Besides, in general, I'm learning a lot, haunting you."

"You mean you're enjoying yourself?" Poppy was both stunned and amused.

"Not in the jolly sense, but in the intellectually stimulating sense, yes, I am," he said with candor.

Poppy took a little time to appraise what he had just said, and she remembered what Aunt Esther had told her about facing fears. "Good," she said. "So am I."

Acknowledgments

There are thanks due to a number of people for their help in the preparation of this book; here they are — on the research end, Michael Plowman, Cheri Mc-Masters, and E.W. Jones — on the reading end, Tania Eggers, Haley Kim, and Philip Horstmann, as well as Stephanie Moss, Margaret Lucke, Tamara Thorne, and Suzy McKee Charnas — on the manuscript preparation and promotion end, Patrick LoBrutto, Libba Campbell, Wiley Saichek, Connor Cochran, Charlie Petit, and Paul Huckelberry — and the just because end, Cedric and Jan Clute, Charlie Lucke, Linda and Wolf Hein, Christine Sullivan, Megan, Gaye, Lucia, Patrick, MaryRose, Steve, Brian, and all the rest of the every-other-Monday-night gang. I appreciate every one of you and all the insights and support you gave to this book.

Chelsea Quinn Yarbro has published over ninety novels and nonfiction works and more than seventy pieces of short fiction. She's known for her bestselling series of historical horror novels featuring the 4000 year-old vampire Count Saint-Germain.

Yarbro lives in the San Francisco Bay Area with the Gang of Two (her irrepressible cats Butterscotch and Crumpet).